Adrian J Walker was born in the bush suburbs of Sydney, Australia in the mid '70s. After his father found a camper van in a ditch, he renovated it and moved his family back to the UK, where Adrian was raised.

He now lives in London with his wife and two children. To find out more visit www.adrianjwalker.com.

FROM THE STORM

ADRIAN J WALKER

ISBN-10: 1477699619

ISBN-13: 978-1477699614

For Mum

PROLOGUE

The French Alps, 1978

HIS EYES opened to a silent, white world. Pure, unbroken light flared before him, obliterating all shape and shadow. He blinked once. His breaths were slow and shallow. There was no feeling, no thought, no memory. Just silence and the bright light swaddling him like a newborn child.

As the flare subsided, his vision adjusted, and the world became two pale halves separated by a single, crippled line. To the right of the line, the space was dark and dense; to the left, the space was light and filled with moving shadows. They floated slowly from left to right, towards the dividing line, the upturned horizon with which they softly joined.

All was quiet. Silence upon silence upon silence. He lay still, his face cold, watching the snow fall upon the ground, feeling it rest upon his hair and brow. For a while, there was nothing but this world. Nothing but this cold, white world and his empty mind. Only the soft falling of the snow into empty silence. Only peace.

But then a slow tide of reality began to sweep across him, trickling thoughts back into the empty pools of his mind. Noise tore through the silence like a blade through thick canvas; an engine stuck on full throttle, a woman's screams. This silence, this emptiness, this peace was not the world at all…the world was terror. The world was pain.

He gasped a lungful of frozen air. Every muscle tensed, every nerve ignited and from his leg there was a sickening sound of bone and flesh moving away from one another. His body convulsed and a scream rose in his throat, but before it could escape he retched and vomited into the snow. He fell down into the sickly mess, mouth agape, what was left of the scream now nothing but a trembling, animal whimper.

He reached down, his fingers touching the wet fabric of his trousers, and beneath them hard, sharp bone. He retched again, spitting bile, and then lay catching his breath, his brain hammering with blood and the urgent sound of the spinning engine behind him.

As the shock of pain left him, his breathing slowed. Eventually, he lifted himself up on his elbow, flinching, shivering, and turned to look across his shoulder. He was a long way from the car, a hundred feet at least, and the impact had thrown him up onto a hill by the side of the road. The car was lodged between two rocks. Its front end had been crushed and its back wheels were raised into the air. Broken glass was strewn across the road, oil and petrol staining the virgin snow. Beyond the devastation was only the empty, white stillness of the mountains. They stood firm and distant, looking back with neither malice nor pity.

Flames rose from the engine. She was still inside, he could see her struggling with the door, banging on the window. But she could not see him. He shivered, a snarl wrinkling his face, fury rising in his blood. Her palms on the window, her face, black and wet, the smoke, his own voice in his throat, growling, howling…an explosion…

What was white became black.

Down the slope behind the car, another man came running. He stopped short of the burning wreckage and crouched down by the body of a woman, brushing the hair from her damp, sooty brow.

'Madame? Are you alive? My God…you're pregnant… Madame? Are you injured? Hurt? Madame? Can you hear me? Madame?'

The woman groaned as she felt an arm around her waist, lifting her from the cold ground.

~2058~

EVERYTHING THEY SAID WOULD HAPPEN

The French Alps

THE STORM came out of nowhere.

Black cloud blustered in and bullied down the sun, the sky darkened, and within minutes the cool Alpine peace exploded into fierce cold and bitter winds. I dropped my pack and caught my breath. Before me was an endless sprawl of mountains, countless darkening peaks smothered by drift and shadow. The world had splintered into black and white and I had no idea where I was.

Everything that they said would happen, happened. Ice melted, seas rose. Animals migrated, perished, thrived. Ecosystems vanished. Economies crashed, economies boomed. People became poorer, people became richer. Nations fought, many were wiped from the map. War, flood, earthquake, hurricane, drought and famine. Doom and gloom; it all happened, just as they predicted.

What they did not predict was how little we would care. The world faced those first fifty years of the century like a smoker faces cancer; meeting warning with denial, confirmation with abandon. The planet changed, life changed, people died. Those who did not, as always, wept and went on their way. Now people are used to the heat in February, the baking, charged skies of August, the drowned beaches, the sodden ground.

People are used the fact that you can no longer go skiing in the Alps. Because there is no longer any snow in the Alps.

Everybody knows that.

The soft and powdery drifts that had once filled the mountains with sport were long gone. Skiing and snowboarding were now impossible, but the barren hillsides made hiking still an option. Yet here, halfway up what should have been a damp and misty valley, I stood watching thick snow smothering the earth against all odds. Night swarmed against the horizon as the dim sun fell. I moved on.

A sharp slope fell to my left and, to my right, a steep wall rose to the summit. I kept close to this wall and staggered through piling drifts as frozen air whipped my face. I deserved the punishment. I had been foolish, pushing on past the village in which I had intended to stay that night. It had a hostel, a shop, electricity and a population of quiet people that would have no doubt let me get on with whatever it was I was doing. But the skies had been clear and there was another village further on, thirty miles up into the hills. I thought I could make it.

The village never appeared. Afternoon came and went and I slipped quietly into a state of numbness, oblivion and, finally, denial: it was not late, I was not lost, I was not beginning to feel ill…

But of course I was. My throat ached, my temples were hot, my eyes hurt when I blinked. Now I was shaking, and it wasn't just from the cold.

I walked on as the conditions inside and outside of my body worsened. It seemed as if the storm and my sickness were working against me. I imagined them bound by some grim union, a symbiosis, two predators united in their conspiracy to tear me from the mountain.

We see ourselves in everything; faces in clouds, evil in the wind, blame in a snowstorm. To be pummelled, abused and judged by a universe that is at least aware of our presence is somehow easier to accept than the alternative.

I came to an overhang which formed a small cave in the wall. I huddled beneath it and caught my breath. My pulse was racing, my head was dizzy, my gut nauseous. I tried to focus by making a mental inventory of what I was carrying. Since I had decided to travel off the grid, it wasn't much - my passport, wallet, a water bladder, energy bars, a first aid kit, head torch, map, cigarettes and some spare clothes.

Where was I? I flicked on my head torch and fumbled in my pocket for the map. It flapped violently in the wind as I peered at it, trying to determine my rough location based on a thirty-mile semi-circle north of the little village. But there was nothing resembling the track I was on, and as I scanned the invisible arc, a chill crept up my already freezing spine as I realised why: I had taken a wrong turn. The rising snow, or my vacant state, had caused me to miss a subtle fork in the track. I had drifted thirty miles away from the village and anything else that resembled civilisation.

I cursed into the freezing gale and shook the map open. There was nothing. No village, house, hotel or campsite - nothing to suggest there was life out here at all.

So much for the road less travelled: perhaps it was like that for a reason.

The nearest place was still the second village, which meant retracing my steps in the dark for thirty miles. I stuffed the map in my pocket and tried to get my bearings. It was dark now and my only reference was the outline of distant peaks on the horizon. They were cruel and watchful, safe in their twilight as I faced my gruelling hike. I cursed again, stood and marched back out into the storm.

With a deep groan and a terrifying crack, the world fell away. Black sky and white mountain cartwheeled as I tumbled down a steep bank. Everything was silent apart from my throat's tight gasps and the thuds of my body hitting snow. I felt oddly calm, not hopeful for a safe landing but resigned to whatever happened next. During one rotation I caught sight of the track disappearing above and the reason for its sudden departure from the mountain became clear. It was not part of the mountain at all; I had stepped onto a gigantic wedge of fresh snow.

I have no idea how far I fell or for how long. All I heard was the soft creak and shuffle of snow and all I saw were the slow sweeps of sky above.

Finally I came to rest beneath some trees. I lay still, hardly breathing, feeling my weight against the earth, the odd reality of lying flat against a planet in the vacuum of space. My atoms seemed to disintegrate, my thoughts melted. Through half-closed eyes I made out a tiny yellow light moving far in the distance. Then all was dark and quiet and still.

When I came to I was lying beneath the light of a wooden porch.

The storm was still raging. Everything was muffled and dim. I couldn't see the figure fussing above me because my jacket was drawn so tightly around my face and its small opening was full of snow. My head was full of the sound of my own blood, but I could hear distant tuts and low, critical grumbles as I struggled to get up. A dog barked somewhere, then whined with excitement. I felt something moving around my feet. I cleared the snow from my hood and peered down to see an overweight Labrador wearing a harness and snuffling at my boots. The harness was attached to the wooden sledge on which I had been lying.

I felt small hands grip my elbows and usher me through a door. The dog loped in behind me, the door slammed and suddenly I was in a warm hall, coughing, the remnant flakes of the banished snowstorm floating down behind me. I waited while the woman — I had established that much by now — tended to the dog's harness. Her tiny frame was covered from head to foot by a long black parka, which she removed and hung on a peg. Then she took me through before a fire and helped to ease the rucksack from my shoulders. I pulled back my hood, releasing an avalanche onto the floor.

'I'm sorry,' I spluttered, bending to rescue her carpet.

'Non,' she said. 'S'il vous plaît.'

She brushed away my fumbling hands and scooped up the snow with a brush and pan she had resting by the fire. When she was done, she straightened up and looked at me. She was old and the years had pulled her face into parchment, riddled with lines like mountain contours. I looked back at her, breathing short breaths and acknowledging to myself, for the first time, that I felt dreadful.

'Désolé…' I said, then 'thank you…' I coughed. 'Merci, I mean.'

'You are sick,' she said. 'What are you doing up here?'

Her accent was soft and her English effortless, but I replied in French. I had spent five years working in Paris in my twenties and was still fluent.

'Walking…' I said. 'I'm on…holiday.'

'On your own? In this?' She gestured to the foul weather outside.

'I know…I should have a partner…I'm…'

'Stupid,' she said, bustling out of the room. 'Very stupid.'

Ten minutes later I was sat by the fire, wrapped in a blanket and trying to eat soup. The old woman sat watching me with her hands knitted together on her lap and her legs tucked beneath the belly of the dog at her feet. The soup was meaty and hot, but I couldn't stomach it. I managed only a few mouthfuls before I looked up at her in apology. The dog whined at me in encouragement. She shushed it.

I put the bowl down on the table next to me. The small carriage clock on the mantlepiece read after midnight.

'Thank you,' I said. 'I don't know what…'

She watched me struggle for words. Her face didn't flicker.

'If I could stay here tonight,' I went on, 'I'll be gone by morning.'

She didn't answer at first. She seemed interested in me, concerned perhaps, yet still scornful of my recklessness. Finally her features stretched into a kind smile. She shook her head.

'I do not think so,' she said. 'Not in this.'

'It can't be far to the nearest village, can it?'

'The nearest village is down in the valley. *Normally* the journey takes five hours.'

'Well,' I said, '...if I make an early start.'

She laughed, a little girl's laugh. Then she got up and pulled back a curtain. Outside was the same dark gale, thick with angry, white particles like a swarm of frozen locusts banging against the pane. The snow was so thick it seemed to be settling in mid-air.

'It is up to you, of course,' she said. 'But I would not put much money on you making it down to the village alive in this. If you do not die of cold, you will die of a fall. I have not seen snow like this...not for a long, long time.'

She let the curtain drop back, as if it shrouded some secret memory, and then turned round. She raised an eyebrow.

'I think you arrived just in time,' she said.

Then she picked up my bowl and disappeared into the kitchen, while I stared into the fire and felt foolish and rotten. The dog looked up at me. I gave the fat animal responsible for my rescue an embarrassed smile and it beat its tail softly against the carpet. When the old woman returned she carried two huge tumblers of brandy and gave one to me. I took a sip and shuddered.

We drank and listened to the clock. At one point the throbbing in my temples synchronised itself with its ticking.

'I can't stay here,' I said at last. 'It might take days for the snow to stop.'

'You might not have a choice,' she said.

'But there must be a way down to the village, it can't be that dangerous.'

She frowned.

'My father did it once. With Zeet.'

The dog raised its eyes.

'Not you,' she said, tugging at one of the dog's ears. 'One of your ancestors.' The dog thumped his tail again, then lay down and let out something that sounded like a soft, broken trombone.

'When was that?' I said.

'A long time ago.'

We listened to the clock again, and the sound of a dog dreaming. This time the woman broke the silence.

'What in the name of *God* are you doing up here, so far from home?'

Home. Hard to say what that was, exactly.

I sighed and rubbed my brow. I thought about telling her that I didn't know why I was there but, the truth was, I did. The truth was the mountains weren't the only place in which I was lost.

I lived in a time and a place from which I wanted to escape. It was the beginning of winter, and London at the beginning of winter is miserable; wet, but still smouldering with sweaty, second-hand heat. The air is like dirt from a shoe. The streets are clammy and hot. Things shrouded by the sun become difficult to ignore; the grime, the barely concealed despair on every third face, the heart rates thundering, for all the wrong reasons, at thirty per cent above the national average.

I had been divorced for three years. Since then relationships had been fleeting and senseless. My friends had grown distant. Each seemed bent on their own brand of self-destruction: work, marriage, materialism, drink. Self-doubt was rife. I knew nobody with purpose.

I wanted to tell her this; I wanted to tell her about what it was like to spend two hours of every day underneath the ground, being shunted back and forth along what may as well be a sewer, sharing the stifling space of an antique tube carriage with three hundred pale and sweaty suicides, each of whom had, despite the desperate urgency of the world, allowed all the joy and ambition in their lives to be replaced with skin conditions, unused gym passes and fashionable diets.

I wanted to tell her what it was like to spend the rest of the time plugged into technology you would never fully understand, pushing buttons for people you would never meet and making friends you would never keep. To spend exactly one-and-a-half hours of every day outside in what meagre amounts of sunshine the city does allow through its bubble of smog, to eat food you are told is good for your health from places you are told are good for your social life.

To wonder, daily, why you live such a life in such a place, but to be terrified of ever leaving it.

Far from home? I wanted to tell her that there was no home. Not really, not like the one from my childhood; the safe shelter I had taken for granted. The world no longer had a home to offer; there was no safe shelter.

I didn't tell her that. I told her that I had needed a break. She shook her head and shrugged.

When I had finished my brandy, she led me to a small room. It had a single bed and an old electric heater that she switched on as we entered.

'There. Please,' she said, pointing at the mattress. Then she left the room, presumably to allow me to undress. I took off my boots and jumper, leaving the rest for warmth. It was a cold room, dim and unused, and the bed creaked in apparent surprise as I climbed into it.

I pulled up the covers and the woman returned with a box of matches and a glass of water. She lit the candle on the table next to me and placed the water beside it. Then she stood at the doorway with her hand over the light switch, looking down at me. I nodded in thanks and she flicked the switch, closing the door.

For a while I watched the candle's flame burn, willing the sheets to warm up, listening to my breathing and feeling strange, unwanted thoughts creep over me. Then I closed my eyes and fever smothered me with dreamless sleep.

DON'T PANIC

THE FIRST day was made of snapshots and loud noises. The old woman's hand in searing white sunlight as it grasped the glass by the bed. The sudden shriek of curtains as they opened, her face next to them, curious, serious, concerned. A cloud of steam, frozen like a photograph, hanging above a bowl of something hot. My foot, protruding from the sheets, dull and pale in the low light. A dog's face like a cartoon at the door, tongue lolling dopily from its mouth. A single pant replayed infinitely and exactly, each one the same as before. A radio babbling in the distance, and then sometimes from inside my ear. The woman's voice, asking me something. The feeling of a long, cool hand on my forehead. Tuts, grunts, shuffles. Heat in my bowels, pain in my temples, my veins sore.

I had a sense of time passing, but not in any place near me. I would wake to peculiar distortions in my body's geometry - one hand balled beneath my chin, as small as a needlepoint; the other like a horse head dangling from a mile long shaft of bone; my feet stretching out impossibly to the far wall of the room. I felt like I was cocooned in the most minuscule nutshell, but lost in an infinite darkness.

I continued this cycle of restless sleep for three days. On the fourth day I awoke suddenly, gasping with lungs full of icy air. The delirium had gone, snuffed out in an instant and replaced with harsh reality: a freezing room and the sound of a dog's whines from outside the door.

I sat up. The fever was gone, but my body ached and I could still taste the sour frowst of illness. The dog whimpered again, then let out a whistling howl. There were no other sounds in the house. The light in the room was eerie and dull. It seemed like dawn, and yet…

Something was wrong.

I got out of bed, reeling as my feet hit the cold floor and quickly finding my boots and jumper. My breath clouded the air. I checked the electric heater; it was switched on, but ice cold.

Then I pulled open the curtains and stopped dead at what I saw. The light was low not because it was early, but because it was blocked by a wall of snow that stood as tall as the window. Through a thin gap at the top, I saw the blizzard raging on. I found my pack in the corner and took out my watch. It was noon.

My feet found some urgency and I marched through the door. The dog met me with howls and barks, his tail wagging but his face wild with panic. I bent to stroke him but he pulled away and ran to the end of the corridor, disappearing up some stairs. I mumbled a low hello into the emptiness of the house, but there was no response. I repeated, louder as I walked up the corridor: still nothing. In the sitting room where I had been four nights before, the fire was out, the hearth full of ash and cinder. The clock on the mantelpiece agreed with my watch: noon. I flicked the light switch without effect. I tried a standing lamp; same result.

'Hello?' I said again, clearer now but still with no answer.

I wandered through the bitterly cold rooms, opening curtains, trying lights, each time in vain, picking up pace and calling out hellos as I went. Nothing. The only sound was the constant whine of the dog from above. In the kitchen I took a glass and held it under the cold tap. For a moment there was nothing but a distant whistle and I thought the pipes had frozen, but after a few seconds water spluttered out in icy bursts. I drank down three full glasses and moved on. Eventually I reached the hall, where I looked up the stairs. One last time I called and, hearing nothing, climbed them. One near the top creaked loudly and I stopped, my hand gripping the banister, nervous and cold.

'Is anybody there? Hello?'

Nothing.

I followed the sound of the dog to a small room at the end of the corridor. The door was ajar. I knocked and went in.

It was a study. A stream of light from a high window fell across a desk littered with paper. Bookshelves and photographs ran around the walls, maps covered the ceiling. Next to a small fireplace was a chair, in which the old woman lay, her eyes closed, her head resting peacefully to one side. I bent over her, peering at the still lines of her face. Then I laid one hand on hers to rouse her, reeling at the shock of cold skin. I checked her pulse. She was dead.

The dog sat quietly with his head on her lap, and to the woman's breast her hands still clutched a worn, open book.

I have no idea how long I stood looking at her. I had never seen a dead body before and I was scared, frozen in this new territory. The stillness - the dense atmosphere of death - seemed to root me to the floor. The dog maintained his mournful vigil at his owner's lap, his tail limp upon the carpet like an old rope.

Don't panic, I thought.

But reality was already gathering like a sea storm. Giddy waves washed through me, bringing with them flotsam of facts and questions. The old woman was dead: for how long I did not know. I was alone in a farmhouse, currently being buried by a raging blizzard. Where this farmhouse was, I knew not. It was bitterly cold. It seemed that there was no electricity. There was a dog.

In the end it was the cold that made me move. I shuddered and shook myself from the trance. Then I backed away from the chair and beckoned to the dog. He assessed me sadly before hauling himself up and padding out into the corridor. I looked again at the body. Then I left the room and closed the door.

Don't panic, I thought.

I found the dog sitting on the landing, quite still, looking out of a window. I joined him and looked out at the grim scene. I had thought I was in a small, solitary cottage, but it was actually part of a farm. Its yard, barn and outhouses were slowly disappearing beneath the merciless blizzard.

I tried not to panic. Really, I did. But things don't always turn out the way you hope.

I bolted downstairs to the bedroom, grabbed my rucksack and emptied it onto the floor. In the pile I found a pair of waterproof trousers, which I pulled on. The rest I put back in the pack. I took my jacket and gloves from the sitting room, where they had dried, and put them on. Then I took my pack and ran back upstairs to the window. The dog was still there, tail thumping with interest.

I scanned the landscape, looking for lights, rocks, anything to guide me away from a hidden cliff or gully like the one I had tumbled into nights before. The old woman had told me that there was a village down in the valley. I marked a downward curve in the snow beyond the outhouses.

I had no plan. I had no choice. I reached up and lifted the latch. The window swung inwards and the blizzard exploded in my face.

The dog barked in alarm and I staggered back, steadying myself against the banister and pushing myself towards the storm's gaping maw. I muttered an apology to the dog that was swallowed by the wind. Then I took a breath and pulled myself out.

A CHILD'S FADED HANDWRITING

ONE HOUR later I was back inside, shivering shamefully in the sitting room. The dog lay at my feet, looking both betrayed and relieved.

I had plunged from the window into oblivion: white noise, white light and air that was so cold it froze the mucus in my nostrils. It was impossible; the blizzard would have taken me within an hour. I had barely made it past the barn before retracing my steps and clambering back inside.

I had built a fire. Now I was on my third glass of brandy and fifth cigarette. This felt far more sensible; better to die in the relative warmth of the house than in the fierce cold outside.

Eventually the dog got up and left. A minute later I heard the sound of metal scraping stone and went through to find him pushing his empty bowl around with his snout. He saw me and whined. I checked the cupboards. They were far from full, but I found a tin of dog food and emptied the greasy cylinder into the bowl. I watched him gulp it down. Then I searched for something for myself. In the lifeless fridge I found some cheese and meat, which I ate with fingers still numb with cold.

I was no longer in a state of panic. I had tried to escape and failed. Now I had no choice but to resign myself to whatever fate awaited me. Maybe the blizzard would lift and I could try again, or maybe it would not. All I could do was keep warm and hope that things would get better. There was nothing more to be done.

This gave me an odd thrill; I had never been so disconnected. If there was one thing this struggling world still did well, it was communication. You were never far from a voice or an ear.

Communication. Suddenly, I remembered: there had been a radio in the old lady's study. It might have been connected to the power supply, in which case it was useless. However, if it ran on batteries…

I ran upstairs.

With some relief I saw that the corpse was in the same state, in the same position with the book clasped tightly to her breast. There had been no visible decay, although the air was fetid. I turned my attention to the radio. It was a brown box, its casing covered with padded leather. A thin cord connected it to a mouthpiece. I guessed it was about a century old. An ancient strip of masking tape was stuck to the front of the box, on which was written in faded ink: *'Ferme de Ferrière.'* Next to it was a switch. I laid a finger on it and closed my eyes, pressing down.

There was a pop, then a crackle, then a low, electric hum. I opened my eyes, smiling. The switch was lit up red and the meters had danced into life. It worked! I turned the dial and heard the whistles, pulses and bursts of static fade in and out with the changing frequencies. I pressed the intercom button, hearing the static silence. I pushed a fist against my lips, nodding. If I kept talking and listening on a frequency for an hour, then moved to another, and then another, if I kept doing this then maybe somebody would hear me. It might work, but if not at least I had a purpose. All I could do was try, and trying was better than dying.

I looked back at the old lady's corpse. If I was going to be here for any length of time then something would have to be done about her. I baulked at the idea, but could not escape it. The body would have to be moved.

I spent a long time hovering above the woman, deliberating about how I was going to pull her from the chair. Nauseously, I peeled her rigid fingers from the book, which I placed on the reading table by the chair. Her fingers retained their sad claw, mourning this last artefact of the living world stolen from their grip. Then I considered the various ways in which I could carry her from the room, realising that the problem with each of them was that I would be carrying a corpse in my bare hands. Eventually, I elected to carry her in the chair.

She was light, and I carried her as slowly and respectfully as I could down the corridor, as if I was a sole coffin bearer at a funeral with only one four-legged mourner. The dog's gaze followed me as I descended the stairs. When I reached the bottom, I set the chair down and considered the best place to put her. The bedroom seemed the obvious choice, but there was no way of knowing how long I would be trapped in the house. Days? Weeks? Either way, I was not keen to share the time or space with a rotting corpse, however much its living embodiment had saved my life. I carried the chair to the front door and opened it.

As I had hoped, the small porch offered protection from the snow. Instead of piling against the door, the drifts had mounted up several feet from it, providing a small, empty space that was colder than the inside of the house. I positioned the chair so the old woman was facing the wall of snow, as if she had fallen asleep watching a sunset, rather than a blizzard. I closed the door.

In the kitchen was a wooden stool, which I broke into bits and carried to the study, along with the brandy and cigarettes. The dog followed and watched as I made a fire in the small hearth. In a little while, the room was warm and the dog fell upon his belly with a sigh, chin on his paws, facing the flames. I sat at the desk, lit a cigarette and took a large gulp of brandy. Then I flicked the orange switch on the radio and pulled the mouthpiece towards me. I pressed the button and spoke.

'Hello…'

The word was cracked and weak. The hiss of the static swallowed it up as if I was calling into the blizzard itself.

'Is there anybody there?' I spoke again.

And so began my vigil at the radio.

I spent over an hour speaking and listening on the frequency

I had found the radio set to. Then I made a note of it and began cycling slowly through its entire range, spending ten minutes on each notch of the dial saying my name, followed by 'ferme de Ferrière'. Sometimes I would catch a crackle that sounded like a voice and leap forward, hammering the button, shouting *'ferme!'*, *'Ferrière'* and *'m'aidez!'* into the mouthpiece. But each time there would be silence again, and when I was convinced that there was nobody there, I would return to my slow journey through the dial's frequencies.

When I had completed four turns of the dial, I stopped. Defeated, exhausted and sick of the sound of my pleading voice, I replaced the speaker grimly upon the shelf. With my head in my hands, I fought back the urge to give up. It was late, after 2am, and perhaps there was nobody listening now. I could try again in the morning.

I turned to the fire. The embers from the stool were almost out and I stood up to look for fuel.

The shelves were packed with books: novels, journals, manuals, ancient classics, dictionaries, encyclopaedias, histories, thick tomes on archaeology, photography, travel, agriculture, war, religion, art and music. I had not seen them before, my attention distracted to this point by fire, radio and corpse. I scanned the spines. They seemed archaic. Nobody had a book shelf any more.

But still, it felt wrong to use books as fuel. As I prepared to search the house for an alternative, something caught my eye: a long series of thin yellow spines running along the bottom two shelves. I bent down and picked one out. They were *National Geographics*, hundreds of them spanning a century. It seemed less of a crime to burn these; certainly it seemed better to do so than to wander the cold rooms of the house again.

I threw five on the fire and sat back in the chair, watching their pages curl and blacken. The sleeping dog growled in appreciation as the room filled with new warmth. I would return to the radio at dawn, but keep it on unless I heard contact. I looked back at the shelves; a book might keep me awake. As I bent forward to pick one out, I saw another from the corner of my eye. It was not in the bookshelf, but on the reading table next to it – the open book the old woman had been holding. I picked it up. It felt ancient and well read, the outer fabric soft and delicate as if it were about to fall away. On its cover was written, in a child's faded handwriting:

The Diary of Claudette Ferrière.

I turned it carefully in my hands to the page at which it was open, sat back and began to read.

~1978~

THE DIARY OF CLAUDETTE FERRIÈRE

7 FÉVRIER 1978

We don't know what his name is or where he came from, but he is living in *my room.*

Papa brought him up to the house this evening as I was finishing feeding the chickens. He was in the wheelbarrow Papa was pushing and had blood all over him like a lamb does when it is born. He wasn't trying to stand like a lamb does when it is born though, because he was asleep and one of his legs was pointing the wrong way. I screamed and ran away and hid because of the blood. Blood on animals is all right, but not on a person. When Papa cut the top of his thumb off last summer I could not keep my hands from shaking as I dressed it and I had to do it three times before the bandage stayed on. Papa was very patient then and just kept his hand still and bit his lip and didn't shout at me once. I think it was because it was hurting him. I don't like seeing blood on a human, it makes me feel sick and I want to fall over.

I hid in the engine shed, but Papa shouted at me twice and I came out and saw him standing in the yard still holding the wheelbarrow in the snow and I could see his breath in the air because it was so cold. He was breathing fast, which meant he was tired and I thought that maybe he had carried him a long way. I wondered where the man had come from and what had happened to him and whether he was alive or dead, because it was difficult to tell. Zeet was barking and jumping up at Papa and running about the yard between us as if we were sheep. Then Papa shouted at me again and told me to help him inside so I put on my gloves and then I helped him.

I opened the door to the kitchen, trying not to look at all the blood or the man's leg or the way it was pointing. Papa pushed him inside and rested the wheelbarrow on the kitchen floor and stood there panting. Then he told me to go and get one of the big empty grain sacks from the barn, so I ran outside. It was getting dark and the snow was beginning to fall more heavily, even though it had been sunny in the morning and there was a blue sky. Zeet followed me and jumped up on me when I got to the pile of old sacks in the barn. I shouted 'Stop it Zeet!' but he was so excited because he knew something was happening and he didn't stop and just kept barking. I ignored him and picked up the biggest sack I could find and ran back with it but it was too big and I dropped it, which made Zeet bark even louder. 'Zeet shut up!' I shouted, but he didn't listen. I picked up the sack again and folded it four times in the snow, then carried it in my arms the same way that I carry the wood in for the fire. I could not see over the top of it but I managed to get to the kitchen and gave it to Papa. I closed the door on Zeet to stop the snow blowing into the house but I could still hear him barking outside and scratching at the door. Then Papa shouted *'ARRÊT!'* and he stopped.

One day I want to be able to do that.

Then Papa said 'lift him up' and I said 'what?' and he said, louder, 'lift him up Claudette we're going to carry him through to your bedroom'. I said 'my bedroom? why are we doing that?' and Papa shouted at me and said 'don't ask questions just lift him up!' and I was going to say that I couldn't and that I didn't really want to touch him and I thought I was going to cry but then I looked up at Papa's face and it looked really angry. So I gritted my teeth and put my hands under the man's bloody shoulders.

It was horrible and I thought I was going to be sick. There was blood all over his face but I could see that he was quite young and handsome, much younger than Papa. There was blood in his hair, which made it matted, and blood all down his neck and soaked into his shirt and I thought *where is it all coming from?* There seemed to be so much of it that he couldn't possibly still be alive and I looked above his ear where I saw a thick, deep cut that looked like it had been made by an axe. That was where the blood was coming from. It made me feel dizzy and I thought I was going to drop him so I looked away, but Papa said 'that's good, hold him there'. He was really heavy but I managed to hold him up and Papa slid the big sack beneath him so that each end was over the sides of the wheelbarrow. Then I let him fall back on it and he groaned, which meant that at least he wasn't dead.

Papa said he was going to lift him by the sack because he didn't want to make his leg worse, and I looked at it and felt sick again. It was going the wrong way in two places so that it looked like one of Zeet's back legs and I prayed that he didn't wake up because I thought *I wouldn't want to wake up and find one of my legs like that.*

I thought *he must be asleep because it hurts so much.* Sometimes your body does this for you. It's as if it is saying I'm sorry but I can't do anything about that pain right now I'm afraid, but there there have a sleep and it will go away soon.

Papa came round to the front of the wheelbarrow and picked up both ends of the grain sack as if they were the legs of a sheep he was moving. The man was much heavier than a sheep and Papa made a grunting sound, but he managed to lift him up because Papa is strong. Then he lifted him all the way through from the kitchen, through the hall and past the mirror where he almost knocked over the jug full of flowers which I picked yesterday and he said I could put there. They didn't fall over, they just wobbled and he stopped for a bit as if he had forgotten something until they stopped wobbling. Then he climbed the stairs and I followed him. The one three steps from the top that always creaks made an extra loud sound because it was carrying two men and I thought it might break under the weight. But it didn't, he made it to the top.

The man made another groaning sound as if he was waking up and I was scared because I didn't want him to wake up and see his leg. Then Papa shouted 'go and get some hot water and a towel Claudette' so I ran back downstairs to the kitchen.

I put the kettle on the stove, which was still hot from making Papa's soup for lunch. It took ages to get hot and I could hear Papa's footsteps creaking slowly along the corridor upstairs like a monster. Outside it was getting dark and snowing really heavily and landing on the old snow and making drifts. I could see Zeet lying in the barn with his chin on his paws taking shelter from the snow and he wagged his tail at me when he saw me looking. His face was asking me what was happening and mine was telling him 'I don't know, Zeet'.

Then I heard Papa upstairs going into my bedroom and my bed made a creak when he put the man down on it. I thought *he's bleeding all over my sheets and I'm never going to sleep there again.* Then the water started to steam and I poured it into a bowl and took it upstairs with a towel. When I got to my bedroom the man was lying on the bed and there was blood all over my sheets just as I thought. He was still asleep though, which made me relieved. Papa took the towel and soaked it in the water and dabbed his own face, which was covered in sweat. He looked thoughtful and sad like he did when he had found a wounded animal and was wondering what to do with it. The man's leg was twisted and broken and I thought if he really was a wounded animal Papa would have shot him by now.

Papa said 'I found him down by the road five miles away, I think he was hit by a car which didn't stop.' I said 'Why didn't they stop?' and Papa told me that some people are like that and would rather save their own neck than someone else's life. He said 'His leg is very broken. I carried him on my back for three miles but then I found the wheelbarrow I had left by the paddock and put him in that instead.' I told him I thought that was a long way to carry somebody on your back, and he agreed.

Papa said that it was too late to take him to the hospital

because we live sixty miles from the nearest town and it was dark and snowing, but that we could take him tomorrow morning. This meant that he had to stay the night with us and that we had to clean him up and put bandages on him before they could do a proper job at the hospital. He started wiping the man's face with the towel and cleaning off all the blood. It was pale like a dead person's and Papa said that this was because he had lost so much of his blood. Then he said 'we also have to do something about his leg' and I said 'what kind of thing?' and he said 'we have to straighten it.'

I didn't say anything.

Then Papa said 'go and get some bandages from the bathroom Claudette' and I did. When I came back he had finished cleaning him and Papa took the bandages and put one around the man's head and one on his arm where there was a big cut. Then he told me to wait there and he went outside to the barn. I stood there watching the man. His eyes were closed but he kept turning his head and making noises and I wondered what he was dreaming about. Then Papa came back with two planks, some rope and a knife.

He looked a bit nervous but started to cut up the trouser of the man's broken leg. I was so scared that he would wake up I didn't know what to do. I must have been making noises because Papa kept saying 'shh Claudette, he needs our help.' He didn't wake up though, but when Papa got to the top he pulled back the material and there was his leg with its knee falling off and two bits of broken bone showing through the skin. I have seen sheep and cows and even a dog like this before, but never a man. I groaned and Papa said 'be brave Claudette I need you to help me'.

'What are you going to do?' I said and he didn't answer. Instead he told me to hold onto the planks and the rope and to give them to him immediately when he asked me. I took them and stood very close behind Papa and held onto the planks and rope really tightly in case I dropped them.

Papa let out a big sigh and looked at the leg and scratched his head. Then he bent over the man and put one hand very gently on where his knee used to be. I think the man felt it because he made a groaning noise and turned his head on the pillow. Then Papa put his hand on the man's thigh and I shut my eyes and bit my lip. He waited for what seemed like forever and then suddenly there was a sound like wood snapping and the man screamed. I opened my eyes to see Papa struggling with the man, who was now awake and reaching down at his leg. The man was sick on Papa but he managed to push him back on the bed and put one of his palms across his forehead to soothe him saying 'shh, shh, shh we have to do this'.

I could see that the man was in agony and his body was trying to help him by putting him to sleep because his eyes kept shutting and rolling back in his forehead. His knuckles went white where they were gripping the sheets, which now had sick on them as well as blood. Papa held his hand behind him and said 'give me a plank Claudette' and I almost made a mistake and gave him the rope but just at the last minute changed hands. Papa put the plank in the man's mouth and said 'here, bite down on this', because another thing you can do to stop pain is to cause pain somewhere else in the body so you don't notice it as much. The body is not very good at stopping pain, sometimes.

The man did bite down on the plank and stopped screaming but was still wriggling on the bed. I looked at his leg and the top bit was straighter now where Papa had put it back in place but the skin around it was black and there was a hole where the bone had poked through. I felt dizzy, but held on tight to the other plank and the rope because Papa had told me to. Then Papa took hold of the man's shin and didn't wait this time so I didn't have a chance to close my eyes. He twisted it round so that the foot was pointing the right way and I squealed and the man screamed even louder than before. Papa said something but I was crying and then he shouted again 'rope and plank

Claudette!' and I pulled myself together and gave them to him. He took the other plank from the man's mouth who was howling like a dog and tied both of them to either side of the man's leg so that it was kept straight. The man kept screaming and Papa said 'wait here and look after him' again and went out to the barn again and I thought *how do I look after him?* He was screaming so loudly and tears were pouring down his cheeks and sometimes he would look at me as if I were something scary who had come to get him. But I'm not I'm just a little girl and I just kept saying 'It's OK it's OK it's OK go to sleep be quiet be quiet shhh' and I thought maybe I should put my hand on his brow like I've seem nurses do in war films when soldiers are crying.

Then Papa came back carrying two big pills and he said 'these should knock him out'. He broke them up and told me to try and keep his head still by putting my hand on his brow and soothing him and I said 'I was just about to do that' and I did and it worked a little bit because Papa was able to put the bits of pill in the man's mouth and make him swallow them. Then he made him drink some water to help them go down. We stayed with him for a while and he began to stop screaming and moving and after about ten minutes he was asleep again, but not because his body had told him to but because the pills Papa gave him are normally given to horses.

It is almost midnight now and I am sleeping in Papa's bed. He is asleep and snoring like a bull and sometimes I can hear the man whimpering in his sleep next door and Zeet barking outside. I want to go and tell Zeet to be quiet but even if I did he wouldn't listen.

Night, night Mama.

8 février 1978

I didn't have to wake up this morning because I was already awake. Papa woke every hour and went to check on the man in my room because of the horrible noises he was making in his sleep and when Papa was asleep he was mostly snoring so loudly I couldn't sleep. The times when he wasn't snoring I was kept awake by the wind outside which was howling around the house. I got out of bed at about six o'clock and looked out of the window. Even though the sun wasn't up yet, it was bright because of all the snow. I couldn't believe how much snow had fallen in the night. The barn and the cattle shed and the yard were all completely covered as if someone had put a thick blanket over them and I could hardly make out Zeet but he was curled up in a ball in the corner of the barn. I felt sorry for him because I wouldn't like to spend the night in a barn if it was snowing hard. But he is just a dog and dogs have thick coats to keep them warm. The path was covered too, and it looked as if all the fields and the mountains around them had been rubbed out by the blizzard.

I went next door to check if the man was still alive, which he was because I could hear him wheezing. He was still asleep from Papa's horse pills but he didn't look very peaceful. I stood and watched him for ages, even though my room smelled the way rooms smell when someone has been ill in them. His leg was all swollen and black and all the bandages were soaked with blood.

Papa must have heard me get up because he came through as well and stood next to me. He said good morning but I just gave him a face for snoring so loudly. Then he said 'We have to get him to hospital now' and I said 'how?' because of the snow. Papa said he didn't know but the man needed medical attention and couldn't stay in my room. Then I got dressed and put on my blue jumper, which Grandma made me when I was seven. It's a bit tight now, but it's the warmest one I have and it looked really cold outside.

We went downstairs to the kitchen and saw that there was even more snow than I thought. It was high in drifts against the front door and all around the side of the house and I didn't know how we were going to get out. Papa made a growling sound and told me to make some breakfast. Then he said 'watch out' and opened the door and loads of snow came falling into the kitchen. Then I made some tea and fried some eggs and sausages while Papa tried to get it all out again. He picked up the shovel by the door and scooped it all out of the kitchen and onto the snow outside. Then he walked out through the snow and it almost came up to his waist. By the time breakfast was ready he had made a little path from the front door through the yard to the barn. All the time Zeet was trying to get to him to help but he was trapped in the barn. He jumped and jumped and kept falling through the snow and disappearing and I kept laughing at him because he looked so funny. He was barking all the time and making whining sounds until Papa picked him up and threw him onto the path shouting *'ARRÊT!'* at him and he stopped.

Then Papa stood scratching his head and looking around and stroking his chin like he does when he is thinking. I shouted that breakfast was ready and he looked around a bit more and came in.

I had one sausage without the skin on and Papa had three sausages and two eggs with some bread. He ate it without talking like he always does and then said 'The road is blocked with snow, there's no way I can drive him to Grenoble. I'll have to call mountain rescue and they'll come and get him with snowploughs.' I said 'when will they come?' and he said he didn't know but that we'll have to look after him until then. Then he got up and went to the study and I washed up.

When he came back he made a huffing sound and said the telephone wasn't working and that the lines must have been affected by the snow. He said he tried the radio as well but that didn't work either and there was just static. Then he stroked his chin a bit more and said that he was going to try and clear as much snow as he could from the yard but that it would be difficult because he was on his own and Phillipe was not back from Grenoble for another week. He told me that it would take him all morning to clear the yard and that I had to look after the man in my room until he came back in. He said stay with him and make him some broth and change his bandages so I said 'OK' even though the thought of touching his dirty bandages made me feel sick. Then he threw Zeet out into the snow, who yelped but enjoyed it really, and Papa followed him outside to start clearing the snow again.

I didn't want to go upstairs on my own so I made a fire and ate some bread with strawberry jam. Then I chopped up some carrots, swedes, garlic and onions and put them in the pot with some beef and dried herbs. Then I thought 'what can I do?' but I realised there wasn't anything else to do while the broth cooked so I plucked up the courage and went to my room. When I got there, the man was awake because his eyes were open and he was staring at the ceiling, wheezing. I was really scared so I stood in the door and watched him for a while. Every so often he flinched or made a noise and eventually I was brave enough to go a bit further inside the room. When he heard my footsteps he turned his head to look at me and I froze. He was white like a ghost and his eyes were bloodshot. His lips were dry and cracked and his breath sounded dry so I said 'Are you thirsty?' At first he didn't say anything but then he nodded his head three times very slowly.

I ran downstairs and came back with a glass of water and went back to the place where I had been standing. He reached out his arm and tried to take it but I was too far away, so I came a bit closer and held it out to him. He managed to reach it but his arms were so weak that by the time it reached his mouth he had spilled most of it all over his face and all over the sheets and he dropped it onto the floor. I ran forwards and picked it up and he yelled out in pain. I said, 'Don't worry I'll get you another one.' I ran downstairs and refilled the glass and saw Papa struggling about in the snow and falling over with Zeet jumping on him as if it were a game, but I didn't laugh because

I was busy. Then I grabbed a towel and ran back upstairs. I put the glass on the bedside table and dried the man's face and hair and the sheets around him taking care not to touch him too hard in case I hurt him. He stared at me all the time and looked like he was about to die so I made sure I didn't look him in the eye because I was scared. Then I lifted the glass to his lips and let him take a sip and he almost choked on it till I held his head up.

He took another sip and I put his head back on the pillow and stood back from the bed. He said 'thank you' in a funny accent. I told him I was making him some broth and that it would be ready soon, but he didn't answer. Then I went back downstairs, sat by the fire and watched Papa and Zeet in the snow through the sitting room window. Papa had managed to clear a wider path through to the barn and another to the engine shed where he keeps the tractor and the car. Zeet was always close behind him but Papa must have beaten him because he wasn't jumping up or barking any more. It looked very cold outside and the snow was everywhere in the air, going up and down and left and right and making big swirly patterns around Papa. His face was completely hidden by his hood and hat apart from a little hole where his nose and eyes poked through. They looked red and raw and I hoped I had made enough broth for him as well as the man upstairs. I was warm and snug by the fire, and watching Papa and Zeet working outside made me feel even more cosy, even though I felt a bit guilty about sitting there when they were out in the cold. I felt sleepy and remembered that this was mostly because Papa had been snoring like a bull most of the night. Then I didn't feel as guilty any more and I fell asleep curled up in the big chair.

It was about ten o'clock when I woke up and suddenly remembered about the broth. I jumped up just in time to see Papa and Zeet coming back down the path they had made towards the house for a break and I ran into the kitchen. The lid was rattling on the pot and I thought *I hope it's not burnt!* as I lifted it off. The broth was bubbling but it wasn't burnt and I gave it a stir and took it off the heat, just as Papa opened the door.

Papa took off his hat and coat and let Zeet in through his legs and shut the door. He said 'Smells good Claudette' and I said 'Mmmhmm' as I was stirring it but secretly I was really shaking and relieved that Papa hadn't come in and found me asleep!

Then he said 'How is he?' and looked at the ceiling. I said 'I gave him some water' and Papa said 'good' and took off his boots and went upstairs. Zeet ran through to the fire so I put the lid back on the pot and followed him. He was standing like he does with his front paws on the hearth, wagging his tail and staring into the flames with his tongue hanging out as if he has just found a ferret to play with. I watched him steaming and started to worry that maybe the man upstairs had died while I was asleep and that Papa would find him and be angry because I was supposed to be looking after him. Then I thought *even if he has died, he could have just died when I was making broth and nobody knew I was asleep, not even Zeet and even so how on earth was I supposed to stop him from dying?* Then I felt sick because if he *had* died then he would have died in my bed and I wouldn't want to sleep there again, unless he had maybe crawled out of bed and tried to get to the door because nobody was hearing him calling out for help and that maybe he died at the top of the stairs and Papa would wonder why I hadn't heard him. And then I really felt bad because I felt sorry for the man and I hoped I hadn't let him die, so I ran upstairs as quickly as I could, expecting to find him in a heap on the landing with Papa trying to rejuvenate him. My heart was beating twice as fast as normal and I tripped on the third step from the top and banged my shin, but when I got to my room I just saw my Papa standing over the man and changing his bandages. I rubbed my shin because it was really sore.

The man was awake and Papa was telling him about the snow

and the telephone not working, but the man was just breathing big, heavy breaths in and out and looking at Papa's face. Papa turned round and said 'come here Claudette, I want to show you how to change his bandages properly' so I walked over to the bed. The man was still pale and his face was wet with sweat and Papa said 'look Claudette, let me show you, we have to change three bandages, one on his head, one on his arm and the one on his leg here.' He taught me how to take the bandages off without hurting the man too much, which was difficult because the wounds were scabbing, but that it was good that the wounds were scabbing because it meant that the man's blood was clotting properly and that his body was trying to help him.

I said that if his body was trying to help him it could have thought of something better than bone to make itself out of, something that didn't snap so easily and tear through his leg and hurt him. But Papa said that the human body is not a perfect thing and it does its best with what it has. He said that nature was not a perfect thing, and that's why there are people like us who live on farms to help it. He said that if everything was perfect then we wouldn't have to have farms and keep cows and dig up the fields because it would do all that for us, and then what would we do all day? He said that nothing is perfect in nature, not even his daughter, and that was the reason it was so beautiful.

Then he showed me how to clean the wounds with special water and put antiseptic cream on the bandages before tying them on. He said the bandages had to be quite tight, but not so tight that it stopped his blood flowing through the actuaries because if they did that then he would get really bad pins and needles and his arm might fall off.

He let me tie the bandages and he said 'well done' and then I asked what we were to do about his leg. Papa stroked his chin a bit and said that the breaks had been quite clean and that he thought he had put it back together properly and that the only thing we could do before he got to hospital was to keep the cuts in the flesh clean and bandaged. He showed me how to do this very gently but no matter how careful I was the man kept shouting at me as if I was deliberately trying to hurt him. I wasn't, I was trying to help him, and at first I was angry at him for making a fuss, especially as he was staying in *my* bed. But I realised that he was only acting like that because he was in pain. I wondered again who he was and where he had come from and whether his family were missing him. I asked Papa and he said he didn't know either, that he only knew the man sounded like he was from Italy, but that he wouldn't tell him his name.

We tried to give him some of the broth but he kept choking and wouldn't swallow it. He couldn't open his eyes properly and all the sweat was running off his face and soaking into the pillow. Papa told me this might be because the man had a fever as well and that might mean he had an infection or it could be because he had been lying in the snow for so long before he had found him. Whatever the reason was he was in need of a hospital and he went to try the phone and the radio again.

While he did that, I put the man's broth back in the pot. You aren't supposed to do this because you might catch something but I knew that the man had only touched a bit of it and I didn't want to waste an entire bowl. Papa came into the kitchen as I was washing up the bowl and said 'Did you keep that broth in the bowl for the man or throw it out? I hope you didn't put it back in the pot Claudette.' I was going to tell him that I had, but then Papa would have wanted me to throw the whole pot of broth away, which would have been a big waste. So I said that I threw it out because it would have got cold in the bowl. He said 'all right then' and told me that the telephone and radio was still not working. Then he said 'I'm going outside to clear more snow' and I said 'I could help, Papa.' But Papa said that I was to stay inside and look after the man like I had done before.

I felt guilty for putting the broth back in the pot, but Papa didn't know and the man only touched a bit of it. Sometimes Papa worries too much.

Zeet followed Papa outside and they went to work clearing the snow, which was already starting to cover the path they had cleared earlier. I sat by the fire again and watched them working, but this time I didn't fall asleep and read my book instead. I went upstairs twice to check on the man, but didn't change his bandages. I tried to give him some broth twice, but he didn't eat much of it and I put it back in the pot.

Papa came in when it was lunchtime and said that it was impossible trying to clear the snow because it was falling so heavily and covering the bits he had already cleared. We ate some of the broth, which was much tastier than the one I made last week because it had cooked for longer and I had put more herbs in it. We went upstairs and managed to give the man some more broth. He ate more of it this time and I didn't have to put the broth back in the pot.

I did some chores in the afternoon and watched Papa and Zeet working outside. It snowed all day long and I couldn't see past the edge of the yard. I imagined that the whole house had been thrown into the air so that there were no fields or mountains around it any more and that it had gone so high that it was floating about in the clouds, like Dorothy's house in The Wizard of Oz. I wondered where we might land if we really were flying and I hoped it would be Italy so that we could put the man back where he belonged.

In the evening we ate some cheese and bread and some more broth and I changed the man's bandages. He still wasn't properly awake and his breathing sounded like a cow that was sick. I did the bandages wrong at first but he didn't fidget or squirm when I took them off, not even when I touched his leg, which means he is really sick.

Papa tried the telephone and radio again for a whole hour but there was nobody there to talk to him. We are all sitting by the fire now and Zeet has fallen asleep because he is so tired from jumping around Papa all day. Papa looks tired too and he is drinking some whisky before we go to bed. I hope he doesn't snore tonight. I think that if he does, I won't hear him anyway because I am so tired. Maybe tomorrow the snow will have stopped and Papa can take the man upstairs to the hospital. Then I can have my room back.

10 février 1978

The snow did not stop last night and it did not stop all day. Papa and Zeet spent the entire morning and afternoon clearing snow away that had filled in the paths they made yesterday but we still cannot get out of our yard. It is still snowing now.

I changed the man's bandages three times. I gave him more blankets and kept the fire strong all day so the whole house was boiling hot, but he is still shivering with fever and crying in pain. Papa gave him another horse pill and I heard him upstairs trying to talk to him and ask him his name and where he came from. But the man just kept moaning and saying 'I come from nowhere', which is a stupid thing to say.

I haven't heard him make a noise since it got dark, but now the quiet makes things eerie. He could be dead for all we know. I went to bed three hours ago and have been up twice to check he is still alive. He was alive, but I could hardly hear him breathing and I watched him for ages last time before coming down to write this in front of the fire. Every time he took a breath I thought it was his last. I wonder who is missing him.

15 février 1978

Papa is sick and it is my fault. It started the day after I last wrote in my diary. Since then I have been too busy and tired to sit down and write but I am staying awake tonight to tell you what has happened.

When I went to bed after writing my last diary Papa was snoring like he always does. He didn't stop all night and when it started to get light and I had not slept I was very angry and decided to wake Papa up and tell him off. When I had checked that the man in my bed was still alive, which he was, I shook Papa and shouted 'Papa! Papa! Wake up!' but he wouldn't wake up properly. When he opened his eyes they were puffy and red and he was sweating like the man in my bed and making groaning noises. I stopped shaking him and said 'What's wrong, Papa?' and he said 'Nothing, Claudette' and got out of bed.

I followed him to the bathroom and he splashed his face with water and put on his clothes, but he was shivering all the time and looked pale and weak. I made him some coffee and some breakfast but he didn't eat it, which is not like him at all. Then he went straight outside into the cold to try and clear the snow again. Zeet was with him but he could tell something was wrong as well and just sat looking up at him. I watched him too through the kitchen window and he was working twice as slowly as he usually does. He kept stopping and leaning on his shovel and bending down to the ground and taking breaths and then his hat flew off in the wind so his head was out in the cold. I shouted 'Papa, Papa, your hat!' but he didn't notice and he didn't hear me and tried to go back to work. But then he just collapsed in the snow and lay there with his shovel on the ground. Zeet went mad and started barking and I screamed out 'Papa!' and rushed out in just my bedclothes. He was shivering and his face was covered in snow like the picture in my book about cavemen from the ice age hunting woolly mammoths. He had his eyes closed tight and couldn't breathe properly.

'Papa, get up!' I shouted. And 'Shut up, Zeet!' but he didn't. I tried to lift Papa and drag him out of the cold but my feet were bare and the snow was cold. I told Papa to wait and ran back to the house, got some boots and a coat and ran back outside again. Then I managed to drag him a bit and he started to wake up and get to his feet. He said 'Claudette, get back inside' and I said 'I'm helping you, Papa, you fell over'.

'I have to clear the snow,' he said. Then he tried to pick up his shovel and he fell over again. I heaved and dragged and managed to get him up again and this time he let me help him inside. I closed the door and took Papa through to the sitting room and put him in the chair while I made a fire. He was shivering and didn't say a word.

When the fire was going I put a blanket around Papa and he and Zeet sat next to each other staring into it. 'I have a fever,' said Papa, 'I must have caught it from the man.'

That's when I realised that it was my fault and that he must have caught it from the broth I put back in the pot. I felt so guilty but didn't say anything. I thought *if Papa is sick then he can't clear the snow and we can't get the man upstairs to hospital and he will die and it will all be my fault.* Then I thought *what would you do now Mama*?

You would have sent Papa to bed and been his nurse so that he got better quickly, and I would have helped you look after things until he did. So I said 'You have to go to bed, Papa, and get better so we can clear the snow'. He just nodded his head at me, and I remember you telling me that when men do this it means they are *really* sick.

That day I cleaned the house, did the laundry, fed Zeet and then I had to feed the beasts. I always help Papa and Phillipe when they feed the beasts but I have never done it on my own. I was scared because you have to get into the shed with them and spread out the hay on the ground with a fork so that it is even and flat, which wouldn't be so bad but the beasts start to stampede and push each other to get to it. Seeing hay is like seeing their favourite dinner and they go wild and make a lot of noise. I get excited when I see my favourite food, which is roast onions, but I would get bored of it if I ate them every day. Beasts don't get bored of hay.

First I had to get the hay into the cattle shed, though, which was difficult because it lives in the hayshed and hay bales are heavy, even the small square ones. Luckily, our hayshed is right next door to the cattle shed and there is a big green door connecting them together. If there wasn't, you would have to take the bales across the yard, and that would be impossible right now even for Papa because the yard is beneath six feet of snow.

But *first* of all, before I spread the hay in the cattle shed and before I even tried to move a bale from the hayshed, I had to get out of the house and into the hayshed. I couldn't open the kitchen door because the entire house was trapped inside a drift. I looked through the porch and saw the snow flat against the window, high above my head. It looked like a giant ant farm you get so that you can see inside a nest and watch all the ants working and carrying things about, except there were no ants in the snow and even if there were they would be dead from the cold. Zeet came and sat next to me and looked at it too and I scratched the top of his head. I tried not to panic about being trapped in a house surrounded by snow, or about the snow that was still falling and might one day bury the house completely. Instead I thought very hard about how I was going to get out to feed the beasts. I could hear them baying from the shed and I knew they were hungry.

Then I had an idea. I ran upstairs feeling excited in the same way that you do when you remember you have finished your chores and you have a new book to read or when Grandma is coming to visit. I slipped on the third step from the top and banged my shin again, which is the second time this week, but didn't care because I was too excited to see whether my idea would work. Zeet followed me up and I said 'No Zeet! Go downstairs, you're not allowed up here!' but he wouldn't listen to me. I tried to grab him and said 'Zeet, you bad dog! Go downstairs!' but he was already at the top and I couldn't stop him. When I got to my room, I stopped at the door and looked in at the man.

The man was awake and not breathing as heavily as usual, and his bandages didn't need changing yet. He was still pale, though, and shivering, and his leg was bruised and horrible. The room smelled and I thought *it's always going to smell like this now.* Zeet was sniffing him and I was worried that he might jump up on the bed and hurt him, but I think he knew he was ill because he just sat down next to him and looked up at him. He only wants to help really.

I closed the door and walked to my wardrobe and put on my hat, gloves, an extra jumper and my thick coat. Then I walked to the window next to the bed and the man looked at me with a worried face as if I was going to hurt him. I said 'sorry' and opened the window. The blizzard outside suddenly came into the room, and a gust of wind blew the curtains about and flapped the pages of a book up and down as if it was thinking about reading it. Zeet barked and snow landed on the bedside table, in the glass of water I left there and on the pillow next to the man, which started to become wet. I didn't want to get the man wet but there was no other way and it had to be my window I climbed out of. 'Stay,' I said to Zeet.

Outside my window there is a pipe attached to the wall. I grabbed hold of it and said 'sorry' again to the man through the window. Then I tried to close the window but before I could reach it, Zeet jumped through it and out onto the snow! I called after him and looked down and saw that he had landed up to his shoulders in it and couldn't move! It was funny but I was angry at him and I shouted 'Zeet, you silly dog' but couldn't help laughing. He was barking and whining and looking embarrassed and trying to get his front paws free so that he could climb on top of it. I closed the window so that it was on the latch and not as much snow was getting into the room, then I looked down and it was only a little jump onto the snow. I prayed that it was strong enough to take my weight and that I wouldn't go straight through and land under six feet of snow because then I would probably die.

I closed my eyes and jumped and landed on my back right next to Zeet. The snow was so soft that it felt like landing on a blanket and I laughed at Zeet again. Zeet laughed too and I threw some snow at him. Then I stood up and tested the snow. It felt quite solid and I knew that if I kept my feet spaced apart then I wouldn't fall through it like Zeet because I don't have paws and skinny legs like he does. I jumped on it a few times and didn't go through, so I decided that it was safe for walking on. Then I helped Zeet get his paws free and got him up on top of the snow like me. He wagged his tail to say thank you. It was strange to be standing so far up above the yard, and if it hadn't been snowing so heavily I would have been able to see over the barn and into the fields, but the blizzard was still hiding everything outside of the yard and making it seem like the only place left in the world.

I put my hood up and we walked to the cattle shed. The snowdrifts went all the way up the sides of the barn, the engine shed, the hayshed and the house. The only places it didn't touch the walls were the cattle shed and the wall where the fire is in the sitting room. That wall was warm enough to melt the snow and make a small path running to the front of the house. It was the same next to the cattle shed because beasts give off a lot of heat, which is how they stay warm together in the winter. The snow stopped a bit before the shed door, which meant I could slide down to it.

Zeet slid down after me and I opened the door and went in. The beasts were all standing round with steam coming off them baying, saying 'We're hungry! We're really hungry! Feed us!' and I said 'I know! But Papa is sick and there's a strange man in my room so you'll have to wait!' Zeet ran up and down the pen sticking his nose in at the beasts and barking at them, and I opened the big green door and went through to the hayshed.

I looked up at all the square bales in the loft and wondered how I was going to get even one of them through to the beasts. I thought about taking handfuls at a time but then thought that that would be a silly thing to do and take ages and I had to think of something else. I couldn't carry a bale on my own and the bale trolley was too big for me to push. Then I saw the wheelbarrow Papa had carried the man in, which was standing next to the back wall. It still had dark red patches of blood on it and I didn't want to go near it because they looked sticky. But because I have been changing the man's bandages I didn't feel as sick as I did when I first saw him in the wheelbarrow, and I realised that it was the only chance I had.

I picked up the wheelbarrow, which was heavy even with nothing in it and put it under the hay loft. Then I climbed up the wooden ladder and went to the section that was directly above the barrow. I pulled a bale out and dragged it towards the edge and looked down and tried to aim it at the barrow. Then I pushed it as hard as I could so that it was balancing on the edge and then I aimed one last time before letting go. It landed on the barrow as I planned but it was so heavy it knocked it on its side so that it was half in and half out. I ran down the ladder and tried to push it in but it was too heavy, so I tried pulling it from the other side but I couldn't do that either. Then I remembered something Papa taught me about using a pitchfork to lift things up from underneath. He said it was called a lever and meant that you didn't need as much strength.

I took the pitchfork from where it was standing next to the ladder and put it under the bale and tried to lift it, but it was just as heavy and it wouldn't move. I pushed and pushed so that the handle was standing as tall as me, but the fork just slid out from underneath the hay and fell over. I felt really angry because all I wanted to do was to give the beasts their hay and I could hear them baying and Zeet barking at them through the pen. I stopped and told myself to think and I thought really hard about what I was doing. Then I realised what I was doing wrong. Pitchforks are bent, not straight, so I turned it round and stuck it under the hay again. This time, the handle was touching the floor instead of sticking up in the air, and the fork had already lifted up the hay a bit. I crouched down like Papa told me to do when lifting things and grabbed hold of the handle and lifted it. At first it wouldn't move and I could feel my face going red like a weightlifter's. I kept trying and eventually the bale started to lift off the ground! I could hardly believe I was lifting a bale, but very slowly it got higher and higher and started to take the barrow with it. Soon it was standing upright!

I was really pleased with myself and had a rest before trying to push the barrow. It was heavy, but I managed to push it bit by bit through to the cattle shed. I don't know why they don't put two wheels on wheelbarrows, which would make them so much easier to balance. The bale fell off twice and I had to put it back on the same way as before.

When I got it through to the beasts I cut the string with the knife hanging from the pen and spread the hay evenly out on the ground. When they saw the hay they opened up their eyes really wide so they were as big as saucers and lifted up their heads and mooed as loudly as they could like wolves do when they howl at the moon. They stampeded around the place and Zeet ran up and down the pen wagging his tail and barking through the gaps in the fence. I had to shout at them and use the pitchfork to push them away from me so that I didn't get squashed, but I got out each time and let them eat the hay and went back to get another.

I fed them five bales and it took me four hours. By the end of the afternoon I was really good at pushing the wheelbarrow.

Afterwards I cleaned the shed and made sure none of the beasts were sick from the cold.

I also made sure Papa was all right in bed. He didn't say anything all day, just slept and shivered, but you always said to me that men always seem worse than they are when they're sick, Mama, and that you should enjoy the peace that comes when they stop talking. When I told him I had fed the beasts, though, he looked at me with wide eyes as if he couldn't believe it and said 'Oooooh'. Then I brought him stew but he didn't eat much of it. Even though I told him he had to and tried to sound like you did when you told him to do something, he still left most of the bowl. I didn't put *that* back in the pot.

The man in my room was still sweating and pale and I

changed his bandages four times. He ate some stew but not all of it. I threw that out too and scrubbed all the pots and bowls extra hard.

By the end of the day I was so tired I fell asleep in front of the fire as it went out with a blanket around me and Zeet at my feet. When I woke up, it was still snowing and the paths outside had been completely filled in again. Then I spent the day exactly like the one before, looking after Papa, the beasts and the strange man in my bedroom. The day after was the same, and the day after that, and at the end of each one I fell asleep in the armchair by the fire with Zeet before I had a chance to write in my diary.

I made myself today though, even though it is past ten o'clock. I am still sleeping down here in the armchair and Papa and the man upstairs are still ill and the snow is still falling. We're trapped and I don't know what to do!

~2003~

DYING IS DEPRESSING ENOUGH

Venice Hospital, Italy

CATERINE WAITED patiently in the dark room, listening to the coarse breaths of her uncle and the slow beep of the machine that told her he was still alive. The only other sound came from a cheap cassette player on the bedside table - Chet Baker singing *My Ideal.* The young man's voice yawned around the walls of the room, finding corners to curl up in, and a lazy-eyed trumpet followed, swaggering across the floor and getting lost in its melody like a drunk in a story before falling asleep.

The room was small and warm, its need for decoration temporarily disguised by the low glow of a reading light. To the right of the bed, opposite the door, was a window with no curtains. The room was next to water, one of many small streams that ran from the Grand Canal like the arteries of an ancient leaf. This one was especially thin, becoming a dead end about fifty metres south of the window, and the deep crevice it created between the walls of the buildings on either side had filled with mist. Caterine could see the orange light of a bridge's lamps burn through it like spots of rust on a muslin sheet.

A water taxi droned by beneath the window, the quiet chatter of its passengers drifting up.

'An odd place to live, Venice.'

Caterine looked down at her uncle. His face was long and drawn, yellowed like goose fat and mottled with brown marks. His eyes were open, cloudy, and surrounded by shadow, but two small points of light peered out from their centres and looked out at the mist.

He turned to her and smiled.

'No cars,' he said. 'So it's always like early morning.'

'You're awake,' she said.

'You came,' he replied.

The door opened and her uncle's mother - an old woman now - walked in. She gave Caterine a nod, then looked back at her son.

'That's them all,' she said, wiping her hands on her black dress as if she had just finished baking. 'Everyone's gone home.'

'Good,' said her son.

'*Elmo*,' she scolded.

Caterine kept her smile hidden.

'Your family love you,' she said. 'The waiting room was full when I arrived. There was hardly any space for the patients.'

Elmo waved a hand.

'Dying is depressing enough without tears,' he said.

His mother tutted and rolled her eyes.

'You should go too,' said Elmo.

'I'm staying till I'm told otherwise,' replied his mother. 'Besides, would you send an old woman out into that?' She nodded at the window and the cold mist behind it. 'Would you like some water?'

'Strega.'

'I don't have any.'

'Beer, then.'

The old woman made a noise of disapproval.

'…and a pile of potatoes covered in greens and gravy…with shavings of pork and lamb. And strawberry tart. Can you manage that?'

His mother smiled a rare smile.

'No last meal then? Even the condemned get a last meal. Somewhere on death row there's a murderous rapist tucking into a pile of steaks, and all I get is warm water.'

'If I could, I would cook it for you,' said Angelina, bending forwards to stroke back the hair from his forehead. 'But I don't think there is a kitchen in this dump.' She plumped up his cushions.

'Careful,' said Elmo, wincing.

When she was done, she stood back and put her hands on her hips.

'I will leave you two alone, then.'

She turned to Caterine.

'You're too skinny,' she said. Then: 'Don't let him waffle. He always waffles.'

Then she left the room. The music on the cassette player had changed; now it was Billie Holiday singing about love and the pain that it offered. Her broken voice sang dustily in the low light and whispered things to them.

'How are you, Uncle?' she asked in a low voice.

'Don't call me Uncle,' said Elmo.

'What would you prefer?' she asked. 'I never liked 'Godfather'.'

'Elmo,' he croaked, raising himself up painfully in the bed. 'Elmo will do fine.' He winced and fell back on his pillow. Caterine leapt forward to help, but he palmed her away gently. She kept hold of his shaking hand as he caught his breath.

'Is there anything I can do?' she said.

'No, Caterine,' he said, easing himself up. 'Any more care and I'll explode.'

He pointed at the door.

'Them out there, my family. They take turns with me. I feel like a parcel at a children's party. One minute it's her wiping my cheek with a spit-sodden handkerchief, the next it's my fat brother trying to talk about a game of football neither of us have watched, then it's my cousin crying and blocking my view of the television. I never get a moment's peace.

'They love you, Elmo.'

'I know. I know. And I'm fifty-three, I'm too young to die, that's why I get all this *pity*. Twenty years older and it would have been sympathy, ten years older still and it would have been resignation, another decade and it would have perhaps been gratitude. But I get pity, Caterine, and pity is not what a dying man needs.'

He coughed painfully into a handkerchief and looked down at it.

'Pity,' he went on, inspecting the spray of red dots. 'Lives in the eyes of those who believe themselves to be in a better place than somebody else and feel bad for it. It stares at cripples and bites its lip. It lasts for seconds before mutating into relief. It looks down like a weeping Samaritan; never up or along like a comrade. It mistakes itself for empathy, but forgets that it is vulnerable too.'

Elmo closed his fist around the handkerchief and looked up at Caterine. She watched him study her face.

'You're a woman now,' he said.

'It's been two years at least,' she replied.

She had never been particularly close to her wayward Uncle. It was true that they had an ease of conversation that both, being natural introverts and more comfortable in their own company, rarely found with others. It was true that there was a warmth and fondness between them, but Elmo had lived abroad for Caterine's entire life. The rare times when they did see each other, at a wedding or a funeral perhaps, it seemed to Caterine that Elmo always turned from her, ignored a genuine bond that they might both have treasured otherwise.

She had not known he had been dying until tonight. Why he had called her here now was beyond her. Still, she sat and listened to the warm and somehow familiar tones of his voice.

For a few minutes they said all the things that were necessary to confirm what was happening, of the mysterious text message from his mother, of her drive from Verona in the dark, of the fact that, tonight, Elmo was almost certainly going to die. Then their conversation faded. The air was still and quiet, punctured only by the regular beeping of Elmo's heart monitor, the clicking of a nurse's heels on the corridor outside and the occasional buzz from a boat passing by beneath the window.

Another song began, a jumpy piano instrumental that Caterine recognised but did not know. Elmo slowly lifted his right hand and began tapping his long finger in time to the music like a baton. The plastic tube stuck into it waggled behind as he picked out invisible notes and stared into the dark air. Eventually he dropped his hand and turned to his god-daughter.

'Still painting, I hope?' he asked.

Caterine shrugged. 'I try to,' she said. 'I do, but it's hard. I work at the library six days a week. Sunday I'm beat. I wish I could find more time, more space.'

'You should travel while you're young,' he said. 'See the world, get some inspiration.'

'That would require cash. I have none.'

Elmo chuckled.

'What?'

'You know you are good, don't you?' he said, ignoring her question.

'Perhaps,' she said with another shrug. 'Sometimes I feel like a fraud, like I'm only half good. To be a real artist I shouldn't really be spending so much time on the day job, should I? I should be skinny, starving, living in a hut and sleeping with the wrong kind of men. Truth is I'm quite happy, I just like painting.'

Elmo shook his head.

'Art is a gift, Caterine, not a burden. Those who say they *have* to paint, they *have* to write, they *have* to spread dung on a twenty-foot canvas and sell it to idiots. That if they didn't they'd die. They're fools. They think their paints and their words and their music are syringes full of filth, parasites sucking at their hearts and souls. But art should set you free, not imprison you. You know I used to play the piano, didn't you?'

She nodded.

'I heard you were very good.'

'I was. But I never *had* to play it; I just did. I had a gravity for the keyboard. It made sense to me, as if a part of my brain was actually shaped like one. Any piece of music I heard, even in the background, even if I was in a conversation or taking an order in the restaurant…'

'Amico's?'

'Of course,' Elmo said, turning to her.

'I knew you played there. I didn't know you were a waiter as well.'

'Everyone was a waiter or a chef in those days, especially those who were learning how to do something that wasn't waiting or cooking. What else does a nineteen-year-old do in Venice that gives him free food?'

'I've never been a waitress,' said Caterine.

'You're different, you're grown up.'

'I'm only twenty-five.'

'Well, anyway, whatever I was doing, taking an order or talking or walking past a busker or getting dressed, whatever, the little part of my brain that was shaped like a piano keyboard would be plonking away, doing its maths and working out the intervals between the notes, again and again and again until all I could see in my head was a blackboard showing the pattern and fingering that made up the piece. It was constantly on, I couldn't stop it.'

'That sounds terrible.'

'It wasn't, it was just part of the gravity. All I had to do was release it onto a real piano and the board would be wiped and ready to go again.'

Caterine struggled. Perhaps this was the delirium of a dying man, yet still there was that closeness again, that ease with which they talked. She decided to encourage it.

'But you said you never *had* to play the piano,' she said. 'What would happen if you didn't wipe the board? It would have been full, your head would have been full of notes, you might have become a lunatic.'

Elmo looked at her sideways.

'You listen too much, you know,' he said. 'I mean you *really* listen, like your mother did. Most people don't, they just nod and hear the odd word that makes a nice introduction to the next story they're going to bore people with. For someone like me who talks a lot of nonsense, that's quite an intimidating weapon.'

'Sorry. So you mean that you actually did suffer for your art?'

'No, not at all, I suppose it was a bit annoying but you get used to it. As long as there was a piano around, which there usually was, it was OK. All I meant is that I think some people take art too seriously.'

'Why shouldn't they if it's something they love?' said Caterine.

'But that's just it, they don't. They drag it around like a lead block around their necks.'

'Maybe that's just a part of their art.'

Elmo shook his head as if it was covered in dust.

'You're doing it again, will you please just let me ramble? I've lost the point.'

'Sorry,' said Caterine. 'What was the point?'

'The point was that there's nothing wrong with letting your art make you happy. I liked playing the piano, but I don't like artists.'

'OK.'

'The first point is more important.'

'Right.'

'The second one I threw in on a whim.'

Elmo sighed like a blocked drain.

'There *is* another point to this,' he said. 'Before Amico's, before I met your parents, the restaurant where I worked was quite small, in a shadowy corner of a tiny square in San Polo. There was only me and another waiter, and sometimes he didn't turn up. He was the owner's nephew, so he never got the sack. In any case, it didn't matter since we never had too many people not to cope. At least to start with. On a usual day it was just the chef, Luigi, and I playing dominoes. He was a big man, a hairy man, ex-army, that's where he learned his trade…you look surprised, don't be. Venice is full of them. Do you know they make meatballs in their armpits?'

'I'll remember that,' said Caterine.

'Do. So, one rainy day, I turn up at the restaurant and Luigi isn't there. Same the next day, and the next. He turns up three weeks later in a deserted farmhouse outside Napoli, five bags of money from the Banco Italia and seven holes in his head, self-inflicted.'

'Seven?'

'Seems he reloaded,' Elmo knocked his knuckles on his head. 'Metal plate from the Second World War, apparently. You have to admire his perseverance.'

'That's terrible.'

'Terrible for us, we had no cook! I guessed I would have to find another job and was looking around but, the owner, he didn't give up so easily. He hires a young chef, my age. Your father.'

Caterine stole her eyes from Elmo's, opened up her hands and looked down at them. 'Mum told me you met Dad in a restaurant. Never told me about his predecessor though.'

Caterine could feel Elmo watching her as she searched her palms sadly.

'I was so sorry when I heard,' he said. 'Truly I was, you have no idea.'

Caterine closed her hands.

'Mum always said she would rather die suddenly when she was young, rather than old, alone and…'

'Stuck full of tubes?' said Elmo.

'Sorry.'

'It's not so bad. I tell you what, though. I could use a drink. Don't you think dying rooms should have mini bars in them?'

Caterine looked behind her at the door and through its glass panel, then she reached down beneath the chair and into her green corduroy handbag that sat on the floor. Elmo heard a light chink, and she pulled out a handful of miniature bottles and placed them on the table.

'I thought you might,' she said.

Elmo brought his two tubey hands together.

'*Angel,*' he said.

Caterine opened one bottle and emptied it into Elmo's water glass. She handed it to him, opened another and raised it in a silent toast. Elmo met it and they both drank. Caterine swallowed and held a hand to her mouth, wincing under the acrid fumes of burnt leaves and pickled earth.

'It's rough,' she choked. Elmo inspected his glass.

'I'll admit it's not the smoothest, but it's wonderful. Thank you.'

He raised his glass to her again and she nodded in response, one eye watering and a hand around her throat. Elmo sighed and continued his story.

'Your father was a fine chef. I would have eaten from his kitchen any day of the week, and I don't even like pasta — quite a curse for a Venetian. He was a natural; his smoked chilli sauce alone would have turned that little restaurant around. Locals became startled at the new smells coming from the corner of the square where previously, as far as they were concerned, there had just been an empty space. They came in and ate, they came back and ate more, they came back bringing friends. We were busier than we had ever been; the owner even sacked his nephew and stole two waiters from a bar in Piazza San Marco. His brother never talked to him again.

'Soon we were famous and every night was a full house. They were frantic times, happy times; your father and I became very good friends. I found him fascinating. He would work a full day in the heat of kitchen and at the end of it he'd come out beaming from ear to ear, throwing off his apron and leading me on into the night to some late-night drinking den I'd never heard of. We'd talk about scams, women and music well into the early hours, getting home at dawn and sleeping till we opened the restaurant again. Not that your father was much of a sleeper. In fact, I don't think I ever saw him sleep; I think he looked on it as a hindrance. A troublesome necessity, something that got in the way of his life. He was ambitious, dynamic…if it wasn't for him we wouldn't…'

Elmo took another slug of Strega.

'Anyway, the restaurant's owner, Giuseppe, did I mention him?'

'No, there's been no Giuseppe,' said Caterine, following his lead with another drink, easier this time.

'We hardly saw him before Luigi's big exit. Every other week or so he'd pop in wearing an old French suit and sandals, poke about, drink an espresso and leave. But now he was in every night. He was a happy man, clearing up, making a lot of money. He would swoop around the tables, preening his customers, throwing free bottles of wine about and enjoying his fame. He decided to expand; customer demand was becoming too high, so he bought the building next door, closed the restaurant for a couple of weeks and combined the two. In the new space he put twenty new tables, twice what he had already. And he also put a piano. He wanted music for his customers.'

'And you played it,' said Caterine.

'No. Not at first. He hired a well-known player on a fixed salary, an easy gig. I didn't like him much. He was a miserable, untalented little man. He'd turn up, usually late, snatch a glass and a bottle of Valpolicella and insert himself behind the piano with a packet of cheap cigarettes for four hours. It didn't matter what he played, he'd fumble about between Gershwin, Mancini and Bernstein, sometimes all at the same time. He had no care, he was just threading together bits and bobs he knew, bum notes everywhere. His favourite trick was to slip in a phrase from a song that was popular that week, see if people noticed. Why? One or the other, surely. He'd put *Suspicious Minds* on the end of *Moon River.* People would laugh, I have no idea why.'

'Frustrating for a true artist such as yourself, Uncle,' offered

Caterine.

'I told you, I don't like artists,' replied Elmo.

'Sorry, I was trying not to listen.'

'But you're right, it was frustrating. Now I had to spend hours every day listening to an endless string of unrelated melodies. For the customers, it was pleasant background noise like a fountain in a hotel lobby, but for my brain it was a waterfall of notes. It didn't stop for the entire evening, it copied down everything that bastard played. By the time we shut up my head was bursting, the blackboard was full, I had to make excuses and leave your father earlier so I could get home and empty it onto my piano.'

'Your neighbours must have been delighted,' said Caterine.

'I didn't care. I suppose it was like pissing in public.'

Elmo finished his glass and looked into it. Before he could ask, Caterine had emptied another miniature bottle of Strega into it. She finished off her own and opened another.

'Go on,' she said.

'There *is* a point to this, you know,' said Elmo.

'I'm listening.'

'Not too carefully, I hope. So one evening maestro finishes early because he's had too much Valpolicella. He sits at the bar and helps himself to another bottle, which he proceeds to drain while treating us to stories about how he could have been so much more successful than he was if it wasn't for all the bad luck he's had to endure. It's quiet, people have finished ordering food and we're just sitting around waiting to close, so I think to myself what the hell, go and sit down at the piano. Nobody stopped me. I started to play quietly and released all his infantile little half-keyed melodies and medleys back onto the keyboard, completing the ones that he'd become bored of and making what I thought were more appropriate links between them. Before I knew it…'

'What did he think of that?' said Caterine.

Elmo shook his head. 'He was not pleased.'

Caterine grinned. 'What did he say?'

'Nothing. Not a word. He waited for the customers to stop cheering — they loved it, incidentally — got up from his bar stool, straightened his jacket, picked up the half-drunk bottle of Valpolicella, looked me in the eye and dropped it on the floor.'

'What an arsehole,' said Caterine.

'Quite. The thing was, it didn't break; it just bounced and landed the right way up, not a drop was spilled. He was mortified, he ran out of the place shouting and screaming; the customers loved it. I replaced him after that.'

Caterine laughed silently behind a mouthful of Strega. When she recovered, she said: 'So that's how you became the resident piano player in Amico's, then? Uncle?' She touched his hand. 'Elmo? Oh God.'

Elmo's breathing had slowed to a shallow, wet rattle. The machine was making a noise that it hadn't been making before. Caterine called the nurse.

HOW DO THE GRACELESS

London, England

'THIS PARTRIDGE slept mostly on its right leg,' said Byron, with a mouth full of meat.

'It has a stronger taste than the other one, which means the muscles are more developed and more supple. Which means...'

He licked each of his fingers, making four wet pops.

'...the little fucker slept on it.'

He took another bite. 'Sure you won't try some?'

Joseph shook his head and looked across the table at the man in front of him. He looked like a partridge himself, eyes curious and head cocked as if assessing a potential predator. It was probably the same expression that the one in his mouth had given him the moment before he blasted it full of shot. Only Byron was using it to request acknowledgement of the interesting fact he had just imparted. Joseph didn't grant it.

'Did you know that partridges sleep standing on *one* leg?' Byron continued regardless.

'No, I didn't,' lied Joseph.

'Mmph,' said Byron, tearing off another piece. 'Always the same one, too.'

Joseph's eyes wandered away from Byron's bird-filled face and landed on a copy of *National Geographic* that had been placed on his desk. On its cover was a photograph of a bright blue, smirking dolphin swimming out from a black sea. He had read the article – it was about sleep research. *'Do Dolphins Dream?'* asked the bold, white letters. Some Norwegian scientists had stalked some marine mammals for five months in a sub-aquatic banana-coloured bubble. When they weren't looking, they slapped electrodes on their blowholes and watched the coloured pulses of their sleep on a tiny electroencephalograph they had rigged up. Their conclusions were weak, but the article itself was quite interesting.

'Now the *dolphin…*' Byron continued between bites, tapping the magazine cover with a greasy finger.

Oh…

Joseph sighed inwardly, the next three moves of Byron's monologue suddenly becoming painfully apparent. He wondered about the partridge. It wasn't unusual for Byron to eat while having one of his heart-to-hearts, but a partridge? Had he got it in deliberately? He hoped not; at least he might have had the decency to be spontaneous.

'The *dolphin…*'

Joseph considered feigning interest, but decided against it. He knew Byron wasn't bothered either way.

'The *dolphin* sleeps with *one eye open*, which means he can eat and breathe and move about, and still have a kip at the same time.'

Joseph's mouth flickered. He held Byron's stare as if it was a soiled bedsheet. With every third or fourth chew his lips smacked open, offering a view of the slurry within. He had eyes that didn't blink, just stared back with a carefully mixed balance of curiosity and aggression, enough of each to suggest he had both intellect *and* authority. Authority, fair enough, he had plenty of that (although how much might have been left if you paid off the big lads standing behind him was another matter). But intellect? No. None whatsoever. All he had was an arsenal of vacuous facts with which to illustrate his threats.

This wasn't the first time Joseph had been made to endure Byron's clumsy, anecdotal gymnastics for the sake of a very simple point. When he wasn't killing, maiming, torturing or eating, the man spent his spare time browsing *Reader's Digest* and half-watching programmes on the *Discovery* channel. He used this muddled knowledge to suggest that he had intellectual weight, that he knew about the world, that he was an interesting man, that he wasn't just, well, wasn't just what he was.

It had to be said though, on this occasion the 'fact' was at least interesting. To sleep with one eye open. What a lucky dolphin.

Joseph was no friend of sleep, or rather sleep was no friend of his. He had once cheated death, her sister, and the payback had been cold and spiteful.

Greek mythology thought of sleep and death as brothers, but Joseph had always thought of them as sisters; cruel and irresistible assassins that waited for you in the dark. They crept up on you, smothered you, folded a chloroform rag across your mouth and shushed you till you dropped. Then they split the takings. Sleep stole a third of your life; Death took what was left.

Since the very day that Joseph Martin had side-stepped death, sleep had started force-feeding him a nightly reminder of just how he had done so. It was a Technicolor dream, twice as vivid and loud as any you could imagine. He had never woken quietly again.

It seemed a nice fantasy, to avoid sleep altogether. Or at least to only half-sleep, like a dolphin.

'Very clever animal, the dolphin,' said Byron, tossing a bone on the plate in front of him. 'Very clever indeed.' He sat up and fixed Joseph with another grubby stare. Joseph resisted the temptation to look away. Here came the finale: Byron was going to tell him to sleep with one eye open.

'You'd do well to take a leaf out of his book, you would Joe. Sleep with *one eye open*,' he said slowly, tapping his thick-rimmed spectacles. 'That's what I'd learn to do if you decide to disappoint me again.'

Jesus, how do the graceless make it so big?

Joseph guessed by the self-satisfied look on Byron's face that he had finished making his point and it was his turn to speak.

'Mr Byron,' he began. 'You have my apologies. Understand

that you won't need them again in the future.'

Byron's face twitched with confusion.

'What I mean to say,' said Joseph carefully, 'is that I won't disappoint you again'.

'I hope so,' said Byron, tapping an Embassy on the table. 'For your sake, Joe.'

He lit the cigarette from the flame offered, predictably, by one of the two big chaps standing behind his chair, and then offered the pack to Joseph. Joseph waved his palm at it. He wanted one, but not one of Byron's.

'You've done a lot of work for me over the years, Joe, but don't think that you're above retribution just because we go back a while.'

Byron paused and took a deep drag.

''Cos you ain't,' he finished, jabbing the smoking tip in Joseph's direction.

Joseph fought with all his will not to wince at this last piece of artlessness. Instead, he closed his eyes and gave Byron a nod.

ALL ATTACHED

Venice Hospital, Italy

CATERINE WATCHED Elmo's eyes open and adjust themselves to the light.

'Uncle,' she said.

'Please, I asked you not to call me that,' replied Elmo.

'Are you OK? You passed out.'

Elmo took a long, rusty breath in and out.

'Have we met your mother yet?' he said at last.

Caterine flinched.

'In the story? No,' she said. 'She sang with you, didn't she?'

Elmo looked at the empty wall as if it shone with projected memories.

'Your dad used to bring his girlfriends to the restaurant. They'd come and wait for him to finish, sit in the corner with a Prosecco about half an hour before closing, then he'd take them out. Sometimes he'd insist on me going along with them; not many of them were too impressed by that.'

'How many were there?' asked Caterine in surprise.

'I don't know, a fair few.' He looked at Caterine. 'More than me, anyway. He was a good-looking man, your father.'

'So were you,' said Caterine. 'I've seen photos, and you played piano – girls love that. I still don't see why you never married.'

Elmo looked back at the wall.

'One evening, one of your father's hussies was sitting in the corner waiting for him…'

'Please don't call my mother a hussy,' interrupted Caterine.

'How did you know it was your mother?'

'It seemed to be going that way.'

'Right, well, your *mother* was sitting in the corner…this ruins the moment a bit…'

'Uncle,' said Caterine carefully, 'you do know I've heard this story before, don't you?'

It was true; Caterine *had* heard the story before. Her mother had told her often of how she had met her father, of the happy times they had had in the restaurant. Though she had never admitted as much, she had always found listening to it an uncomfortable experience. The tender, distant care with which her mother treated those memories and the sad, desperate look as she revealed them; it was too much. It was as if she was showing Caterine parts of some priceless, fragile thing that could never be touched or fully seen: a secret story of a secret man who she would never be allowed to know. Not *her own* story; not the story of her father.

'Not like this you haven't,' said Elmo, his breathing suddenly more laboured. 'Not like this.'

'I was just saying,' said Caterine, 'time isn't…'

'Stories…stories don't start and end at definite points, you know. You can't isolate them, they're all attached.'

For a while, they just looked at each other's face: hers young and confused, his old and resigned. Eventually, Elmo turned slowly back to the wall.

'Your mother came in,' he continued. 'I was surprised, she wasn't stunning, not like the others. I watched her as I was playing. She looked off-balance. And nervous; I think she thought she was out of her depth, bidding higher than her reserve. With your father, I mean. Her face was odd…'

'Uncle, it's only been four months since she died,' said Caterine suddenly. 'I'd rather we didn't…'

'Don't misunderstand me, Caterine,' Elmo broke in. 'Your mother was a very beautiful woman. In every way, in the best way, but you had to be next to her to find that. You had to hear her, watch her move, listen to her laugh, let her smile at you.

You knew real beauty when you were with your mother. Real beauty looks at you in odd ways.'

'All the same,' said Caterine, her eyes glistening, 'talking like this, of her before I was born, it's…'

Elmo grasped her hand tightly, urgently.

'Caterine, you need to hear this,' he said. 'I have waited too long already. I should have called you when she died. But I didn't. I didn't do a lot of things. Please…'

'Go on,' she said at last.

'I didn't know she was musical at that point,' Elmo continued. 'I suppose I put on a bit of a show for her, a few more fiddly bits and clever finishes.'

'You were showing off?'

'I showed off to all of your dad's girlfriends. Maybe I thought they might come to me after he'd dumped them. They did sometimes. Anyway, *she* wasn't impressed. The three of us went over to one of your dad's nightspots and she corrected me on the inversions I'd used for my Oscar Peterson medley. I was pissed on Campari, and transfixed. I'd never met a woman who knew about music before.'

The machine hummed, clicked and beeped.

'It would be three years before your father asked her to marry him, but he knew he'd found his bride. We became strong friends, the three of us, and pretty soon your mother became a part of life in the restaurant. She waitressed, cleaned, chatted with the customers. From my piano stool I could see through the hatch between the kitchen and the bar. Your father would sometimes just stand there watching her; even at a busy time when he had three ducks to prepare or zabaglione to mix, he'd just watch her smiling. Other times, she'd sneak back and I'd see her put her arms around his neck and he'd kiss her, still holding his whisk. I was envious.'

'Envious? You mean, you liked her?' She frowned. 'Loved her?'

'I loved them both. They were never exclusive, they never

made me into a gooseberry. Sometimes they set me up with girls; mostly dancers and actors whom your mother knew. I got lucky with a few of them, but they never really lasted.'

'Couples are useful friends to have,' said Caterine.

'Good pimps,' said Elmo.

The sound of a nurse's shoes echoed softly in the corridor outside. Caterine glanced at the clock by the lamp; it was past two o'clock in the morning.

'There really *is* a point...' said Elmo.

Caterine blinked slowly at him in assurance. He eyed the two remaining bottles of Strega. She smiled and prepared them.

'The restaurant kept on pulling in the crowds, and Giuseppe basked in its success like a sun-drenched seal. But eventually he decided to sell it. He wanted to leave Venice, start something new in Rome. He thought he was suddenly a natural entrepreneur and wanted to make it big. The fool, he didn't realise it was your dad's cooking...'

'And your piano playing,' said Caterine.

'...and my piano playing that had made him. We were worried, we wondered who the next owner might be. We guessed it would be some faceless idiot who'd tear through it and change everything. We didn't want that to happen. Then, as the three of us sat round discussing it after closing, your mother had an idea: why didn't we put an offer in? Why didn't we buy Amico's?

'Of course, at first I snorted at her. Buy *Amico's*? A pianist, a chef and a waitress, in their early twenties? Not a chance. I mean, I had some money saved up, but not much; it wouldn't have bought one of its plates. Your mother just smiled and looked me in the eye. She was rich, she told me. Inheritance from a wealthy aunt.

'Well, your father leapt at it. He picked her up and danced her round the room, then he grabbed me and messed up my hair, laughing and smacking me about the head. He was sold immediately. But I wasn't as easily convinced. Running a restaurant isn't just cooking and playing the piano, it's book-keeping and ordering and staff management, long hours and long debts. It was a huge risk to stake an inheritance on. I argued against it for hours with them, but they had an answer for everything, and they wouldn't let me out of the bargain. She told me that they could only afford to bid if I put in my savings, my measly share; I knew she had more than she said though. She just wanted me to be part of the fun, and I buckled under the weight of her good nature. Excuse me…'

'Uncle, are you sure you want to go on? Your breathing doesn't sound good.'

Elmo coughed another lungful into his handkerchief, hiding it from Caterine. He frowned and gulped, closing his shaking fist around it, waving his other hand at Caterine to brush off her concern. After a few deep breaths, he continued.

'We got the restaurant, Giuseppe sold it to us. It was a lot more work, but your mother got on top of things. She did the accounts, organised the waiting rota, dealt with the orders, even kept waitressing herself. And towards the end of the night, when things were slowing off and there were no more orders for food, she'd sing with me. She'd put down her tea towel, slide over and lean on the piano and sing with whatever I was playing.

'Now, I'd like to be able to tell you that she had a beautiful voice, that she sang like an angel, but I can't I'm afraid. She was no good really, cracked and unsteady, mediocre on a good night.'

Elmo blinked and smiled.

'But such honesty. Every note she sang was from deep within her soul. She couldn't help it, it was as if she was showing you around every broken, imperfect corner of her heart. It was beautiful. That's when I really fell in love with her.'

Caterine felt the words before she heard them. They hurt her in a strange way, like a wound opening.

'I couldn't turn the music off, Caterine. When you share that with someone, it's hard to. I bet your mother never told you that, did she?'

Caterine just looked back at him.

'No, I bet she never told you the next bit either.'

He cleared his throat and sat up slightly, taking a sip from his glass.

'Book-keeping, staff rota, food ordering, cooking and piano playing, they aren't the only things you have to keep on top of in order to run a successful restaurant in Venice,' he began.

'The other thing you have to keep on top of — the main thing you have to keep on top of — is the Mafia. It's a fact. Everyone gives up a little to the Mafia; that's just the way it is. Giuseppe never told us about it until he gave us the deeds to the restaurant, but it seems he had quite a good deal going with them. Very amicable, twenty per cent – not a bad price to keep them from burning the place down. And other people, of course.

'Every month we'd get a little visit from a man. He wore nothing you'd expect somebody of his trade to wear. Very simple; white shirt and grey slacks. Brogues. He had a stick too, I remember, and he always carried some book. I don't know if he dressed like this just to seem natural, or whether he actually was. He called himself Pepe. I liked him, actually. He'd stay for the evening; sit in the corner reading his book while we gave him food and wine. Every now and again, when I'd finished a piece, he'd look over at me, nod and lift his glass in appreciation. He enjoyed Amico's, everyone did. And when we closed your mother gave him a little bag to take away with him. He just seemed like another cog in the business, nothing threatening.

'But your father,' Elmo looked back from the wall. 'Your father didn't like it. He didn't see why we should be giving a fifth of what we took in that place to criminals he'd never met, especially not when he'd been the one to turn it round. He wasn't stupid, though; he knew we'd lose the place if we didn't pay up, maybe lose even more. So he talked to them.'

'To Pepe?' said Caterine, still dazed by Elmo's recent announcement.

'Yes, became friends with him, of sorts. He sat with him and talked with him when he visited. Your mother and I were worried, we didn't want anything to get messy. As far as we were concerned, we were happy to just write off twenty per cent every month for peace of mind. Not your father.

'One day Pepe visited and went away without the cut. Your father looked pleased with himself, told us he'd made a deal.'

'What kind of deal?' asked Caterine.

'The worst kind. He agreed to Amico's being used as a drop-off.'

'What does that mean?'

'Apparently our restaurant backed onto a very dark canal that made a nice, discreet beeline for the shore. Very handy for driving boats in from the sea, making drops from Serbia, Croatia, even the Middle East. Stolen goods, drugs, cash, jewellery, documents. They'd pick it up later.'

'Shit.'

'That's exactly what I said, and your mother, among other things. We were furious; he hadn't even consulted us…'

Caterine wrapped her fingers together as she struggled with what Elmo was telling her. She had never known her father, he had died before her birth, but her mother had painted him as a kind, creative, loving man. Not one who would knowingly become involved with organised crime. Now her mother was dead, and the man who was distorting her last memories of them both was dying too.

Elmo, seemed to sense her turmoil and laid a hand on hers.

'Your father was a good man, Caterine,' he said. 'A very good man, and a very good friend.'

'I never knew him,' she said.

'I know. But I did.'

Elmo took away his hand.

'We tried to get him to go after him, cancel the deal, stick with the agreement we'd inherited from Giuseppe, but he was having none of it. He didn't see the problem; to him, all we had to do was hide a few suitcases once in a while. He didn't see the implications; that we were no longer just a pay cheque for them but a vested interest. Your father pulled us right into a pocket nobody wants to be in. Besides, the deal had been made. They're strict about that kind of thing.

'Things were different after that. Business went on as usual, of course, but we didn't talk. Your mother went cold and the atmosphere in the restaurant became dense with anticipation – we didn't know what to expect or when to expect it. As it happened, we only had to wait a couple of months.'

'What happened?'

'We got a call. Your father took it, it lasted about seven seconds. When he hung up, he told us that somebody was going to make a drop that evening. We had to pull in three metal crates from our delivery hatch at 3am and stash them till the following week. We weren't told what was in them. I didn't want to know.

'That evening was terrible. One of our waiters had called in sick, so I had to cover for him while playing between orders. It was very busy; two large birthday parties had booked in and wouldn't leave. They kept ordering more sambucas, competing with each other, getting drunk and fighting. It was after 2am and your mother was starting to panic. Your father was keeping his cool; nothing was going to faze him and I think this made her worse. I tried to keep her calm, keep the atmosphere in the restaurant normal. But I was nervous too. I remember playing very badly; I kept forgetting what I was doing. I was heckled.

'We sent all the other staff home and eventually managed to remove the revellers, the first time we'd ever kicked a customer out onto the street. Any other night and we'd have let them drink and eat until they'd had enough; more money for us, we didn't care. But not tonight. We sent them outside. Two or three of them stuck around banging on the doors for a while and cursing us. We ignored them, praying for them to leave, and finally they did. Then it was just the three of us, sat around a table with a second-hand bottle of wine from one of the parties, your mother chain-smoking. We didn't look at each other, or say a single word. Then we heard three low thuds coming from the back. Somebody else was banging on the door.

'At first, nobody moved. Our hearts stopped and we just looked at each other. In the end it was your mother who broke the silence. She stubbed out her cigarette and marched through to the delivery hatch, your father and I running after her. When we opened it, there was nobody there, just the dark, quiet water rippling below. But we heard a whisper and looked below the hatch, and there was a small fishing boat with a man at its keel. I don't know what we were expecting, some flash speedboat with machine guns, perhaps. He handed up the crates to us one at a time. They were very light, very small; easy to hide. And then he chugged away into the night.

'And that was it?'

'That was it, the first drop. We hid the crates in a broken refrigerator that lived in the upstairs room and went home without saying a word. The next week, the same thing happened, but in reverse. A fisherman turned up, banged on the hatch, took the crates and left.'

'I can't believe my mother did this.'

'We got used to it. We'd get a drop-off every month on average, although at one time we had one twice a week for a few months. The drop-offs were the most difficult to bear; sometimes we didn't know what to expect. I remember the worst: it was a person.'

'What? Who?'

'Not a fucking clue. He just lived in our attic for a fortnight. We fed him from the restaurant. He came out about two stone heavier than when he came in, and never said a word.'

'He could have been anyone,' said Caterine.

'I know, but as I said, we got used to it. Very used to it. It got to the point when I even thought your father had made a good decision making that deal. We were considerably better off, and all we had to do was keep boxes and suitcases and fatten up the odd mute. Working for the Mafia didn't seem so bad after all.'

Elmo's face suddenly creased and he retched four long heaves from his chest. He spilled the last of his Strega on the bedsheet and the glass dropped and smashed on the floor.

'Uncle…I'll get the nurse,' Caterine got up from her stool, but Elmo gripped her hand and shook it. He spat into his handkerchief again, wiping some blood and mucus from the side of his mouth. Then he fell back on his pillow, staring at the wall and pumping short, shallow whistles from his throat. He closed his eyes.

THE WHOLE DAMN BUSINESS

London, England

JOSEPH PARKED his black Saab and limped up the two flights of stairs to his door. Once inside, he threw his keys on the table and poured himself a Talisker, which he took across to the window. It was high and wide and gave a good view of the city, one of the reasons he had taken the flat. He had quickly learned that living in a city as revoltingly overpopulated as London was all about finding some space. Not just physical space, but space for your mind, somewhere you could let your thoughts off their leash for a while, a sanctuary.

When he had first moved there, money could afford him nothing but the coldest and dirtiest of the north-western bedsits he had looked at. It was below street level, it was tiny, it was noisy, damp and uncleanable — but in all other ways it suited him. No need for questions, no need for documents, just a name (not his, not yet) and a rent book, which the youngest of the French sisters who owned the place wordlessly stamped every Sunday in exchange for a bunch of crumpled notes from Joseph's pocket.

That first place, a room with a cracked sink and a buckled single bed, was to be his sanctuary. Somewhere to come back to, to regroup, to sleep, however fitfully. But it wasn't enough. Its window was nothing more than a thin crack at the top of the wall beneath an overground tube platform, so close that he would wake to the shuffling of shoes and murmur of morning conversations from the early-rising office workers who lived in the area's real flats and houses. Even on the brightest of days, it offered barely enough light by which to read a book. Safe haven though it was, it became a cell for his mind, so Joseph took to wandering outside late at night, early in the morning, through the day, any time he felt the walls closing in. He walked through parks and along the grey riverside, often through the centre of town as far as Soho and Piccadilly, sometimes further. Outside became his sanctuary, he let his mind free in the city itself.

That had been twenty years ago, and he had lived in many places since. He didn't walk so frequently now, but having a view from a window two floors up at one of the highest points in Greater London had become sanctuary enough. It felt like coming up for air.

He took a sip of whisky and watched dusk creep slowly over the skyline, dimming the detail in its landmarks till they all became silhouettes and his mind became calm. It *was* a fine view. A cigarette would have gone well with it, if he'd had some. He thought about going to buy some Dunhills from the garage on the corner of Maida Vale, but knew that by the time he returned the sun would have set completely and his whisky would have lost its first-glass appeal. He didn't want to ruin his mood. He could get some later.

He thought back to his meeting with Byron, his rap on the knuckles, a threat that was meant to sound sinister but was so formulaic it was childish. Most of the people Joseph had contracted for in his years had at least something that set them apart from the rest, something that made them unique, whether it was a style of dress, a method of killing or a genuine, misinformed passion for some generic style of art. Even those who didn't have such a totem had at least the dignity to just be who they were — common thieves and murderers — without the need to place themselves above the scum with whom they dealt. Byron, however, was neither of these types. He was a walking stereotype; an East End mobster who would be more than what he was, right down to the shiny suit, the coat of arms, the cheap country retreat and the affected love of game hunting.

None of that mattered, though, did it? He had the money, the power, the big lads behind him. He could be whoever he wanted.

Joseph knew he had fucked up. The last job he had pulled was sloppy to say the least; half-planned, badly timed and poorly executed. On paper it was simple — a small flat in Dollis Hill, unexposed territory, unsuspecting subject. A job like that, done in the home of the target itself, should have been quick and quiet. As it was, the man he had almost failed to kill (one of Byron's many traitors) had managed to let out so many half-strangled screams and break so much furniture in his death throes that half the street woke up. Lights were lit, heads were rubbed, dogs barked, voices grumbled. Joseph had had to finish the job and bolt without the body. The police became involved, there was evidence that could have led back to Joseph, back to Byron, if it wasn't for a contact inside the force from which he had plucked a favour. It had all been a little too close.

He had fucked up, of course he had, but that didn't make being told off by such a tortuous little prick any easier.

If the roles had been reversed, if he had been wearing the shiny suit and had two big lads behind him, he would have dispensed with Byron there and then, without a word. True to his stereotype though, and probably because he thought it gave him an air of mercy, Byron had given him another chance: a high-risk job abroad, non-optional.

By all accounts, it was more than he deserved. Certainly it was more than he wanted; what he wanted was out. Out of the whole damn business.

MICE EAT THEIR YOUNG

Venice Hospital, Italy

'TWO YEARS,' rasped Elmo.

Caterine opened her eyes like a commuter in an empty carriage at an unfamiliar station.

'Two years,' she repeated as she unfolded her fingers, uncertain of what either word meant. She blinked. 'How long was I asleep?'

'I don't know. I was just thinking how like your mother you are. She was undemanding, and she didn't like small talk. She said only what was important and listened to everything. She was like an open page, an empty record onto which you could spill all the music in your heart without worrying about mistakes.'

Elmo leaned his head towards her.

'Be careful whose music you listen to, Caterine.'

He heaved himself up on the pillow.

'Two years,' he confirmed. 'Two whole years we helped the Mafia like that. They became part of the routine, part of the running of the restaurant, and whatever we were looking after at the time we treated as indifferently as eggs or peppers. Have we ordered enough sugar? Do we have enough staff for the weekend? Have we hidden those heavy sacks well enough under the stairs?

'We stopped thinking about it. Whereas before we had a suit in the corner of our restaurant, drinking our wine, eating our food and taking our money, now the only human contact we had with them was a face in the dark for a few seconds a month. It became very easy to forget they existed. I expect your mother and I began to forget the implications, just like your father. Nothing seemed likely to go wrong…you look angry, Caterine.'

'I'm sorry,' said Caterine, rubbing her eyes. 'It's just hard to accept that my parents did this. Being the victim of protection racketeers is bad enough, but to work with the *Mafia*? What were they *thinking*?'

'Money and pride. To your father, it seemed like a good idea at the time, I suppose,' said Elmo. 'Most bad ideas seem like that at the time…mind you, sometimes you just know they're bad.'

'What do you mean?'

Elmo looked seriously at the wall, as if the memories were becoming troubling. He breathed a crackling sigh.

'As I said, we got used to the routine. Things came in, things went out, but we never knew what they were. We decided that we wanted to.'

'You didn't look…' said Caterine.

'It was actually my idea. We were having a good month at the restaurant and it was my birthday, so we shut up shop and set about getting drunk. All the awkwardness there had been after the deal was first made had long since gone, and we were all best friends again.'

'But you said you loved her. How could you stay friends? How could you stand to be around them?' said Caterine.

'Love is relentless,' said Elmo, after a pause. 'It is the Mafia of the heart. It owns all of your emotions.' He clenched the fingers of his right hand. 'Holds you in its fist, has the power to break you. With one call it can assassinate you with grief. It has to be paid off, it must be satisfied, even if you can only manage a look or the brush of a hand. I could have found work elsewhere, left them with Amico's, but if I had then I wouldn't have seen her. Or your father.'

Elmo turned to Caterine.

'Don't forget that I loved him, too. He was a dear friend.

You can't understand how badly I felt about my feelings. But love was holding me to ransom. I had no choice.'

'What happened? Tell me.'

'So, we were sitting round drinking and the conversation fell upon the drop-off we'd had the week before. It was small, just one bag sealed in another plastic one. For the first time, amazingly, we began to speculate on its contents.'

'What did you think it was?'

'I thought it was diamonds, your father thought it was the thumb of a kidnap victim, your mother thought pills.'

'I'd have been with you,' said Caterine.

'And you'd have been right. It took about five minutes after I suggested we look inside for the other two to agree.'

'You looked?'

'What harm was a look? Anyway, at 4am, after thirteen Stregas, the Mafia don't seem quite as nasty. We all ran back to the kitchen, where we'd hidden the bag beneath the fridge. It all felt like nothing but a drunken game.

'We took it out and placed it on a large chopping board on the table in the centre of the room. Then, for a while, we just looked at it. We were nervous and excited, looking around us to check if anyone was there. Eventually, I picked up a potato peeler — I don't know why, there were plenty of sharp knives around — and went to work on the sealed plastic.

'Sealed? How were you going to seal it again?' said Caterine.

'*Thirteen* Stregas, Caterine,' said Elmo, inexplicably holding up just three fingers.

'It came apart quite easily, then there was just a large black leather wallet wrapped up with string, the kind that might hold legal papers, bonds, that kind of thing. We looked at that for a while too. I was beginning to wonder whether your father's guess was right, about whether we were going to like what was inside.'

'Who opened it?' said Caterine.

'I did. I flipped it open with the potato peeler.'

'And what came out?'

'Lots and lots of diamonds.'

'*Shit...*'

'All uncut, all different sizes, all on our chopping board.'

'Bet you were glad it wasn't a thumb.'

'I wish it had been, otherwise we wouldn't have done what we did next.'

'What did you do?'

'We took some,' said Elmo.

'What?' whispered Caterine, as if the Mafia were there in the room.

'It really is quite incredible, you know, alcohol.' Elmo turned the half-empty miniature of Strega in his hand. It caught the light and glinted.

'The conversations you can have, the thoughts you think, the revelations, they can be truly wonderful. But there's a point you hit during an evening's course, and when you hit it they drown like rats. One minute you're talking about music, life, friendship, physics, religion...the next you're stealing diamonds.'

'How many did you take?'

'It didn't take long for us to agree. There were so many of them, all different sizes, none of them looked the same and we didn't think they could possibly be missed. After all that we'd done for them, we figured they owed us. Why would they miss them? We could build another extension, take a holiday...we took six medium-sized rocks and closed up the bag.'

'Six? But...how did you reseal it?'

'That was the tricky bit. We tried holding a lighter to the plastic and trying to melt it back together but it just shrivelled up and went brown. Eventually we managed it by clamping it in the oven door, which was still hot from the evening. It acted as a heat sealer and then we just trimmed the edge. Good as new.'

'But what if they knew exactly how many diamonds to expect? What if they counted and found them six short?' said Caterine.

'Ah...well, that's what we began to wonder after we'd sealed the bag. The Strega was wearing off you see, we were sobering up. Suddenly stealing six sizeable diamonds from the Mob didn't seem like such a wise idea.

'We argued for a bit,' he said. 'In the end, though, we each agreed we should put them back. Only problem is, we never got a chance,' he said.

'What? Why?' said Caterine.

'No sooner had I picked up the potato peeler than we heard a very bad sound. A soft, slow knocking sound on the delivery hatch. The pick-up had come early.'

'We froze. We didn't know what to do. We still had the diamonds but we didn't want them any more. There was no time to open up the bag, put them back and reseal it and the fishing boat was waiting outside. None of us said anything, we just looked at each other and waited for some idea to present itself. It didn't, and in the end we did the only thing we could do, which was to open the hatch and give him the bag. I had the diamonds in my pocket as I handed it down.'

Caterine shook her head.

'You stole from the Mob. Weren't you scared?'

'*Terrified.* None of us slept that night, and the next few weeks were hell. We expected trouble any moment, that some party of thugs would burst through our doors and shower us with bullets, or that we'd be ambushed when we walked home alone, pulled into a boat and garrotted with our own hamstrings.'

'Do they really do that?'

'I've no idea, you know how your imagination plays when you're scared. Everywhere I went I expected some gloved hand to reach out and drag me into some alley. You know those days when you think more people are looking at you than usual? I had them every day, I stared at everyone in the street, even old women, children. I was swamped with paranoia.

'It got worse when a month went by and there was no sign of any call for a drop-off. We were certain they'd got wise to us, that they knew we'd stolen their diamonds. We thought about shutting up the restaurant for a while, going somewhere, leaving town, but your mother managed to calm us all down. The last thing we wanted to do was attract attention to ourselves, so we decided to carry on, business as usual.

'That evening, we had a full house as normal. I played, your mother waitressed, your father cooked. Playing relaxed me; I could lose myself, forget about what was worrying me in real life.'

Elmo let the scene run on the wall and looked at the young woman.

'I don't normally make mistakes either,' he said. 'But I did when I looked up to find Pepe sitting in the corner.'

'Pepe? The man?' gasped Caterine.

'Pepe the man, yes. My heart…' he said, gulping. 'My mouth must have fallen open and my fingers stiffened when I saw him. The music stopped and he looked up, catching my horrified eyes and smiling serenely. He held my stare and the bastard raised his glass at me.'

Elmo had started to speak more slowly. His voice was becoming little more than a breath, and his eyelids had drawn together.

'Then it all happened rather quickly. I was aware of your mother hurrying across to the kitchen, running to tell your father, no doubt. The room slowed down and I heard nothing but the pounding of blood in my head, it must have been fifty per cent adrenaline.

'I think it's the only time in my life when my conscious mind has truly given up. Luckily, you have reinforcements in situations like that. Your instincts take over. Did you know that mice eat their young when they're under attack? I don't know why, maybe they're thinking if anyone eats their kids it might as well be them. Keep it in the family and all that.'

'I think it's because…'

'Well that's what I did. Except I ate some diamonds.'

'What?'

'I ate the diamonds. They were hidden beneath my piano stool. I reached beneath it, pulled them out and swallowed them.'

'You could have choked!' said Caterine.

'I did,' said Elmo, 'I fell off the stool and collapsed in the middle of the restaurant. I remember the noise of shouts and gasps rushing back into my ears and your parents carrying me through into the kitchen. They tried punching me in the back, the Heimlich manoeuvre, but nothing moved those diamonds. Everything seemed to just work them deeper down inside me. Eventually I stopped choking and found my breath, then I told them what I had done, and started babbling at them about Pepe and that we had to escape.

'Then they both did exactly the same thing. They put their hands to their mouths, gasped, shook their heads and then creased up with laughter. I thought they'd gone berserk, and I told them so. Pepe was outside waiting to kill us and all they could do was laugh. I was furious. I started to make my own escape and made for the delivery hatch, but they stopped me. They just kept laughing, as if nothing was the matter.

'As it turned out, nothing was. They calmed down and told me what had happened. Pepe had talked to your mother, told her he was sorry he hadn't been in for a while, that he'd always liked it in Amico's. He also said he had a message to say that they were sorry the drop-off had been late this month, but to expect one that evening.'

'So you ate the diamonds for nothing?' said Caterine.

'Well, I wasn't so sure. I was still suspicious, I thought it might be a clever way of telling us we were going to be knocked off that evening. Turns out I was wrong. The drop-off was made and everything continued as normal.'

Caterine looked at Elmo sadly. He was weak, his breathing now no more powerful than a moth's wing-beat. The inevitable was closing in.

'What about the diamonds, Uncle?' she said.

'I spent three months pawing through my own stools as if I was panning for gold. One came out eventually; we had it valued. It turns out they were worth more than we'd thought, uncut and especially rare — $30,000 a piece.

'$30,000?'

'And that was thirty years ago.'

'That makes $180,000!' said Caterine.

'Not quite,' said Elmo looking down at his belly. 'The others never made an appearance, they seem to like it inside my intestine. Apparently they're lodged firmly in one of the more inaccessible areas of my gut, a spaghetti junction of nerve and artery, completely irretrievable without certain death, but no real threat to my health where they sit. Although I'm certain they gave me this.'

Elmo lifted his tube-laden hands an inch off the bed and let them fall back down. He looked at Caterine through two threads of eye.

'They're still inside me,' he whispered.

Caterine looked back at him in disbelief.

'For all these years, you've been carrying around five $30,000 diamonds?' she said.

'That's the truth,' replied Elmo eventually. 'They're worth millions now, I'm sure.'

'Is that why you left Amico's?' she asked.

Elmo nodded. 'I don't think your father ever really believed that I hadn't taken the diamonds for myself. He eased up a bit when I showed him the X-ray, but even so he blamed me for losing a small fortune. We weren't ever quite the same friends we had been after that. I left and played in other places. I still saw them, but it was mostly just your mother; he always had some excuse or other. I don't blame him.

'They married soon after. I went to the wedding and Fidelio and I acted as friends, but we soon lost touch. Then,' he said, carefully studying Caterine as he delivered her the words, 'when

I was meeting your mother once, she told me that he had been doing some work for the Mafia.'

Caterine's face fell apart.

'Why?' said Elmo, addressing her disbelief. 'I don't know, perhaps he felt coerced, perhaps he wanted to earn some quick money. I didn't like it and I know your mother didn't either. She never spoke about it again, and I never asked. When she told me they were leaving Italy, making a new start…' he turned to Caterine and smiled, '…that she was pregnant…'

Caterine blinked, expressionless.

'I was happy, truly I was, Caterine. Happy because she was happy, and that you were going to be born into a good family, a happy family.'

'I don't understand,' she stammered.

The machine picked up pace as she gripped his hand.

'…tore me apart when I heard of the accident,' Elmo continued gruffly, turning back to the wall. 'No trace of his body. Dead. Gone. And your mother hurt and alone in a foreign country…'

He stopped and looked back at the wall, his frail ribcage pumping short, fast breaths into his dying lungs.

'When she returned, I met her. She was still bruised from the crash, her arm in a sling, her face…her face was not the same. It had lost something. She had lost something; she had lost Fidelio. But at least she still had you,' he said, turning to her fragile face. 'You were still inside her, still alive.'

'She only told me that my father had died in a car crash,' said Caterine blankly. 'Not that he was never found.'

'Your mother spent her whole life keeping the memory of your father as pure and good for you as she could,' said Elmo. 'She didn't want you to have to live your life wondering as she had.'

Caterine stared blankly at Elmo.

'I wanted us to make up,' he continued, ignoring her silence. 'To be friends again…'

A rattle in his throat sent Elmo into a sudden convulsion. Caterine leapt towards him as he shuddered and coughed and the machine into which he was plugged beeped urgently. She soothed him as he rested back against the pillow, taking no time to breathe as he continued the last words he would ever speak.

'…to be friends, at least to be friends,' he gasped. 'But it was too painful. It wasn't the same. So I decided to leave Venice.'

Elmo gulped, his throat dry. The heart monitor was slowing.

'Before I left, she called me, said that someone had been to see her to ask about Fidelio. *Joseph* as they liked to call him.'

'Who?' said Caterine, desperately searching Elmo's face.

'The people he had been working for, the people they had tried to escape from.'

He gulped twice, nothing to soothe his dry throat, no water to cool his lips as they searched for air, for words.

'And she told me that I would be your godfather, when you were born.'

Elmo smiled. 'That was a good way to part company, I think.'

Caterine nodded.

'So then I left, travelled, travelled far. Movement became an almost permanent state of affairs for me, such was my paranoia over my little 'cargo'. Hearing that your mother had been contacted scared me, I suppose…but I didn't just travel because of fear.'

Elmo's face fell and he took another dry gulp of air.

'I wanted to escape Venice, escape its memories,' he went on. 'Strange that I would want to lose such happy times.'

For a second he was quiet, shaking his head.

'Eventually I found Laos. It's a peaceful place, slow and forgetful. I felt happy there, safe. I made friends, lived my life. I would have liked to have died there, but this…' he threw a hand at the tubey, grey body before them both. 'My family…you know?'

Caterine looked back, still and quiet. Elmo blinked back at her.

'But I'm going back, Caterine…after tonight, I'll be buried there. Caterine,' he said, drawing her closer to his weak voice. 'This is important: before I'm buried, I've arranged for a…post mortem…'

She shook her head, bewildered.

'…go to Laos, Caterine, collect your inheritance…someone will call you…'

He broke off suddenly, as if remembering something.

'Your father, he wasn't a bad person, Caterine,' he began again. 'I made a mistake, that's all. Two mistakes.'

Caterine shook her head. 'Two mistakes…?' she whispered.

'Someone will call you…'

'What mistakes, Elmo? Tell me, please…'

Elmo breathed a long, slow painful breath and his eyes widened.

'I told you I swallowed the diamonds…well I swallowed something else as well. A secret. Your mother…When I said I loved her…it wasn't entirely…one-sided.' He pulled in some more air.

'Before they married, before you were born…when I met her and…your father wasn't there,' he said. Caterine's eyes flicked across his face.

'I have a child…' he whispered.

'…Uncle…' said Caterine.

'I told you…not to call me that,' said Elmo.

And with one last breath, Elmo closed his eyes and left the world.

SOMETHING UNCOMFORTABLE

London, England

JOSEPH TOOK a sip and held the warm, peaty taste on his tongue before letting it flood down across his torso. He looked at the pieces of paper in front of him. It was dark, but he had left the curtains open so he could still see outside, and the only light was a small desk lamp he had placed on the table. He was alone, late at night, apart from Miles Davis and the bottle of Talisker.

Joseph had always told Anita that he would have rather lived and died alone than spend his life beside somebody who only half interested him. It was a common compromise, he believed, that many people were prepared to make just in order to spare them the ugliness of their own company. The reason he wasn't prepared to make such a trade-off, he would happily claim, was that he genuinely liked his own company. He didn't need the affections of others to fill any gap made by solitude. He thrived on it; it was when he felt most at home. He could have easily lived and died without anyone else, least of all that half-hearted excuse for love they called 'companionship'.

It was integrity, and finding Annie had seemed like his reward. She had fulfilled so much more than even his most perfect womanly ideal that there had been no need for anything like a compromise. It had been like a bonus prize from fate, for sticking to his guns, thinking down the road less travelled.

It was easy to imagine the same fate being responsible for tearing her away just as quickly, within the space of those few terrible words. But he knew that wasn't the case. Fate had nothing to do with that.

Since then, his own company had never seemed quite such a

cherished thing. But even so, late nights with a bottle, a stack of CDs and a light-polluted silhouette of London's skyline was always better than giving in to sleep. A bottle, good music, good view, pack of cigarettes…

He realised that he had forgotten to buy any earlier, and now he really wanted one. He wasn't a full-time smoker, he lit a cigarette only occasionally, usually one or two every other day or a pack when he was drunk. He saved them for a good view, or after a meal, or for late nights alone. This made each and every one enjoyable, probably akin to the hardcore smoker's first morning drag. Personally, the idea of sparking up when still in his dressing gown — or worse, still in *bed* — repulsed him. In fact, the whole idea of cigarettes disgusted Joseph, right up to moments such as these. The upshot of this was that he very rarely bought them during the day, which meant that he very rarely had any to hand. The garage would be closed now.

Joseph muttered a curse and studied the sheets of paper in front of him. One was a torn piece of notepaper on which he had scribbled the few facts Byron threw him regarding the job. He copied these out more legibly on a clean piece of A4 next to it.

<u>*6th November - facts*</u>

22nd October: Byron received word from contact on road in Laos, South East Asia.

13th November: corpse is to arrive in autopsy ward of hospital, Luang Prabang.

Corpse contains a number of high-value diamonds.

Young female due to collect, no id.

Nothing further from contact.

Diamonds. How predictable. If he could credit Byron with a shred of wit, Joseph might have thought this was a joke, sending him on a wild goose chase through Asia as some chummy payback for his error. But Byron was not chummy, and neither was he funny. This was a real job, and as jobs go this had to be one of the worst. A corpse, no ID, just a date, a whiff of cash. Vague bits of information made all the worse by their source, some faceless pervert, a crony of Byron's *en route* to Cambodia for some dubious holiday Joseph would rather not think about.

Joseph had stolen bodies before for what was inside of them. Usually they were smugglers, hit after an otherwise successful run and still with the goods in their bellies. In his early career it had been drugs, later it was stones. Either way, he always knew the ID of the carrier, their background and any associated threats. And he had never had to travel any further than eastern Europe to collect. This, on the other hand, was a phantom corpse in a place he had never been.

He looked out of the window. A corpse full of diamonds. Something uncomfortable stirred in his memory, the same thing that had stirred when Byron first told him.

He dismissed it and turned back to the facts in front of him, trying to build upon them, at least form some questions about them in his mind. But they were all dead ends. This was opportunistic crime of the highest order, the equivalent of a sly flick of a car's door handle as you passed it, or some adolescent warehouse break-in based on a tip-off from a mate. It was a crude, low waste of time.

A rude beep sounded from the laptop in the corner of the room. Joseph walked over to it and brought up his email inbox, one new message waiting with an attachment.

```
From: gkelly@trmail.sk.net
To: jmartin@vnet.co.uk
Subject: RE: Schematics.
_______________________________

Joe,
Hope attached is what you need.
G.
```

Joseph opened the attachment – a large, single-page PDF showing the floor plan of Luang Prabang Hospital. He printed it off and took it back to the table, sat down and looked at it.

It was, predictably, useless. The detail was fine, but it told him nothing more than where the morgue was. He could have found that out from the hospital reception. He threw it back on the table with the other bits of paper and shook his head, not knowing what else he was expecting to find. His only choice was to go to the place and watch what happened. The diamonds were leaving the hospital anyway, so all he had to do was identify the girl carrying them, dispose of her and take the stones. It would have been so much easier if he had had some kind of handle on her, knew who she was so he could just intercept her on the other side of wherever she was going next. The idea of smuggling diamonds through South East Asia did not appeal.

He looked at the clock, it was past 2am, probably time to let sleep have its greedy fix. Joseph drained his whisky and turned off the lamp, finding his way through to the bedroom by the cold light from outside. He took off his trousers and shirt and hung them in his wardrobe. Then he took off his right leg, propped it in its place by the bedside table, and rolled himself into bed.

~1978~

THE DIARY OF CLAUDETTE FERRIÈRE

20 FÉVRIER 1978

Papa is still not well enough to leave his bed even though he tried, but he couldn't even put his boiler suit on. He said that the fever is making his bones hurt and that he wouldn't like to have it with a broken leg like the man in my room. He asked me how he was and I told him that he was just the same, which he is. He still hasn't talked.

21 février 1978

It is still snowing and the drifts outside our house are getting bigger and bigger. They almost reach to the top of the door to the yard so the sunlight cannot get into the kitchen or the sitting room and downstairs is always dark. Until today I have had to stay downstairs in the dark because there is a sick man and a sick Papa upstairs. The man is more awake now but the room smells really bad like something died in it so I keep the window open as wide as I can now when I go out to feed the cows, even if it does mean the snow blows in and gets the man wet.

Papa's voice is croaky and he still cannot leave his bed without falling over. He told me today that I should try the telephone and the radio, which means I get to go in his study!

Papa's study is on the top floor and right at the end of our house. It has a lock on the door and he never lets me go in it, even though I know that there is just a desk and a radio and a few bits of paper and some magazines with pictures of ladies in them. I know that because he left it unlocked once when he was out in the fields and I went inside. He almost caught me but when he asked what I was doing at that end of the house I told him I was cleaning the stairs, even though the stairs hardly ever need cleaning.

When Papa told me that I should use the radio, I felt so grown up and excited, especially as I have already worked out how to feed the cows on my own. I pretended that I wasn't excited, though, and kept my mouth from grinning when he was talking to me by biting the inside of my cheeks. Papa told me that if I hear a buzzing noise on the telephone when I pick it up it means that the line is fixed and I can call Doctor Moreau on the number by the phone. If I don't hear a buzzing noise I should try the radio for an hour in the morning and an hour in the afternoon and that all I have to do is switch it on and say my name *clearly* into the mouthpiece and say 'over' after everything I say. I have to keep doing this and turn the dial very slowly from one end to the other and back again.

He also said that whatever I do I am not to look in the drawers of the desk, and I promised him I wouldn't. That's where he keeps his magazines, which I think he looks at because he misses you, Mama.

I was excited about being in Papa's study even though I had been in there before and it felt the way you do when you need to go to the toilet but you don't want to because you are doing something interesting like reading about spiders or cavemen or dinosaurs. I went down to the kitchen and poured myself some milk, then I went into the study and shut the door and looked around it. When I looked inside it last time I was so nervous that Papa would come in that I didn't really see what was in there, apart from the desk and the paper and the radio and the magazines. But this time I was *allowed* to be in there so I took my time and had a look around. It smelled sweet like smoke from a pipe and the walls were covered in old maps of places I had never heard of. He even had maps of seas on the ceiling, stuck up with rusty brass tacks. On one side there was a bookcase I hadn't seen before full of magazines called *National*

Geographic and some of them were from years and years ago and had gone the colour of tea. They were about places I had never heard of as well, and had black and white photographs of people who looked like cavemen but were actually living now without any clothes on or any house to live in. There were other pictures of mountains and valleys in South America, in a place called *Patagonia* that looked like the mountains around our farm only much, much bigger.

I spent ages there drinking my milk and looking at the pictures and imagining I was riding horses through them and picking out places where I would build a farm if I lived there. I chose a place by a big lake where nobody else lived, and there was a forest and a mountain range behind me where I could ride my horse, and two flat fields where I could keep sheep, and in the mornings and the evenings I could go swimming in the water if it wasn't too cold.

It made my head dizzy to think that there were so many different places in the world and so many strange people living in it. It made me even dizzier to think that the magazine was written years and years before I was even born and that everything is so big and different and far away and I just live on a little farm in France with my Papa.

I decided to try and find where Patagonia was on the maps stuck to Papa's walls. It took me forever but when I found it I saw that it was almost as far away as you could be from where we live. I wondered how long it would take to go there if you just walked and the oceans had all dried up. It takes me three hours to walk down to the village in the summer and I tried to find that distance on the map of the world but I couldn't. It was such a small distance that the map couldn't show it!

I thought it must take days and days and days and days to walk to *Patagonia*, maybe you would never even get there, and even if you did you would have to walk across a dry sea bed with lots of dead whales and sharks and everything else that used to live in the ocean, and they would start to smell after a while. I felt dizzy and sat down on the floor and drank some milk and remembered that I hadn't tried to use the telephone and the radio yet. I wrote down how you spell *National Geographic* and *Patagonia* on a piece of paper and put the magazines back on their shelves.

Papa's desk is under a window that looks out across the fields and down the mountains to the valley, but the view didn't look right because the drifts were so high it looked as though I was on the ground floor of the house. The snow was heavy but not as heavy as it was last week and I could see some of the valley and the river far below and the tops of the trees poking out from the snow near the village. The village is where Doctor Moreau lives and I had to call him.

I picked up the telephone, which is black and heavy, and put it to my ear. I couldn't hear anything so I tapped the two buttons again and again like they do on films, but all I could hear then was a clicking sound and no buzzing. I turned the dial a few times but still couldn't hear anything, and then I quickly put the phone down because I thought *maybe I have called someone and they can hear me but I can't hear them.* Then I thought *maybe it was someone on a farm in Patagonia* and imagined asking them what the weather was like down there. They would say 'windy' because the magazine said it was a very windy country and if they asked me what the weather was like here I would say 'snowing, snowing, snowing!' because it *still* is.

The radio was next to the telephone. It was a brown box covered with leather and had an orange plastic switch, three white things like clocks but with different numbers on them, a black dial and a speaker. The thing you speak into was standing next to it and had another white switch, which Papa told me you pressed when you wanted to talk and then it sprang up again. I pressed the orange switch and it lit up and the speaker started humming. I was nervous but excited and felt like a spy and knelt up on Papa's chair so that I could see down to the village that I was trying to talk to. Then I turned the dial all the way to the left and pressed the white switch.

The speaker went quiet and I thought I had broken it so I let go, and then the speaker started humming again. I pressed it again and the speaker went quiet and then started humming the moment I let go. This means that if you have the switch pressed down you can't hear whether anyone is there, so I thought I will have to listen for a while after I have said my name just in case there is someone there but they aren't sitting at their radio like me.

Then I thought that if I was speaking to someone and I didn't like what they were saying, like if they were talking about how cold it was or how one of their cows had died or how much they had sold a sheep for at the market that weekend, I could just press the switch and turn them off and read *National Geographic* until they realised I wasn't listening and shut up. Then I could talk to them instead and tell them about the wind in *Patagonia*.

I pressed the switch and said 'Claudette Ferrière here. Over.' and let go and listened. There was just a hissing, humming noise so I tried again. 'Claudette Ferrière here, is there anybody there? Over?' but again there was just hiss. I kept trying but nobody answered and so I moved the dial round a bit. The speaker made a funny noise like Papa when he is outside with Zeet and trying to whistle a tune he only knows a bit of. Then I thought I heard a voice and quickly pressed the button and said 'Hello! Hello! Claudette Ferrière here who is that!' But the voice just kept mumbling and muttering about something until I realised it wasn't a voice but just a beeping noise in the background.

I kept moving the dial and saying 'Claudette Ferrière here, does anyone want to hear about the wind in Patagonia? Over?' and I spent an hour going back and forwards through the dial but there was nobody there so I turned it off.

I went and told Papa and he said try again tomorrow, so I went to feed the beasts. The man's bandages didn't need changing on his arms, head and shoulders today, which I think means he is getting better. But his leg looks black and horrible and the bandages are covered in smelly stuff.

22 février 1978

I tried the radio and the telephone twice today again and read *National Geographic* about people who live on the bottom of the world in a place called *Australia*. It is an orange place full of big snakes and giant spiders that want to kill you and there is a big desert where people called *aborigines* live without any clothes because it is so hot, and they have black suntans and paint their faces and sing through a thing that looks like a drain pipe called a *didgeridoo* because that is what the noise sounds like. There are other people who live there too in cities and on farms like us but they mainly live near the sea because it is cooler there. *Australia* is even further away than *Patagonia* and I want to go there.

I tried to talk to someone on the radio about *Australia* today instead of *Patagonia* but there was still no reply.

10:23pm

Did you know, Mama, that there is a wall in China that is so long you can see it from up in space? I tried to tell somebody on the radio today but there is still nobody there.

It is still snowing.

28 février 1978

Papa is better today! He got out of bed and I made him a special breakfast that he ate at the table. He dressed himself and I showed him the man, who looks better too, apart from his smelly leg. Papa took one look at him and said for me to go and do something else while he tried to talk to the man alone. I said 'shall I go and feed the beasts?' and Papa looked worried but said 'yes' and rubbed his chin as if he wasn't sure. I said that it was OK and that I had worked out a way to feed them on my own and that if he didn't believe me he could come and look at them because they all looked fine and healthy. He rubbed his chin again and said 'why are you standing by the window?' and I told him that it was the only way out to the shed and he could follow me if he liked. He said 'maybe later, go now and let me talk to our guest', so I did.

When I got back through to my room, Papa had left but the man was still awake and looking at me. He didn't look so pale any more and his eyes weren't bloodshot. I stood at the window for a while and he just kept looking at me and I got scared and ran past him. Before I got to the door, though, he said 'thank you', and I stopped. I turned round and looked at him and he said 'for the room, and for changing my bandages. Thank you'. And then he smiled, but it was a sad smile as if he had nothing to be happy about and it made me sad too, but I smiled back anyway. He said 'what is your name?' and I told him, and he said that his name was *Joe.*

Then I ran downstairs and told Papa that the man had talked to me, and Papa said he had talked to the man too and he seemed much better apart from his leg, which he didn't like the look of at all. I asked if I could try the radio again to get a doctor but Papa said that he had just tried that and there was still nobody there. He said that the only way to get a doctor was to try to go down to the village on foot. I told him that was a dangerous thing to do because the whole mountainside was covered in snow and he wouldn't be able to see where he was going, but Papa said that it wasn't snowing as hard any more, and anyway he had been up and down that mountainside thousands of times and knew it like the back of his hand. He knew where the path was and where the cliffs were and which bits you shouldn't walk on. He said it was the only way and that the man couldn't stay here any longer without medical attention for his leg so he *had* to go. I said that if he was going then I was going with him, but he said 'no Claudette, you have to stay here and look after the man. It might take me all day to get down to the village in which case I will stay there overnight and come back with the doctor tomorrow. You have to look after things here, just like you have been doing'. Then he stroked my head, which he never does.

I put some bread, ham and cheese in his shoulder bag and filled a flask with tea and put that in as well. Papa put his big coat on and his hat and gloves and boots and took his shotgun from the wall in the porch and gave it to me. Then he said 'it's not loaded, just point it at anyone if they give you trouble'. I told him there was nobody about to give me trouble, and he looked at the ceiling and said 'you can't trust anyone, not even people with broken legs, now how do I get out of this house?' and I took him up to my room and showed him. It took a bit longer for him to get out because Papa is much bigger than me but eventually he made it. I threw out his shoulder bag and Zeet followed, and then Papa picked all his things up and said 'Now Claudette I'll be back tomorrow with the doctor. Keep trying the radio and if I'm not back by tomorrow evening, well, just keep trying the radio. OK?' I nodded and then he went trudging off through the snow high above the yard as if he was floating on a white cloud. I watched him and Zeet disappear into the distance and every now and again Zeet fell through the snow and Papa had to lift him up like I did. I watched them until they were little black specks in the distance and then the snow swallowed them up.

Then I turned and realised that the man was looking up at me and I wondered if he had been looking at me all that time and if he really was to be trusted. I thought *maybe his leg has healed and any moment he will leap out of bed and attack me*, so I started to back away from the bed.

But I think he knew I was scared of him, and he didn't want me to be, so he said 'You are a very brave little girl, Claudette'. And I stopped. Then he said 'Your Daddy thinks so, too. He'll be back soon and he's very proud of you'.

So I told him about the wind in *Patagonia* and the drainpipes that go *didgeridoo*.

Midnight.

Papa did not come back today. I know he said he was coming back tomorrow but I was still worried about him and Zeet and by the evening I thought they might have fallen or died of being pneumatic which means you die of the cold.

I talked to Joe for hours after Papa left. It was smelly in the room but I wanted to talk to him so I left the window open wide even though it was freezing cold. I told him about the wheelbarrow and about how I learned to feed the beasts and about how hard it had been snowing. I also told him that it didn't normally snow as hard as this and that this time last year Zeet and I could play outside without getting out of my bedroom window. He told me that he used to live in a city that was so close to the sea that the roads were made of water and there were no cars so it was the most peaceful city in the world. He said the city is called *Venice*, so I wrote it down to see if I could find anything about it in Papa's *National Geographics*.

He told me that there were some mountains quite close to Venice but that you still had to go a long way to get as high up as we were now and they became covered in snow in the winter as well. I asked him how he was going to get back there and if he was missing his family, but he said he had no family to miss and looked sad. I said that everyone has some family unless they had died and I asked him if they had and he said 'something like that'. Then I told him about you, Mama, and he listened but didn't say anything afterwards.

By the time we finished talking it was late in the afternoon so I made two omelettes with onions and bacon and Joe said it was the best omelette he had ever had. I'm not scared of him any more, Mama, not now that his eyes aren't bloodshot and his face isn't pale and not now I've talked to him and found out that his family are dead or something like that. He told me thank you for the omelette and thank you again for my bed which was really comfy, and I said that it was all right and that

I'm glad he's feeling better.

Then it was evening and I was worried about Papa and Zeet and wondering whether they had got lost or fallen. I didn't like not knowing where they were so I went to Papa's study to see if there was anybody there to talk to in the village.

The telephone was still not working so I tried the radio. It still just made the same hiss and whistle it always did and I turned the dial backwards and forwards four times and heard nothing that sounded like a person. I was beginning to wonder whether the radio ever worked or whether I was doing something wrong and was just about to give up, Mama, but then I heard something!

It was only faint at first, but it sounded like somebody talking! I quickly took my hand off the dial and said 'Hello hello! This is Claudette Ferrière speaking to you! Who are you? Over?' and then there was silence and I heard it again. I turned the dial a bit and it got louder and heard that it was definitely a voice. Then I turned it again and all of a sudden the hiss got quieter and it was as if someone had stepped into the room. 'Hello Claudette Ferrière, this is Angelina Michel. Are you OK? Over?'

I got such a shock that my heart started beating twice as fast and I didn't know what to do. 'Hello? Over?' it said again and I slammed my finger down on the button. 'Hello! Hello! Madame Michel! I'm Claudette Ferrière from the farm on the hill! Over!' She laughed and said 'I know my dear, are you all right? Over?' and I told her I was and that I was just worried about my Papa, who had gone down to the village in the snow, and I told her all about Joe and his leg and the snow and that I just wanted to know whether my Papa was all right.

Madame Michel laughed again and said 'Calm down, my dear, calm down, we've all been worried about you because of the snow. You see we've been trapped down here too; it's very deep isn't it? Over?' And I said yes it was and the telephone wasn't working and nobody had been on the radio till now and she said that she knew. Then she told me that Papa had made it to the village and that he was staying with the Beauforts, who own the café on the corner! I was so happy. She said that she knew this because everyone knows everything about everyone else in the village and so she had kept her radio on because she thought I might try and call.

How lovely Madame Michel is!

She told me to keep the dial exactly where it was and that she would go and get Papa immediately from the café where he was busy drinking wine with the Beauforts. When she went I had a look through the *National Geographics* to see if I could find anything about *Venice* but there wasn't anything so I read about things that live really deep in the sea where it is so dark that you cannot see anything.

Quite soon the speaker made a noise and I jumped again, and then I heard Papa!

'Hello Claudette I made it, are you all right? Over?' He sounded a bit drunk and I laughed just because his voice was all crackly on the speaker but I could tell it was him. I said 'Hello Papa, I'm fine, is Zeet all right?' and he said that Zeet was fine too and so was he. Then he said 'Sorry if I took a long time to get to the radio, I was with the Beauforts and some wine', and I said 'That's all right, Papa, I wasn't bored, I was reading your magazines.'

Then Papa made a noise and didn't say anything for ages, so I said 'The yellow magazines, Papa.'

'The yellow ones!' said Papa, 'My *National Geographics*?' and I said yes and that I'd been reading about things that live really deep in the sea. Then Papa said he had read that one too and I think he was relieved because he thought I was looking at the *other* ones. But I wasn't, I don't know why you would want to look at pictures of naked ladies when you can look at pictures of bears fighting wolves in *Alaska* and real-live cowboys in *Kansas USA* and volcanoes erupting in *Ecuador* instead.

Papa told me that he was staying in the village with the

Beauforts for the night but that he had found Doctor Moreau and that they were both coming back very early tomorrow morning and that I was to make a big stew and make sure there was lots of hot water to hand. I asked him why but he wouldn't tell me and said it was important so I will boil some in the big pot.

Tonight I get to sleep in Papa's bed because he is not here. I had to change the sheets because they stank of sick people and now they are all clean and white, although I can never get them as crisp as you did, Mama. I'm tired and I think I will have a good deep sleep now. I miss you, Mama.

1 mars 1978

Two horrible things happened today. I don't know which thing I have been crying about the most but I wish that neither of them had ever happened and I wish that *she* wasn't here.

I got up really early and put the big pot of water on the stove like Papa said. While I waited for it to boil I made some breakfast and took it up to Joe. He was asleep when I went into my room and the window was shut and the room smelled like dead animals. I opened the window and held my nose and shook him, but when he woke up he jumped up and cried out as if he was having a bad dream but then fell back on the bed because his leg was so sore. I gave him his eggs and asked him if he wanted me to change the bandage on his leg. He said 'Is your Papa coming back today?' and I told him yes, so he said 'no, then.' I didn't understand why then because it looked like it needed changing. But I do now.

When the water had boiled I put the lid on it to keep it hot and then went outside through my window to feed the beasts. I am so good at it now it only takes me three hours instead of four to get all the bales through. I missed Zeet today because he is funny when he goes up and down the pen barking and the beasts were braver because he wasn't there and almost ran me over. I had to stab one of them in the bottom with my fork so I didn't get squashed.

When I had finished feeding the beasts I felt really happy because I was proud of myself and Papa and Zeet were coming back with the doctor to make the man's leg better. It had stopped snowing too and everything was quiet and the air smelled clean and new as if nothing around me had ever been touched before.

I climbed the pipe and went back inside through my window. I said hello to Joe but he was just staring at the wall in front of the bed and not listening. I asked him why he hadn't eaten his eggs but he just kept staring at the wall, so I took his plate downstairs and closed the door so that the smell from the room wouldn't get out into the house.

Then I spent the rest of the morning in Papa's study reading about monkeys who live on a big rock called *Gibraltar*, which is at the bottom of Spain and nowhere near as far away as *Patagonia* or *Australia* or the bottom of the *Pacific Ocean*. After every bit I read I looked out of the window and down the mountainside to see if I could see Papa and Zeet and Doctor Moreau. I could see much further than yesterday because the snow had completely stopped and there was even a bit of sunshine. I kept seeing black specks in the distance and thought it was them, but they just turned out to be crows looking for worms who flew off across the valley.

But at last one of the specks didn't fly off and I saw them. As they got closer I saw that Papa was in front and Doctor Moreau was behind trying to keep up, and Zeet was running around them in circles getting his feet stuck in the snow. Papa ignored him and let him get out on his own. He must have got sick of helping him.

Then, when they got even closer and I could see their long shadows stretching out behind them, I saw that there was another person with them whom I didn't recognise. I watched them as they walked all the way up to the house and tried to work out who the third person was. At first I thought it was Phillipe back from Grenoble, but it wasn't him and after a while I saw that it wasn't even a man, it was a woman. I thought *why have they brought a woman with them? Maybe it is Doctor Moreau's nurse to help Joe*, but she was too old to be a nurse and too fat. Then, when they had almost reached the farm I saw that it was Madame Beaufort, who runs the café where Papa stayed. *What on earth is Madame Beaufort doing here?* I thought. But I didn't find *that* out till later.

I could hear them talking as they got to the farm and then they disappeared behind the engine shed. I ran through to my bedroom and held my nose and said hello to Joe but he didn't say anything back, then I opened the window just as Papa, Zeet, Doctor Moreau and Madame Beaufort came into the yard walking on snow about as high as a man from the ground. I waved and shouted 'Hello!' and Zeet saw me first and barked and fell through the snow. Then Papa looked up and waved at me and Madame Beaufort pointed and waved as well, but Doctor Moreau was too busy trying not to fall over.

They were all wearing big hats and boots, but I don't think Doctor Moreau was used to walking anywhere far. He was carrying a big bag too and Papa was carrying a rolled up stretcher under his arm, like the ones football players are taken off the field in when someone has pushed them over. He couldn't believe it when Papa told him the only way into the house was through my window and he and Madame Beaufort started laughing. First I thought they were laughing at me and I was cross because I've been feeding beasts all week and I don't have my own bed and all they have to do is make coffee for people and look in their mouths when they're ill. They don't have to push five wheelbarrows full of hay every day or poke cows in the bottom with pitchforks just to stop themselves from getting squashed, and if it wasn't for me then nobody would have thought of getting out of my window and all the cows would be dead.

I think I must have had a cross face on because Doctor Moreau stopped laughing and said I was a *very brave girl* and *very clever* for finding out how to get out of the house and feed the beasts, and Madame Beaufort looked embarrassed and agreed.

Madame Beaufort lit one of her cigarettes then, and I said 'Hello Madame Beaufort, what are you doing here? Where is Monsieur Beaufort?' and Papa interrupted her and said 'Madame Beaufort is here to help us Claudette and her brother is back in the village looking after the café. So I said 'But what about Monsieur Beaufort?' and he said that her brother *was* Monsieur Beaufort.

They all stood round above the yard for a while having a rest after their walk and waiting for Madame Beaufort to finish her cigarette. Then Papa said that we couldn't spend all our time getting in and out of the house through my bedroom window and he said they were going to dig the snow out from around the door. He slid down on his back into the engine shed and brought out three shovels, one for him, Doctor Moreau and Madame Beaufort and they all started digging. Doctor Moreau was useless and his spectacles kept falling off. Sometimes he dropped the snow back into the place he had shovelled it from and I could see Papa didn't think much of his digging. Madame Beaufort was much better and he kept looking up and watching her. She wasn't as good as you were though, Mama.

It didn't take them that long to dig the hole, and when they finished there was a big area around the kitchen door so that you could open it and walk outside and climb up a small slope and onto the snow. They were all very pleased with themselves — even Doctor Moreau who had hardly moved a snowflake — and they came inside.

When I ran downstairs to meet them I wanted to hug Papa but I knew he would be embarrassed so I hugged Zeet instead. Zeet never gets embarrassed and jumped up on me and almost knocked me over. They all took their gloves and hats and coats off and hung them up in the porch and I didn't like it when

Madame Moreau put her coat on your hook, Mama. Then Papa said that he was going to take Doctor Moreau up to see Joe. He said 'You stay down here in the kitchen with Madame Beaufort and make her a cup of tea and keep her company and we won't be long.'

Then they disappeared upstairs and I was left alone with Madame Beaufort who stood with her back against the kitchen sink and looked at me smiling as if she wanted to be somewhere else. I asked her why she married her brother and she laughed out loud and covered her mouth and giggled. She said that she hadn't and that Monsieur Beaufort was just her brother and that they had inherited the café from their Mama and Papa when they died. I told her that my mother was dead too. She said that she knew and she was sorry but I told her it wasn't her fault but a disease.

Then I asked her who her husband was and she said that she didn't have one and I asked her why not because she was much, much older than me, and she said that she had never met anyone who wanted to marry her. I told her that Joe didn't have a family either and maybe they could get married when he was better. But she just smiled then, so I made some tea.

When Papa and Doctor Moreau came down they both looked very serious and Papa sat me down and said that they had to do something very important with Joe. I asked him what and he said they had to do an operation on him because his leg had gone bad like a piece of old meat. I said 'Is that why he smells?' and Doctor Moreau said yes and he wasn't going to get better unless they did the operation. They said that if they didn't do it soon then Joe might get really, really sick and might even die, and that they had told him this and he had said that they should do it.

I asked them if Joe was going to go to hospital but Papa said that even now the snow had stopped they couldn't take him because the roads were completely covered, and that they couldn't even take him down to the village with his leg as bad as it was, so they had to do the operation here at the farm. I said 'In my bed?' but Papa said no, they wouldn't do it there they would take him into the engine shed instead.

I said what sort of operation? And Papa said it was very simple and wouldn't take long.

They took the stretcher and brought Joe downstairs in it. As they went past he looked at me and looked really frightened so I put my hand on his forehead like nurses do and told him not to worry because it was a very simple operation. Then he gulped and blinked because Doctor Moreau had bumped into the doorframe.

Madame Beaufort and I followed them out as they carried him up the slope across the yard and down into the engine shed. Madame Beaufort carried the pot of hot water I had boiled and then came back for Doctor Moreau's big bag. Then Papa closed the shed door leaving me and Madame Beaufort sitting outside on the snow. Zeet started barking at the door and I said 'Shut up, Zeet!' three times but he wouldn't stop until Papa shouted *'ARRÊT!'* from inside the shed.

While we waited she smoked cigarettes constantly and asked me how I managed to feed the beasts when I am only eight years old. I told her all about it and I didn't mind talking to her even though she was a stranger and smelled of smoke all the time because I was happy that Doctor Moreau and Papa were making Joe's leg better so he could get well and go and find a family.

I thought they were just going to take the bad, smelly bits out of his leg so that good bits would grow back.

But they didn't, they *cut it off.*

That was the first horrible thing that happened, Mama. When Papa opened the door there was blood all down his overalls and he was carrying a bag with something big in it which he took away somewhere. I could see Doctor Moreau packing up his needles and tubes and knives and there was blood all over him too and blood all over the table and blood all over the saw that was next to it. And on the table Joe was lying asleep with bandages around a stump where his *leg should have been.* That's when I realised and I shouted after Papa 'What have you done? Papa! What have you done?' but he just strode off into the furnace room. I can't remember much then because I was crying so much and my face felt red, but I think I ran back into the engine shed and Madame Beaufort tried to grab me but I shook her off and ran up to Doctor Moreau shouting 'What have you done? What have you done? What have you done with Joe's leg? Put it back on! Put it back on!'

Doctor Moreau tried to calm me down and told me that they had to cut it off because it was bad but I wouldn't listen and banged my fist on his chest and said 'You're a doctor, you're supposed to make things better not chop them off! Now Joe doesn't have any family *or* a leg any more! Put it back! Put it back!'

I ran back across the yard and slipped on the snow and hurt my knee. Madame Beaufort dropped her cigarette and came running after me, but before she was even halfway across the yard, I was already sliding down the slope to the kitchen. Then I ran upstairs to my room and slammed the door and fell onto the bed and cried and cried and cried into the sheets, even though they smelled of dead animals.

I heard Papa and Madame Beaufort outside my door whispering. I think she was trying to tell him to leave me on my own, and it must have worked because they went away. I don't know how long I was crying for, but when I got up off the bed it was starting to get dark. I crept downstairs and saw that Doctor Moreau was sitting by the fire on his own, staring into it. He was drinking a glass of brandy. I wasn't as upset any more, but I was still angry and didn't understand why they had to cut off Joe's leg. I was about to go and ask him, when I suddenly realised that there was a light on in the old family room and shadows moving about inside it. Nobody ever goes in there any more, it's dusty and cold and full of old furniture we don't use and some of your things too.

I went in and saw Madame Beaufort settling Joe into the old bed. She had put some new sheets on it and was cleaning his face and neck and putting a new bandage on his arm even though he didn't need one any more. She had also lit a fire in the hearth, which was smoking because the chimney had not been used or cleaned for two winters.

'Claudette,' she said and looked at me, but her smile didn't work properly. I looked at Joe, who was still not awake because Doctor Moreau had made him go to sleep for a long time so that he didn't feel anything when he *CHOPPED HIS LEG OFF*. I could see the shape of his stump underneath the white sheet, and all the bumps of the bandages that were wrapping it. I wondered how he would feel this time when he woke up and saw that his leg wasn't just broken but *wasn't there at all.*

Madame Beaufort waited for a while holding another set of sheets to her chest and wondering what to do, I think. Then she said 'I'll go and change the sheets on your bed,' and I told her that I could do it myself and didn't need her help, but she didn't listen and walked right past me.

I watched Joe for a while. It was the second best part of winter days when it isn't quite dark and not quite light so the curtains are still open and you can see the sky getting darker before your eyes. The fire was crackling and the smell of burning wood was filling the room, and outside the deep snow kept everything still as if it was freezing the land and the trees and stopping anything that was alive from moving.

The first best part of winter days is the morning when the frost is still fresh and the sun starts to make icicles trickle.

I walked up to Joe and looked at his face flickering in the light. I put my hand on his forehead and stroked it once. He looked sad, even though he was fast asleep, and I wanted to tell him something interesting from *National Geographic* that would cheer him up. I thought that maybe his body knew what had happened to him and was telling him in a dream.

Then Madame Beaufort's footsteps hurried past the old family room and I heard her go up the hall. Then I heard whispers and things coming from the kitchen and Papa's voice low and gentle like you hardly ever hear it. I went to see him, thinking I would ask him straight out why they had chopped Joe's leg off, but when I got to the doorway I stopped dead. That was the second horrible thing I saw today, Mama, and I'm afraid to tell you about it in case it upsets you like it upset me. Papa and Madame Beaufort were cuddling next to the sink. She had her arms around his neck and her head buried in his shoulder, and he had one arm around her back and the other one was stroking her hair. He was saying 'shhh, shhh' and rocking her slowly as if she was a baby. I couldn't say anything, my mouth was wide open and my heart felt as if it had stopped. Then Madame Beaufort lifted up her face from Papa's shoulder and sniffed and wiped her eyes as if she had been crying. Their faces were really close and they smiled at each other and then she kissed him on the lips for three seconds.

My face went red and I felt my throat was going to burst. I shouted 'WHAT ARE YOU DOING WITH MY PAPA?' and they both turned round suddenly and pulled away from each other. Papa tried to say something but I ran away upstairs again and into my room and locked the door and ran to my bed. It didn't smell of dead things any more, but I ripped off the clean sheets from my bed because *she* had put them on.

Soon Papa was at my room with Madame Beaufort. He was using his best gentle voice and saying 'Claudette, please don't be angry. Claudette, please don't be angry. Madame Beaufort is a friend and she wants to be your friend too', so I covered my head with a cushion and cried until they went away.

Now it is properly dark and I can hear voices downstairs and even people laughing, probably Doctor Moreau boasting about how many people's legs he has chopped off in his life. I'm hungry because I haven't eaten anything all day, but I didn't want to go downstairs because I didn't want to see any of them.

I've put all the sheets in the corner and am wrapped in two blankets from the wardrobe. I'm confused and unhappy and hungry and tired.

I do not understand what grown ups do or why they do it.

~2003~

LIFE CAN ALWAYS RUN FASTER

Bangkok, Thailand

A WARM evening wind snakes down the street. It starts high in the tree canopies next to Chakrapong Road and moves north-west towards the river, over the walls of the temple and the broken rooftops of the low-lit bars and guesthouses facing it. It turns and falls down between the gutters and onto the orange earth, where it breaks like water on rock and sends tendrils of itself spilling out in all directions. It finds a broken beam leaning on the open front of the Surokhat Hotel and inspects it for splinters. It ducks beneath the wooden table next to it, where two young American men are growing small beards and drinking alcoholic milkshakes with an Italian girl who rubs her calves together in a way that makes the men's groins ache. It skids across the cool gravy that remains on a discarded plate of noodles, rattling its fork before a shy waitress, eyes fixed on her feet, picks it up and hurries it away to the kitchen.

Later, the same waitress will walk home thirty-eight blocks and sleep in a single bed with her mother who snores, watching her white blouse, crisp and perfectly clean, swing slowly in the moonlight from a rusted brass hook.

The wind finds its way down the three stairs from the hotel's veranda and crosses the street to the metal tables sitting next to the high white temple wall, shaking up some dust that gets in its way. There it gatecrashes the loose material of brightly coloured sarongs and linen dresses smelling of sweatshops and mosquito repellent, and slaps the soft, brown, eighteen-year-old, puppy-fatted thighs beneath them. It bristles the hairs on the long ankles of a German dive instructor and moves onto four microbiology students from the University of Stockholm, flicking up the cheap leather straps on their sandals.

Skinny dogs run low to the ground. The wind worries their balding legs. It batters the balloon held by a child who is giggling, running up the street away from the plump arms of a pink-dressed lady. It whips up the salty smells rising from the hot food carts cooking sweetcorn, banana fritters and Pad Thai noodles. It swoops into the wide, open door of a cushion retailer and tickles the nasal hair of its owner, cross-legged and asleep on a bean bag, who is having one of his cigarettes expertly stolen from the pack in his shirt pocket by a delighted shop assistant. It swoops back outside again, dives and crash lands in the dust. Everything is free and far away.

Ashley Gritten is far away too. He is far away typing words into a white box on his fifteen-inch monitor and pressing buttons that send them halfway across the world to a router in Los Angeles. There they sit briefly in a queue, which is not really a queue at all but a set of electronic charges, before launching themselves back across ten of the United States and all of the Atlantic Ocean. They check in to a server in west London, and then transfer to another white box on the monitor of Ashley's friend, Damien. Damien's white box is periodically hidden and revealed beneath an open copy of a document describing the sales management techniques he has employed in the last six months, because Damien is at work and doesn't want his boss to know that he is chatting to his friend Ashley, who has gone travelling in Thailand, which is cool because Damien is three years older than Ashley and went there a couple of years ago and can give Ashley tips on the best places to visit and where the fittest girls are. Damien likes chatting to Ashley because it reminds him of when he was away, even though now he thinks he's got that out of his system and doesn't need to do it any more, and now he can concentrate on his career, which is in sales and which is earning him a fuck of a lot of money, which is essential when you live in London because it's so expensive? But so so worth it? Because everything's on your doorstep? And he's having such a wicked time, just met a bird the other night in a Czech bar on Old Street, really fit, and he's hoping to buy another flat, on top of the one his family bought him in South Kensington, which is cool but a bit far away from work.

The words Ashley writes are clipped and stylised, interspersed with faces made of punctuation marks. They require the bare minimum of keystrokes, yet are painstakingly crafted so that they carry the totem of his own dialect. It is a type of poetry, like haiku.

Ash Trés says: yeh, bk in bankok dude. fucking hot :-p

Damien says: fucky fucky land yeh hope you packed rubbers man don't want you coming back with cockrot ;-)

Ash Trés says: ha ha lol no way

Damien says: you dicked a thai chick yet?

Ash Trés says: no

Damien says: :-0

Damien says: man how long u been there for now?

Ash Trés says: dunno man five weeks i think

Damien says: shit dude pull ur finger out and stick in ur dick! thai girls r bendy

Ash Trés says: yeh man but ive been in the islands, no licky sucky fucky down there :-(

Damien says: cool where u been

Ash Trés says: met a danish girl though

Damien says: koh samui or pan yang?

Ash Trés says: at a full moon party, i was wasted couldn't stand

Damien says: shit boss coming hold on dude

Damien is offline and may not respond.

Ashley's booth is number sixteen of twenty-five in the

Internet café, a place which charges 80 baht for one hour at a computer. Ashley considers this more expensive than normal. However, it is reliable and offers a high-speed connection, which means he gets better value in the long run.

It's eight o'clock in the evening, and every other one of the twenty-five booths is occupied. Two twenty-one-year-old women from Kent sit in the pair behind Ashley. They have been in Bangkok for four nights of their month-long trip and have seen the palace and the river. The rest of their time has been split equally between drinking banana milkshakes, watching pirate copies of American films in bamboo-stilted bars and talking to other people of their own age about where they come from-where have they been-have they been to the islands yet-where are they going. They're now talking excitedly about the online conversations each is currently having with friends back home, one with a marketing trainee called Kate and the other with a web designer called Mark. Mark and Kate slept together for the first time at the weekend and neither is aware that they are both now simultaneously plugged into two computers in Bangkok, where their own shy and radically different versions of events are compared mercilessly across a thin, plastic partition separating the two women.

The woman who is talking to Mark is unaware that Mark is masturbating between sentences because he has secretly harboured sexual fantasies about her for over five-and-a-half years.

Kate, too, is unaware that she is now pregnant with Mark's child and in three months' time, when the young women return, all four parties will face varying degrees of strife in their respective relationships because of things that cannot be said or known through gossip alone and because life can always run faster than you.

Next to them, a middle-aged divorcee from La Rochelle, France, tries desperately to think of the right words that will make his ex-wife believe he is a dynamic man enjoying a new lease of life, when all that the wet heat of Bangkok will allow him to think of is the smell of her neck and the curve of her lower back and how he would do anything to have her again.

Next to him, a first-year undergraduate from Leeds feels sick as he realises he has just accidentally copied in his mother on an email to his mates which vividly describes a sexual experience he had with a girl from Luton the night before.

The girl from Luton is also in the café, but neither is aware of the other's presence. She is writing an email to her best friend, explaining why she thinks she has been raped.

Ashley brings up the inbox of his Internet email account and feels a dull stab of arousal when he sees a new one from the Danish girl he fucked against a rock three nights ago at a beach party. He can't entirely remember fucking her against a rock because he was drunk and had swallowed three ecstasy tablets during the evening. When he had woken up, though, they were both lying next to a rock and he saw that the girl's left arm was over his bare chest and her pink face was in the sand and her sarong was hitched up over her bottom, revealing the fact that she wasn't wearing her underpants, which were instead crumpled in a messy ball by her feet. All of this told him that he must have fucked her against the rock, and they would have done it again if she hadn't had to get her boat that morning.

Ashley wishes he had some more tangible memories about fucking the girl because she was very pretty and had a beautiful, tanned backside that he's pretty sure he remembers massaging. He contents himself instead with her email, which contains lots of cute superlatives about him in badly translated English, particularly about the size of his penis, which pleases Ashley because it strengthens his conviction in the memory that they did indeed copulate.

Outside the Internet café a gaunt, rat-faced man with an East London accent walks past, confidently escorting a four-foot-five-inch prostitute back to his dark room, where two cockroaches will watch them have joyless sex before he sends her back out, alone onto the street to find her own way back to the club where she works. Even though this is about four miles away, the young prostitute doesn't mind that much because she has just made enough money to pay for the drugs that keep her from losing her mind. She does not know that it is already lost.

Before Ashley has finished reading the email from the Danish girl who he definitely, definitely fucked against a rock three days ago, a box starts flashing at the bottom of his screen. He clicks it.

Damien is online.

Damien says: sorry dude so what u doing now?

Ash Trés says: no probs matey just chilling now, catching up on emails, grab a beer i think

Damien says: lucky cunt wish i was there too how long u staying in bangkok?

Ash Trés says: not long. bangkok's alright but think I'll go north, reckon im done partying for a while, join a trek or something yeh?

Damien says: sounds dull mate

Ash Trés says: might meet that bird as well

Damien says: gotta go meeting Mikey for lunch

Ash Trés says: 'k take care mate

Damien says: try and get laid before you leave bangkok yeh?

Ash Trés says: i did i fuckd that danish girll.

Damien is offline and may not respond.

A small window pops up on Ashley's computer screen showing him that he only has ten seconds left of his time on the computer. He clicks the button saying 'log off' and stands up to leave. As he walks to the door he catches the eye of the young woman behind him who is talking to Mark, the web designer. She gives him a smile and he returns one, running a long brown hand through his hair, which is now at its perfect length, sleek with perspiration and streaked with natural highlights from the tropical sun. Although he is not entirely conscious of it, he has in his head an exact mental image of how he believes he looks to her.

Thousands of miles away, Mark has finished masturbating and is cringing in his own shame. He asks for God's forgiveness, despite the fact that he has masturbated exactly one hundred and ninety two times previously under the same conditions and will do so again in four days' time.

Relax now. We are on the street in Bangkok, enjoying the cool late evening and, although it is near the Khao San Road (that itchy, rancid mecca), it is not the Khao San Road, and, anyway, anything is better than home…

Ashley returns to his guesthouse on Soi Ram Buttri, an open-fronted building with a deep, wide room that opens onto the street. Around its walls are worn beanbags and soft cushions that cradle the backsides of people in transit; groups, couples, singles, lonesomes. Four speakers hang above them in the corners of the room, gently squeezing out electronic music that drifts around the walls. It is designed to relax, and reminds the people of the feelings they had two years ago, when they took drugs and danced on a hot Spanish island.

There are a hundred places like this within a one-mile radius of Ashley's guesthouse. They are rest stops and junctions for those who are *en route*, Bangkok being the centre of any journey's line through Thailand, never its destination. They are wayfarers' comfort stations, harbours, pitstops.

But if you are looking for some spirit of travel, don't look here. It lives somewhere else, in the glances exchanged between businessman and bell-boy in the lobby of a Budapest hotel; in the coffee steam rising from a polystyrene cup on a dashboard at 5am; in the reflection of a child's face in the backseat window as her parents drive her onto a cross-channel ferry for the first time.

But not here. Here you find people who sit and whine about where-you-come-from-where-are-you-going-where-have-you-been, and the feelings they had two years ago when they took drugs and danced on a hot Spanish island.

Ashley sits down on a beanbag near the entrance, stretching his shoulders as if he has just returned from a hard day's work and orders a beer in Thai from a girl called Tsuk, who is standing by the bar. He ends all of his sentences with a question mark, regardless of whether or not they are a question. The effect is that every statement he utters requires some confirmation that the listener has understood it. This is confusing for Tsuk, because Thai words rely heavily on intonation for their semantics and at first she thinks he has asked for something else. After a brief and embarrassed rejection, Tsuk suddenly understands and laughs and then complies, even though she is not yet seventeen and only employed by the guesthouse to clean the toilets. She brings him the beer and smiles maniacally at him, saying something with a voice like rubber bands. He takes it and thanks her, again in Thai, before stretching out and lighting a cigarette with the Zippo his brother gave him as a leaving present. It is bronze and has some words engraved on it which Ashley thinks are really cool.

He looks out onto the colourful night and feels relaxed. It is a dirt street without tarmac and only wide enough to fit one vehicle at a time. People are walking in both directions, talking mostly in English but sometimes in German and Swedish. The occasional tuk-tuk, a three-wheeled taxi, splutters past, swerving between them and honking its horn, causing giggles and hoots. One of them is parked on the other side of the street, its driver stretched out asleep in the back, his small hat covering his face.

Next to him, in the shadows, Ashley sees a woman. She is Thai, her face is smeared with dirt and her hair grows wildly around it like black weeds. She wears a long shawl and an old dress beneath it that reaches the ground and covers her feet. As she shuffles them in the dust, Ashley sees that they are bare and blistered and a brown bandage hangs from her left ankle.

Her long fingers grip the handles of a tall wooden cart, on top of which is a heap of old blankets and plastic bags. Ashley drinks some of his beer and watches her adjust something on one of the cart's wheels. She is slow and seems old, although he wouldn't place her over thirty. As he starts to wonder what's in the bags, he sees one of them move, then one of the blankets pops up its head and looks around, causing the other blankets to shift irritably and make noises. Ashley looks closer – the blankets are dogs, there are about fifteen of them on the cart – flea-bitten, hungry-looking things with small eyes and bony frames. Some of them growl as the pile is disturbed, three others drop off onto the road and start sniffing about in the ground, picking at their legs with their teeth.

'Hey there, Dog-Lady!' says a Texan voice. Ashley turns round to see a man sitting on the other side of the room to him, also looking out onto the street. He wears a baseball cap and a muscle vest and lifts up a bottle in toast to the woman, his wide, flat face pulled into a grin. The woman yabbers something back at him, frowning and throwing up a hand in the air. The man chuckles and raises his beer again, before turning to Ashley.

'Ever seen so many dogs on a cart, buddy?'

Ashley grins back, because it's easier to laugh with someone who is laughing than to ignore them, even when they're not funny.

'Up and down this street all day long,' says the man. 'I been here since 10am, I should know.'

The man takes a swig of his beer and Ashley hears a low growling noise by his feet. He turns his head quickly to see one of the dogs looking up at him. Its ribcage stretches the thin flesh of its torso and a long strip of bald skin shows through the hair on its back. Its lip quivers and it flashes him some of its teeth.

Ashley isn't scared of dogs, though. His parents have three Labradors: Jack, Angus and Sam. He has known them since he was fifteen, when their first dog Lucinda died of liver failure, and he still takes them walking in the glen near their holiday cottage in Scotland. When Ashley visits home, they clatter through the oak-floored hall of the family home and lay their paws on his chest and wag their tails.

There is no tail on the dog by his feet, but if there was it would not be wagging. Nevertheless, Ashley is not afraid of dogs, he thinks that all they need is to be told their place. He puts down his beer and fixes the animal in the eye. Knowing how much this will impress the American man and the three Irish girls sitting near him with whom he has been exchanging glances, he holds out a palm for the dog to sniff.

'Don't touch the fuckin' dogs, you idiot!' says the Texan. 'They're fuckin' dirtier than a whore's asshole!'

The dog doesn't sniff it. Instead, it peels back its two black lips and lunges forwards with a loud bark, snapping at it and catching Ashley's knuckles with its rotten fangs. Ashley reels back and pulls his hand to his chest, almost falling off the chair and knocking his beer bottle onto the bamboo mat beside him.

The Irish girls laugh and the Texan curses, flicking his bottle at the dog and showering its face with frothy beer. The dog flinches momentarily and begins to frantically lick its face with a slavering tongue, its lips still pulled back, still growling, still staring at Ashley.

Ashley inspects his hand: two light grazes score the knuckles of his thumb and forefinger, and small beads of blood begin to ooze from the broken skin.

'Mother fucker,' he whispers, picking up the spilled beer bottle from the mat and pouring some over his fingers, dabbing it with his T-shirt.

'Fucking mother fucker,' he repeats, glaring at the dog. It raises another growl and Ashley lashes out with his foot, sending one of his flip-flops flying off and clipping the dog on its snout. It yelps and backs off, but then another yelp comes from across the street. The woman, who is now staring furiously at Ashley with deep-set white eyes, throws up her hands and starts to shout.

'Shit dude,' mutters the Texan behind the mouth of his beer bottle. 'Now you're in trouble.'

The woman strides across the street, pointing at her dog and at Ashley, shaking her hands and hurling curses at him as if they were items of cutlery. Her shawl billows behind her and the dust in the street is whisked up by her feet. People walking by stop in their tracks and begin to make low warning noises that always accompany trouble in public. Ashley looks around.

'Your fucking dog? Your fucking dog bit me?' he shouts back at her, but the woman continues to curse and her face becomes angrier. As she reaches the entrance to the guesthouse, the dog starts barking up at Ashley and he takes a step backwards. People are gathering in the street, watching with open mouths, and people inside the guesthouse are standing, craning their necks to watch. The electronic music bumbles along, ignoring the disturbance and whistling. Suddenly the woman is upon him, standing inches from Ashley's face and screaming murderously into it.

'YOUR....DOG...FUCKING...BIT...MY...HAND,' he explains, holding up his bleeding knuckles, but the woman shouts louder, snorts and then spits at him. A cry of mild disgust rises from the crowd, and then becomes alarm as the woman throws her arms forward and grips Ashley by the neck. But before Ashley can struggle she is yanked back from him into the street. He hears a painful yelp and sees the sleeping tuk-tuk driver, now awake, pulling both woman and dog yelling and snarling back to the cart. The crowd parts for them and several men make hesitant attempts to help without actually touching either culprit.

When they reach the cart, the dog scurries beneath it and the woman springs to her feet. She makes to return across the street to Ashley, who watches wide-eyed and open-mouthed as the driver pulls her back again. He pushes her against the cart and says something quickly and firmly in her face. This seems to work, and he stands back from her. She is quiet now, but still stares at Ashley. She picks up her cart and, keeping her eyes fixed on him, throws one last curse into the dirt with a ball of dust-covered spit and rolls away down the street. The dog leaps up onto the cart and finds a warm hole to lie in, and the tuk-tuk driver resumes his place in the back of his cab, looking suspiciously at Ashley and replacing his hat on his face.

Ashley looks around as the crowd dissolves, muttering and tittering, and stretched necks are pulled back into their beanbags. The Texan laughs into his bottle.

'Reckon you made a friend there,' he says.

Ashley looks down at his wound, now smeared with a thick string of phlegm.

'Fuck's sake,' says Ashley.

He wipes his hand on the material of the chair with a grimace and drains the rest of his spilled beer, glaring down the street. The Irish girls titter as the Texan joins them.

Ashley says 'Fuck's sake' again and goes to bed.

He dreams. He dreams that he is in a house somewhere in the country. It is not an old farmhouse cottage with low ceilings and an iron stove, nor is it a mansion with sleek steps, butlers and long greens. It is a pebble-dashed bungalow with thin walls, formica tables and linoleum floors. Everything inside it is brown, because everything inside it has been designed to be brown. It stands in the middle of a deserted terrace that constitutes the main strip of a deserted mining town; it is blight; it is vomit from the exorcism of a 1960s architect's worst nightmare.

In the dream, in the house, Ashley is trying to plan his journey in one of the bedrooms. The bedroom he chooses is the smallest, long and thin with a low single bed in an alcove and a window that will not close. Outside, four builders are working noisily, mixing cement in a neglected garden full of dying grass and weeds. Ashley takes five paintings of dogs playing Playstations down from the sunflower-strewn wallpaper, and replaces them with three sheets of A3 paper with torn edges, on which he writes his travel itinerary.

In the dream Ashley likes the fact that the edges are torn, because it makes his trip seem like an old-fashioned voyage like Around The World in 80 Days, even though any plans laid out by Phileas Fogg would have been done so on perfectly new paper with sharp, straight edges from a stationer's on the Charing Cross Road.

Ashley likes his edges torn because his most certain belief is that nothing born within his lifetime can have soul. He does not yet realise this.

He goes to the kitchen to check on some tinned ravioli he is cooking in a second-hand saucepan, but when he walks back into the bedroom he stops dead in horror. All of the dog pictures have been carefully replaced on the walls, and his itinerary is in a neat pile on the bed. He is terrified, cold, frozen to the spot. Outside, there are no builders and the sky is dark with black cloud.

He discovers he has a flatmate. It is Damien, although nothing in his demeanour or appearance says so. Ashley tells him that he believes they are haunted, to which Damien's response is to escape through a secret door on the urinal wall of a nightclub toilet.

That night, within the dream, Ashley tries to sleep in the bedroom but cannot because it is too cold. He doesn't understand why it is cold, however, because the window is now shut. He is scared, he wraps himself as tightly as he can in the sheet and faces the wall next to the bed, but the air around the exposed area of his face rapidly starts to feel colder, and although his eyes are shut he knows his breath is visible. He frowns and whimpers and suddenly feels the sheet moving behind him. Very slowly, it lifts up and lets in an icy draught that shoots up his bare back. Then it starts to flap angrily up and down as if somebody is shaking it. As he cringes further into the bed and the sheet flails violently around him like the unlashed mainsail of a yacht, he hears a soft female voice.

It asks him if he will share his bed.

Now he is frozen with fear, but to his horror he finds that the voice's request has aroused him and he wakes in his guesthouse room to the sound of his own stifled moans and traffic noise from the road outside, wet sheets twisted around his clammy body and a large erection clamped between his trembling legs.

From: Byron, T [T.Byron@multicorp.co.uk]
Sent: Tuesday, October 21
To: Mylo [m.rappeli@gmail.com]
Subject: Goods delivered

Mylo

I just had a meeting with our mutual friend. During this meeting I informed him of his trip East and of the 'goods' I want him to collect when he is there. He accepted the offer. Very gracious of him. He leaves in two days.

I have also arranged the welcome party of what you spoke. It will be quite a small party ten I think. They will be waiting for him when he gets to Laos you know there number.

Allow me to recap: you will already be at the hospital when Joseph is at the party and you will collect the goods on his behalf so to speak, save him the trouble I suppose, very good of you. Then you will join him at the party. All very nice and cosy and what you get up to at that party is none of my concern.

Oh by the way if he happens to leave the party early – he might do, sneaky cunt – then he will no doubt scamper off to the hospital to get the goods as planned. If that happens then you will have to look after him. Consider this a warning. He is getting on a bit but he's still one vicious fuck excuse my French.
Either way as long as I get my goods then I am happy. He's all yours after that.

Yours truly,

Byron.

A GLIMMER OF A MEMORY

Somewhere over the Indian Ocean

JOSEPH WOKE, as he always did, to the sound of tyre and metal and his own strangled screams. He searched the muscles in his body. He was tense and rigid. His arms were crossed tightly and his left knee was squashed against its prosthetic brother, his chin tucked into his chest and his brow crumpled into a thick frown. He opened his eyes and lifted his head, swallowing slowly before taking in a lungful of sterile cabin air. As usual, sleep had taken more than it had given.

He unfurled his hands and flexed his fingers, straightening his back and looking around. The cabin was dark and quiet, apart from the odd reading lamp still on and light snores from a few seats. Most people were unconscious, or trying to be. He shuddered. Flight was at its most disturbing at night. People were sleeping — actually sleeping — while their bodies were busy hurtling through the upper troposphere at five hundred miles an hour, an utterly outrageous, deeply unnatural thing for anyone's body to be doing.

But, tucked in by tight-bloused cabin crew, with a good dose of drink and a film or two, the horror of flight simply fell away. It was a moment when sleep and death were at their closest, touching fingers through the glass, working together. Sleep drugged you, then death, which circles anyone going at that speed so far above the earth, tried to bring you down.

Somebody behind him chuckled under their breath at some comedy. Joseph thought about putting on a film himself, but the collection didn't interest him. He stretched out his legs. He had been too late booking the flight to get a business class ticket, but at least his disability bought him a good seat at check-in, in front of a cabin divider. He was by the window on a three-seater, nobody between him and the woman on the aisle seat asleep. It was cold, so he took the spare blanket on the empty seat out of its polythene wrapper and added it to his own, massaging his stiff fingers beneath it.

He turned to the small, dark window beside him. It was just before dawn but there was enough light to see the dark, barnacled fists of cloud rising up above the Indian Ocean. Probably five hours till they arrived. He felt like having a cigarette; maybe he would break his morning rule and buy some when he landed.

The woman at the end of his row gave a wheezy snore. Joseph watched her lolled head and gaping mouth and, almost subconsciously, he mulled over the various methods he could have used to kill her right there and then. He briefly considered asphyxiation and poisoning, but decided that a sharp twist of the neck would be the safest option, probably allowing him to be off the plane before anybody noticed.

Planning a stranger's death was a skill he had developed over some time. The first had been twenty years ago, two months after he arrived in London. He had already killed a couple of people, so the act of life-taking had already lost its nauseous rush, the toxic cocktail of power and guilt served with the first hit weakening and giving way to curiosity and interest.

One day, during one of his walks, he bought a paper from a street-seller, placed some coins in his hands, looked at his face and then suddenly imagined cleaving it in two with a machete.

He turned and walked away without a word. It wasn't a conscious thought, just a flash as if he had closed his eyes and seen the burnt outline of something at which he had been staring too long. It was a shock, having his retina subjected to such an unplanned and violent image. What he found to be more of a shock though — and this he might have found shocking in itself — was that the method of murder his brain had thrown up was unquestionably inappropriate. If he had wanted to kill a newspaper salesman, he wouldn't have done it in broad daylight, and he certainly wouldn't have done it by splitting his head in two.

After that, almost in an effort to protect himself, he had started to think consciously of ways in which he would kill. He began to keep his walks to the same times and in the same places and soon he spotted familiar faces, nine or ten people interesting him at first. He monitored them as they went about their daily business, following a route that allowed him to watch them go in and out of buildings, shops and offices from a safe distance that ensured he wouldn't be noticed. After a while, he concentrated on a few with more engaging movements than others, and finally whittled the group down to one winner, whom he then tracked exclusively — a woman who worked in the printing shop three streets away from his bedsit. He chose her because he wasn't attracted to her, didn't want to have the stigma of stalker hanging over his conscience, and didn't want to be distracted. He dedicated his days to finding out everything about her life, filling a little notebook he had bought with her diary, which soon contained more information about her life than even she wanted to know. Every spare centimetre of each page he wrote was covered with a code he had made up; tiny abbreviations, symbols, times, postcodes and arrows scrawled in thick blue biro.

Her flat was on the fourth floor of a tenement crescent that curved round so that the rear windows of each building looked over a shared green courtyard. He stole an already stolen pair of binoculars from a second-hand shop and found a way of getting up onto the roof of the building opposite, through a hatch in the ceiling outside the top flat's door. He discovered that people don't close their curtains when they can see other windows out of their own — probably because they want to be seen just as much as they want to see in.

Every evening he stationed himself behind a chimney pot

and watched her. Sometimes she left to go out, in which case he ran down and followed her. She never noticed him. The times when she stayed in, which were most nights, he tracked her movements throughout the flat, the television she watched, the music she listened to, how much she drank, who stayed, when she was at her most vulnerable. He left only when she turned off the bedroom light. Sometimes he stayed longer to check on any nocturnal visits to the bathroom.

After two months of observation, he pinpointed the optimum time of attack as 9:45pm on a Wednesday, when she took the rubbish out into the concealed alley behind her flat. The method would employ a short length of washing line.

He didn't make the kill, of course; he had no reason to. Instead he became interested in her partners. During those three months he recorded, she slept with five people. One of them was a woman and two of them were brothers, one of whom cried every time. He started to follow these, too, then the people whose lives touched theirs. Pretty soon he was on his fifteenth notebook, each chapter ending with a brief description of a murder method.

He spent very little time questioning why. At times, he felt as if what he was doing should make him feel guilty. But it didn't. He didn't feel anything any more. Something vital left him when he lost Annie and now nothing he did made any sense or mattered. He was a shadow; just a glimmer of a memory of what used to be a man.

But he was fascinated by the routines people kept. The lies they told, the contradictions in their actions, even the ways they moved and the expressions their faces made as they went about the strange business of living. He often wondered how they would react if he caught up with one of them and sat them down in a chair, introduced himself politely and then began to recite to them their life, translated from three months of scribbled code. If he read back to them their exact actions, second by second from the moment they woke to the moment the bedside light went out, all the wrong rooms they had entered, the time they had spent looking for lost keys, chewing pencils, staring at walls, all the involuntary facial spasms and noises they made, all the nonsensical things they had said, everything they had laughed at, everything that they claimed one day and denied the next — he guessed that they would not believe him. He learned that life's static was louder than its tune, but people just didn't hear it any more.

He never considered the idea of getting a job, of earning some money by joining the noise he was monitoring. He had some cash left from before; he didn't know exactly how much, but to sustain his existence further by increasing his funds just didn't seem right. Though he never admitted so consciously to himself, he was allowing himself to die. His money would dwindle, his rent would go unpaid and he would be out on the street, where he wouldn't have lasted long. He just wanted to keep himself occupied while he waited for it all to happen. And happen it would have done, if it hadn't been for Martine Huttner.

Martine Huttner was in her mid-thirties, and Joseph had started to watch her during the winter, after she became romantically involved with a young city banker he was monitoring in Greenwich. It was a passionate affair, sadly for all the wrong reasons. Their evenings together were always tearful, and the lack of conversation married with the almost cinematic desperation of their bedroom habits meant only one thing: adultery, in some form, was stirring things up. Sex like that only ever happened when something was at stake.

Since Joseph knew that the banker's bed was a one-woman show (he even slept on her side of it when she wasn't there), the infidelity had to be hers, so he dumped the banker and moved his operation across town. She lived just three miles from his bedsit, on one of St John's Wood's smugger streets, one that smelled most strongly of wealth. Her flat had three bedrooms, Joseph guessed, and was on the ground floor of a white-washed building with a red-gravel drive.

It had been difficult at first, since there was no obvious position in which Joseph could station himself without being noticed; none of the rooftops around the building were flat and the street was very wide. It was impossible to watch her for any longer than a few minutes at a time, until he found a thin, overgrown pathway that ran between her street and the one behind it. Her garden, which she rarely used, ended with a thick hedgerow that backed onto the pathway and offered clear views into the kitchen, bedroom and bathroom, which were almost always lit and hardly ever curtained.

She usually woke between 6:30am and 7:00am to the breakfast show of a London radio station, which she displayed no signs of enjoying. For twenty minutes she would stay in bed, sometimes getting up to look at herself in the mirror for a minute before falling back in. Occasionally, when her fiancé stayed (there lying the victim of her infidelity), she would screw him lazily for a few minutes before getting up and showering.

She washed her hair every third day and blow-dried it loudly in front of the mirror by the kitchen door for about ten minutes. This she did while eating toast and marmalade and drinking fresh coffee. Then she brushed her teeth and spent two minutes repeating something to her reflection in the bathroom cabinet. She left for work no earlier than 7:20am and no later than 7:53am, driving her 1969 blue Mercedes 280 SL convertible the two miles to her office on Baker Street, where she managed a branch of a high-brow estate agent covering the north-west central London area.

Her time in the office was impossible to record because the building was too high and too exposed. However, since her work took her mostly outside, it didn't matter. She usually left at 10am and went to meet one of a string of wealthy clients in the market for a flat. She would eat long, expensive lunches with them and throw them property deeds like meat to fat hounds. Occasionally, if they were men, she would sleep with them to close the deal.

Joseph had found adultery almost everywhere he found life. It was usually kept guarded, a guilty passion that was snuffed out and ignored after a few months. But for Martine Huttner it was serial, a part of her existence. She felt no shame and no worry, and it made hatred ache in Joseph's memory.

It hurt him to watch her guiltless abuse of trust, hurt him to see the ignorance on her fiancé's face. For a while he tracked him instead, hoping to find him doing something similar, but he was clean. He considered stopping, forgetting about her and backtracking to the banker, but something masochistic drove him on, until one evening, as he was just about to leave the hedge and walk home, Joseph saw a shadow creep along Martine Huttner's wall.

He froze and watched it stop by the kitchen window, through which he could see Martine cooking some pasta on her large steel hob. The shadow's head turned in Joseph's direction, presumably at the brief rustle he had made, but then turned back when it heard nothing else. It slowly peered around the window-frame and into the kitchen, jerking back when Martine turned to pick up her glass of wine from the work surface behind her. Joseph watched her pause and do a double-take, glass halfway to her mouth. She kept still for a while, watching the corner of her window where she had seen movement, then took a large slug of wine and put the glass down again. She then picked up a cigarette (a Dunhill) and lit it from the flame on the hob behind her, before marching over to the door that led out into the garden. It was on the other side of the window to the shadow, which, sensing something, retreated behind the corner made by the window's bay.

The door opened and Martine's head popped out, blowing a tight jet of smoke violently out into the cold air and looking around. Joseph watched them both, the shadow tucked tightly behind the corner and Martine's foggy silhouette peering suspiciously up the wall. They were no more than twenty feet apart, separated by the warmly lit square that framed her comfortable kitchen.

Finally, she gave up and flicked the cigarette into the garden, blowing out the last of the smoke from her mouth and slamming the door behind her. In the time it took her to walk across the kitchen, retrieve a key from a drawer and return to the door in order to lock it, however, the shadow had sprinted across the window and had his hand upon the handle. As she inserted the key, the door burst open and she fell back across the kitchen.

Joseph remembered that he didn't hear her scream. He remembered that he came forwards into the garden and stood wide-eyed in front of the kitchen window. Remembered that he saw the shadow — a tall man with a black balaclava — grasp her throat and struggle with her for a few seconds. Remembered that she had made a few choking noises, but had reached behind her and brought the pan full of bubbling pasta round against the man's head with such force that it knocked him sideways and onto the floor, showering his back with boiling water. Then he remembered Martine bent double, holding her throat while the man struggled silently to get up from the floor, stunned and scalded. He remembered walking to the door, grabbing the discarded clothes line on the ground by the hedge and going into the kitchen. Remembered the look of shock on Martine's face when he had looped it around her neck and jerked it tight. Remembered the stench of stale smoke on her last breath. Remembered wondering calmly, as she slid to the floor, why cigarettes always made you smell worse when you smoked them outside.

Once the shadow had managed to stand up, he had a gun in his hand that he pointed at Joseph's belly. He used it to usher him out of the house and into a car, and made him drive them both to a dark room beneath a pub at the bottom of the Kilburn High Road.

There, Joseph had stood in front of a desk with a gun lodged in the base of his skull, searching himself for traces of feeling. Guilt, remorse, exhilaration, horror; anything to describe his reaction. But there was nothing. He had just done it. Self-analysis was pointless, because it seemed as if there was no self to analyse. He felt detached like he never had before, impervious, weightless in a gravity of morals.

Behind the desk had been a large man whose forehead rose at such an angle that he could do nothing but stare across it. This he did, directly at Joseph, while the shadow summarised the events of the evening for him, holding a damp towel to the burns on his neck. When he had finished, the man continued to stare for a minute before speaking.

'Tell me who you work for,' he said.

Joseph said nothing.

'I won't ask again,' he said, nodding to another shadow in the corner, who stepped forward with a pistol.

'I work for nobody,' said Joseph, trying his best to keep his accent as neutral as possible.

The man didn't move for a few seconds. Then he turned and whispered something into the ear of the man with the pistol, who stepped forwards and aimed it directly at Joseph's head. Joseph didn't move, didn't close his eyes, just stared at its thin, black barrel and felt nothing. But then the barrel moved, three inches to his right, and fired a bullet across his shoulder. Joseph heard a thud as the shadow hit the ground. He looked at the man.

'I think it's safe to say that's no longer the case,' he told Joseph.

Arnold Blackwater was his name, the man who added Joseph to his payroll and made a hired killer from a suicidal stalker. Blackwater, among other things, made money by killing people. Rather, he took people's money and got other people to do their killing. Joseph smiled when he learned that the five thousand pounds he was paid for finishing the shadow's botched job came directly from the pocket of Martine Huttner's fiancé.

Dawn came and the cabin was roused by streaming, orange sunlight. Words were muttered, jaws were yawned, legs were stretched. The light clatter of trays announced breakfast from the trolleys at the back of the plane. Everyone was waking up, back to the business of flight, gently roused and comforted by the whistles of the jet engines on either side of them.

Why anyone would find the sound of explosive thrust at thirty-thousand feet comforting was beyond Joseph. The woman two seats from Joseph arched her back, smiled and looked around sleepily.

'I hope I didn't snore,' she yawned, picking up a book from her lap. 'I was dead to the world.'

Joseph smiled back at her silently, wondering what position her neck would make broken.

LOSE HIMSELF

Thailand

THE TRAIN travels north through wild jungles, rice fields and steep mountains. It is long and painted green, the same shade as the country it passes through. All of its doors are open for ventilation, and warm, wet air floods through its carriages.

There are two classes of carriage. One is designed for maximum capacity and houses mostly large families who face each other on hard-backed wooden benches. Those who do not sit on the benches, the youngest of the families, sit on the floor and lean against the rattling door frames. The journey to Chiang Mai takes twelve hours.

Passengers in the other class of carriage have had to walk through the first kind to get to their seats, carrying rucksacks on which are strung heavy boots swinging wildly in the faces of old women. Their seats are soft and wider and when it is time for bed a small man comes to flip up the table and drop down a flap, thus creating a double bunk. They also get a meal, which they choose from a menu, and electric fans under which they keep cool.

In these carriages, there is some glimmer of life. Everyone here who isn't a long-distance commuter or a brand-new ladyboy has, until today, been sitting on beanbags watching American films and drinking milkshakes and beer. Now they are actually travelling, and the realisation of this is as thrilling as the green spray of jungle sailing past their windows.

Bangkok is fading and the north tugs them slowly up with its promise of elephants and jungle-bound exercise. There is chatter and movement and those who aren't commuting or still smarting from the clinic walk up and down the aisle, meeting people by accident. Voices are excited, the conversations loud and forgettable. On every third table, music plays through portable speakers retrieved from the recesses of a deep rucksack side pocket. It is electronic and designed to relax and remind them of the feelings they had two years ago, when they took drugs and danced on a hot Spanish island.

Ashley sits on his black plastic seat with one bare foot tucked tightly beneath his leg. He looks out of the window, sucking the toothpick he kept from a noodle bar at Bangkok station and trying desperately not to think about his dream. It is fresh in his mind from the night before and the fear is still in his mouth. He feels nauseous; the heat tugs at his clothes and the babble of the passengers hammers on his eardrums. He nibbles the toothpick and watches the country move past him.

The train's movement makes it seem as if they are travelling on a gigantic green disc, which revolves immediately about himself and a point somewhere far on the horizon. It is hypnotising, and he tries to forget about the dream and think about Danish breasts.

'HELLO.'

Two soft, pink nipples flutter away from Ashley's cranium like startled moths and he looks at the seat opposite him. There is a young Thai man smiling at him with interested eyes. He has black messy hair and is wearing a beige jacket and jeans, even though it is sweltering and humid.

'DAVID BECKHAM,' he says.

Ashley takes the toothpick out of his mouth and says 'Ash Gritten.'

'DAVID BECKHAM,' says the man again, raising his eyebrows and nodding at Ashley's chest. Ashley frowns and looks down, noticing the Union Jack that makes up part of the design on his faded T-shirt (sixty pounds from Retro Metro on King's Road). He flicks back his head in understanding and smiles blankly at the man.

'David Beckham,' he says.

'MANCHESTER UNITED,' says the man.

Ashley shakes his head.

'Not for a while now,' he says.

The man nods, agreeing with whatever Ashley just said. For a while they smile at each other, then Ashley replaces his toothpick and looks out of the window again.

'ENGLISH,' says the man.

Ashley turns back and nods with the toothpick stuck somewhere in his lower right molars.

'London?' he says.

'LONDON,' nods the man.

'South Kensington?'

The man nods again and starts rustling with something while Ashley looks out of the window, watching the illusion of wide, green arcs form in the fields they are rushing through. The only train journeys Ashley normally makes are on the Tube between his flat in South Kensington and the office where he works on Charing Cross Road. The journeys are cramped and long, the view from the window just a black reflection of what is inside the train: tired and serious people on their way to and from work. Ashley thinks about this and the fresh, steaming countryside before him now and feels happy about his decision to travel.

He is still unsure of the reason he made it, however. He has a good job in a television company owned by his brother-in-law that pays him five times the salary of the French woman who sells him champagne and continental cigarettes in the delicatessen near his flat. It offers him a lifestyle of good-looking girls and fashionable bars. On Friday and Saturday nights he socialises with glamorous people. On Sundays he plays golf with people who own ski chalets in fucking Chamonix. He can afford a bucket of cocaine every weekend. He is thinking about buying a sports car.

But he is twenty-six now and his brother-in-law told him he

can have his job when he gets back, no problem at all. So Ashley booked his tickets and spent two months telling people all about where he was going and why he was doing it: the parties, the beaches, the drugs, the girls. Parties, beaches, drugs and girls — things that Ashley enjoys. He has already spent a month enjoying them. He took three ecstasy tablets and fucked a Danish girl against a rock last week. Probably.

But Ashley has a suspicion that these things aren't the real reason he is here. There is a small bubble of thought rising steadily from the deepest part of his mind, and soon it will reach the surface and burst into his consciousness.

Ashley is starting to believe that he wants to FIND HIMSELF.

The mating call of the traveller, cried out by all who trade ties and trouser suits for beads and sarongs. It is overused, vacuous, a parody, yet still said (in all seriousness) by people who (in all seriousness) scrawl blue tattoos on their shoulders, ankles, backs, knees, anywhere that is not easily visible, and shun paganism for a package holiday up Buddha's backside.

What Ashley doesn't realise is that he doesn't need to FIND HIMSELF, he needs to LOSE HIMSELF.

He still cannot stop thinking about his dream.

'SMOKE?'

Ashley jerks around to see the man smiling at him, holding a six-inch joint vertically in his fingers. The man nods at him encouragingly and Ashley takes a worried glance at a guard who has just passed. The man understands.

'NOOOO PROBLEM. NOOO PROBLEM,' he says, tapping the joint on his knee.

'LIGHT?' he says, popping it in his mouth.

Ashley looks around again and then searches in his pocket, he pulls out the Zippo from his brother and flicks it open with his thumb. It makes the sound that always precedes a crackle, a suck and a long outward breath — and in films, monologue or explosion — and Ashley holds up the thick flame to the joint's tip. It blackens instantly and the man narrows his eyes and smiles as he draws on the yellow smoke. After two foggy puffs, he sits back slightly and Ashley closes the lighter on the flame. The man takes three long drags, looking at the burning tip between each and blowing warm billows of smoke through the corner of his mouth and around his head. He passes the joint to Ashley, who inspects it and takes a pull, instantly filling his mouth with the taste of strong, meaty herbs. He breathes in slowly and deeply, holding it for a few seconds before releasing it against the window. As he does, the man leans forward and rests his elbows on his knees, cocking his head, grinning and nodding at Ashley. Ashley smirks. Then he takes another drag, and this time feels a heavy canvas being pulled from his brain, letting in all light and colour. A curtain is lifted, the world is revealed. How wonderful. Trees outside become curled and wide, miming the shapes of unheard stories. The mountains beam like big-bellied giants, rivers flow backwards, birds make lines on the sky. Sound becomes acute and perfect, as if a kitchen radio had suddenly turned into a full orchestra. Ashley begins to laugh.

The man starts to chuckle back.

'SMOKE?' he says. 'SMOKE?' again and again. Ashley laughs harder, and the sound of his voice reaches an apex and becomes silent, his face stretched in a grin and his shoulders jiggling as he looks out of the window at the rubbery world. The man's chuckles become louder and open-mouthed as Ashley descends into hysteria. 'SMOKE? SMOKE?' he repeats between them, until he is laughing loudly and uncontrollably.

Ashley takes another drag and a bird flies past the window in the wrong direction. He splutters out a huge lungful of smoke and doubles up, hugging himself with his head to the floor, rocking backwards and forwards and crying with laughter. He manages a deep breath and starts again, looking back at the man's wide, happy face. Outside, the great green disc spins, and the fields turn faster and faster. The sound of the train rocketing on its tracks becomes more focused in his ears, like a beat getting louder, all the while the man's laughs rolling in the smoke-filled air around him. Ashley has tears streaming down his red cheeks.

But then, things turn. They change. Like a flipped mirror, Ashley suddenly sees himself, and in an instant his face is no longer creased in laughter, but creased in grief, the tears streaming down it becoming those of misery. It as if his emotions were a song that has reached its end and has started to play backwards. A terrible, unspeakable sadness overcomes him and he begins to sob silently, while the man's chuckles fall down to a low, mocking cackle and the rhythmic rattle of the train becomes a single drum beating deeply, solemnly and slowly. The sky has turned black, the turning world frozen, the birds have all fallen dead on the ground. Everywhere is dark.

The man stops laughing and there is silence but for the beating drum. Ashley looks back at the carriage and sees no passengers, but in the man's place sits a girl. She seems young, fifteen, and sits with her palms folded neatly in her lap over a wilted lily. Her shoulders are straight and her head is bowed down so that he cannot see it. She wears a veil, and a white dress like a bride's, decorated with intricate designs, spirals and marks running down its seams and across her breast.

But when Ashley looks closer he sees that the decorations are moving. They are insects and bugs, maggots and cockroaches sewed into the dress, crawling and wriggling around beneath the clear fabric. The dress looks alive, squirming and writhing on her young body. The drum booms.

Ashley stares at the girl and whispers.

'Who are you?… What do you want?'

The girl lifts her head and mumbles something that Ashley cannot hear.

'What? What do you want?' he says, feeling panic rising as the drum beats slower and deeper all around him.

The girl lifts her head and looks straight at Ashley. Her face is pretty, dark-skinned and delicately made up. But the two lips of her mouth have been sewn together. A thick, coarse thread makes a rough zigzag, piercing her flesh in random points and tied off at the ends in crude knots. Ashley gasps and lets out a cry of horror as she tries to open her mouth. The threads move painfully as she speaks, and for a second the drum stops and there is nothing but silence.

'You,' she says, and a smile breaks on her lips and snaps the threads between them, revealing a set of sharp, rotten teeth, brown and broken in her grinning mouth.

The beating drum starts up again, furious, pummelling, deafening, and Ashley screams as the girl's face wrinkles under its bloody smile. She drops her flower, snarls and lunges at him hungrily.

'Are you OK?' says the girl sitting on the other side of the carriage to Ashley.

Ashley is breathless, curled up in the corner of his seat with his arms across his face and his knees tucked into his chest like an orphaned monkey. He peers at her through the gap made by his elbows. The drum has faded to the sound of his own blood throbbing in his temples, and the train rattles sleepily in the background.

'You were making a noise,' says the girl. 'Like crying.'

Ashley raises one arm, increasing the gap between them so that he can see the girl more clearly. Her silhouette against the bright window begins to gather detail and he sees that she is holding a book open in her hands. He can't see what it is but the cover is made of images that suggest he wouldn't enjoy it. She is reasonably pretty, short dark hair and large eyes. She's wearing a blue linen blouse that hangs from small yet ambitious breasts.

There is a part of Ashley's brain that floats outside his skull. It is untouched by fright or the will to survive and no other part of him understands it or questions it. Every man has it, it is the thing which remembers the smell under the arms of a girl just as a tiger's claw breaks belly skin; it notices the moistness in the lips of a paramedic as she pulls you from the dual carriageway; pumps your groin full of blood when your fingertips go white, gripping to the crumbling cliff-edge; it will lie back and think of sex when all the rest of you is fighting to live. Ashley is still sweating from the foul clutches of a nightmare, yet he still registers attraction in the silhouette of a stranger.

He discovers that he has an erection, so he lowers the other hand and adjusts himself. His mouth is dry and his nose wet, so he swallows and sniffs and wipes his wrist across a damp cheek.

'Sorry,' he says and coughs.

The girl smiles and makes a noise.

'Bad dream?' she says.

Ashley looks around and rubs his hands on his shorts.

'There was a man…was there a man…?' Ashley points at the seat in front of him and frowns at the girl. She looks blankly back at him and shrugs. The laughing man has left no trace of himself, no joint stub or smoke. But the smell is still in Ashley's nose and he rubs his dry throat.

A small man in dungarees walks down the carriage towards them swinging a bucket full of ice and bottles. Ashley buys a Singha beer from him and takes three gulps from it. His hands are still shaking.

When Ashley was six years old he had dreams in which a giant hen was sitting on his chest. It would cluck slowly and comfortably, and push down so hard on his body that he couldn't breathe. He'd wake up gasping for air and crying at the bottom of his bed, in the arms of his mother who shushed him and stroked his hair. When he calmed down, his father would wink and tap a finger against his temple, and then he'd be left alone and could not get back to sleep.

Ashley was scared by dreams about chickens, but he has never been scared by dreams since. From the age of seven to thirteen, his dreams were like the fronts of the birthday cards he received from his parents. They had racing cars, boats, footballs and tennis players. They had no sound, sometimes they didn't even move. Then, when he was a teenager, his dreams abandoned sports and became interested in what lived beneath the pleated skirts of the hockey team that shared his school playing field. They were restless dreams, hot and largely inaccurate until pornography found its way into the dormitory. After that they were of women in hairspray and make-up who looked you in the eye and smiled as they spread their stockinged legs.

At seventeen, the pornography dwindled and he began sleeping with the hockey team. After that day, any dreams he had were abstract and mindless, repeats of a day's events or suggestions of tomorrow's. Dreams of sex were still high on the list, but they were streamlined and serious, decorated with taboos. Mostly his nights gave way to nothingness, especially when alcohol and narcotics began sharing his bed.

Not one single nightmare. Demons would not touch Ashley. Not until now.

Ashley takes another sip of beer and looks at the girl. He feels better.

'Sorry,' he says again, smiling in a way he knows will make him look cheeky and embarrassed.

'Don't be,' says the girl, returning to her book. She has an accent. Ashley thinks it might be Spanish — he has never slept with a Spanish girl.

'That's a nice accent,' he says, shifting his body so that his bare knee is aimed at her. 'Where are you from?'

The girl says 'Italy', but doesn't look up.

Ashley nods in understanding.

'Cool,' he says. 'I'm from England?'

'I know,' says the girl, still reading, and then 'Caterine, two days, no and no.'

Ashley looks vacant. 'Huh?' he says.

'Caterine, two days, no and no. The answers to your next four questions.'

Ashley raises an eyebrow and curls a lip, pouring beer through it.

'Oh really. And what would they be?'

'What's your name, how long have you been in Thailand, are you staying in Chiang Mai long and have you been to a full moon party yet.'

Caterine stares all the while at her book, which Ashley guesses she can't possibly be reading while jibing him so smartly. He guesses wrong: women are good at that sort of thing. He repeats the lip and eyebrow curled beer slug but says nothing back. Instead he looks up the carriage and notices a young Israeli man smiling at him. He has dark brown curly hair greased back beneath a black and red striped bandana, which could easily make him look like a girl were it not for his tanned and muscular torso. He wears a white vest, which shows off his biceps and pectorals to the three Irish girls who are sitting with him, smiling and squirming.

He likes listening to Aerosmith, working out, smoking dope, looking at himself naked and making breathy grunts. Sometimes he does all of these things together. He grins and winks at Ashley, holding up a bottle of beer in congratulation.

Ashley looks out of the window and sees that evening is beginning.

Tits too small, he thinks.

From: Rappeli, Mylo [m.rappeli@gmail.com]
Sent: Tuesday, October 21, 2002 5:49 PM
To: Byron [T.Byron@multicorp.co.uk]
Subject: RE: Goods delivered

Dear Mr Byron,

Many thanks for your last missive. Thank you also for your time and efforts in setting up this surprise for our good friend, Joseph.

Please do not worry for my safety. I have been watching Mr Martin for some time now and, although you are quite right, he is both a sneaky cunt and a vicious fuck, I am sure our party will run smoothly for all concerned.

Expect your goods in early November. I regret that we will not speak again.

Ciao,

M

SQUAT IT COULD NOT

Vientiane, Laos

THE CONNECTING flight from Bangkok was late and bumpy, and Joseph arrived in Wattay International with seventeen hours of flight, three lines of longitude and ten of latitude wrapped around his shoulders. He stared at the small, mechanical departures board in the lounge.

```
1:27
ALL INTERNAL FLIGHTS CANCELLED BECAUSE FOR
STRIKING
- LAOS AVIATION -
ALL PASSENGERS ARE INSURED THANKS YOU
```

For a few minutes, he willed it to change, but it didn't. He looked at his watch and adjusted it to read 1:30, then picked up his holdall and walked across to a small information desk along one wall of the lounge. The dumpy woman behind the glass tilted her head in the universal gesture for 'HOW CAN I HELP?'

'When is the next flight to Luang Prabang, please?' he said through the window.

The woman grinned fatly at him through the glass.

'No planes,' she said.

'What? No, I need to get to Luang Prabang,' said Joseph. 'Look, I have a ticket, here.' He produced a ticket from the inside pocket of his suit jacket and slid it under the glass. Without looking at it, the woman slid it back and stretched her grin even wider.

'No planes,' she repeated. 'Striking.' She stretched out a tubby arm and pointed cheerfully at the board behind Joseph.

'Yes, I saw that,' he said.

'Ha ha ha!' said the woman.

Joseph paused. He was used to customer service reps utilising fixed, painted grins like the Joker in *Batman* and singing pre-recorded jaunty knockbacks at him, but this one seemed genuinely delighted. It was an unfair tactic. He pushed the ticket gingerly under the glass again.

'You don't understand, I have a ticket to Luang Prabang and I need to be there by tomorrow. This is my tick…'

'Hee hee hee!' squealed the woman, pushing the ticket back as if they were playing a retarded card game. 'No planes! Striking!' she repeated, covering her mouth and pointing at the board again.

'Yes, I KNOW, but when is the next one?'

The dumpy woman's grin was so wide her eyes were shut.

'WHEN NO STRIKING?' said Joseph.

'One week,' said the woman with one finger aloft, her face suddenly dropping into one of childish seriousness.

'One WEEK?' said Joseph.

The woman nodded her head, smiling again.

'Bus,' she said, pointing over Joseph's shoulder. He looked round and saw a row of small single-deckers at a stand outside the airport doors and several queues of people scattered about next to them. He looked back at the woman, who was busying herself with some paper in front of her. She gave him the universal gesture for 'DONE HELPING YOU NOW, GOODBYE.'

Joseph picked up his holdall and walked from the desk. *Drowning*, he thought to himself. *In acid.* He found a small toilet in one corner of the lounge and went into one of its two cubicles. There was no lock on the door, so he tried the second one, finding it to be the same. Still, it was clean and the door reached from floor to ceiling without a gap, so he lodged his bag against it and stood for a moment in the sealed capsule he had created for himself. He closed his eyes and slowly rolled his shoulders, then his neck. When he opened them again, he was relaxed. He started to unbuckle his belt and looked round for the toilet seat.

It was a squatter.

Joseph was used to having to make certain physical compromises. The prosthetic leg he had had made for himself before he arrived in London had been basic to say the least. It was uncomfortable, made of plastic and didn't bend fully at the knee. It buckled around the middle of his femur, just above the stump, and his long walks around London, although succeeding in rehabilitating him, had always left him with sores and bruises around what was left of his leg, not to mention stress pain in his lower back. The best that could be said about it was that it carried his weight and allowed him to hobble around as if it were a crutch.

After he began working for Arnold Blackwater, and subsequently his peers and successors, he was able to afford a better limb. He bought a new one every year or so when the technology moved on. His latest model was a TrueStep Thrust XK1, a top-of-the-range leg built for the active amputee. It had a transfemoral docker with self-adjusting seal and breathable, moisturising inner layer that locked comfortably onto flesh with its patented SkinGrip™ technology. Its ankles employed an active rotation system modelled on the foot pronation of Olympic athletes.

The knee, its greatest selling point, was built from a carbon fibre frame, with a titanium rear joint, needle bearings and shock absorption technology borrowed from the design boards of Ferrari. It featured an artificial intelligence chip that learnt the user's walking patterns and bent or locked in response to varying pressures from the ground and electrical impulses from the muscles in the upper leg. It could run. It could jump. It was, in many ways, better than his other knee.

But squat it could not.

Joseph growled and dropped his trousers and boxer shorts. Then he took off his jacket, hung it on the hook by the cubicle door and stood for a moment, hands on his hips, looking between his ankles and the door handle. He released a loud, impatient fart and decided upon a strategy. He lifted his real leg out of the trousers and unthreaded the belt from them, buckling it and looping it around his false shin. He looped the rest of the belt around the door handle, so he was balanced on his left leg. Then, carefully, he lowered himself over the ceramic hole, pressing his hands against the walls for support until his left leg was fully bent and his other, metallic blue and shiny, was stretched out, suspended in his belt.

A smile of satisfaction visited his face for a second and he relaxed, the belt and the overdeveloped muscles in his left leg easily holding his weight. He hung motionless for a moment, like a cyborg cossack dancer switched off mid-jig.

He inspected the leg, slipping his hand into a long, hidden pocket in his trouser seam and feeling under one of the metal supports for a slim button. He pressed it and part of the thicker metal below it flipped open, producing a curved, needle-pointed knife sheathed within it. He checked it and sheathed it, clicking it back into place invisibly.

He did his business and lifted himself up again, buckling himself and collecting his jacket. Outside the cubicle he took off his shirt and splashed his face and torso with cold water from the sink. Since he hadn't left the air-conditioned luxury of Bangkok airport, this was the first time he had tasted Asian heat on his journey. Next to the frost of London's November, it was sweltering and humid, and the effort from the toilet had left him sweatier than before. He dried himself on a paper towel, and put on a black T-shirt from his bag, stuffing the shirt and jacket back in its place.

He looked in the mirror at his face, grey and coarse from the journey. Recently, it had begun to seem different every time he looked at it. So much older, less vital, more resigned than it had been. Perhaps the acceleration of age had finally reached its apex, he thought, just like a chemical reaction nearing its conclusion.

This kind of thing used to be so much easier.

Back in the day, he had been hot property. Once he had extricated himself from Blackwater's grip, a feat that was remarkably easy after somebody shot him, he became freelance. Nobody owned him. He was already well known, for both his success at executing the job and his avoidance of its investigations afterwards. He was quick and efficient, left no trace, never got caught.

His price doubled, his value heightened considerably by the novelty of his disability. He didn't really understand why this should be, but guessed at the time that it made him seem more dangerous, perhaps tougher. His notoriety was boosted further by the rumours of his connections with the Italian Mafia. Rumours which were, of course, true. He had worked for the Mafia. Although he never let anyone know the truth about that.

He thought for a while about giving himself a nickname — The Splint, Hobbler, Legs or something. Then he toyed with the idea of just giving himself a new name, until he remembered that he already had. He stuck with Joe.

Flexibility was also his forte. He didn't just kill, he spied (of course), kidnapped, robbed, tortured and delivered, sometimes all of them in one job when he was on a high-earner. Joseph watched the beads of his own sweat break through the skin of his face and join the drops of water from the tap and he remembered one, a man called Bruno Dickson.

Dickson was a thief, a talented one, and made most of his money holding up small banks and building societies. One day he had had the misfortune of doing so an hour before a respected client of Joseph's had planned to do a similar thing at the same place, the team watching helplessly from their car as a masked man bolted from the bank with their haul. It had been planned for a month and the client, Clayton, had sent Joseph off to find his unknown trespasser, deter him and take what should have been his. Joseph traced the robbery to Dickson, tracked him to a high-rise in Park Royal and paid him a visit. When he broke down his door, he found Dickson in his bedroom, bearing down upon an eight-year-old boy. His remorseless child-abuse hitherto unknown, Dickson jumped up and reached for his shotgun. But he was fat and slow, and Joseph's bullet reached his left kneecap first. As Dickson lay yelling in agony on his grimy carpet, Joseph suddenly recognised the crying boy from a photograph on Clayton's desk. It was his nephew.

He took Dickson, his money and the boy back to Clayton's building, invoicing for three times the amount based on the bonus discovery. It was a coincidence that cost Dickson the last few hours of his life in a room with Clayton, his brother and an arsenal sponsored by Black & Decker.

Not that Joseph particularly cared back then. Morals had left him. He never thought of himself as above or below anybody else, simply that he was outside of their world. Whatever kind of hole Dickson had crawled out of, and whatever kind of pain he ended up in, it didn't matter.

Joseph splashed some more water on his face and wondered whether that still held true, wondered whether his last job had been sloppy because of old age or because he had stopped to think, stopped to feel; wondered whether the morals that had been hacked away twenty years ago were starting to grow buds again. He picked up his bag and walked out.

Outside, he realised that the airport had been air-conditioned — badly — after all. It was even hotter, a wet sun blinding through dark, heavy clouds. Everything smelled of sweet, overripe fruit. There was a man selling food and cold drinks at a small barbecue near the bus stand. Joseph bought a can of something too warm and too sweet and a tray of noodles, which he ate next to a queue of people, sat on his bag with his right leg outstretched. The buses weren't moving but were clearly ready to board, people just milling about them, the drivers smoking or sleeping in their seats.

He threw the plastic tray in the dust and drained the sickly liquid from its can. Then he took out a map from the side pocket of his bag and studied it. Luang Prabang was roughly 200 miles from Vientiane along a hilly, winding road, which he hoped was tarmacked. He should have been here earlier so he could have had more time to case the hospital and locate the girl, but as it stood he would arrive just two days before the corpse did at most.

He replaced the map and saw a driver flick a butt onto the ground. Just as he was wondering where the nearest cigarette machine might be, there was suddenly a flurry of movement as an engine started. Joseph joined the crowd who were handing up their bags to a man on the bus's roof. When he reached the front, he looked up at the man and said 'Luang Prabang' at him, who nodded and snatched his holdall, hurling it into the pile behind him.

It was one hour before the bus left the airport, during which time it stopped and started its engine three times. Joseph was near the back, lodged against a window by a man who was tall and full of sharp angles. He had too many bones with not enough to cover them, and he felt like a broken clothes horse in Joseph's side. It seemed as if his skeleton was trying to escape from his skin. He arranged himself in the seat, rotating his bones like the wings of a vulture. Joseph suffered three major bruises to his torso before grabbing the man's chopstick fingers and dropping them on his metal knee. The man recoiled creakily, protecting his hand with the other one. He looked at Joseph's face with horror, then down at the knee, then back at his face. Then, whether through understanding or fear, or maybe because he had never met anyone bonier than him, the man twisted his pelvis like a corkscrew across the seat, still staring in disbelief at Joseph. Joseph spread out into the extra room and looked away, deciding on death by woodchipper.

He guessed he had about seven to eight hours on the bus as it pulled away. Without warning, sleep mugged him of five.

DOG THE DOG

Thailand

LATER, WHEN it is dark outside and the low yellow lights of the train buzz blearily to life, Ashley takes a wander up and down the carriages to stretch his legs and see what is about. He goes first in the direction of travel, sauntering slowly between the seats and rocking as the train rolls about on the tracks. Businessmen and brand-new ladyboys are dozing or looking at their reflections in the darkened jungle that swarms outside their windows. Those who aren't businessmen or brand-new ladyboys, those with large rucksacks from the high street, find groups in which to drink and chatter in the sealed gaps between carriages. Ashley squeezes between them as he passes from one into the next, nodding and grinning as he goes until he finds the second-class carriages with the wooden benches. Then he turns and retraces his steps back to his seat. In one carriage, he buys a beer from the bucket man and recognises two people sitting at one of the tables. Plumbers' apprentices from Hackney; he remembers them from the party with the Danish girl. They're drinking bottles of weak Thai bourbon with one can of Coke shared between them and laughing about nothing while one crumbles bright green weed into an open joint on his lap. His fingers are dirty because the last water they saw was a tepid dribble in a wooden beach hut before they left the islands for Bangkok. All of their clothes fit into two small daypacks, which also keep their passports and money: four-hundred and twenty-seven pounds' worth of baht between them, minus the price of the three more bottles of whisky they will buy during the rest of the evening. Neither of them has a ticket home. One of them notices Ashley and flicks up his head.

'Darren, it's that geezer from that party.'

Ashley returns the flick and smiles with one side of the mouth, while stooping to count out coins into the bucket man's palm. The plumber making the joint turns his head and watches Ashley walk cagily down the carriage towards them.

'Him? Yeah, I remember. Ashley. Posh, wasn't he? Fancied that blonde bird. Wonder if he fucked her.'

'Hello Ashley mate,' the other says, grinning up at him. 'What brings you here?'

Ashley can't remember their names. He is afraid because they talk in accents that make him feel rich, and afraid because his natural reaction to people like this is to talk like them. Ashley has a real live friend back home called Lee, who actually does speak in an east London accent because he went to university in Limehouse and drank in pubs where bank robberies are planned across the pool table on Sundays. But despite the fact that Lee is a friend, Ashley still drops his 'g's and 't's and says the words 'muppet' and 'geezer' a lot with him, even though he doesn't want to, Christ he doesn't want to, and even then he still goes up at the end of his sentences.

Aware of his affliction when he first met Darren and Keith, Ashley played a trump card and tried on a different accent. He called on the vague Scottish heritage his father insists on perpetuating through clan crests and pictures of glens on his study walls, a heritage made barely possible by a great-great-great-grandfather from Sussex's union with a Dundonian needleworker while on holiday in the north. A heritage as weak as a thimble of single malt in the English Channel. But not as weak as the accent Ashley tried out on the two plumbers before discovering that Keith could do a brilliant Rab C. Nesbitt and are you from fucking Wales or what?

'Hey, how's it going guys? You going to Chiang Mai too yeah?'

'That is where the train is heading, Ashley,' says Darren,

folding a torn piece of cardboard from his pack of cigarettes and placing it on the papers. 'Am I right, Keith?'

'I believe you are, Darren,' says Keith, nodding sagely and sipping from his bottle.

'Cool,' says Ashley. He pushes a hand against the roof of the carriage and leans forwards, taking a drink of beer and looking around. 'So, you guys doing a trek or something, yeah?'

Darren the plumber makes a short sniggering sound beneath his breath as he licks the top edge of the papers.

'Probably not, Ashley, mate, no,' says Keith.

Ashley is quiet. There is a pause while Darren seals the joint and bites off its tip. Keith breaks it.

'You fuck that blonde bird then?'

Darren snorts again and says 'Fuck's sake, Keith.' Ashley snorts too and lets out a few loud laughs.

At this point, the two French girls playing cards on the table beside them look cross. They have been listening to Darren and Keith for seven hours and have said no to them five times. Later, after the ninth rejection and three plastic cupfuls of their warm whisky cocktails, the girls will buckle and one of them will let Keith stuff his grubby hands down her underpants. But until then, they will remain disgusted. They want Ashley to undisgust them.

Keith puts his glass on the table and looks up at Ashley, folding his arms.

'Did you?' he says. The French girls bite their lips and look up at Ashley, waiting for his answer. Ashley stops laughing and keeps his beer bottle pressed to his bottom lip like a microphone.

'Yes,' he says quietly into it, 'yes, I did.'

One of the French girls tuts and their game resumes. Keith unfolds his arms and picks up his glass.

'Nice one, she was fit.'

'Fucking fit,' says Darren, putting the joint between his thin lips and lighting it.

'Stay for a puff?' he says, blowing smoke up at Ashley.

Ashley remembers his dream and feels light-headed. He says no and that he's going back to his seat.

'Posh cunt,' says Keith after he's left.

'Yeah well, you still fucked her first, Keith,' says Darren.

When Ashley returns to his carriage, he is passed by two men in white jackets pushing a trolley full of sheets. They nod silently at him as they enter the next carriage and he sees that the seats have been converted into bunk beds. Most, including Caterine's, have curtains drawn across them and are making noises, but reaching his own he sees that the top bunk is free. It is covered with a white sheet, and two grey blankets are piled on top of it next to the pillow. Guessing it is time for bed, he climbs the thin ladder.

'Hey man,' whispers a voice behind him.

Ashley turns and sees the Israeli lying diagonally opposite him with one hand behind his neck. He's still grinning, the muscle vest is off and he has lain a book face down across his corrugated belly. It's about snowboarding and zen — Ashley thinks he has read it.

'You tired?'

Ashley says 'No.'

Bandana rolls his eyes and makes a breathy groan, still grinning.

'Me neither,' he says, 'I'm fuckin' WIDE awake, man.'

He sits up, knocking aside the book so that his stomach muscles can flex unhampered, and swings his legs over the side of the bed so that they dangle down. His shorts are fashioned into a neat tear around the base of his knees and the calves are brown and sleek.

He grooms his ankles with a nasal-hair trimmer and a jar of baby oil, but nobody knows this.

Bandana reaches back and plucks a joint from the canvas bag by his pillow, inserting it into his mouth and lighting it.

'J?' he says.

An old voice beneath him complains and the curtains thump outwards. Bandana chuckles and thumps them back playfully with his heels, stretching over to pass Ashley the joint. Ashley accepts it and inspects it before gingerly taking a drag. Bandana bobs his head in encouragement.

'Cool man, name's Mehdi,' he says, offering a hand and two silver rings to Ashley.

'Ashley,' he says as he exhales. 'Ash.' They perform a complicated handshake for which neither is prepared. Both have been learned from different films.

'Cool,' says Mehdi again, making a deep noise in his throat. 'Saw you bum out with Italian girl, huh? Bummer.'

Ashley shrugs and smiles.

'I wasn't chatting her up? I was just like talking to her? But she obviously didn't want to be…'

'You been to the islands yet?' Mehdi says.

Ashley pauses.

'Yeah, last month?' he says, back on track. 'Koh Pan Yan? Koh…'

'Cool,' Mehdi nods his head deeply again. 'Been diving yet?'

'I kinda went diving in Australia last year? To the Great…'

'Barrier Reef, huh? Cool.' Everything has a nod.

'Cairns.' Every conversation is a new opportunity to impress.

'You go to Cindy's Rum Bar..

'Yeah, I went th…'

'…you tell them Mehdi says hi. They'll treat you well, give you a good night man, I'm serious.' A very deep nod for this one. And a pause. Ashley pounces.

'I was hoping to go south to dive later on…'

'Big fish in Oz man, but the water's clearer here, huh?' Mehdi takes a drag.

'I'd heard…'

'I'm a dive instructor, two years, all over the world. I should know, yeah?'

Ashley nods. 'Cool,' he says.

'Definitely cool, man,' says Mehdi about his own life. 'I'll give you a good place to…'

'I'm taking my snowboard instructor exam this winter.'

Ashley interrupts successfully and Mehdi stops speaking. He doesn't like doing this and grimaces slightly as he does so. He smiles as if it is from the smoke in his throat.

'In France? Chamonix?' Ashley goes on. Mehdi nods. He's a relaxed kind of guy, he can take a bit of interruption.

'And my teacher's like a really good friend? Says I should pass no problem…'

'Cool, I used to snowboard,' Mehdi tries to dull Ashley's triumph, but he's too slow.

'…and then he's like offered me a job any winter I like …'

'…but I'm more into diving now…'

'…which is cool 'cause I've got some really good friends with chalets there…'

'…means I can do it all year round…'

'…and the nightlife's wicked man…'

It's a dead heat. Both take a rest and Mehdi passes Ashley the joint. This is a conversation Ashley feels comfortable with. He feels comfortable with it because he has had it a thousand times before and all they require from him is to make himself sound great, which is easy because he is a good-looking twenty-six-year-old with enough money to buy a bucket of cocaine every weekend — good timing, here's the man with the bucket. Throw him a few coins, Ashley, and have a beer with your new friend.

They talk for an hour and learn the following things:

1. Ashley plays golf with people who own ski chalets in Chamonix.
2. Mehdi has recently finished military service and is travelling on the money his parents gave him as a reward.
3. Ashley once grew marijuana with his friends in his

parents' disused greenhouse and made three thousand pounds selling it.

4. Mehdi once had sex with a Dutch dive student twenty metres beneath the surface of the Indian Ocean.
5. Ashley once met Richard Gere and was fellated by his make-up artist in his dressing room.
6. Mehdi has a job in the oil industry waiting for him when he gets back.
7. Ashley has a job in TV waiting for him when he gets back.
8. Mehdi has done some modelling.
9. Ashley has snorted cocaine with the headlining DJ of the main club on a hot Spanish island, who let him mix on his decks for a whole twenty minutes on the last night of the season and said he was the dog's bollocks.
10. Mehdi surfs.
11. Ashley surfs, too.

And that's all they need to know. At 1am they say goodnight and Ashley lies down behind his closed curtain feeling good.

Wrong, Ashley.

He sleeps. He dreams.

On a country road, running: Ashley. It winds up around the side of a hill halfway up its slope, so that on his left there is a steep bank of grass going upwards for a mile or so and on his right a steep bank going down. As far as his eye can see, the terrain is the same: thick scrub, no hedges or trees, no towns or cities, just a dull green, jagged landscape stretching out to a distant horizon. The sky is still and dark grey, and the road is empty of cars or people.

He knows that he is being chased by a dog, which is about fifty metres behind him and gaining. The dog's name is Dog. At times Dog the dog is running on its hind legs, sprinting after him silently with its mouth closed and eyes fixed on his. Then there are moments when he can smell hot, reeking breath and feel fangs snapping at his ankles, but then suddenly Dog the dog is very far away again, barking and snarling in the distance.

His legs won't work, the coordination around his knees is twisted and he stumbles and stops as if they are made of rubber. In his mind he wonders how he has ever been able to run, but he keeps moving, his heartbeat echoing out across the plain.

As he rounds the corner of the hill he sees a row of three grey houses. He recognises one as the house in his first dream and ducks through its fence. The door is shut and locked, but somehow he gets in through the letterbox. Once inside, Dog the dog's barking ceases and there is silence. Ashley catches his breath in the house's hall, with its suffocating low ceiling. The air smells of old cigarettes and tinned meat. The carpet is deep purple and worn and covered in dust, dirt and bits of rubbish, sweet wrappers and tinfoil.

On the wall is an old school photo of Ashley as a child, one of those with a picture of the sky in the background. But in this one Ashley is facing the wrong way, and all that can be seen is the back of his head.

Suddenly Ashley hears a noise coming from the back of the house. A whir and a click; it sounds like a washing machine. Someone must be in, he thinks, they should know about Dog the dog. He walks back through the house in the direction of the washing machine to investigate, going through the kitchen door, which is a multi-coloured collection of vertical plastic strips. There is a pan on the hob, with blackened ravioli stuck to its bottom. A breeze blows in from the open window and whips up some pasta ash onto the floor.

Opposite the cooker is the washing machine, which is on its soak cycle. The drum rotates lazily for ten seconds and then stops for another ten. Inside there is something soapy squashed against the glass. Ashley bends down to look, and sees the face of his favourite childhood teddy bear. It was blue, even though bears are not blue, and had a serious pursed mouth and orange eyes. His mother used to wash it like this when it became too covered with child, because teddy could hold his breath for a long, long time and didn't mind the soap in his eyes.

But Ashley can see that teddy has his eyes shut and his mouth open and that he is dead. Ashley looks at him sadly for a while, feeling the light grow terrible and the clouds outside blacken. Suddenly he is overwhelmed by the same sadness that clutched at him on the train, and he starts to weep with his hand against the washing machine door. The feeling is as if all hope has been torn away from him, that he is stripped and naked of joy. Everything is slow and final; his heartbeat, the gathering of the clouds outside, the dead bear's movement in the water. It is like the funeral of a soul. He strokes the glass; he has never felt sadness like this.

Still sobbing, he stands up and turns around, but immediately falls back against the wall. There in front of him, standing with her back turned, is the girl from the train. Her dress is still crawling with bugs and maggots, and she has her head bowed, the nape of her neck stretched at Ashley like an archer's bow. Ashley's heartbeat becomes a drum again, deep and threatening, shaking the skin around his ears and his temples. He begins to hyperventilate, clutching at his chest, feeling shock, fear and sorrow in one wretched ball of emotion.

The girl mutters something into her neck, and then slowly walks forwards and out of the kitchen door. To Ashley's horror, his blood begins to burn and pump with excitement, and he feels his body follow her. He tries to stop himself, but the rubber in his legs is now jelly; uncontrollable, paralysed. Possessed.

They move steadily past the hall, and Ashley notices that his school photograph has changed. The child of him has turned to look back over his shoulder, and his face is screwed up into a wrinkled mess, crying and miserable and full of reproach. He wonders what he has done to warrant such a look, but then suddenly jumps as he feels his hand brush against something coarse. He is close behind the girl now, close enough to touch her dress. Close up, it is even more filled with crawling life than he first saw. Long worms and black insect shells move about awkwardly, crawling over each other and scratching at the seams. At some points there are black lumps, which Ashley now sees are the corpses of birds in various states of decay. He gulps and gags; the smell of death is overpowering, not just from the dress but from the girl's skin itself, and yet still Ashley feels desire unhinge itself between his legs. Revolted, confused, filled with lust, he follows the girl into the bedroom.

It is the same room as his first dream, but no pictures are on the wall now. The girl is standing by the bed, her head still bowed and her back still turned, and Ashley feels his body pull uncontrollably towards her, his muscles twitching and his bones tugging as if they are not his own. He starts to whimper and tries to hold on to the door handle behind him with his right hand, but his left hand stretches out in front of him towards the wriggling cloth of the girl's dress. For a second, he is stuck between each direction, and he cries out as his toes begin to lift off the carpet, trying with all his strength to keep himself from stumbling forwards.

But then the girl begins to mutter something low again. The muttering becomes a growl, and the growl becomes a snarl, and suddenly she turns to face him. Ashley screams. The stitched mouth has broken and grown forwards into a huge, wrinkled snout. It barks and snaps its frothy yellow teeth at him while the girl's blue eyes stare into his — she seems to be milking his soul as he stretches, paralysed towards her. He feels sick as the stench of dog breath reaches his nose, and sicker still as he feels his erection grow against his leg. He turns his face away from her, closing his eyes, and with a growl the girl springs forward onto him.

Ashley lets out another scream and stumbles back against the wall. The snout is over his shoulder, snapping its jaws against his ear and smearing thick saliva on his neck. His eyes begin to water and he retches at the smell, simultaneously feeling his arousal grow as he feels the warmth between the girl's legs rub against his hip and her breasts pressed hard up to his back. The girl's right hand is moving down his belly.

Suddenly, Ashley feels a rage rising within him. He feels it at the foul creature on his back, at the thin wall it is squashing him against, at the grotty house he has had to take refuge in and the grim, spiritless country it sits in. He didn't ask for this. He lets out a stifled cry and stands up as straight as he can. The girl growls and barks louder, gripping on tighter with her thighs and arms, but Ashley feels his anger growing into fury. He takes a breath and bursts out with his arms and shoulders. The barking becomes deafening, but the grip around Ashley's body is loosened, and he smashes his back against the wall, denting it, falling to his knees and sending the girl flying, yelping to the ground.

Ashley staggers to his feet and runs back through the door and into the dark corridor. The barking has stopped behind him, but he feels a few low woofs and the scrabbling of claws against the carpet. He turns left and pushes forwards, finding his coordination again and running properly on his feet. There are no other doors off the corridor but ahead of him, at the end of it, is a set of steps and a wooden handrail going down into the floor, down to what Ashley assumes is a cellar, a dead end. He stops and looks back at the door. A snout appears at it, followed slowly by a dog. Dog the dog. It looks dazed and disorientated, whining, rubbing its paws against its eyes, snuffling and scratching lazily at the ground. Ashley watches and catches his breath as the dog pokes about randomly in the corners of the corridor, but suddenly it finds his eye and stops in its tracks. For a moment its eyes flash blue, then fangs appear and a growl begins in its throat. Ashley turns back and runs. Once again there is barking and snapping and the clatter of claws behind him, but in a second he is at the stairs. He has no choice but to follow them down into the darkness.

Halfway down the staircase, Ashley falls, and he lands on his front at the bottom. He cries out and scrabbles to his feet and runs forwards, but it is pitch black and silent; no sound of barking, no smell of dog, no light from the corridor above. He stops and hears only his breath. The air in his lungs is damp and hot.

As his eyes adjust to the darkness, Ashley sees a red glow ahead of him. It looks as if it is coming from around a corner to his left. He widens his eyes and stretches out his arms. His hands hit two stone walls to his left and right, and he walks forward down the corridor towards the glimmering light. As he moves he starts to hear sounds. Wet sounds, and breathing like low laughter from a well. Ashley hesitates, but walks on. Suddenly he starts to smell something again, an alkaline tang in his nose, sharp, salty and hot.

He keeps moving his legs, a fear beginning to grip him by the base of the spine as the corner draws nearer. The sounds become louder, the smell more powerful, the red glow brighter.

Ashley reaches the corner. When he sees what is around it, his lungs fill with fetid air and he screams until he falls to the stone floor.

Ashley wakes with his head hanging over the edge of his bunk. His body is taut in spasm and drenched with sweat, the sheet and curtain wrapped around his neck and torso. He opens his eyes and sees that all the other beds in the train carriage have been made back into seats and that the passengers are dressed and moving about, gathering up their bags. Outside it is morning and the countryside is giving way to city. He blinks. It is hot, and the sun streams through the window and burns his forehead.

Below him, his bunk partner — a balding Thai man in his fifties — is sitting on his bed patiently waiting for Ashley to organise himself. As he does, he coughs and spits into a plastic bag. A voice sounds on the train tannoy saying something that Ashley cannot understand. He blinks again and sits up, immediately realising that his erection is sticking through the sheets and out into the carriage. He plunges his hand down and covers it with a sheet. A few of the passengers catch his eye, some smirking, some looking at him with something like pity. He swallows and tries to collect himself, and suddenly notices the Italian girl, Caterine, looking at him as she stuffs a book and a bottle of water into her rucksack. She gives Ashley a half-smile and he clutches the sheet against his chest.

'You were crying again,' she says. 'And moaning.'

Ashley doesn't answer, just shakes his head once and swallows. She picks up her bag and looks at him.

'And shouting,' she says. 'We're almost at Chiang Mai.' She nods down at his chest. 'You should go to a doctor.'

Caterine smiles again and follows the crowd of passengers down the carriage towards the door.

Ashley looks down at his hand; it is swollen, red and weeping with yellow fluid.

~1978~

THE DIARY OF CLAUDETTE FERRIÈRE

2 MARS 1978

It was light when I woke up this morning. The clock said it was eight o'clock and I was still wearing the clothes I had on yesterday. The sun was up completely and it was streaming through the window, it was warm and bright and made a big dusty shaft through the air in my room. I could hear noises downstairs, the smell of smoke from new fires and bacon cooking. Doctor Moreau's voice was loud and he was talking to Madame Beaufort about the snow and the weather and if he could get back to the village on his own.

I unwrapped my blanket and yawned and rubbed my eyes and looked out of the window down onto the yard. The snow was still there but the sky was completely blue with no clouds at all, which meant that the sun could start melting it away and Papa could clear it. I heard him in the cattle shed feeding the beasts, and saw Zeet running around the outside of the yard poking his nose into rat holes.

Then I remembered all of the things that had happened yesterday and I felt all the anger and tears well up inside me again. I turned away from the window and was about to get back into bed when I saw something yellow on the floor by the door. I walked over and picked it up. It was one of Papa's *National Geographics*, and it had a long piece of paper marking one of the pages. On it was written 'Papa' and a kiss.

I opened it up and there were seven pages about a place called *Cambodia*, where there are lots of bombs called *landmines* hidden in the ground, which only go off if you step on them. They were dropped there during a war that happened before I was born. It's finished now and all the soldiers have gone home, but the bombs are still there and people step on them and get killed, even children and dogs. Lots of them don't get killed though, and instead their legs get blown up. There were lots of photographs of people who had stepped on a landmine. Some of them had no legs or arms; some just had one leg missing and were walking on legs made out of *bamboo*. There were words next to each one saying what had happened to them. A lot of them had not lost their legs at all when they had stepped on the bomb, but had injured them so badly that they had to be *amputated*. If they weren't *amputated*, then the leg would have gone rotten and killed them.

I realised that Papa must have slipped the magazine under my door when I was asleep and was trying to tell me that Joe had to have his leg *amputated* so that he didn't die. I understood this now. But I didn't see what this had to do with kissing Madame Beaufort on the lips for three seconds.

When I had finished, I looked up and got a shock because Papa's face was at my window looking in. He had climbed up the drainpipe and was trying to hang onto it. I don't know how long he had been there, but he smiled at me and tapped on the glass, and almost fell off before he grabbed the pipe and clung to it like a *Koala Bear* in *Australia*. I went up and opened the window and looked at him with my crossest face.

'Good morning, Claudette,' he said. He was shaking a bit. 'Did you read the article?'

I nodded and held the magazine tightly in my hands. Then I said 'Did Joe step on a landmine?' and Papa said 'No he didn't,' so I said 'THEN WHY DID YOU CHOP OFF HIS LEG?'

Papa sighed and said that it wasn't just landmines that hurt people. Lots of things did, and Joe was hit by a car that smashed up his leg and turned it rotten, just like people whose legs get exploded by bombs, and that if they hadn't *amputated* it then he might have died. But I understood all of this already. I was just angry at him because of *her*.

I kept staring at him crossly and I think he knew why. Eventually he said 'Claudette…your Mama would…' really quietly. I said 'Mama would *what?*' and he took one of his hands off the pipe to reach out and touch me — which he *never* does. I stepped back a bit and he stretched his arm further, but suddenly there was a creaking sound and the drainpipe came away from the wall. Papa's face went white and I saw him fall backwards, still gripping the pipe.

I shouted 'Papa!' and held both of my hands to my mouth, but he was struggling and suddenly I couldn't see him any more and I heard him yell out and then a heavy thumping sound and a noise like 'oooff'. Zeet started barking and I gasped and ran to the window, thinking about how much heavier Papa was than me, and how much harder he would have hit the snow, and that he might have broken his leg like Joe, and then I imagined Doctor Moreau down in the kitchen, looking out of the window at Papa and stroking his little beard and wondering if he needed to sharpen his saw first…

But when I got there I saw Papa lying in the snow with Zeet barking and licking his face shouting 'Zeet! ARRÊT! ARRÊT! Get your smelly tongue out of my nose!' but for once Zeet didn't listen.

I laughed because I was so relieved to see him moving and with both legs pointing in the right direction. I jumped out of the window after him and landed lightly next to him, still laughing. I grabbed some snow and threw it in his face and then some at Zeet, who barked and tried to eat it. Papa spluttered and wiped the snow from his eyes, but I threw some more at him before he could get it all off. Then he shouted 'Right!' and pulled me down to the ground and rolled me around in the snow and I squealed and laughed and felt like I used to when he carried me on his back to the paddock in the summertime.

I couldn't remember the last time Papa laughed like that, big rolling wheezy laughs like a giant, and it made me so happy that I laughed even harder till my sides were hurting. Then Papa sat up in the snow grinning and brushing himself down and I stood up and did the same, still giggling. When I had finished, I looked down at the kitchen and saw Madame Beaufort looking through the window at me. She was smiling like she didn't want to smile again and pointing at a frying pan full of bacon.

Suddenly I was angry again. I turned back to Papa and picked up the biggest pile of snow I could carry. Then I threw it down on his bald head as hard as I could and ran off to the cattle shed.

Later on, Papa came and found me where I was sitting up in the hayloft swinging my legs off the edge. There were hundreds of icicles hanging from the doorway, and I was squinting so that I could see the sun making funny shapes in them as it melted them, and listening to the sound of the water dripping on the stone floor and the beasts shuffling and huffing around in the straw next door.

He climbed the ladder and sat next to me with his legs over the side as well. I could smell bacon and coffee and cigarette smoke on him, which made me even hungrier than I was already and also sick. I shifted away from him and made myself keep squinting at the icicles and not look up at him. He didn't move any closer.

'Claudette, your mother…' he said again, but didn't finish. I said 'What *about* my mother?' just like before.

Then he said 'Your mother has been dead for over a year, you know'.

This made me want to cry so I bit my lip, but one tear escaped and rolled down my cheek so I wiped it away quickly on my sleeve so he wouldn't see it.

'I know it upsets you to talk about it,' he said, and I nodded my head and tried to concentrate on counting how many icicles there were.

'And I know I'm not very good at talking about it with you…'

I said 'I don't want to talk about it with you,' and Papa

replied 'Well, that's fair enough, neither do I particularly, I'd rather we get on with our lives.'

Then I said 'Good', and he said 'Good' too and I said 'Why don't we just do that then?' and he said 'I'm trying, Claudette'.

I didn't know what to say then, so I started counting the icicles again because I had lost count. Papa took a big, big sigh though and carried on. He said 'I miss your mother, I miss her every one of the days she's not been here. There have been three-hundred-and-ninety-five of them'. I turned and looked at him then and asked him how he knew that, and he said that he had counted them, and that he could remember when it had been a week, then two weeks, then fifty days, then a hundred days, and then a year, and that next week it would be four hundred days since you died. I turned back to the icicles.

'I miss her,' he said again, 'and I know you miss her too. But it's time to move on. That's what Mama would want us to do. We can't run this farm on our own, Claudette.'

I said that we could run the farm on our own, and that I had learnt to feed the beasts on my own in deep snow without anybody's help and I could cook and clean and wash up and help him in the fields. But he said 'I know, and I believe you, but I don't want you to have to. You won't be here forever, Claudette, and what about when you go to school?' I told him I didn't have to go back to school, and that he could let me read his *National Geographics* to learn about the world instead of learning arithmetic and biology, and I said this even though I like going to school and biology is my favourite subject.

But Papa said that there was more to the world than a few pictures of dolphins and people in places I might never go, and anyway what was wrong with a little help around the place? I said that I didn't see what any of that had to do with kissing Madame Beaufort on the lips for three seconds, and he told me off.

Then he rubbed his chin and said sorry, and I said it was all right.

We didn't speak for a while, and I counted thirty-seven icicles and loads more tiny ones which hadn't had a chance to grow into proper ones yet. Then Papa said 'I need you to understand Claudette, please. I know how strong and helpful and useful you are. The men in the village sometimes make fun of me and say *'Victor, I bet you wish you had a son to help you on that farm, don't you? A son rather than a daughter?'* but do you know what I always say to them?'

I said 'What?'

'I say: *'My daughter is twice the son any of you shamefaced drunks could hope for, and I am twice as proud of her as any of you are of your children. She can cook breakfast, clean the house,* and *chop turnips,* and *clean out the chicken shed* and *feed the cattle* and *help me at harvest time, which is better than any of your sons who spend their time on mopeds and chasing girls, drinking beer and growing their hair long."*

I tried not to smile, but it was so hard and I blushed. I could sense Papa was smiling too.

Then he said 'but Claudette, I need you to understand, I like Madame Beaufort and she wants to be your friend and help us'. He rubbed his head again.

'And…I…it's difficult to explain, Claudette. Perhaps when you are older.'

I said that I understood, which was a lie because I don't, but I think it has something to do with the magazines that aren't *National Geographics.*

Then Papa told me that Joe was awake and was wondering where I was and so I jumped up and ran down the ladder to the house. Papa called out and ran after me, catching me up before I made it to the kitchen door. He made me eat some breakfast first, which I didn't mind because I was so hungry my stomach hurt. Then he made me wash my face and hands and say thank you to Madame Beaufort for breakfast, which I did without looking at her face, and then ran through to the old family room, where Joe was lying in front of the fire and looking out at the miles and miles of white, melting snow that covered the valley.

He had his hands crossed on his tummy and was sitting up in his bed as if he was just getting better from a cold. 'Hello,' I said, and he turned his face towards me. It didn't look sad any more, but it didn't look happy either, even when he smiled and said 'Hello' back. I was expecting him to be crying or something, even though he is a man, because anyone would cry if they woke up and found that they only had one leg. But Joe didn't cry. His eyes were dry and empty. I thought *someone has turned him upside down and shaken out all of his feelings.* That's what it seemed like.

I looked down at the shape of his stump through the sheets. He saw what I was doing and looked at it too. For a while we both just stared at it as if we were both trying to make it grow back using our minds. Then I said 'does it hurt?'

'It still feels as if it's there,' he said, 'but it feels like it is trapped under a really heavy rock.'

'That must really hurt,' I said, and he said that it would do if Doctor Moreau hadn't given him a special injection. Then I asked him if he was angry at Doctor Moreau and Papa for taking away his leg, but he shook his head and said that it didn't matter any more. Then we both looked at the stump again.

'More stories to read me?' he said after a while. He was looking at the *National Geographic* that I had rolled up in my hands, the one Papa slipped under my door. I said maybe. Then I said 'It's not snowing any more,' and he said that he could see that and how beautiful the valley looked. 'You're very lucky to live here in such a place,' he said.

'I know, it's pretty,' I said, 'everyone always says that. There are other pretty places in the world too, though, probably prettier than here.'

'Like *Patagonia*?' he said, and I said 'like *Patagonia* and *Australia* and *Alaska* and *Tibet.'*

'Tibet?' he said, and I sat down on the floor and read to him about the mountains there and the goats that live on them.

When I was finished, I told him about *Cambodia* and the bamboo legs that children make for themselves after their real ones get blown up.

In the evening, Madame Beaufort and Doctor Moreau ate dinner with Papa and me. Doctor Moreau was discussing with Papa how long he should stay to watch Joe and make sure he heals properly. They agreed that he would stay for at least a fortnight, or until Joe was ready to start trying to walk with a false leg. Doctor Moreau said that he should start doing this as soon as possible. Papa said 'How will we get a false leg?' and Doctor Moreau said that once the snow had cleared they could get one in Grenoble. 'In any case,' he said, 'he should go to a proper hospital soon enough. A farm is no place for an *amputee.* No offence, Victor.'

'None taken, Doctor,' said Papa. Madame Beaufort said nothing all through the meal, she just kept smiling at me badly across the table every time I caught her eye. She looked like she didn't want to be there, and part of me felt sorry for her. When I was finished I excused myself and went to read more things to Joe. I think he fell asleep halfway through *Caterpillars in Puerto Rico.*

2:38 in the morning.

I have just woken up and realised that I am in my bedroom and Joe is in the old family room and Doctor Moreau is sleeping on the couch. This means that Madame Beaufort must be sleeping in Papa's *bed!*

5 mars 1978

For three days the sun has been out from morning till evening, melting big craters in the snow so that the valley looks like the surface of the moon. Between helping Papa and playing Astronauts outside with Zeet (which he doesn't really get) I have been reading *National Geographic* to Joe. On Thursday I read about finding dinosaur bones in England, Friday was about things called *microchips*, which I didn't understand, and yesterday I found something on a place called *Pompeii*, which is in Italy, so I thought Joe would like it.

This morning was *Kenya*. Joe asked me if I ever wanted to go to all these places I read to him about and I said that yes I would but I couldn't go anywhere until the snow melted properly. When I said that, he laughed for the first time ever and I was so happy that I didn't even ask him why.

I said that the snow would melt, and that it was already melting outside if he looked. But I spoke too soon, didn't I? After lunch, the snow came back out of nowhere. The sky stopped being blue and became dark grey and filled with blizzard, and the valley is once more invisible, as if we have been pulled up into the clouds again. Papa has spent the last three days clearing away the drifts, and now the snow is having fun building them all up again.

I'm sad that the snow has come back because if it is as bad as last time, then Joe cannot get to hospital to get a new leg. But secretly I'm happy as well, because it means he will have to stay with us longer.

6 mars 1978

The snow is as bad as last time. In fact, it is worse. The drifts are already halfway up the windows!

7 mars 1978

The phone is not working again and the radio just crackles and hisses. Madame Beaufort tried to speak to me today but she didn't know what to say and just stood by the sink fiddling with a tea towel. I was polite and said 'Sorry, Madame Beaufort, but I have to read to Joe', and she nodded and I went to teach Joe about a special gorilla called *Koko* who can talk with her hands.

8 mars 1978

I have never seen so much snow. It is like somebody is pouring it in giant buckets from the sky. I can't see past the engine shed. For all I know I could be in the *Arctic*, which is the snowiest place on Earth.

Doctor Moreau made Joe do some exercises today and he started to walk around on crutches Papa made for him from some old brooms.

In the evening, Papa told me not to call Madame Beaufort *'Madame Beaufort'*. I said 'Why? That's her name.' He said that it would be like him calling me *'Madame Ferrière'* and I said I didn't mind at all if he called me that and he said well we'll see about that.

12 mars 1978

Today Papa said 'Please let me stop calling you *'Madame Ferrière'*, Claudette, I'm tired of it,' and I said 'but I like it'. Then he said 'OK, if I keep calling you that, will you start calling Madame Beaufort *Jeanette*?'.

I told him I didn't like it *that* much, so he said a rude word and stomped off through my bedroom window to feed the cattle.

15 mars 1978

The snow around the farm and down the valley is worse than it was before Papa came back with Madame Beaufort and Doctor Moreau. It stopped for a bit this afternoon, so that you could see some of the way down the hillside, but there was nothing but white, no trees or houses, and even the river was completely covered. It was like looking into a patch of nothingness held right in front of your face, like the opposite of what you see when you close your eyes. We all looked at it through the stair window and Doctor Moreau shook his head and tutted.

'We'll never get him to Grenoble through this,' he said. 'It's been a fortnight since…the operation, and he needs to start trying to walk with a *prosthetic* leg.' I had heard this word before but I couldn't remember where, so I asked him what it meant. He smiled and patted my head and said 'It means false, you know, like Long John Silver.'

'Or people who step on *landmines* in *Cambodia*,' I said, which made his mouth shut and his eyebrows jump up like springs.

As we all looked at the snow, I noticed that Madame Beaufort was holding onto Papa's arm tightly. I suppose she was scared because we were trapped on our own up here on the farm and just wanted to feel comfortable, but I didn't like it. I gave her a cross look but she didn't see it, so I gave her a crosser one, but she just gripped his arm tighter and kept looking out at the snow. So I kicked her on the shin and ran off to my room.

I heard her yelling and hopping about on the landing, and suddenly all my anger turned into fear because I could hear Papa's voice booming behind as he ran after me.

'GET BACK HERE RIGHT NOW YOU SELFISH LITTLE BITCH! HOW DARE YOU!' and I could hear myself squealing and his footsteps getting closer and I could feel big angry puffs of his breath on my neck. I got through the door of my bedroom and suddenly I found myself being lifted off the floor by a big hand gripping the collar of my dungarees and choking me.

I screamed out and flew around in mid-air, kicking out my legs, and saw his big, red, angry face glaring at me. 'How dare you! How dare you!' he shouted again, and then smacked my legs three times so hard that it knocked all the noise out of me. Then he dropped me to the floor and I crawled towards the bed, but he walloped me twice on the bottom again before I got up onto it and cried, curled up in the corner.

He looked down on me with his sleeves rolled up and his red face panting and his teeth gritted and I looked at him over the tops of my arms.

'I'm sick of this behaviour! Madame Beaufort…*Jeanette* has been nothing but friendly to you since she came up to help us! What ever has she done to you to make you kick her like that? Haven't I taught you to respect people? HAVEN'T I? WELL?'

I didn't say anything, I couldn't think of what to say. I had got used to Papa being quiet around me and calling me *Madame Ferrière* since Madame Beaufort came along because he didn't want to upset me. Now he didn't care, and I had forgotten that Papa gets angry.

'WHAT HAVE YOU GOT TO SAY FOR YOURSELF?' he bellowed. Even the air around him seemed to be red and furious. I tried to say something but it only came out as a whimpering sound.

'WHAT?' he said.

'I said she was holding your hand!' I shouted suddenly. 'She was holding your hand like Mama did!' The sound of my own voice frightened me and I thought Papa would explode, but he just stood there glaring at me and puffing like a dragon.

Then I heard Madame Beaufort's voice, soft and scared like a mouse. 'I'm sorry Claudette. I was only touching his arm.'

She was standing at the doorway, fumbling with her fingers. Her shin was getting blue.

'I don't like it,' I sobbed into my arms. 'She's trying to be *Mama* and she's *not!*'

I expected Papa to tell me off again, to blow up and shout at me for saying that. But he didn't. When I looked up again, he had walked out of the room and I could hear him stomping downstairs. That left me and Madame Beaufort looking at each other. She didn't try to smile this time, she just said sorry again and closed the door.

I missed dinner because I just wanted to be on own in my

room. I should remember to keep some food up here when these things happen. Later, I heard a knock on my door and I said 'come in' very quietly. It was Madame Beaufort, carrying a plate. She didn't say anything, but came and put it down on my bed. It was piled with bread and sausages and mashed potatoes and gravy, which made my mouth fill up with spit like Zeet does when he's hungry. Her leg had a big bruise running up it, which means I must have kicked her really hard. I didn't mean to, I really didn't.

Then she went back to the door without a word, but halfway through closing it she stopped.

'I want to be your friend, not your Mama,' she said, and her voice was trembling. 'I would never expect you to call me that. You don't have to call me Jeanette either, you can call me Madame Beaufort if you like.'

She looked sad, and I felt sorry for her.

'In fact you can call me whatever you want,' she said. 'I just want to be your friend.'

We didn't say anything for a while. Then I told her that there is a tree in Canada that has been alive for two thousand years.

Her mouth made a funny shape and she almost said something, but she changed her mind at the last minute and closed the door instead. Then I ate the sausages, mashed potato and bread in three minutes flat.

~ 2003 ~

DUST WAS BEGINNING TO SETTLE

Chiang Mai, Thailand

IT WAS late afternoon as Caterine walked from Chiang Mai railway station and into the centre of the city. It was different from its southern sister, Bangkok. Instead of the hellish maze of hot, dusty streets and rubbish-strewn alleys that sprawled across the capital, Chiang Mai seemed to have been built with at least some design in mind. It was quieter, cleaner, less brutal. People kept their distance more. The air was lighter, although still thick with the wet, organic heat of the equator. Streets were cobbled. The city itself was surrounded by walls, green banks and a moat that reminded Caterine of Europe and home.

Tuk-tuks tuk-tukked past on the main road, followed by children on old bicycles, three to a seat. Modern hairdressers and newsagents sat comfortably next to open-fronted bars and wooden shacks selling strange assortments of ointments, chairs, fruit and bottled water. Everywhere sold cigarettes. Caterine bought a pack from two smiling woman sat in deckchairs, draped in old dresses and T-shirts, fanning themselves in the dying, amber sunlight of the warm dusk. She said thank you and smiled back, floating away down the street and lighting one of the cigarettes. For the first time since her flight from Venice, Caterine felt a mild form of peace; a loosening of the muscles in her tired mind.

It had been five days since the night in Venice hospital. When Elmo had died, her place at the bedside had been swiftly taken by nurses, doctors and his mother. She had backed away in the corner, and made herself small while the necessities of death were dealt with. The pulse, the charts, the declaration, words uttered softly, tubes extracted, switches flicked and tears wept as the great machine of Elmo's life ground quietly to a halt in that dark room.

That night, she had stayed with Elmo's mother; her grandmother, as it turned out. Both were polite as they ate breakfast the following morning, but the circumstances meant that neither had to be overly friendly with the other, and Caterine was glad of this. She had little enough idea of how to process what Elmo – her godfather, her uncle, *her father* – had said to her, let alone discuss them with another person. It was as if the words had yet to be absorbed. She was aware of them hovering somewhere - colossal, world-shaking facts that were yet to find a way of fitting into her consciousness.

She had returned to Florence and taken leave from work. It rained. She spent a day trying to paint, staring at a blank canvas and thinking of nothing at all while the world span idly around outside her flat. Then the phone rang. *Someone will call you*, Elmo had said. She answered, a strange and kind voice replying, adding more unwanted facts to the ones she was already ignoring. *Luang Prabang hospital, Laos…the mortuary…four days' time…strange, I know, it must be difficult for you to take this all in…but your father, he was a good friend of mine…a good man…we'll all miss him…I'm sure you will, too…but you will be there like he asked?…you'll be there…call this number when you arrive…goodbye, Caterine.*

She listened blankly to the voice, making noises when noises were required, said goodbye and replaced the handset when it clicked and buzzed.

…your father…

She returned to her canvas and painted nothing, ate nothing for another 24 hours. When she awoke the next day, her cheek smudged against the easel, she showered, packed and left for Laos, lost for any other course of action, Elmo's words still floating patiently like dust around her head.

But the journey to Chiang Mai had taken almost two days, and the dust was beginning to settle. Aside from the disturbances from the young man on the train, there had been very little to distract her attention from slowly absorbing the facts. The truth was that she had never had a strong image of her father, such were the impossibly romantic and private descriptions her mother had given her. This made accepting the possibility of Elmo being her real father easier, but what made it easier still was the fact that, in some strange way, she had always known it to be the case. It was an uncultivated, unrefined, raw and forgotten instinct that had lain dormant for her whole life.

Now he was dead, along with her mother and the sugary dreams she had pedalled of the father who had never really been; dreams she had pedalled because of her own guilt, Caterine now realised. She had, after all, betrayed her own husband.

Through the grief, Caterine's anger bit through; anger at three parents who had failed each other and failed her.

As the sun reached its lowest point and night began in Chiang Mai, Caterine checked herself into a small guesthouse in a quiet alley and, leaving her rucksack unpacked, wept soundlessly until she fell asleep.

Damien says: duuuuuude! whassup, where u now?

Ash Trés says: chiang mai

Damien says: where?

Ash Trés says: chiang mai

Damien says: heard u 1st time dickhead wheres that?

Ash Trés says: oh north. inland

Damien says: wot no beach? :-)

Ash Trés says: no

Damien says: u ok u sound fukt

Ash Trés says: sorry mate tired. not been sleeping well, how r u?

Damien says: heh heh yeh bet u havnt, got some thai pussy yet?

Ash Trés says: no

Damien says: christ whats wrong with u man get it together

Ash Trés says: yeah, heh heh, dropped the ball a bit i guess. had to go to doctor yesterday

Damien says: fuck!

Ash Trés says: fucking dog bit me

Damien says: fuck!

Ash Trés says: yeh got it cleaned still swollen tho

Damien says: fuck

Ash Trés says: going out tonight tho

Damien says: fuck?

Ash Trés says: no met this bloke on train, going out on pull in town

Damien says: s'more like it mate! shit dude boss

Ash Trés says: danish bird in chang mai too

Damien is offline and may not respond.

SILENT AS HE SPEAKS

Chiang Mai, Thailand

ASHLEY WALKS out of the Internet café and scoffs at the sign advertising its 120 baht per hour price. It is the slowest connection he has yet had to endure on his trip and it has taken him all afternoon to send an email to his brother, read one from the Danish girl saying that she'll be in Chiang Mai by the evening, check his bank account and chat to Damien. Unacceptable. Why don't these people get their shit together?

It is an overcast day, much the same as any in autumn back home if it wasn't for the stifling heat. He turns right and walks down the east wall of Chiang Mai's old town. After a couple of hundred metres he comes to a wooden-fronted bar with ten tables and chairs set out on its covered porch. Ashley chooses an unoccupied one and sits down, yawning and looking out onto the street. It is a main road — a dual carriageway that skirts around the east and north side of the city — but it is quiet and only the occasional tuk-tuk bluebottles past. Beyond it lies the still moat, and a cyclist freewheels along its path. There is something pastoral and village-like about the scene, even though Ashley is in the centre of the second-largest city in Thailand.

After a few minutes, the waitress scratches her neck and looks out from under the hat on her face. Seeing Ashley, she slowly swings her legs off the bench in the corner and rubs her eyes. She wears a polo-shirt, jeans and flip-flops, which she flicks out with every step as she shuffles across the floor to Ashley's table.

She says hello like a chicken swallowing bubble gum and

leans sleepily on the back of his chair. Ashley asks for a beer and she shuffles away through the door of the bar. After another minute, she shuffles back with a bottle of Singha, says something like a chicken blowing bubbles and returns to her bench. Ashley takes a small sip from the bottle and then yawns again. Rain starts to hammer lightly on the wooden roof above him.

He looks about at the other tables. At the one by the waitress's bench sits a man with a moustache. He is eating a steaming bowl of chicken soup and reading a guidebook about Prague at which he laughs occasionally, splattering broth on the hairs above his mouth. Next to him are two empty tables and then one with a young couple. He has bony knees and is wolfing down a plate of beef. She has diarrhoea and stares straight ahead trying to ignore him.

Ashley looks at the other tables and begins to wonder whether any of them — himself included — could muster up an adventure between them. Ashley doesn't usually have thoughts like these. It confuses him. A lot has confused him over the past few days. He tries to put the image from his last dream out of his mind, rubbing the bandage on his hand as if hoping for some antiseptic genie to emerge. He is beginning to dread his own imagination.

As he flicks his eyes between the tables, he suddenly recognises a face on the one nearest his. It is Caterine, on her own, drinking a glass of rum and reading a new book — Ashley doesn't like the look of this one either. It takes them both a few shared looks to accept the fact that they have seen each other, then a few more from Ashley before Caterine puts down her book. The whole thing takes about four seconds. She looks at him, her eyes quite still and her mouth lifted into only the barest of smiles. Ashley feels like he is being studied.

'Hello,' she says. 'How are you?'

'Hey,' croaks Ashley. 'HEY,' he repeats, gulping. 'I'm fine, you?'

Caterine nods.

'Really fine?' she says. 'Only you didn't seem it this morning.'

Ashley fidgets and shrugs.

'Bad night's sleep, that's all,' he says behind a swig of beer. 'Don't sleep well on trains.'

'No, it didn't sound like it. I wouldn't like to meet it, whatever it was,' says Caterine, picking up her book again.

Ashley swallows. 'Meet what?'

'Whatever it was that was you were dreaming about. Must have been some monster.'

Ashley says nothing. The rain suddenly becomes heavier. Drops of it seem to be competing for the same space to fall through the air, colliding with each other and creating wet explosions on the flooded tarmac. It roars on the wooden roof and a deep belly roll of thunder sounds from the sky. The spectacle causes the waitress to look out from under her hat. Caterine seizes the chance and lifts up her empty glass, and the waitress trudges through to the bar, returning with a generous rum.

'You have nightmares a lot?' she says, after a sharp sip.

'No,' says Ashley. He thinks for a while. 'I used to dream about a giant hen when I was a kid,' he says at last. He looks at the sweeps of rain stroking the moat and the city wall of Chiang Mai like huge hands.

'Sitting on your chest?'

Ashley swings his head around.

'How did you know that?'

'It's quite common for someone with your…'

She breaks off.

'My what?'

'Just a hunch,' she says. 'Tell me about them.'

'It just sat on my chest, that's all.'

'No, the dreams you have now.'

Ashley grimaces. He is uncomfortable about people trying to see inside of him. He only sees the outside of other people, only the outside of himself. Life does not require a great depth of field.

Yet something, perhaps the beer or the heat or some weak sense of adventure, drives him to try something new.

He sighs and sits back in his seat, tells her all about the dreams, starting with the first. He tells her about the house and the pictures and the ghost, then the man with the joint and the girl on the train and the dog chasing him, of the photograph, of the washing machine, of the dress and of the bedroom. Caterine keeps silent as he speaks, resting her cheek on her right fist and taking occasional sips of rum while looking at his face. Ashley expects her to make mmm sounds or understanding nods, or even a few 'fuuuuck's when he elaborates on the more gruesome areas of the nightmares. But she doesn't make a sound. When he's finished he takes a large pull on his beer and inspects the white label on the bottle.

'Did they turn you on?' says Caterine.

Ashley snorts and blows a raspberry.

'Did they?' she says again.

Ashley picks at the label. After a pause, he says 'kind of.' After another, he says 'yes. Yes, they did.'

'What happened in the end?' says Caterine.

'That was it,' says Ashley, still scratching at the label.

'But you got away, didn't you?'

'Yes, I ran out of the bedroom and down the corridor, like I just said,' he says, his fingernail increasing in its velocity.

'So why the scream?'

The label comes off in Ashley's hand and he crumples it in his palm.

'What?' he says.

'You screamed before you woke up.'

Ashley slams down his bottle on the table in front of him and shoots two fierce eyes at Caterine.

'Well, I'm glad you've taken such an interest in my sleeping habits,' he says. 'Especially when you wouldn't even talk to me on the train.'

The man with the moustache looks up momentarily from his book, munching on a bit of chicken.

'Sorry,' says Caterine, 'but it was pretty loud. Actually it was deafening. Everyone heard you.' She picks up her book again.

'And saw you,' she says, looking briefly down at his shorts.

'Great,' says Ashley, adjusting himself and pulling down his T-shirt. He crosses his arms and shakes his head. Caterine buries her head in a page.

After two minutes of silence, Ashley shakes his head again, unfolds his arms and picks up his beer.

'It's not very nice,' he says finally.

'What?' says Caterine.

'How it ends, my dream. I'm not very proud of having imagined it…I don't know what it says about me.'

'You'd be surprised what you can imagine if you put your mind to it,' says Caterine.

'Maybe,' Ashley says, tipping back his bottle and letting beer swill against his tongue.

'I found…'

'What did you find?'

Ashley sighs.

'I found the devil m…'

He breaks off, the word stuck.

'Go on,' says Caterine.

'I found the devil masturbating in a cellar.'

After five minutes, Caterine is still laughing silently into her hands. Between Ashley telling her that he's glad she finds it so funny and that he doesn't know why he told her anyway, she comforts him with sympathetic noises and waves of her arm before starting up again.

'I don't think you'd find it so funny if you saw that in your basement,' says Ashley.

Caterine's chuckles eventually ripple away and leave an amused smile. She directs it at Ashley, who has his arms folded and is staring at his beer bottle.

'Succubus,' she says.

'Suck what?'

'Succubus, you have a Succubus.' The word rolls against her teeth like a mouthful of rum. 'At least some would say so. It's a spirit. A female demon who wants you for her own ends, lusts after you. She'll visit you when you sleep, try to seduce you. Men have talked for centuries about it, stories of being pinned to the bed and taken by evil nymphs. The female version is called Incubus, although I think you men fare better. At least you seem to enjoy it. For us it's more like rape.'

'So you're saying some…randy…hell-whore has taken a shine to me and wants to get it on?' says Ashley.

'Exactly, but not just that,' says Caterine.

'What else?'

'If you give in to her, if you succumb to her seductions…' Caterine's eyes widen and she smiles, '…then she takes your soul back to hell.'

Ashley snorts and takes another swig of his beer, looking across the road.

'It's quite common,' says Caterine. 'Research puts it down to hormones released during REM sleep. A lot of people report dreams of chickens sitting on them too.'

Ashley frowns. 'Where do you get all this stuff?' he says.

'I read a lot.'

'Yeah well, like you say, the imagination can be pretty weird sometimes,' he says.

'It can. Thing is, there's quite a big difference between a giant hen and a girl with her mouth stitched up who keeps turning into a dog. Isn't there?'

'Maybe it's just because I didn't know about sex when I was younger.'

'Maybe. Or you could have been cursed,' says Caterine.

'What?'

'Cursed. Have you been to Laos?'

Ashley looks blank.

'Laos. It's the country next door. The Americans blew it up in the Vietnam war.'

'I know where Laos is. What do you mean I could have been cursed?'

'I'm telling you. There's a cave there, it's called the Sleeping Cave; do you know why?'

Ashley shakes his head.

'Because when the Americans were busy blowing up the countryside around it, the people who stayed in the villages nearby used it to hide in. Two thousand of them stayed inside it altogether, spending their time shitting in a single hole and eating bats. A river ran through it, so they always had water. They had to keep quiet, and they didn't light fires for fear of alerting the Lao mercenaries hired by the Americans to spy on their own people. So they lived in dark, cold silence eating raw bat meat while they listened to the hills around them getting slowly blown into pieces. For two years.

'The other thing they did to pass the time was pray to the cave's spirit to keep them safe. Because they had a lot of time, they did a lot of praying, and when the bombs started to run out they found themselves to be all alive and in one piece, and they left the cave, blinded by the sunlight, and went back to their villages. The cave spirit had saved them.'

'More like the bats,' says Ashley.

'Perhaps, but to this day the deepest recesses of the cave — where the spirit is said to live — remains holy and sacred and is not to be disturbed. Sacrifices are made outside the entrance all the time.'

'Sacrifices?'

'Chickens, pigs.'

'Did you read this, too?'

'No, a friend told me. He went there last year and joined a kayaking trip.'

'So what does this have to do with a curse?' says Ashley.

'The tour guide on the kayaking trip was a young man called Sarat, and he told my friend a story. He was a good kayaker and ran the company himself. He knew all the caves in the area, he made good money from tourism and all he wanted to do was to find better, deeper and more exciting routes to take his tour.

'He knew well enough about local folklore, and many of the older people had urged him not to use the Sleeping Cave as a tourist attraction, not to take people deep inside it. They were afraid he might disturb the spirit and bring war back to the country. But Sarat didn't hold with ideas like spirits or prayer, he had long since shunned his family's religion. So one evening he took his kayak and followed the cave's waterfalls right down to its deepest pools.

'He got to one chamber where there was no light or sound and the water was still. He began to get an eerie feeling that something was watching him so he stopped his kayak and looked around. Nothing. But then, suddenly, he saw two orange lights shoot out at him from the darkness. He paddled back away from them, but heard a ripple behind him. Turning around, he saw two otters swimming around his boat.'

'Otters?'

'Otters, and then a snake. A huge snake, sliding into the water. Sarat was freaked now and reverse paddled out of the chamber. As he did so, he was chased by a huge hoard of bats that suddenly appeared from the ceiling. He paddled home as fast as he could.

'What were otters doing deep in a cave?'

'That night, and for some nights afterwards, he had the same dream. He dreamed of being in the cave again, but this time there were two women, one young and one old. Each time the younger woman approached him and claimed him for her husband while the older one looked on cackling, and each time he retreated from the cave, followed by the same hoard of bats.

'It got to the point where he couldn't sleep because of the dream, he had it every time he shut his eyes, three or four times a night. Eventually he couldn't take it any more, so he decided to visit a local monk, who agreed to tell his fortune. Sarat told him about his trip into the cave, of the lights, the otters and the snake…but before he could even mention the dream, the monk's face went white and he told him that the cave spirit was angry. She wanted him for her daughter!

'That evening, Sarat was so scared that he couldn't think of anything else to do but make a sacrifice. So he killed a chicken and left it at the entrance of the cave.'

'Chickens and bats don't get a very good deal out of this story, do they?' says Ashley. 'So did his dreams stop?'

'I don't know,' says Caterine. 'Want me to ask him?'

'How do you mean?'

'I'm going to Laos tomorrow.'

'Just to see the cave?'

'Yes,' says Caterine, '…among other things.'

Ashley fidgets again.

'So you're saying I'm cursed, and I have to kill a chicken if I want my dreams to stop.'

'Just an idea, but have you done anything to offend any spirits lately?'

Ashley grunts and rubs his injured hand, remembering the dog lady in Bangkok.

'How's the hand?' says Caterine.

'Hmm? Oh, OK. Still infected but the doctor said it would clear up soon.'

Caterine pauses, as if considering whether what she is about to say is wise.

'I saw how it happened you know,' she says, finally. 'With the dog and that woman. I was sitting in the bar next door.'

'Eh? Have you been following me?'

'Only you seem to be everywhere I've been — Bangkok, the train, here.'

'It's hardly surprising, this is Thailand after all,' she says.

'Exactly, it's a big country and I don't know you.'

Caterine raises an eyebrow.

'Yes, it is a big country, but you only know that from looking at a map. Most people divide their time here between the islands, Bangkok and Chiang Mai. Fair enough, they might do a trek for a couple of days while they're up here, but it's not exactly off the beaten track, is it? Forty miles out into a national park, walking a few miles up and down a muddy road?'

'So? What's wrong with that?' says Ashley. 'Nobody's pretending they're climbing Everest. Besides, it's still a bit different, at least I'm seeing something new, and anyway, you're doing exactly the same so what gives you the right to slag it off?'

'I'm not slagging it off.'

'You have very good English, you know.'

'Thank you. I'm not slagging it off, it's a beautiful country and a great place for a holiday, you just shouldn't be surprised if you bump into the same people again and again throughout your trip. It's the equivalent of bumping into someone from your hotel on a Spanish beach. Anyway, I have a reason to be here.'

'What is it?'

Caterine doesn't answer, just drinks her rum and holds up her glass to the waitress, pointing at Ashley's empty beer bottle as well. The waitress mooches back into the bar.

'So what did you say to her? Why did she spit and shout at you?'

'The dog lady? Nothing. All I did was try to make friends with one of her dogs. Little fucker bit me.'

'You shouldn't touch them; they're filthy. Look.' Caterine points across the road at two dogs next to a rubbish bin. One is raking through its contents while the other divides its tongue's attention between its two scrawny testicles and a swollen boil on its leg. Ashley curls his lip in disgust.

'Well I know that now,' he says. The drinks arrive with a sigh from the shuffling waitress.

'After she walked off and you left,' says Caterine, 'I went to ask the tuk-tuk driver what happened.'

'He told me the woman's name was Thukra. She's famous around the area, although notorious would be a better word. Apparently she used to be a dancer in a club during the Vietnam War.'

'A prostitute?'

'She used to be a beautiful woman, so he said, a favourite among the soldiers. But one night some marines got heavy with her, tried to make her do things she didn't want to, bad things.'

The part of Ashley's brain that floats outside his skull lies back and daydreams nastily.

'So she ran to the club owner, crying and asking for his help. But he didn't give it. It was the Vietnam War and western soldiers were big business, so he pushed her back into the fray and the marines had their way with her.'

Ashley looks at Caterine suspiciously, but she doesn't see him and continues.

'After that night, she left the club and never danced again. Now she lives only for her dogs, believes she is one. Any stray she finds she picks up and carries with her, feeds it, looks after it, scavenging from the waste of all the westerners who come to feed and lie about in bars on the streets where she walks. She scrapes food off plates, discarded noodles from bins, old sweetcorn cores, fruit.'

'So now she's just a tramp,' says Ashley.

'Not just a tramp, she doesn't take too kindly to people.'

'Sounds like most tramps to me.'

'Most tramps don't practise witchcraft.'

'Witchcraft?' he says, trying to sound more incredulous than frightened.

'Just a local legend. That's why the bar owners and stallholders tolerate her. They believe she's capable of the odd curse.'

'Curse,' spits Ashley, mostly at himself. Two opposing sides of his rational mind begin arguing. His dreams had started that night after she spat at him. What did she scream at him? A curse? Curses don't exist. Everything about her said 'witch': the wild hair, the dirty rags, bandaged feet. Witch…ridiculous. The savage dogs on her cart — maybe they were hell hounds. Hell…you idiot, there are no witches and no hell hounds and curses don't work. She was a tramp, a bag lady, except this one had a temper and a pack of dogs, one of which you pissed off.

But the dreams — Ashley has never been this scared, not of dreams, not of anything.

'After her night with the marines, she ran away from Bangkok and roamed the country looking for shelter. The one place that she found it was with a colony of Hmong people, themselves refugees struggling to avoid being captured and bombed by the Americans. She travelled with them around the north-east and into Laos, became one of them, learned their ways, their skills, their trades. They were big on voodoo, so they say.'

Ashley looks suspiciously at Caterine again.

'So eventually the war breaks apart the tribe she's travelling with and she finds her way back to Bangkok with a cart full of dogs and a head full of curses.'

'How does he know all this, the tuk-tuk driver?' asks Ashley.

'Like I said, she's a local legend. Anyway, he told me he had her on side, that he was the closest thing that came to being one of her friends. And with good reason. He told me he once saw a bar owner try to shoo her away from some half-eaten plates of pad choi. He didn't like her or her dogs bringing down his establishment's reputation.'

'Not surprised,' says Ashley.

'Apparently he's never walked properly again.'

Ashley begins to shake his head.

'You're fucking with me,' he says. 'You're making this up.'

'Oh really?' laughs Caterine.

'Yes, really. I think you have an overactive imagination and I'm fair game for it. In the last two hours, three rums and four beers, you've given me ghosts, sacrifices and witchcraft, all of which you seem to suggest have some relevance to my… predicament. I think that's a bit of a coincidence.'

'Imagination? You're the one dreaming about horny dog-girls and self-abusing Antichrists.'

Ashley shuffles in his seat and drinks.

'In any case, even if you aren't making them up, I still don't believe them.'

'What do you believe in, then?'

Ashley frowns. It's not a question he's used to answering; it's easier to answer things like that in the negative.

'I don't believe in witchcraft, curses, ghosts, goblins…God.'

'I asked you what you believed in, not what you didn't,' says Caterine.

'I believe that there are a million things out there which don't exist, and I believe that people believe in things just to make themselves feel better about that. I believe a person is a clingy, desperate mollusc that will grab anything, anything to stop itself thinking that there's nothing waiting for it other than a big, black, empty void.'

'So you don't believe in the soul,' says Caterine.

'I don't believe anything in our lifetime has soul,' says Ashley, surprising himself.

'In our lifetime?'

'W-What I mean is, I think things are lost,' Ashley stammers. 'There's too much to believe in, nothing's real any more.'

He frowns, wondering where the words are coming from. This is not a conversation he's used to, since his achievements and lifestyle don't feature too strongly in it.

'Life's difficult, even when you have it easy, even when you have money and a job and friends with money and jobs and…'

He breaks off, retreating to his beer label again.

'So what are you trying to do, Ashley,' Caterine makes mocking rabbit ears with her fingers. ''Find yourself'?'

'Maybe…' suggests Ashley.

'Sounds more like you need to lose yourself,' says Caterine, opening her book.

'What about the last bit?' Ashley says after a while.

'Last bit of what?'

'My dream.'

'The devil?'

'Yes.'

'I think maybe that's just your imagination waking you up with a joke.'

'Do you think?'

'Or maybe you just like dreaming about Satan's cock.'

SOMETHING'S NOT RIGHT

Chiang Mai, Thailand

LATER, IN another bar: Ashley. It is about 8pm, and he sits on a stool stroking the neck of a bottle and thinking about his conversation with Caterine. The idea that he is being haunted by a demon is ridiculous. But he has never had dreams like this, never woken up dripping with his own sweat, never felt lust and dread in one needlepoint of emotion before.

Lust, sex, desire. He has never taken them seriously. He doesn't even know the name of the Danish girl he fucked against a rock; her email address is cryptic, she signs off as 'D xxx'. Nevertheless, he thinks he should know the name of a girl he fucked only last week. The fact that he doesn't makes him feel empty, whereas usually it would make him feel good. He starts to pick at the label.

The bar is dark with an open front made of bamboo stilts. There are wooden tables and chairs and a montage of posters — Jimi Hendrix, Bob Marley, The Who — road signs, album covers and photographs spread across the walls. At the back is a pool table, where a small and serious Thai girl with tattoos over her bare shoulders is about to pot the black in a game in which her opponent — a tall man from Berlin — has failed to pocket a single ball. The Doors rattle 'The End' through the three speakers hanging from the corners of the room and a couple of tall prostitutes sit at the other end of the bar to Ashley. He recognises the one with the largest Adam's apple from the train.

Ashley wonders whether he should have agreed to see Caterine this evening, instead of meeting Mehdi as he'd arranged. She is leaving the next day for Laos; he probably won't see her again. Well-rehearsed parts play out in his mind when he thinks this. Tits too small. Not blonde. Trouble. Too smart for her own good. What's the point?

The point is, Ashley had spent four hours talking with her. She had made him laugh, despite the fact that she had clearly been playing games with him, and yet not once had he made a play for her, despite the best efforts of his libido.

Lose yourself, Ashley.

Mehdi arrives and slaps him on the back like an old friend. A more fluid handshake than the last ensues and he raises a finger at the barman. This is awkward for the barman because Mehdi has never been in the bar before so he doesn't have a usual. He realises that the finger means 'one please', but 'one' could mean 'one' of anything. The barman looks at Ashley's drink and opens one of the same, placing it cautiously in front of Mehdi. Mehdi swigs it and grins delightedly because he has just ordered a beer in a strange bar without saying a word. How fucking cool is that?

'Hey, what you do to your hand, man?'

'Oh, it was nothing, just a…'

'I just had a fucking massage from this girl man, she was fucking *beautiful*.'

'Yeah?' says Ashley, still rubbing his bandage.

'Yeah, but she kept massaging the backs of my thighs, man, and I don't like that, you know what I am saying?'

'Yeah…'

'So I said to her, listen, will you please spend more of your time rubbing my lower back and my shoulders, because the beds on those trains, Ashley, Jesus fuck Christ they are sore, aren't they sore, Ashley? They're fucking sore, aren't they?'

'Yeah…'

'*Fucking* sore, but…'

Mehdi's shoulders hunch up and he squeaks like a mouse hiding cheese.

'…you know what she says to me?'

'No...'

'You will fucking love this, Ashley,' he giggles.

Mehdi puts on a voice.

'So solly, you legs so nice! Legs so nice! Handsome man! Muscles! Like you, like you lot handsome man!'

Mehdi can hardly control himself and he laughs, slapping Ashley on the shoulder.

'She fucking loved me, man, you know what I am saying? But I think, hey, listen I'm paying you 320 baht, you shouldn't be getting off on me, you know? Not cool. Definitely not cool. So you know what I do? I roll over and…'

Mehdi draws nearer to Ashley's face and lowers his voice excitedly, squeaking again.

'I put her hand on my dick and say, hey, you can rub me anywhere you want, but I'm not paying if it turns you on.'

Mehdi laughs in Ashley's ear and grips his shoulder.

'You know what she does? You know what she does? She fucking sucks me off dude! And she fucking loves it too! And I don't even pay for anything!'

Ashley gulps some beer and lets Mehdi have an approving nod. Mehdi stops laughing and tries on a serious face.

'I never fucking pay for a whore, man, it's one of my principles. I'm very strong on principles, I think you are too, am I right?'

Ashley raises an eyebrow.

'Right. That's probably why we get on, a lot of these motherfuckers…'

He swings a finger around the room behind him.

'…they pay for any fucking piece of second-hand meat that shows them their legs.'

He shakes his head and looks about, moving the finger to his chest and scratching his front tooth with the other hand.

'That's not what I'm fucking about, you know? You neither.'

He prods Ashley in the shoulder, he responds with another nod and Mehdi becomes conspiratorial again.

'Guys like us, we don't fucking *need* to pay for whores,' he laughs. '*They* fucking pay for *us!*'

This is too much for him and his face wrinkles into a red, hysterical prune.

'*They fucking pay for us!*'

Eventually he calms down and finds his breath and runs a tongue around his mouth, clicking his jaws together twice.

'Took some fucking *COKE* before I came out, man,' he says, his eyes swelling at the word.

'You want some?'

Ashley opens his mouth.

'Huh? You want some?'

Mehdi takes Ashley's hand and places a small triangle of cardboard in his palm, staring at his eyeballs. Ashley wonders again whether he should have met Caterine.

After a few more beers, though, and one line of coke that Ashley snorts nervously in the small toilet at the back of the bar, Mehdi begins to seem less intense. They talk, streams of words running faster and faster between them, each story with less meaning than the last.

About one hour into the conversation, Ashley suddenly registers that — bizarrely, impossibly — he hasn't yet told Mehdi about the Danish girl he fucked against a rock last week. He is midway through listening to Mehdi's tale of the Czech gymnast when he realises this, so he endures the rest of the story in zipped-lipped excitement, mentally embellishing his own and waiting for a nice, quiet slice of air in which to release it.

As he waits, it strikes him that most conversations are like this. The things people say, the stories that they tell are just cues and reminders for others to tell their own. You can usually think of your own story — probably better — just a few words into the one you're waiting for to end. After that, it's just a case of finding the right moment to make your move, slide in, crank it up, interrupt. This is an art in itself, because the longer you let the other person's story drag on, the more likely it is that they capitalise on the airtime and think of something else, and consequently the less relevant your story becomes. Then you have to store them up like a hand of cards and deal them out appropriately. If relevance matters, of course. If you accept that the other person is doing the same as you, then it doesn't.

Another realisation follows: the conversation he'd had earlier with Caterine had not been like this. That one had *listening* in it.

The two thoughts begin to buzz frantically against his skull's window frame and he begins to feel something tepid and edgy. His back becomes cold and his teeth tired, there are parts of his brain doing things he doesn't want them to. He feels like biting his nails. Instead he stops Mehdi and asks him for the coke, which he takes into the toilet and snorts liberally.

He walks back to the bar, feeling ice, zinc and electricity flood through his skeleton. The edginess crumbles and by the time he reaches the stool it is dust. His gums are hot. Mehdi stops talking to the man beside him and turns back to reignite his story, but he's too slow and Ashley gets there first.

There is joy in his voice as he recounts his tale. At first he realises that he's going too fast and slows down — he doesn't want to miss out anything even though he can't remember all of it. Not too slow though, Mehdi's not getting in on this one. He squeezes out every detail of the evening's seduction, uses hand movements and voices too, and Mehdi seems to be actually enjoying it, contorting his face with every twist and grope.

When he gets to the actual bit with the rock, Ashley catches a movement over Mehdi's shoulder. He registers exactly what it is the moment he sees it, but keeps talking to Mehdi for three whole sentences before taking another look. This time he stops and doesn't look back.

'Then I….then I…' he says.

'Then you what?' says Mehdi.

'I…I…'

'What happened next, you mother fucker? Come on, tell me!'

'I…it's her…it's fucking her…don't turn round! Shit Mehdi.'

Mehdi spins round on his seat, his black, wet hair flicking against his cheek as he dots his eyes around the small crowd of people standing in the middle of the bar, until he notices a tall blonde dipping a straw in and out of a fresh drink.

'Hey what? Her? The blonde? You fucker man, she's fucking hot!'

Ashley keeps his head low, smirking with his mouth open and nodding as he looks at her. She's wearing very little, a short sarong wrapped low around her waist showing the tops of her hip bones, and a white cropped top that hangs down happily from her upturned nipples. It is hot in the bar, and tears of sweat nestle in the soft, light down on her shoulders and run down the groove of her belly and into its button. He's sure he could get an erection just looking at her. Finally she looks at him, and although she noticed him fifteen minutes previously when she walked into the bar with her friend, Claudia, she bites her bottom lip and blushes, flooding his gaze with lechery and mischief.

In four seconds, she is next to him, Claudia by her side. Claudia is shorter, with dark brown, salt-curled hair to her shoulders and a wide smile. She bites her lip too and stands next to Mehdi, whose smile is now bulletproof.

'Hello, how are you, I am Mehdi…Claudia? Very pleased to meet you, Claudia…yes, that's right, Mehdi, I'm from…Israel yes! Good guess! And who is this lovely, lovely friend? Daniella? A lovely name…yes, Mehdi, Israel…I am very pleased to meet you too…aha…Denmark? Wonderful place….beautiful…I love your skirt, Claudia…do you want a drink? Some coke? I have some coke? OK maybe later…yes of course…and this is my new friend Ash…Daniella, Ash…oh do you know each other?'

Daniella. Daniella. The word is like a fanfare. Three syllables trumpeting in his ears, heralding the arrival of lost memories from the beach, smells, sights, dancing, even conversations. Ashley could kiss Mehdi, but he already has an arm around

Claudia's waist and two of his fingers are stroking the bare skin at the top of her left buttock. A kiss would be inappropriate.

The next two hours are dedicated to the pleasantries of ego grooming and self-promotion. Each of the four faces standing at the bar simultaneously carries the smiles of salespeople and the greed of a consumer. Trading begins, presentations in pocket, credit cards in hand. Mehdi listens to Claudia talk — they like that. His face is a piece of art: serious and searching but accommodating enough for a smile and the occasional wink. She rewards his interest with longer, deeper looks and warmer strokes of his arms. For a while they talk about his muscles, during which he feigns modesty while mentally he is breathlessly playing out the lead role in every single scene that has ever appeared in a shaving advert.

Ashley talks to Daniella. He definitely fucked her, didn't he? Had to. She stands so close to him he could flick out his tongue and taste the dew on her skin, her breasts are warm and squash against his shoulder. Everything is exactly as his pubescent dreams told him it should be.

They have beers, they have tequila, they have more of Mehdi's cocaine, and, at 2am, they get into two tuk-tuks and zip along the dark streets back to Mehdi's hotel. The warm breeze blows through Ashley's hair and brings with it good smells. People are still on the street, smoking and laughing, tugging at each other, tumbling in and out of the bars on the main strip, music throbbing all around them, through their bones and under their feet. The troubles of the last few days fly out of Ashley's skull like dust, and Daniella replaces them with a warm, wet tongue.

Caterine is sleeping in a small guesthouse next to the river. She has packed, and has to be up in three hours to catch the bus to the border.

They reach the hotel and Mehdi leads them up to his room, flicking on a low light and closing the door behind him. He has thought ahead. It is big, far bigger than necessary for a man on his own, built in an L-shape with a double bed against the far wall of each section. Between them is a table, on which Mehdi has laid out glasses and some candles. A guitar stands in the corner and he has thrown a red sarong over one of the beds.

The girls coo over the room, while Ashley leafs through the pile of CDs on the table and Mehdi roots around in the mini-bar. The air is still filled with thermals of narcotics and alcohol, and half-finished conversations glide aimlessly around on them, never finding the ground. Daniella stays close to Ashley, looking through the CDs, their heads close to each other, their breath on each other's hands. The excitement bubbles in Ashley's belly. He is high and drunk, but not wasted — memory has not yet made its excuses. He will remember everything.

Mehdi surfaces with a bottle of vodka and pours it liberally into the glasses. They toast and drink and do another line, then Daniella finds an album she likes and inserts it into the portable CD player next to the pile. But before she can press play, Mehdi yanks his guitar from the wall and falls back on the bed. He sings Aerosmith and Bryan Adams as Claudia curls up giggling at his feet with her head on his knees and Daniella and Ashley lie together on the other bed. Before long, the songs stop and Mehdi props the guitar back in its place and starts the CD. Then he returns to the bed. The music starts — it is electronic and designed to relax, and seeps around the room like warm mist. Other sounds start happening as well. Wet sounds.

Ashley turns to Daniella, who is on her side already looking at him. She smiles and blinks slowly, twice, her eyelids not quite touching each other. Ashley blinks back and puts his left hand on her waist, kissing her.

They do things to each other.

While they do the things, Ashley is vaguely aware that Mehdi and Claudia's progress is somewhat more advanced. Mehdi is making long, breathy grunts as if whatever he is doing to Claudia is extremely difficult, possibly perilous, the work of a trained professional, and Claudia responds with small, encouraging hoots of pleasure.

Focus.

He is pretty sure that Mehdi and Claudia are both almost completely naked, whereas the only thing on the floor behind Daniella is her sarong and his T-shirt. Her cropped top grants excellent access to the breasts, and her underpants are very small. But still…

Ashley pulls up her top, and she whips it off obligingly. Her breasts are as perfect as he believes he remembers them to be — round, evenly tanned, firm and decorated with soft pink nipples looking up innocently to the sky. He twists one of them gently, and it hardens obediently between his fingers. Daniella squirms and sighs. He immediately gives the other one a tweak to honour symmetry, but before he can watch it stiffen she rolls him onto his back and starts kissing his cheeks and neck, flicking out her tongue and running it up and down his throat.

Jack, Angus and Sam, his dogs, welcoming him home.

Something's not right.

His hands fall on the muscles of her lower back, and he feels them curve upwards to the softer flesh of her bottom. She twitches her abdomen, thrusting her pelvis gently up and down like a wasp on a spring leaf. Her skin is exactly how he imagines a woman's skin should be — sleek, firm and warm with a thin, wet film of perspiration. Her arms are slender, her legs smooth and toned, and she smells of every sexual fantasy Ashley has ever had. She is a walking wet dream.

He begins to run a finger under a thread of elastic. It feels a bit loose. Ashley wonders how old it is.

Something's *definitely* not right.

Daniella moves her hands beneath her and presses them down against Ashley's belly as she smears her lips down his bare chest. Soon she is at his hips, and she kisses them deeply as she begins to peel down his shorts. Mehdi is beginning, expertly, to synchronise his grunts with Claudia's hoots.

It dawns on Ashley — he doesn't yet have an erection.

Shit. Focus.

The ceiling above him is white. Shadows leap across it from the flickering candles, bobbing and ducking like a dark fire. First they move randomly, shapelessly, but as Ashley watches them and the rest of the room disappears into darkness, something changes. It is nothing to begin with, just a collection of dark spikes as if the candles have been brought together. But then something starts to appear, a shape, still, slow and controlled…a face, with features made of shadow, the rest of it empty ceiling. Ashley widens his eyes and looks closer. He studies it; the two eyes are upturned ovals, the nose small and round, the mouth an undefined line beneath it. An optical illusion.

It blinks.

Ashley lets out a tiny gasp, and Daniella — taking this as encouragement — tugs harder at his shorts. He feels her fingers moving against his thighs, pulling the tight waistband with them. The face blinks again, slower this time as if in greeting, and Ashley puts his hand across his mouth, his eyes wide and helpless as his shorts slip down his legs.

Suddenly the face's mouth starts to move. It twitches twice, up and down, then begins very slowly to open. At first it is imperceptible, just a swelling of its lips, but as they part they reveal a gap between them, a gap that is strung together with rough, cord-like lines as if the mouth has been sewn with thick string. Soon it is a snarl, and the two shadow eyes crease together with pain.

Ashley cries out and sits bolt upright. Daniella is at his feet, holding his shorts in her hand and looking scornfully down between his legs. If a needle could scratch across vinyl, it would. He takes long, fast breaths through his mouth and follows her eyes down to his penis, which is flaccid, squashed and wrinkled. It is sleepy. It looks like a creature that has been left under a rock for too long.

'You don't have to make the sounds,' Daniella says. 'It's obviously not working.'

'No…no…' pants Ashley. 'It's not that…I'm…I'm…'

'Sick? Yeah,' says Daniella, tossing his shorts onto the floor and getting up off the bed.

'That's what you said last week.'

Ashley watches as she turns her back on him and walks away from the bed, rolling down her underpants and wriggling out of them so they drop to the floor. He falls back onto the bed, still trying to catch his breath. The shadows have returned to their normal states, weaving and jumping lazily about the ceiling. Ashley turns onto his side and curls up his knees to his chest. From the other side of the room he hears a few small laughs and the sound of bed springs. Then wet noises, grunts, hoots and a long, Danish sigh.

Ashley lies curled up in a ball on the bed. For three hours at least he hasn't moved a muscle or made a sound. He hasn't slept, hasn't dreamed, the cocaine still ticking over in his blood. Eight noisy climaxes have been announced during the night: four for Mehdi, two each for Daniella and Claudia. They were very loud, and Ashley has spent a dark night studying the various combinations of moans, sighs and fumblings forming in his mind — against his own will — the positions and acts that each might have represented. Now the only sound from the other bed is light and peaceful snoring, and grey dawn light is starting to sift through the balcony window.

He is naked, and the air conditioner above him is freezing. He decides to risk movement. Very slowly he starts to extend one of his legs out to the edge of the bed, then the other, while easing himself up on his elbow. He gets up off the bed and stands on the chilly marble floor, stretching his back and swallowing. His throat is dry and his spine is cold, the night before has made his guts feel rotten and empty. He shivers, picks up his shorts and his T-shirt and puts them on. The clock by the bed says 6:34am.

Ashley turns round to look at the other bed. Mehdi is lying in the centre with his head resting comfortably on a pillow. His left arm is around Claudia's neck, and her face is nestled between his bicep and wrist as if it were a blanket. His other arm is stretched out above him and beneath it lies Daniella, her fine curves wrapped perfectly around his body. Each is sleeping, smiling serenely, sated and at peace. Even Mehdi's penis seems to be lying with its hands behind its neck, resplendent in its thicket of black curls. It might as well be chewing one like a wheat straw.

Ashley opens his mouth to mutter something. But then he closes it, and leaves.

Chiang Mai is a beautiful place in the morning.

SOUND OF TYRE AND METAL

Laos

JOSEPH WOKE, as he always did, to the sound of tyre and metal. But this time the reality that flooded his head did not dampen it. Instead it became the noise itself, before shouts of alarm joined it, then screams. He opened his eyes to find the world hurtling past him at different angles and the muddy ground outside rushing backwards and upwards towards the window. They were crashing. People were being thrown from their seats, grabbing out for handrails and missing, smashing into each other and being flattened against the left side of the bus. Everything inside had become like socks in a washing machine as the vehicle toppled onto its side.

Joseph slammed his hands hard against the seat in front. The girl occupying it had her face squashed against the glass, the weight of her partner and four other people steadily pushing against her as the bus's angle reached forty-five degrees, producing louder and more desperate noises from her throat. It was the same story in all the seats ahead of them, and Joseph wondered why he hadn't yet been punctured by the bones of the man next to him. He turned to look, immediately seeing why.

The man had managed to get to his feet; perhaps he had done so a few moments before when the bus first began to crash. He had grabbed the metal pole rising from the seat and now his shoulder was jammed hard against it, but his long legs had somehow been pushed backwards behind the seat itself, and six or seven bodies were now piling into him. Their weight was causing him to roll slowly around to face Joseph, his expression widening into horror as the metal pole started to squeeze against his windpipe.

The effect was that the length of his body from neck to knee had become a natural barrier, shielding Joseph from the weight of flesh and bone bearing down upon him. Instead of being crushed against the window like the others, he had a whole seat, a protective empty space around him.

Suddenly the sound of the bus engine changed from a struggling growl to a piercing, high rev as the tyres left the ground. As the ground folded up to meet them, Joseph saw through the window that they were on a steep mountain road, a clump of trees the only barrier between them and the drop they were heading for. There was a bang and a smash as ground met bus, but the slick mud beneath them kept them sliding forwards at the same speed. Voices were momentarily silenced, through either expectation or strangulation. But then the air was filled with even greater sounds of panic as the windows began to break.

Joseph's, free from any internal pressure, held firm. But all the rest splintered, exposing the other passengers to broken glass and ground beneath. He looked between his window and the bony man, who was either unconscious or dead with his neck crushed against the pole. Either way, his body retained its hold of those behind it.

Everything happened quickly after that. The bus slid and flipped as it left the road on its side. Then there was silence as it flew over the precipice, the weightlessness lifting the piles of people for a few seconds before slamming them down again on top of each other as the bus collided with a large boulder. The roof tore open, and bodies began to leave the bus through the cavity and the broken windows, being whipped outside like skydivers from a plane. The sound of screams gave way to terrified silence, and the bus ploughed into the thick canopies of the trees on the mountainside. It exited briefly into open air, then entered another set, finally slamming into a trunk and stopping.

All sound had stopped. There was no voice, no crying, no whimpering, no engine, no whistle of steam, no creaking noise as the bus rocked precariously. Nothing at all but the rhythm of Joseph's breath as he orientated himself in his seat. He was lying against the window, bodies and sky above him, branches and God knows how much air below. The bony man's buckled body was still strung across the pole and the seat, a few others lying on his back. His neck was bent forwards too far and blood was dripping from his mouth onto the glass. All around him were dead faces with open eyes and mouths, and he had his long arms stretched straight out in a cross.

Joseph tried to turn, but his left leg was jammed beneath the broken seat in front. He struggled, lifting up his other and jamming his boot against the pole beneath the man's head, pushing. His leg came free, but as it did his thigh caught a sharp piece of broken metal from the seat frame. Joseph yelled and grasped the wound, cursing as blood instantly seeped into the fabric around it.

One of the dead heads around his saviour wore a bandana, which had come loose. Using his arms to pull himself up the length of the seat, Joseph yanked it down and unfastened the knot, checking to see whether there was any blood on it. It was clean and had a gecko pattern. He slipped it around the top of his thigh and tied a tight double knot.

Joseph managed to shift around so that he was facing the window. It was dusk, getting darker, but he could see that there was not as much height beneath him as he imagined. They were on a shallow slope, stuck in the branches of a tree that was at most twenty feet above the ground. Beneath him were branches that he could safely fall onto.

Bracing himself against the seat, he stamped his prosthetic leg down onto the glass, which shattered easily, and kicked away the shards around the frame. Then he lowered himself carefully through the opening and dropped onto the branch below, landing messily and sliding down it, but managing to steady himself and hang on.

He looked up at the top of the bus, which was now facing him. All the luggage which had been strapped to it had been jettisoned somewhere in the crash. Gripping his thighs to the branch, he turned carefully to look back at the road. It was nothing more than a thick mud track, unsurfaced, ploughed up by tyres and heavy rain. No great surprise that they crashed, then. There was no other vehicle wreck to be seen, nothing that they could have crashed into, but a long, wide gash in the mud marked the bus's helpless trajectory off the hillside. It stopped at the edge, the ground beneath it strewn with dark, still objects — the bodies and luggage spewed from the crashing bus.

Joseph turned back so that he was facing the bus again. Its front was crumpled around the tree trunk and the bonnet had been ripped away, exposing a smoking engine. He let himself slide down a few feet till he was closer to another nearby branch, which he grabbed and transferred himself onto, letting the other branch snap back up. He slid down again, till he was only six feet from the ground, and then let himself drop, landing on his back, winding himself and rolling awkwardly down the slope.

Scrabbling with his hands in the dirt, he managed to stop himself falling any further and raised himself onto his wounded leg. Steadying himself, he lifted his prosthetic up and stood, immediately hobbling as quickly as he could up the slope towards the road. Dusk had given in to a rapidly darkening sky and everything was dull and blue, but suddenly something orange lit up the earth around his feet. He looked back quickly to see a small fire break out around the engine cavity of the bus, and tried to accelerate his double limp and hurry away from the tree. All around him were twisted and muddy bodies, some broken beyond hope, others lying on their backs so normally that they might have been sunbathers in a meadow if it wasn't for the vacant, dead expressions on their faces. There was no movement except his own and the flickering of flame.

The fire was spreading, and Joseph followed the debris as fast as he could to the edge of the road, clutching his left leg. Out of the corner of his eye, he spotted his holdall sitting behind a rock. It was covered in mud but undamaged, and he scooped it up. As he reached the road, he fell back with his bag on his chest and caught his breath. He lay watching the burning bus calmly, like a man does leaning on his rake next to an autumn bonfire. A cigarette would have been a fine thing.

A second later there was a small bang as the flames reached the petrol pipes, then a larger one as the tank exploded and spat flames and black smoke high into the air. The inside was flooded with a molten tidal wave, and jagged blades of fire flicked out of the windows and through the gaping hole in the roof, lighting up the hill and reflecting bright pinpoints in the lifeless eyes scattered about it. Joseph felt the heat and remembered. He had crawled from a wreck before and watched it burn. That had been twenty-five years ago, and it had taken his leg.

It was supposed to have been an apology, a way of clawing back three lost years of marriage. They were away from everything in a snow-drenched paradise, winding around that high Alpine road like flushed lovers lost in the end credits of a film, or the opening titles of another. It felt like both, the close of one story and the beginning of the next, the point at which two tales were touching, the second much happier than the first. He had felt the rush of volition and dignity that follows every difficult decision made purely with the heart, the virtue that comes from doing the right thing, however much it went against the grain. He was going to tell her the truth about what he did, tell her everything. If only she hadn't got there first.

As he watched the bus blacken, Joseph heard a noise to his left. A human noise. There was movement, too, and he saw a small figure struggling to get to its feet. It shook on its arms and one of them buckled, but it regained its balance and paused, quivering on all fours like a newborn calf finding its feet. It let out a long, mournful wail and began to crawl through the dirt.

Joseph unzipped his bag and searched around inside of it, pulling out a three-cell Maglite and shining it in the direction of the child. She froze and stared into the beam, crumpling her round, brown face in confusion and releasing a squeal of terror. He turned off the torch. Her mouth trembled and she started sobbing three woeful, descending notes. *Sob-weeee…Sob-waaaaa…Sob-wooooooo.* They repeated over and over again, as if for comfort, and she returned to her crawl, looking hopelessly around her at the pile of bodies from which she had emerged.

Joseph watched her for a while. He turned the torch on again and the child froze, squealing in the blinding light. Then he clicked the switch off, and she returned to sobbing and crawling. He repeated the experiment twice more, each time getting the same results.

Joseph wondered what to do. The child, still crying, was making quick progress down the hillside towards the inferno in the trees, presumably drawn by the comfort of heat. He replaced his Maglite and put the bag to one side, sitting up. Then he let himself roll forwards and then down the slope towards her, his injured leg smarting and his other one clattering as he bumped over rocks and debris. He overshot the child, but gripped onto the earth and stopped so that their faces were six feet from each other, each illuminated in the flames. The girl stopped in her tracks, startled, and stared at Joseph's face. Joseph stared back for a few seconds. Then he grinned widely and winked at her.

'Hello,' he said. 'Where do you think you're going?'

The girl blinked back and then let out a terrified cry, struggling away from Joseph and closer to the burning trees. She fell back onto her shoulder and struggled, but got back to her hands and knees and began to wriggle desperately away, wailing as she went.

'No,' said Joseph. 'No, come back here. I'm not going to hurt you. I WON'T HURT YOU.'

He tried to get to his feet, but his injured leg gave way and he growled with pain as he fell back to the ground. Then he started to claw his way up the slope after the child, grimacing as his cut flesh rasped against the grainy mud.

'COME BACK,' he said as he wrenched his body up with his arms. 'I WON'T HURT YOU.' But the girl kept crawling further towards the bus, each impact of her limbs against the ground sending wobbles into her high, panic-driven squeal.

Just then, as he was coming within arm's reach of the girl, he heard another noise from further down the hill. From its direction he saw other beams of light, six or seven of them, swaying and bobbing up the slope towards them. Voices and some laughter. Joseph wondered what kind of rescue party would find something to joke about as they approached a burning vehicle and fifty corpses. Indeed, what kind of rescue party would be so quick to find them on the top of a mountain.

He looked back at the child, who had crawled clear of a fresh patch of bodies and was approaching the trees. Joseph launched himself up and leapt for her. She squealed, kicking him in the crotch, but he grabbed her, wincing and holding a hand over her mouth. He pulled her down to the ground, but the voices had stopped and the torches had all moved their beams in their direction, scanning the ground around them. One of them froze on Joseph's face. Then he heard a voice, and the lights came running with guns around their necks.

~1978~

THE DIARY OF CLAUDETTE FERRIÈRE

16 MARS 1978

Joe is not really called Joe. That's not his real name.

Today Papa and Doctor Moreau faced each other at breakfast and ate eggs with their elbows on the table talking seriously at each other. They were discussing how they were going to get Joe to Grenoble so that he can get a false leg.

'Amputees should start practising on a prosthetic at least ten to fourteen days after the operation,' said Doctor Moreau. 'This is very important, now is the most critical stage of recovery and can save the patient months of turmoil, both in the body…and up here.'

He tapped his head when he said 'up here'.

'There is no way we can drive to Grenoble,' said Papa, who had grumbled good morning to me earlier but said nothing else to me since. 'Even if we could see where the road is, it is probably still beneath ten feet of snow.'

'If we can just get down to the village, though, there's a chance they've cleared enough of the roads from there.'

'It's still too dangerous,' said Papa. 'You can't see fifty metres in this blizzard, and one wrong turn could send us over the side of the mountain.'

Joe was eating with us because he is trying to move around as much as he can on his crutches. He didn't say a lot because I don't think he understands everything that is said because he doesn't speak French properly. I think he knew they were talking about him, though. I watched him as I ate my toast; he looked uncomfortable and nervous.

I hope he understands what I read him from *National*

Geographic.

Madame Beaufort sat opposite me and ate without talking. She looked at me a few times, but she didn't try to smile badly and I preferred that. When everybody had finished their eggs, somebody did a motorboat that smelled really bad. We all groaned and Papa shouted at Zeet and smacked him, but as he was throwing him out into the porch, Madame Beaufort looked at me and wrinkled her nose. I saw that she was pointing a secret finger at Doctor Moreau and tried hard not to giggle.

Doctor Moreau cleared his throat. 'Isn't there any other way we can take him down?' he said. Papa grumbled into his coffee.

'What about the sledge?' I said. Papa grunted 'What?'

'The sledge,' I said, 'you know the big one we used to carry turnips on last winter. Joe could lie on that with blankets on him and you could pull him down like huskies in *Alaska*.'

Papa grumbled again. 'The runners on that thing are loose and the wood has perished, it would break under his weight. Besides it's still too dangerous.'

'I agree,' said Joe suddenly. Everyone turned to look at him. 'I mean…I mean I don't want people risking their lives for me.'

'But you could fix it, Papa, couldn't you? I know you could.' This made Papa start rubbing his chin. 'And you could be really careful, we could work out exactly how to get down on one of your maps first.'

'Well…' he said.

'No,' said Joe, but Doctor Moreau interrupted him.

'It is crucial that we get a leg to him as soon as possible,' he said.

'And you could go high along the ridge and cut down through where the forest is, so you don't go near the cliffs,' I said.

'I suppose I could…' said Papa.

'You could, Papa, you could all go today and Joe would have a leg…'

'NO,' said Joe suddenly, and everyone shut up and looked at

him again. 'What I mean is…you've all done so much for me already. I don't want you doing anything more. I'll be fine until the snow melts, then I can go to Grenoble myself, I'm sure there are buses. That is, I mean if you don't mind me staying. I could pay you…'

Doctor Moreau made a snorting sound. 'Go to Grenoble on your own? Two weeks after you've had one of your legs amputated?' Then he laughed, which I thought was cruel.

Papa was still rubbing his chin, but he was looking at Joe and frowning as if he didn't trust him all of a sudden.

'Why don't you want to go to the village?' he asked. Joe looked scared.

'It's not that I…'

'I'm beginning to think that it's possible, and what if we waited a couple of days for the snow to stop…'

'If it stops at all,' said Madame Beaufort. Papa shot her a look.

'You could be on your way to hospital where they could check you over properly.'

'That's not necessary, I mean I can do that on my own,' said Joe quickly.

'And there's the matter of the police,' said Papa, still rubbing his chin.

'What?' said Joe.

'The police still don't know about the accident. Don't you want to find who did this to you? You could tell them at the village, they could pass on descriptions all over the country.'

'I've already told you about that. I can't remember what happened.'

'All the same,' said Papa, 'I think they'd like to know what happened. It can't hurt, can it? Can it, Joe?'

Joe didn't say anything, and neither did anyone else. Madame Beaufort began collecting everybody's plates.

'Well,' said Papa as he got up from the table. 'I'm going to the engine shed to see about that sledge.'

He went upstairs and we heard my bedroom window open. Then there was another 'oooof' noise and crunching footsteps above us getting quieter as he walked across the yard.

Doctor Moreau excused himself and took Joe into the sitting room to do his exercises, which left Madame Beaufort and me. She was washing up and I brought some cups from the table to the sink. I was about to leave and go up to my room, but before I got to the door she said, 'It must be a very big tree.'

'Pardon?' I said. She still had her back to me and was scrubbing the frying pan.

'The tree in Canada that's two thousand years old. It must be very big by now. Huge, I'd say.'

I asked her if she wanted me to show her a picture. She said that she did, so I did.

Later on, after I had told Madame Beaufort all about *Canadian Redwoods*, I went to the engine shed to see what Papa was doing. He had the old sledge out on the floor and I saw what he meant earlier about the wood and the runners. It looked bad even for firewood, and the runners were all rusted and had holes in them. I wouldn't like to go down a mountain on it.

'It might take longer than I thought,' he said, and I left him rubbing his chin.

Then I went to see Joe, who was lying in the old family room after his exercises with Doctor Moreau. After telling him about fruit bats in *French Polynesia,* I asked him why he didn't want to go to the village with Papa.

He took a long time to answer, but eventually he did.

'It's not that I don't want to go to the village, Claudette,' he said.

'Then why don't you want to tell the police what happened? I would want to tell them if somebody ran over me.'

'I can't tell the police, if I tell the police then…'

'Then what?'

He looked at me as if he was trying to decide whether to tell me something or not.

'Claudette, sit down.'

I did.

'Can you keep a secret?' he said. I nodded.

'I mean a really important secret that nobody must know? Not even your Papa? Not even Zeet?'

I nodded and said that I promised. He thought for a while again and told me to shut the door.

'My name is not really Joe,' he said.

'What is it then?'

'I'm not going to tell you that. You can still call me Joe, because that's my name from now on.'

'I don't understand,' I said. Why do you want to have a different name?

'I'm not going to tell you that either. But if I tell the police what happened, then they will find out that I'm not really called Joe and I'll have to go back to a place that I don't want to be.'

'Where?'

'A place I cannot be.'

Now I was frustrated.

'What's the point in telling me anything then?'

I really was frustrated, but Joe…or whatever he's really called…sighed and looked unhappy.

'Do you ever…do you ever just want to fly away, Claudette? Just fly away and disappear?'

I watched him looking away as if he could see something I couldn't. He looked so sad. He looked as if there was a part of him hurting badly, but it was deep down inside himself, so deep that he couldn't reach it to look after it and tell it that everything would be all right.

'What happened?'

'I'm not going to tell you that,' he said, which made me even more frustrated and I made a loud noise. 'OK, OK,' he said. Then he sighed. 'How did you feel when you saw your Papa kissing Madame Beaufort?'

'How did you know about that?' I said.

'He told me. How did you feel?'

'I felt really angry and upset and everything I could see went red and I could hear my blood thumping around my head, even though I thought my heart had stopped beating.'

'Because of your mother?'

'Yes.'

'And did you want to see either of them?'

'No. I ran to my room and I didn't want to see either of them again and, even though Madame Beaufort is being nice to me, I'm still angry with them both.'

Joe nodded as if he understood, and then he said, 'Now imagine how your Mama would have felt if she was still alive and had seen them doing that.'

It took me a while to work out what he meant.

'Did you see someone kissing someone else?' I said after a while.

'A bit like that,' he said, 'and that's why I don't want to go to the village and I don't want to tell the police because...because I want to fly away, Claudette. Do you understand? Just fly away, be somewhere else.'

He looked away again.

'But your Papa and Doctor Moreau don't understand that.'

'What about Madame Beaufort? Would she understand?'

'I don't think she would either,' he said. I agreed with him.

'Do you understand, though, Claudette? Do you see why I don't want to go to the village just yet?'

I nodded. Sometimes I want to be on my own.

17 mars 1978

Papa spent all of today working in the engine shed on the sledge. Doctor Moreau is helping him, although I can't imagine he is very good at woodwork.

They came in once for lunch and went into Joe's room to talk with him. I couldn't hear what they were saying, but their voices were raised and when he came out Papa looked troubled and went straight back to the shed. He wants Joe to go.

~2003~

JUNGLE HOVEL

Laos

THIS WASN'T the first time Joseph had been captured.

He sat in the back of a truck with his hands tied and a sack over his head, and he knew that the child was there too because he could hear her crying. As the men had approached him where he lay on the ground and before they beat him around the ribs and back till he let go of the girl, he had counted six of them in total, and he could hear at least that many voices around him now. A man sitting next to him was chain-smoking home-made cigarettes rolled with leaves, and the smoke was billowing up into Joseph's hood, tantalising him so much that for a second he considered asking him for one. He was the comedian; he had the loudest voice and tended to dominate the conversation among the group. He kept saying something with glee and nudging him, which caused the rest of the truck to laugh each time and the girl to cry even louder.

Joseph tried to ignore the smoke by doing some calculations. He guessed that the bus had crashed at about eight pm, which meant that it had to be after nine-thirty now, the truck having left the scene twenty minutes ago and the men who took him having spent half an hour beforehand looking through the belongings of the dead passengers. This meant that the bus had been travelling for about five hours, which meant that they were about two or three hours away from Luang Prabang. Sixty miles.

Since they had left, they had been driving downhill all the way and taken two sharp turns, one right, one left. They had been across rough terrain, no roads, just fields and streams, but now they were on a smoother track and the engine sounded different, as if they were under cover. They were in jungle.

Joseph did not know a huge amount about firearms, since the weapons he tended to use were less noisy and more difficult to trace, but he could tell by the state of their guns — all different, cheap imitations of Russian rifles — that the group that had taken them were dangerously amateur. They were bandits, common thieves, but disorganised and therefore unpredictable. There were a number of groups like this in central Laos, and the guns they carried were certainly not for show. They would shoot you as soon as steal your wallet, and they were one of the many reasons a plane would have (in this rare instance) made better transport. Muddy roads and old buses aside.

After another half hour of driving, the truck pulled to a halt and the driver cut the engine. The rear latch was opened and the men in the back clambered off, two of them yanking Joseph by each arm and pulling him with them. Joseph heard the girl cry louder as she was taken, too. It was almost completely dark, apart from a dim electric light in the distance, which he could vaguely make out through the fabric of his hood. He was marched in that direction, hobbling, dragged when he stumbled on either his prosthetic or his injured leg.

The men had stopped talking, and the only sounds now were the loud hiss and chirp of insects in the trees around them, the thud of boots against earth and the doleful cries of the girl stumbling along behind. Joseph heard another noise getting louder as they approached the light. It was music, electronic but not western, tinny and disjointed, punctuated with the worst kind of drum beats from the worst kind of sticky euro-pop, and decorated with a warbled, tuneless screech that suggested the girl singing it didn't want to be a singer, never had wanted to be a singer, didn't really understand why she was still singing.

They stopped walking and Joseph heard the sound of a latch being flipped and a wooden door squeaking open, the music suddenly becoming louder. There were voices, greetings and wordless sounds from men inside the building that suggested delight at seeing the two hooded figures of him and the girl. Behind the conversation there was the fizzing, chinking sound of large bugs and moths hitting a bulb above them, which swung under the barrage, dimming and brightening intermittently. Further still in the background was the growling hum of the diesel-engined generator powering it, presumably devoting most of its energy to the musical horror blaring from inside.

In his head, he tried to create a picture of the environment. They had driven quite some distance into the jungle, at least two hours' walk. It might be less in any other direction, but Joseph decided to assume the worst – that they had taken the shortest route from the jungle's edge to where they were. The track was narrow, because the sound of bugs had been close to their right and left as they walked from the truck. But when they had stopped, it had opened out to their left, so the building was in a clearing. In addition to the ten men who had found them, there were no more than five inside, at least those who were awake, and there were no more lights to suggest other buildings. They were at a shed, a little jungle hovel for a group of sloppy outlaws.

The girl had stopped crying, but Joseph hadn't sensed any movement behind him and he guessed that she was still there, fear now silencing her rather than making her cry. There was more movement, laughter and a pause followed by some mumbled words, suggesting that a decision was being made. Then there was a shout, and the sound of a trigger being cocked. Joseph's muscles tightened and his eyes widened inside the dark hood, and he suddenly felt a sharp prod of gun metal in his left temple. There was silence, the barrel pushing harder against his head. He took a breath and raised up his head, but the gun was pulled away and there was more laughter, and the man holding it cracked Joseph's forehead with its butt.

They dragged him, stumbling, away from the light and round

the side of the building. He heard the girl behind him whimper as she was pulled after him and the sound of the generator drew nearer. They were in darkness, closer to the jungle, and then they stopped. He heard an altercation, then a jangle of keys and another door being unlocked. Then he felt himself being thrown into a dark room, and he clattered into one of its corners. He lay, scrabbling his legs against the floor, feeling blood drip down over his eyebrows and hearing the girl's bubbling squeals as she was pushed in after him, stumbling into the opposite corner.

Then the door slammed shut, the men disappeared and everything was dark and silent, apart from the sound of sniffs and sobs and the humming of the diesel engine in the room behind them.

Damien says: yo

Ash Trés says: alright

Damien says: guess what

Ash Trés says: give up

Damien says: got the fucking henley account

Damien says: whos ur fucking daddy bitch

Ash Trés says: whats the henley account?

Damien says: u shittin me? only the fucking biggest break ive ever had

Ash Trés says: nice one mate, that's really cool

Damien says: bet your bloody bollocks its cool ill be earning twice what I earned last year in the next six months! u got laid yet dick boy?

Ash Trés says: kind of

Damien says: kind of? whats kind of? whats going on mate, what happened to my old buddy ash 'fucked-amy harris-and-jenny fox-in-one-night' gritten? u a batty boy now or what? :-0

Ash Trés says: leaving chiang mai today, going to laos

Damien says: wheres laos? boss reckons if i pull off henley account ill be on the board by next summer

Ash Trés says: country next door to thailand

Damien says: fucking big time or what?

Ash Trés says: got bombed a lot apparently

Damien says: right. you doing a trek or something

Ash Trés says: not sure

Damien says: phones ringing

Ash Trés says: Damien I feel fukcing weird

Ash Trés says: You there?

Damien is offline and may not respond

ACTUALLY BROWN

Mae Khong River, Laos

THE MAE Khong water is brown. This isn't just an illusion caused by light and the riverbed; it's actually brown. The slender-faced woman who boarded at the last village sits next to Ashley and fills a bottle with it. She gives it to her young daughter who knocks it back greedily like milk. Brown milk. Ashley tries to look disgusted but he is too tired.

It's been two days since the night at Mehdi's hotel, during which he's been on seven buses and not slept for more than an hour at a time. Every time he does sleep, he wakes almost immediately from shock, images of dogs, the girl and the house lurking in the shallows of his consciousness. To fall asleep is to plunge himself into a permanent nightmare.

Now he is on a boat. The last boat Ashley travelled on was a gleaming white yacht owned by his cousin Rupert. They sailed for an afternoon around the north Cornish coast, stretching out in leather seats, sipping Chablis and talking about Rupert's shares in Korean plastics. The spray from the surf was cool, the sun was warm, and life was as grand as it always had been and always should be.

The boat Ashley travels on now is a rotting barge making its way south towards Luang Prabang. It is low and narrow, with hard wooden benches along its sides and open windows. In the cockpit sit three smoking crew members, and behind them young monks in orange robes lie dozing on a pile of rucksacks. The owners of the rucksacks sit on the benches behind, facing each other. In the twenty-four hours since the journey began, jovially and excitedly like a school trip, the population on board has doubled with the addition of bona fide passengers — mothers, fathers, babies, toddlers and dogs travelling from the small villages that dot the banks of the river. For them, although uncomfortable, it is only for an hour or two between stops. Those with rucksacks have signed up for two days solid.

His fatigue, the heat, the hard wooden seat and the sounds on the boat are all playing a balancing game that suspends Ashley between wakefulness and sleep. If his head lolls forward, then his pelvic bone grinds against the wood, jerking him awake. If the sun beats against his eyelids and they shut, they open again only when a baby starts bawling.

Opposite Ashley sits a group of Australians getting drunk on the contents of a plastic bottle. One of them is a freckle-faced girl with white teeth and blue eyes; she looks at Ashley now and again, never for longer than a glance. He wonders what he looks like these days, not having been able to bring himself to look in a mirror since Chiang Mai. His eyes feel puffy and his shoulders hunched.

Next to the Australians is a young Frenchman reading something Ashley doesn't like the look of. He has managed to maintain the same position for the last half hour, leaning forwards, legs tightly crossed like a woman, arms loosely draped across them, one hand holding the book. He reads intensely, never looking up, never distracted, never fidgeting. He is doing it deliberately.

Next to him is a willowy, hairy couple who will not stop sucking at each other's faces and next to them is a fat man with a tattoo of a whore on his shoulder. *Fat man likes whores*, thinks Ashley.

Ashley considers the effort involved in striking up a conversation with one of them, but the very act of doing so exhausts him. Not for the first time, he wonders what he is doing in Laos. Wouldn't it have been wiser to head back south? Back to the islands? Get stoned in a hammock? Meet girls? He shudders. The image of Daniella holding his shorts and the look of disdain on her face makes him cringe, and the very thought of trying the whole thing again with another unsuspecting nymph fills him with dread.

All Ashley really wants to do is find a dark, cool room and sit in it for a while, maybe with a cup of tea to collect his thoughts. But there are no such rooms for hundreds of miles and the idea of turning back is unthinkable. He would have to go through Chiang Mai, and he might meet Mehdi there. Maybe he'd still be entertaining Daniella and Claudia. He's probably doing exactly that right at this moment, making them squeal and squirm with his golden wand.

Something else drives him on, though, something other than the anxiety of retreat. The last time he can remember feeling vaguely comfortable was with Caterine, and the story of Sarat and the Sleeping Cave – that somebody else has been troubled like him – makes him want to be back in the bar talking with her. True, she is a stranger, but no stranger than anyone else he has met. He holds no hope in finding her, doesn't even know where she is, but he remembers what she said about bumping into people, about how you keep meeting the same people when you travel. He hopes this might be the case with her, since it's happened several times already. For now in his exhausted, feverish state, a general direction away from things anxious and closer to things more settled is enough.

His body is starting to ache. Something other than the sun is making him hot.

'You all right there, buddy?' says the girl with freckles opposite him.

'Yes,' he says, his eyes half-shut.

'Only you look like you're burning up. Maybe you got a fever.'

'I'm fine,' he says, and falls face first into a nightmare.

A cool, dark room. It is empty apart from the wooden chair Ashley sits on and the dog lying in front of it. There is no window, and the only light comes from a low-watt bulb hanging directly above him. The dog is watching him; it doesn't blink.

Ashley tries to get up from the seat but finds his hands and legs tied to it. The dog growls but doesn't move. He struggles against his bindings but they will not shift and the chair is stuck down. The dog's tail slaps the floor lazily; its eyes never leave him.

Everything seems still beyond stillness. It is not just that nothing moves; the air, the walls, the light itself seems to be trapped inside a moment. As Ashley struggles he feels as if it is against some inertia, not the rope around his wrists and ankles, and when he moves his head and his perspective of the room changes, it is like looking around a photograph in two dimensions. He feels that he is himself still, flat and lifeless, that any movement he makes is in his imagination, every position just the same as the last. Sounds in his throat or from the rope against his skin become stifled and crushed before they start. He cannot breathe, cannot suffocate; his heart is stuck between two beats.

Something cold touches the back of his neck and he sucks in a slow gasp of air. It is a finger, then two fingers, and gradually a thin hand wraps itself around his right shoulder. Another one joins it on the left; they are like ice on Ashley's skin and the stiff air around him seems to freeze into crystals. The dog wags its tail again, gets up and trots around behind Ashley — it seems to find no difficulty in moving. From the corner of his eye, Ashley can see it greet the owner of the hands, raising up its snout and resting it on the hem of a white dress full of black, wriggling things. Ashley closes his eyes and weeps with fear.

The hands on his shoulders strengthen their grip and move down over his chest. Ashley shuts his eyes tighter, but the more he does so, the more he can feel the fear creeping across his ribs and through his heart. A head is next to his; it is cold too, and the collar of the girl's dress is so close to his ear that he can hear the clicking and snapping of insect legs inside it. He hears a dreadful whisper. He cannot understand it but shakes his head, and the girl's hands move down further over his stomach. His whole torso is freezing, and yet beneath it he feels himself stirring, blood beginning to pump into his groin. He begins to shiver and gasp for breath.

She whispers again, louder this time, and Ashley whimpers, shaking his head and screwing up his eyes into knots. The dog barks and Ashley's legs and arms begin to shake violently with the cold. Still he feels himself becoming erect.

'Lie with me,' the girl says out loud, her hands reaching the base of his belly.

Ashley cries out. The only part of him that isn't numb is bursting against his trousers, hot and swollen.

'No!' he shouts. 'No I will not! I will not! Get your hands off me!'

He wakes with every muscle tensed and clamours for breath. He hears the quiet growl of the barge's engines and the lapping of the brown Mae Khong water against its hull. But the passengers are silent. The Frenchman looks up from his book, the freckle-faced girl holds a bottle halfway to her mouth, the hairy couple have stopped kissing and the fat man has crossed his arms. All are looking in his direction, most of them down at the massive, wet bulge in his shorts.

ANOTHER CHILD HE HAD ONCE KNOWN

Laos

THIS WASN'T the first time Joseph had been in a cell.

Three hours had passed since the door had been locked and the girl had finally stopped crying. Joseph had managed to prop himself up in the corner where he sat with his legs outstretched and his hooded head against the wall, his wrists bound awkwardly behind him at the base of his spine. He had tried making sounds, sounds he thought might be useful to a frightened little girl. But they had only seemed to make things worse, so he had stopped, realising that he didn't even know what sounds to make at a little girl who was happy, let alone one who had survived a bus crash only to be kidnapped by bandits in the middle of the jungle and thrown in a room with a foreign man making stupid noises at her.

For a brief moment he had considered singing a lullaby, but decided that it would have the opposite of the intended effect. Apart from the fact that he couldn't remember the last time he had sung a note, nothing, not even the sweetest cradle-rocker, could have sounded soothing above the caterwauling of the strangled girl-gibbon blaring from the stereo in the room next door. Eventually he had given up and let tiredness go to work on her tears. Now, sleep had finally given her the dose and her sobs had given way to short, tight, irregular breaths that could only be from tiny lungs fighting their way through troubled dreams.

The music had stopped too, and Joseph now heard only the quiet pulse of insects and the drone of the generator. A door opened and shut and two men walked past outside, slurring things to each other and laughing lazily. He heard them relieve themselves into the trees, then one of them belched and opened a gate. A switch was switched and a lever pulled and the engine coughed itself out, and Joseph was surprised to find that what he thought was pitch black became blacker still as the bulb around the corner of the building was drained of light. The men walked back past the door and out of sight, back into the shed. Then there were some mumbles, shuffling from next door, then nothing — just the sounds of a jungle at night.

For a while, Joseph enjoyed the relative silence — a strange kind of bliss for a bound man in a hood. As he suspected, a few more of the men trudged out to purge their bladders and spit into the jungle before there was peace proper. He waited another half an hour after the last zip had zipped, the last glob of phlegm had hit the mud and the last fist had banged lazily against their door on the way back. When he was sure they were inside and asleep, he shifted himself from where he had slumped down the wall.

His left leg felt numb from lack of movement and the bandana tourniquet. His arms were stiff from having been tied behind his back for four hours, his head throbbed dully and his neck ached from the pistol butt against his head. He took a deep breath and stretched down his forearms. Pushing against the base of the wall, he raised himself up for a second and then relaxed so that he was sitting on his hands. The pressure made the wound in his leg throb as a surge of blood passed by it, and the revived circulation filled his foot with pins and needles. Taking another breath, he pushed his fists hard against the ground so that his entire weight was on his arms and tried to rock his legs backwards so that his hands passed under his thighs. But the bindings around his wrists were too tight to give, and lack of strength in his leg meant he couldn't push himself up any further. He fell back on his hands and panted, tried twice more and then gave up and let his head fall back against the stone, thinking.

Manoeuvring himself into an awkward position with limited resources was a skill, like murder, that Joseph had acquired over many years. Like managing a squatting toilet in an airport, it was just a matter of careful planning. Life with one leg was full of such things, which meant that even the simplest of tasks sometimes had to be preceded with deep concentration, during which all thought became three-dimensional and all perception gave way to spatial and physiological awareness. This had been especially true in the first few years after the accident. Getting in and out of bed, bathing, using stairs; it was as if his body had become a puzzle to unlock, a spatial riddle to solve, each move beginning with a brief bout of furious thought and then an execution of some gymnastic combination of limbs that either took him swiftly where he wanted to be or sent him tumbling, cursing to the floor. Daily locomotion required active, conscious thought. Nothing was left to instinct any more.

Sometimes, when sitting with someone in conversation, Joseph would seem suddenly distant, his face glazing over and his eyes settling into the middle distance. Whoever was talking at the time would think that he had become disinterested, but Joseph was really just working out how to go and take a piss without falling over.

Getting his hands free now was just the same, just another puzzle. He let himself fall onto his left side and his hands sprang back behind him. Then he slowly pulled up his thighs halfway to his chest, bending his left knee and letting the chip in his right do the same automatically in response to the muscle movement above it.

He lay for a while in that position, letting blood circulate further around the veins, which had been all but empty beforehand. Once the paraesthesia had died, he closed his eyes so that he shut out the blackness outside and concentrated on the image in his head of his own position. He stretched down his arms again and managed to slide them more easily underneath his pelvis, but they still reached a point at which they could go no further. At that point, he stretched his left arm further and pulled with the other so that his right hand was against the top of his thigh. Then he strained, grunting as he twisted his wrist around and his fingers touched metal. Stretching all his muscles to their limit, he felt around underneath a stem and found the button, pressing it to release his knife. One further stretch of his fingers released it through the seam and it clanged noisily onto the stone floor.

Joseph froze and waited for silence to assure him that he hadn't been heard. After a few minutes, he relaxed and rotated his wrists to ease the pain in their muscles. Then he slid himself across the floor to the point at which he thought the knife had fallen, finding its sharp edge with his left thumb and feeling it bleed moments later from a long, thin cut. He grasped the handle, turning it so that the blade was hard against the rope, and a few small slices cut it from his wrists. He breathed in relief and immediately brought his hands around to his chest, placing the knife on the floor and massaging them together.

He sat up and removed the hood from his head, sucking in the fresher air and rubbing his face vigorously. Opening his eyes as wide as they would go, he darted them around the room, getting them accustomed to the light, the only threads of which were coming from stars and a small crescent moon. There was no window, but there was a grill by the door through which Joseph could see black sky and foliage. In the corner, he could see the girl curled in a grubby bundle. He watched her breathing, tiny breaths of dreamful panic. He imagined that she looked much the same as he did when he was asleep.

He picked up his knife and replaced it in its sheath, clicking the compartment back into his leg. Then he felt his other leg around its wound, checking for any fresh blood from the exertion. Finding none, he undid the bandana and tucked it into his pocket, and then raised himself up so that he was standing, stretching his back and shoulders, rolling his neck. He felt his forehead — that had stopped bleeding, too; the only fresh wound now was on his thumb. He took it across to the wall and examined it in the bone-coloured light, squeezing it and sending a thick globule of blood running down his palm. He wrapped it in the bandana and looked out through the gap. It was bright enough to see the truck they had been taken in next to another one. They were old, ex-military vehicles with canopies across their backs and thick muddy tyres.

The clearing that Joseph thought the building had been in was actually a tight bend in the road, and behind the trucks he could see that the jungle was actually on the beginning of a steep slope. They were high on a hillside, and the jungle fell away from it and stretched out into the distance, a wide green mattress of treetops bathed in dim moonlight. It was a good view. Joseph wanted a cigarette.

He wondered what motives a group of unprofessional drunks would have in taking a middle-aged foreigner and a little kid from the wreck of a bus crash. Were they hoping to get some ransom? From whom? The British Embassy? He hoped not. Any friendly debriefing from a consulate once he was released would only involve questions he didn't want to answer, not least of which would be his business in Laos, and why it involved him having a knife secreted in his leg.

Besides, the red tape involved in such a ransom would take months, and in any case they didn't seem like the kind of outfit who would want to get involved in such a risky trade. They were the kind who would stumble upon a bus crash, loot the dead bodies and take the survivors because they didn't know what else to do. They had made a mistake. And given that they would wake tomorrow with fifteen hangovers and two more strangers in their hideout than usual, it wasn't a mistake that was likely to end well. Not for him, and not for the unconscious little creature fretting on the floor next to him.

He looked down at her. She seemed calmer than before, her chest moving more steadily and her breathing now barely audible above the insects, she had obviously fallen into some deep, anaesthetic illusion offered up by a dream. He would have felt relief for her, had he not known that when sleep wore off she would find herself bound, blind, parentless, hungry and soiled, with nothing to comfort her but her own innocence of the fact that all she had to look forward to was a bullet.

Joseph felt a sudden well of protectiveness, which simultaneously surprised and worried him. It surprised him because he never felt protective about anyone, not lovers, not friends, not children, not even himself, which was what made him so good at his profession. It worried him for the same reason.

Children were a mystery to him: he didn't know how they thought, how they spoke, how they saw the world, how much they knew. He didn't remember being one, didn't even remember being young. He had never had kids. He had come close, of course, but that chapter of his life had been torn away half-read, and he had never revisited it.

Suddenly he thought of another child he had once known. A little girl he had said goodbye to once, shivering alone in the snow with a dog at her feet, the whole of her life rising out before her like the mountains into which he had been headed. He had watched her as the dim lights of the farm faded and the only thing left was a tiny dot behind him. The whole of her life and the rest of his own rising out like the mountains, to be faced like everyone else's: alone.

He had never killed or kidnapped anyone under the age of eighteen. But that wasn't for any moral reason; he just hadn't been offered the contract. It would have been a revenge job, he supposed, killing the daughter or son of a traitor — a worse punishment than killing the traitor himself, for some. Part of him was glad that he had never had to, but another was curious. Would it have been as easy as any other? Could he shake off that last moral? Could he cut a child's throat?

If someone had asked him that right there and then, the answer would have been no.

He spent the rest of the night quietly exercising his legs and muscles, listening out for any movement in the room next door and watching the early dawn light grow outside. By three o'clock he would have given his other leg for a cigarette. By four he would have swapped that for food and by five he would have swapped anything for water. He realised that he hadn't drunk anything since the can of warm, floral syrup he had bought from the noodle man, and the thought of that made him thirstier still.

But by six o'clock it was light, and his nerves over what he was about to do made him prepared to re-trade all for nicotine.

He paced a few times up and down the wall next to the door, rubbing his beard and nervously eyeing the trucks outside, which were now completely illuminated in the rising sun. He tried to keep his steps noiseless, and thought about how he would wake the girl without alarming her. He couldn't risk her crying, but with any luck she would be sleepy, and perhaps she wouldn't remember what had happened before she was fully awake. By that time he could be away.

In one movement, he slipped his hand into his hidden pocket, unclipped the knife from his leg and drew it out. Sliding it through one of the grills, he went to work on the padlock outside, closing his eyes and concentrating on what he could not see in front of him. A few times the padlock banged against the door and he froze. Each time, he waited for a few minutes, listening for a reaction from either the men or the girl before trying again. Eventually, the padlock came free and fell into the dust. Joseph stepped back and slipped his knife into his belt. He looked at the door; there was no other lock or latch on it and it should have swung open when the padlock was opened, but it stayed tightly shut. He prodded it. It rattled. He pushed it harder and winced as it creaked in its frame. It was a bad fit, jammed. Joseph gritted his teeth and shoved both of his hands against it sharply, and the door swung open with a single loud rasp of wood against wood that seemed to echo around the room for an eternity. He shut his eyes tightly as the quiet morning air regained its hold over things, and then opened them again, looking out onto the bright road outside. He heard no movement from the room behind, but the girl had stirred and was fidgeting on the floor, making the muffled, disorientated noises only made by a child who wakes up blind and unable to move. Joseph sprang down by her side and ripped off her hood. Her eyes were terrified and she squeaked as he cut through the bindings around her wrist. Then he tried with everything he had to find a friendly face and placed a finger against his lips. It seemed to work, and the girl understood, stifling her fear. Joseph reached out a hand and pointed at the door. For a while, she looked between him and the light outside, weighing up the few options she had. Then she slowly stood up and took his hand and he led her quietly outside.

But before she had stepped through the doorway, Joseph stopped dead in his tracks. Footsteps were coming from around the corner to the right, where the other door was. One of the men appeared and walked towards him, head down, oblivious to either the open door or Joseph, standing in mid-stride, wide-eyed, long knife in his hand.

The man looked up and stumbled to a halt, his jaw agape and his bloodshot eyes fixed on Joseph's. For a few moments they looked at each other, neither making a move. The bandit eyed Joseph's knife, and Joseph eyed where the bandit's gun should be. The bandit turned and ran.

In a split second, Joseph had pushed the girl back into the room and turned on his left leg, hurling his knife at the fleeing man and catching him in the back of the neck as he reached the corner. It pierced his throat and stuck out through his jugular, and Joseph saw a thick squirt of blood shoot from his artery. He fell with a single gurgle to the ground as if his skeleton had collapsed, and then he lay still, a red pool growing in the orange dirt around his head.

Joseph turned to the girl, who was standing terrified in the middle of the room, and placed a finger to his lips again. Then he spread his palms down, mouthed 'stay here' and hobbled out up the road. He grabbed the corpse's feet and dragged it back, causing the girl to squeal when she saw its surprised face float by the doorway in the dirt. When he got to the roadside, he slid his knife out of the dead man's neck and rolled him over the edge, where he fell some way and landed beneath a clump of trees. Joseph looked out across the landscape — a very fine view indeed now that the sun was up — and briefly noticed that the otherwise bright blue sky had a wide black band of cloud growing on its distant horizon. He brushed his hands against his trousers and turned back.

When he got back to the open doorway, the girl was still standing, rooted to the spot in the centre of the room. She looked at his silhouette with mistrust, slowly clenching and unclenching her tiny fists by her side as if she were weighing up an important decision. He had blood on his hands, his own and a dead stranger's, his trousers and T-shirt were sweaty and covered with filth, as was his face, he expected. He tried once more to make himself seem an appealing option over incarceration, bending down with his hands on his thighs, the servo-motors in his right knee twitching slightly in response to his touch. He smiled sweetly.

'Come on, then,' he whispered. 'Let's get out of here.'

He flicked his head towards the door. It was a gesture that worked for both dogs and toddlers, but not when accompanied by the sharp ricochet from the right shin. Joseph's legs were swept from underneath him and he landed heavily on his ribs, feeling a splintering pain in his left calf. His prosthetic felt as if it had been knocked off kilter, its seal twisting around his thigh like a gigantic Chinese burn. He gripped his leg and winced as he heard the men approach, shouting sharp, angry orders all around them. He felt a boot connect with his lower back and another to his stomach, winding him and making him drop the knife. He reached out to grab it, but before his fingertips reached it, somebody had scooped it from the dirt and stamped on his hand.

Joseph curled into a ball as three of the men stood around kicking him. Through their legs, he saw that one of the others had noticed a patch of blood in the ground that hadn't been there before, and that others had been following its trail to the hillside and were looking down over the edge. He took another boot to his ribs and saw the rest of them close in on the little girl, who had reverted back to shameless, terrified bawling in the commotion. Two of the men kicking him stopped in response to an order. The man standing by the door who had shouted it hailed them to join the others at the hillside. Joseph saw that he was wearing a red, faded Liverpool Football Club cap. The two ran off, and the one remaining launched a foot at his head, but before it made an impact Joseph had caught it in both hands, catching its owner off balance and twisting it sharply in its ankle socket. It snapped like raw broccoli and the man shrieked as he crumpled to the ground, but before anyone could respond Joseph had pulled himself up agonisingly on his left leg and launched himself into the room, through the four men who were advancing on the girl, and pushed her out of their way and into the corner. He turned and fell to his backside, scrabbling back along the floor so that he was shielding the girl, who cowered behind his back.

One of the silhouettes standing over them laughed and pointed. Another cawed in mock sympathy. The third brought back the stock of his assault rifle, but before he could bring it down on Joseph's skull there was a garbled shout from the man at the door and they all turned round. There was some movement outside, two of the men had fallen against one of the trucks and others were yelling angrily, all of them, apart from the man whose foot Joseph had dislocated, still writhing around in the background, were standing around the dead man's body they had dragged up the slope.

Joseph took the opportunity to count the men. There were twelve in total, fewer than he had thought.

One of them had fallen to his knees, wailing with grief.

The brother, thought Joseph. *Fucking great.*

As if in response to Joseph's thoughts, the man suddenly turned and glared at him. Then he stood and stormed through the doorway, screaming murderously, pulling off his gun and ramming its stock in Joseph's face. He felt a blinding smart in his nose and looked up to see that the angry brother had cocked the gun and trained it on Joseph's face, proclaiming things violently into the air.

Joseph stared back. It wasn't the first time he had seen a gun from this angle. Still, it never got any easier, the temptation to go out kicking and screaming — or on your knees with soiled underwear and a tear-stained face — was always strong. Joseph relaxed, ignoring the pain that had erupted over the various parts of his damaged body. Fighting the last temptation to close his eyes and grit his teeth, he looked calmly up at his executioner's face.

'Fanculo,' he said lazily.

The brother stopped shouting and gripped the trigger, but before could squeeze it the bandit in the Liverpool cap had reached him and pulled back the gun, gripping his shoulder and calmly ordering him away. The brother resisted and retrained the gun at Joseph, but two others helped drag him away outside, where they pinned him against the truck and calmed him down.

Joseph looked up at the Liverpool fan, the leader he supposed, who was regarding him thoughtfully with his hands on his hips. He heard the girl whimpering behind him, suddenly remembering she was there. The man shifted and looked briefly past Joseph's shoulder, as if just having noticed her too.

'English?' he said.

Joseph said nothing.

'English? Speak English?' he repeated, snapping his fingers.

He ignored Joseph's silence and looked past him at the little girl again, who cringed under his flat gaze. For a moment he looked her up and down as if assessing some second-hand bargain he was only half interested in.

'Little girl,' said Liverpool.

Joseph frowned.

'L-i-t-t-l-e…g-i-r-l,' he repeated, rubbing his chin and drawing out the words as if deciding on a price. Then he strode forwards, knocking Joseph to the side and grabbing the child by her wrist, pulling her squealing and kicking into the air.

'No,' said Joseph, struggling to get to his crippled feet. 'Stop.'

Two of the men pinned him back against the wall and he watched helplessly as the girl was carried out of the door, dangling from the man's hand, her mouth wide open and bent down into a wide, black crescent. She was crying and reaching her hand back to Joseph.

'What are you doing? Come back here! Come back here!' he yelled, wriggling in the men's grip as the girl disappeared outside. He heard her cries getting quieter as she was taken round the corner to the front of the building.

There was a slap and the crying suddenly became shocked squeaks, then some scuffling in the dirt, a single word, a single click and a terrible bang, after which there were no more cries.

Then Joseph felt the sharp crack of a rifle butt against his head, and unconscious, dreamless sleep was suddenly upon him.

Damien says: the bank said no problem to 290k considering my projected earnings now ive got the henley account so its sorted. dads check clears next week so ill be able to put down the deposit then, move in in a fortnight. you should see it dude its such a cool pad

Damien says: you there dikwad?

Ash Trés is online

Ash Trés says: sorry connection shit here

Damien says: where ru?

Ash Trés says: vang vien laos

Damien says: out in the stix?

Ash Trés says: not really, backpackers sitting get drunk much

Ash Trés says: getting drunk much

Ash Trés says: getting drunk a lot

Damien says: er…yeah

Damien says: you still there?

Ash Trés is online

Ash Trés says: lost you agen, what u say to me

Damien says: nothing mate, van van or whatever the fuck its called sounds alright, better than a hut in the middle of nowhere. rather be in a beach myself but its your holiday

Ash Trés says: im tired

Damien says: more heavy nights eh? nice one

Ash Trés says: i cant remember shere ive been

Damien says: sounds like you should take it easy matey!

Ash Trés says: im going on a tyre

Damien says: you what? fucking hell mate what you on!? gotta go, fri night, going out on piss with work take it easy

Ash Trés says: big tyre

Damien is offline and may not respond

HAVE A GO ON A TYRE

Vang Vien, Laos

ASHLEY TRUDGES heavily out of the Internet café and throws a tired glance at the sign lying about its high-speed connection. He's on Vang Vien's main street, a dirt track lined with bars and guesthouses inside which western faces stuff themselves with milkshakes, noodles and beer while watching American films. Just like Bangkok.

If asked how he had found his way between the last traveller-friendly outpost and here, Ashley might describe some uncomfortable hot bus trip just like all the others he has taken in the last…week? Or has it been two? He can't remember; all the journeys and all the places have rolled into one. The truth would not surprise him. The truth is that he has travelled twice back and forwards between Vientiane, Luang Prabang, Vang Vien and Phonsovan, the last being a dangerous choice owing to its location at the end of one unfinished road, riddled with bandits. He has not slept in any hostel or guesthouse; he has simply travelled with no rest. He has not seen Caterine, and he has forgotten he is looking for her. He is a zombie, memory like mush and eyes permanently half-closed, letting in so little light that he cannot see the looks of shock and concern on the faces that pass him. His body is hot and his shoulders and spine ache, his hearing is muffled, and he has already vomited four times today. A distant part of his brain puts this down to some kind of malnutrition, since he cannot stomach any food.

Sleep is not an option. It no longer exists; in its place is a restless nightmare, a hundred times worse than the weariness of being awake.

A strangely comforting feeling, however, is that he cannot fully remember a time when he was not like this. He cannot recall what it feels like to be rested, to not feel like an empty husk, to not be afraid, to not walk around with a demon on his back.

And a demon is exactly what it is. The word no longer troubles him; he no longer scorns it. All his cynicism, all his arrogance, all his lust, his vanity, his greed; all that he was has been drained. He has lost himself, and all he has left is a walking body. With a demon on its back.

Despite all this, he has decided to have a go on a tyre.

Vang Vien has one more tourist attraction, in addition to the sitting and the eating and the drinking and the watching of films. For the equivalent of thirty pence, visitors can float down the river on a large rubber tyre, and a desperate part in Ashley's brain has deemed this a good idea. Maybe it will help him clear his head, maybe it will act as the cool, dark room he craves.

He stumbles up to the stall where the tyres are stacked and puts down 6000 Lao kip, his thirty pence, and listens to the man behind the stall explain something. The words sound like they are coming from three streets away, but he makes out that a truck will be along shortly to pick him up and take him to the river. Ashley nods and remains standing by the stall, not wanting to sit in case he falls asleep.

Soon a small wagon approaches, tooting its horn twice, and Ashley is guided onto its open back by the driver, who slings in a tyre behind him. There are other people there too, five of them, but Ashley doesn't look up. Instead he concentrates all his energy into resisting the temptation to fall asleep under the truck's rocking motion. He counts the number of times he can scratch his fingernail against the tread of his tyre, managing one-thousand-nine-hundred-and-sixty-three before the truck pulls up by the riverside. The other passengers step nervously around Ashley's hunched body as they disembark, and he gets off last.

It's a bright, sunny day, hazy and warm, weather more suited to an English summer fête than to the banks of a wild, equatorial river. Ashley follows the others down to the water, about fifty steps behind. Each carries their tyre slung over their right shoulder, the base of it resting against their left hip. They look like a troupe of lost tuba players. Ashley begins to laugh weakly at this image, but his right eyebrow begins to twitch and he stops.

At the bank, he watches the others place their tyres half in the water and throw themselves in backside first before being swept downstream, whooping. He does the same, falling in the first time, but struggling back onto his tyre and kicking away from the bank with his face touching the river surface. For a while he floats like this, vaguely enjoying the sensation of cold liquid on his nose and forehead, but eventually he manages to right himself and lies back with his face turned up to the sun. He doesn't close his eyes.

After a while, once he's used to the motion of the tyre, Ashley adjusts himself and looks around the river. Its current is strong but not fast, and he's moving in a straight line down its centre, spinning slowly so that the surrounding scenery is presented to him like a slide show. The bank to the left of his direction of travel is lined with thick trees, most of which dangle their branches in the water as if they were taking a drink. The bank to his right has fewer trees, and behind them green paddy fields stretch out towards rich, lush forest, sweeping up into a steep curve and finally becoming three gigantic cliff faces. Their rock is jagged and red like rust, and they tower above him like three giant cardinals. The sky is still blue and the sun warm, and the sound of the water reminds him briefly of his cousin's boat, although the feeling is no more than a flashback, a suggestion. It feels like there is a blind spot in his memory, that anything he tries to recall burns up immediately in his cerebrum like an overexposed photograph.

Still, tangible or not, it's the first semi-pleasant feeling Ashley has had for a long time. In fact, as far as he's concerned, it's the first semi-pleasant feeling that has ever existed in the entire history of Ashley.

A breeze washes across his eyelids, closing them gently.

When Ashley wakes up, he is on his side screaming on a bamboo floor. There is a sound of thunder. His knees are touching his chest and his arms are curled up under his neck. He feels two other arms cradling him and the sound of shushing as he's rocked back and forth by their owner. Gradually he calms down and catches his breath, focusing his eyes. He swallows and looks up, and sees Caterine's face looking down on him. She gives him a smile.

'Try to calm down,' she whispers, another roll of thunder sounding in the distance.

Ashley raises himself up on one elbow, but Caterine increases her grip and tells him to stop.

'Where am I?' says Ashley. 'What happened?'

'Shh,' says Caterine, 'you're OK.'

Ashley falls back into Caterine's arms and looks at the wall. It's made with a mixture of stone, wood and twigs, as if none of the materials was abundant enough to be used alone. Halfway up the wall is a small, glassless window, through which Ashley sees heavy rainfall against thick, black cloud. He hears the water hammer against the tin roof and a deep rumble in the distance.

'It's dark,' he said. 'How did it get dark? Why is it raining? How did I get here?'

Caterine strokes his hair.

'You fell asleep on your tyre, just as a storm rolled in. You span out of control and were taken downstream, about five miles further than you were supposed to. We were supposed to get out at the bathing area, don't you remember?'

'No.'

'No. I told you that you shouldn't get in in the first place, the state you're in, but you didn't seem to be listening, so I held on to a branch and waited for you to pass me. Then I followed you. When the storm hit the river and you missed the bathing area, I had to follow you again. All the way here. The current became strong and I thought I was going to lose you, but I managed to catch up, grab your tyre and pull you to the bank.'

'I didn't even know you were there,' croaks Ashley. 'I was looking for you. Were you on the truck, too?'

'Yes, I tried to talk to you but you just kept scratching your tyre. You looked like you were sleepwalking; you didn't say anything, didn't register anyone. Ashley, what's happened to you?'

Ashley sighs and looks straight ahead.

'She won't leave me alone,' he says. 'Whenever I fall asleep… I…'

He sighs again.

'Where are we?'

'We're in a village,' says Caterine. 'About ten miles out of Vang Vien, the people here…'

Suddenly, a young man hops into the room, muttering and shaking himself free of the rain. He has a wide, fresh face and smiles as he gives two brown blankets to Caterine. Then he looks down at Ashley and nods his head in acknowledgement. He holds his gaze, searching Ashley's face with something like empathy.

'Hello,' says Ashley, released from Caterine's arms and getting to his hands and knees. 'I'm Ash.'

'Ash,' says the man.

'Bit of a coincidence, really,' says Caterine. 'Ash, this is Sarat.'

'Sarat?' says Ashley, dull synapses firing.

'The man I told you about. The Sleeping Cave. He lives here.'

'Hello, Ashley,' says Sarat, reaching down a hand. Ashley takes it and stands, realising that he is soaked to the bone.

'You are both very wet,' says Sarat. 'My grandmother has lent me these blankets. She lives five houses away and I am as wet as you just from getting them! I'll have to go and get another for myself now. Please put them on and I will try to dry your clothes in the other room.'

Sarat turns and lights a lamp in the corner of the room before leaping out into the rain again, yelling. The darkness outside is growing and the lamplight fuses with what natural light there is left into a warm orange glow. Caterine gives Ashley a blanket and for a while they stand looking at each other before simultaneously turning their backs on each other and getting undressed.

A few weeks earlier, Ashley would have recognised this as an opportunity and made some attempt to abuse Caterine's trust; he would have snuck a peak. But the thought does not even occur to him. The part of him that floats outside his skull is long gone.

'Thank you,' he says.

Caterine, who has already taken two sneaky peeks at Ashley's bare back and legs is caught off guard.

'What for?' she says breathlessly, jerking back her head and going to work on her bra hook.

'For saving my life,' says Ashley. He wraps the blanket around him. It's large and warm and acts like a massive toga.

'Oh,' says Caterine, 'that's all right. You owe me one.'

'Are you decent?'

'One moment, please,' says Caterine, struggling with the blanket around her small shoulders. 'There.'

Ashley looks at Caterine. Before, when he met her on the train, she looked pretty. But she was also severe, closed. Now she seems to have opened up, to have become herself, and smiling in the lamplight she looks beautiful.

'Hail Caesar,' says Caterine, with a hopeful smile.

Sarat bounds in once again, cursing, with a new set of clothes for himself, some jeans and a black T-shirt. He laughs briefly at their outfits and then gathers up their clothes, taking them wordlessly into a side room. Ashley watches the wooden door close behind him and then looks around the room. It is bare, apart from a single bed in the corner, low, with a thin mattress on top of it. The rain outside is no longer torrential, but still heavy, and it splashes in through the open doorway making small puddles on the bamboo floor. The wall opposite him is also covered in a bamboo weave, and he supposes that wall made of sticks, wood and stone is to be covered with the same eventually. They are in an unfinished building.

He places a hand against the rough surface of the wall, and it suddenly and unexpectedly occurs to him that this building is what being alive is like: incomplete, only ever half built, at the mercy of storms and floods and the slow disaster of time itself. Why, he thinks, why seek happiness, completion, security and self-satisfaction, when there is always a storm ready to tear off your roof? Better to live in the storm itself.

The thought is fleeting, but it comforts him in a way he cannot describe. He removes his hand and takes a step towards the window. Although he guesses it to be mid-afternoon, the heavy cloud has dimmed the light so much that it feels like dusk. It is still very warm, but the storm has carried with it a cool breeze so that hot and cold currents of air curl around each other. Everything is still, apart from the movement of water: through the air, down tree bark, creating rivulets in the muddy road outside the building. To his left, he can just make out the brown swell of the river he was rescued from, a few hundred feet away. The dirt road leads away from it, making two lazy curves past him and up to his left. It is lined with trees and other small buildings. Huts, some made just of bamboo, others made of more sturdy stuff like his. Each has an orange glowing window, in which he occasionally sees the moving shadows of villagers taking shelter from the rain.

Ashley is about to stand back from the window, when he suddenly hears a small voice coming from outside. He turns his head left and looks up on a dirt ridge at the side of the road. There, holding a broken umbrella, is a little girl. She is wearing a white, tattered dress, unbelievably clean and dry in the mud and rain, and has long, jet black hair combed down around her shoulders. Ashley's face twitches with surprise, and the girl smiles back at him, a sweet, delighted grin. Then she starts to sing. Loudly. Ashley's face twitches again; he has never seen or heard a little girl singing on her own in the rain.

He listens for a while, trying to lock on to the tune, but it is unfathomable; there seems to be no sense to its rhythm or melody. It twists and turns without root or resolve, winding around itself like a snake curling into endless question marks. There is no verse, no chorus, no key, no time signature to speak of, no beginning, no middle, no end — like a music box played with an unsteady hand, backwards and forever.

Life is like this.

The girl cries out the song, her face turned up to the rain, and her eyes looking happily down at Ashley. For the second time that day, he experiences something approaching pleasure.

Suddenly, Ashley notices a movement from the house next to the little girl. A woman darts out and sprints up the bank, grabbing the girl by her waist and tearing back to the door, scolding her. The song stops and the sound of giggles disappears back into the hut.

Ashley continues to look at the empty space where the girl had been standing, now a growing stream of muddy water running down the bank, and admits something to himself. When he first noticed her, when he first saw her standing there, he half expected to see insects crawling about in her white dress.

He doesn't remember the storm, doesn't remember falling asleep in the tyre and doesn't remember what he dreamed. He guesses from his memory of his waking screams that it was the usual. All of his dreams, like the most recent days of his life, have been smeared together. Even reality feels like a dream, most of it dull and without substance.

'How are you feeling?' says Caterine behind him.

Most of it.

Ashley turns round, swaying on his feet. She's sitting on the bed, her legs crossed and her blanket wrapped around her, her hair illuminated by the lamplight. There is something simple about her face that Ashley has just noticed. It seems primal, wild, eager, yet tempered and concerned. There is no judgement in her features, nothing to say right or wrong. There is just calm. He feels envy and desire: to be her and to have her.

'I ache all over, and I'm cold. I can't focus, my eyes hurt, and my stomach's tight. I'm a wreck. Christ, if you hadn't been there…'

'Come and sit down,' says Caterine.

'No, I don't want to sleep again.'

'You should try, you're ill, you need rest.'

'I'm not ill,' says Ashley, rubbing his head with both hands, 'I'm fucking possessed.'

At that moment, the door to the side room opens and Sarat comes out dressed in his dry clothes. He is shorter than Ashley, wiry and taut with a mop of dark hair. Bright eyes. Sickeningly healthy.

'You're hungry,' says Sarat, looking Ashley up and down. 'We'll eat. I'll just go and get the bomb.'

~1978~

THE DIARY OF CLAUDETTE FERRIÈRE

18 MARS 1978

Papa and Doctor Moreau have made a leg for Joe!

They spent the morning in the engine shed like yesterday, and at lunchtime Doctor Moreau came into the kitchen and said they had finished. I was worried and saw that Joe looked worried as well, because if they had finished the sledge then it meant they would be taking him to the village. But then Papa came in carrying something in his arms. It was two thick wooden poles joined together, and the top one had something that looked like half a bucket filled with rags at the end of it.

'What's that?' I said, and Papa said that it was a leg for Joe. The sledge was going to take longer to fix, and Doctor Moreau insisted that Joe had something to practise walking on while they completed it.

We all looked at the leg. The two poles were different shapes. The bottom one was thinner than the top one and had a flat wooden block at the bottom. The block had a rubber sole that Papa had cut from a tyre melted onto it. This was Joe's new foot.

The top pole was much thicker and stronger, and at its top Papa had attached more of the old tyre. Inside he had put some foam covered with sheets so that it was soft, and some thick leather straps that came out of the rubber and strapped together above. This is where Joe would put his stump and the straps were so he could tie it on.

Between the two poles was Joe's new knee, which was a solid lump of shiny metal. Papa had cut it from the old bumper he had taken from his Deux Chevaux. He had bent it into shape so that it wrapped around the two bits of wood and welded bolts to it. From these bolts were four thick springs that hooked onto other bolts up and down the wood. These springs meant that you could bend the leg, but that it snapped back straight when you let go. There were different holes up and down the wood so that you could tighten and loosen the springs. Doctor Moreau said that this had to be adjusted for Joe's weight.

They were both very proud of the work and Madame Beaufort and I clapped our hands when they showed us it working. Papa was very proud, but he kept himself looking serious because I know he doesn't want Joe here any more. I know he doesn't trust him; he thinks he should be in Grenoble hospital and that he should be talking to the police. He doesn't understand why Joe doesn't want to.

Joe didn't say anything, but Papa gave him the leg and he held it and flexed it in his hands. It made a twanging sound like an old mattress.

'We should try it on,' said Doctor Moreau. 'Now.'

We all went to the sitting room and Papa and Madame Beaufort cleared all the furniture away so that there was a long space in the floor. Then Joe stood at one end on his crutches, while Doctor Moreau knelt at his feet and undid all the straps. Nobody spoke, and all you could hear was the wind outside and the ticking of the big clock in the corner. It was quite dark because the snow was still reaching halfway up the windows, and the flickering light from the fire made funny shadows out of Doctor Moreau fiddling about on his knees in front of Joe.

'Shall we try?' he said at last, and Joe nodded, even though I don't think he wanted to. Doctor Moreau held the leg upright and bent back the top towards Joe's stump. Then Joe carefully pushed himself over it. His crutches were wobbling and his face was creased up, and when his stump first touched the foam inside the leg, he gasped and pulled it out.

'It's OK,' said Doctor Moreau. 'It's going to hurt, but the wound is healed, you'll just make it stronger by walking on it.'

Then Joe tried again and managed to get all his stump inside. He trembled and winced and gritted his teeth as Doctor Moreau adjusted it around him.

'I'm not going to tie the straps just yet, let's just see if you can put your weight on it.'

Joe nodded, but he was shaking so much and I could see he was in pain. I went up and stood next to him.

'See if you can stand up, Joe,' I said. 'Just see.'

Gradually I could see him leaning forwards and putting more and more of his weight onto the leg. Every time he tried he pulled back and spluttered and let out big puffs of breath with sweat running down his face.

Eventually he managed to put enough weight on it that both his real leg and the wooden one were next to each other, and we all made 'well done' noises. Then, when Doctor Moreau had made sure Joe's stump was inside the new leg properly, he said 'shall we try without the crutches, Joe?'

Joe tried, even though he was shaking so much with the crutches that I thought he would fall over anyway. But as soon as he let Doctor Moreau have the crutches, he let out a high squeal that I have never heard a man make before, and he fell back out of the leg and into a pile on the floor. He struggled about for a bit, grabbing the carpet and wiggling his stump up and down like a blind worm as if he was trying to use his old leg to stand up with. We all ran to help him up and Doctor Moreau gave him his crutches back.

'I'm sorry, I'm sorry,' he kept saying, but Doctor Moreau said that they would try again later. As we took him through to the old family room, Joe was still panting, but I heard him say 'thank you, Victor,' to Papa. Papa raised his eyebrows at him. He looked out at the new snow that was landing on the surface, halfway up the kitchen windows.

'It's still coming down hard,' he said. 'I'm going to work on that sledge.' Then he went outside to the engine shed and let Doctor Moreau and Madame Beaufort help Joe back to bed.

Later, while Madame Beaufort and Doctor Moreau sat talking in the sitting room with big glasses of wine, I read to Joe about a village in a country called *Thailand* where there are so many spiders that the people who live there eat them like bananas.

It's late now and I'm going to bed, but I can still see the yellow light in the engine shed making long, Papa-shaped shadows on the snow in the yard.

~ 2003 ~

DON'T CARE ABOUT MUCH

Laos

JOSEPH WOKE, as he always did, to the sound of tyres and metal. This time they crescendoed and were cut short by a child's crying and a gunshot, so that he jolted up from where he was lying on his side, tensing his neck and shoulders and crying out in pain as his cut, battered body rebelled against the sudden exertion. Reality silenced the dream, and he fell back onto the ground. Like before, there was a hood over his head and his hands were tied behind his back.

It was cool, and rain roared on the tin roof above him, some of it dripping through holes and landing in puddles. The whole of the stone floor was wet. It was dark too, but it felt like the darkness caused by heavy cloud as opposed to the onset of evening. He could have been unconscious for only a few hours, although he wouldn't have been surprised if it had been more considering that he hadn't slept since the five hours on the bus and that he'd taken a gun stock to the temple as a sleeping pill. His throat was dry and swollen from thirst and he wheezed, the pain in his head, ribs and leg making him cough.

Outside, he heard the sound of boots turning in the dirt. Through the weave of the hood he saw a figure behind the stone grill. It stood near the wall, out of the rain, looking at him quietly. Then it tapped its gun slowly against the door three times, made two mocking tuts and turned its back. Now he had his own private guard. He was short and wiry, his face full of sharp bones.

'What time is it?' said Joseph. The guard ignored him.

'Hey, dickhead.'

The guard turned and eyed him lazily, tapped his gun barrel against the door again and tutted. Deep thunder growled in the distance.

Joseph rolled onto his back and shuffled himself up so that he was sitting with his back against the wall, where he began to wander his concentration around his limbs and muscles for a damage report.

His prosthetic was still holding firm to his right stump, despite the fact that the rest of the leg had twisted horribly to the right so that the foot was pointing inwards. He imagined that the men must have noticed it, maybe tried to remove it and given up when the SkinGrip™ did its business.

It had to have taken the bullet first. On his left shin, he could make out a patch of blood where it had been grazed by the ricochet. It wasn't bleeding now, though, but he could feel the bruise on his bone. His head felt cut and swollen and his ribs ached. Maybe two were cracked, one almost certainly broken.

'I suppose there's no point me asking why I'm not dead?' he said.

'You can ask,' replied the guard, raising his voice above the rain. Joseph's eyebrows flickered in surprise, aborting a full lift to avoid the bruise on his head.

'I didn't know your line of work required learning a foreign language.'

'Useful to know what people say,' said the guard. He spoke slowly, carefully pronouncing each word as if they were on a blackboard in front of him. His consonants were clipped, his vowels long. Joseph nodded in his hood.

'True. It's nice to understand people when they're begging for their lives,' said Joseph, his sarcasm tasting uncomfortably hypocritical. 'Nice to understand the final pleas of a child,' he amended.

'You would know,' said the guard, pulling something from his shirt pocket.

Joseph frowned under his hood.

'What?'

A sharp flash of lightning filled the air suddenly, followed shortly by another low rumble nearby. The guard said nothing, moving further back from the rain. He struck a match against the wall and protected it with one hand as he lit a cigarette from his pack. The smoke from his first puff drifted into the room and found its way under Joseph's hood.

'Tell me then,' he said, his nose twitching with envy. 'Why am I still alive?'

The guard turned and looked at him as he took another drag. He rubbed his thumb and finger together for a while, then turned back and blew smoke out into the downpour.

Joseph laughed. 'Money?' he said. 'From whom?'

The guard didn't respond.

'The Embassy?' suggested Joseph.

Embassy, thought Joseph, *Regal, Mayfair, even John Player Special. Anything would do.*

'Good luck,' said Joseph, 'but I doubt the British Embassy has time to trade for a man like me. Least of all with amateur child murderers who live in a shed.'

The guard swung around and made what Joseph presumed was a scowl. Then he flicked his butt through the grill. Joseph followed its arc and saw it land two feet in front of him. His body gave a sudden twitch as if to pounce on it, but he held back for dignity's sake. He watched sadly as its dull, orange embers quickly extinguished themselves on the damp stone.

'It might at least help your cause if I was British,' mumbled Joseph. He looked up from the wet fag end. 'I don't suppose I could have a cigarette?'

The guard laughed and spat through the grill. Another flash of lightning snapped at the air, and thunder chased quickly behind.

'How long?' said Joseph. 'How long before I'm traded?'

The guard released a sudden, girlish giggle. He shrugged.

'I'm not a patient man,' said Joseph. He pushed his fists back against the wall, lifting himself up like he'd done before and sitting on his hands, just as he remembered that they'd taken his knife.

'Nooo noo nooo,' said the guard, shaking his head and still laughing, his back still turned. 'You have long time, Joe. Long time.'

Joseph stopped wriggling and sat up rigid.

'How do you know my name?'

The guard laughed breezily and lit another cigarette.

Joseph wondered whether they had found the passport he kept secreted with his tickets in another compartment within his leg. It was the only piece of identification he carried, and the only way they could have known his name. But even if they had, what were the chances that a Laos bandit knew the derivative of 'Joseph'?

The rain suddenly doubled in strength, the way a shower does when turned from hot to cold. Another flash, another rumble. The thunder had almost caught up.

'You're not asking a ransom for me,' said Joseph. 'It doesn't make sense, I don't believe you.'

The guard shrugged again.

'Don't care,' he said through a long flume of smoke.

'Who are you working for?'

Nothing from the guard. He seemed uncomfortable. The storm was almost on top of them.

'I don't think you even know who you're working for, do you? I think you just do as you're told.'

'Don't care,' snapped the guard again.

'You don't care much about much, do you, amico?'

Just then, two things happened. First, the guard swung around and pointed his gun in the air, furiously jabbering in Lao at Joseph and spitting through the bars of the grill. He fired a shot into the air and, at that exact moment, the second thing happened: a bright, white blade of lightning struck the tip of his barrel and blew him into the air like a fluorescent jack-in-the-box, the deep boom of thunder that followed it swallowing up the sound of gunfire.

Joseph watched with astonishment through the thick weave of his hood, as the guard hurtled up out of sight with a single yelp, then landed some seconds later, ten metres back from the door, in a limp, blackened heap. He squinted, trying to make out some movement, half-expecting the guard to get up and rub his head and then walk back to his post and light a cigarette. But he didn't, he just lay there curled up around his gun, three wisps of smoke rising from his body like steam from a wet dog.

For a moment, nothing happened, just the rain. Then, suddenly appreciating the unexpected change in circumstances, Joseph shuffled across the floor and jammed his prosthetic in one of the stone grills, pushing forwards on it and slowly rotating his stump in its seal. The action gradually released the SkinGrip™'s suction and it began to loosen, finally letting go altogether and falling away. Joseph pushed painfully away from the wall with his other foot and shifted himself back to his sitting position. He then yanked his hands down, feeling something go in his wrist but managing to push them far enough forward so that they cleared the stump of his right leg and were now only behind his left. Summoning all his strength, he then drew his knee up to his chest and strained in agony as he pulled his wrists underneath his foot, falling back, gasping and panting with his hands on his lap.

He tore off his hood and looked at the blue metal limb stuck between the grill on the other side of the room. Rolling onto his side, he crawled across the floor on his elbows towards it and raised himself up against the wall. Twisting his head around and flattening his face against the stone, he opened his mouth and filled it with rainwater and greedily gulped it down, taking two more mouthfuls immediately afterwards. It was warm and tasted how the air smelled.

He pulled out the leg and examined it, removing its boot. One side of the knee had taken the impact of the bullet and shattered, the electronic components blowing inside and the support beneath it twisted and broken. As an emergency protective measure, the artificial intelligence chip's last action before it died had been to lock all motors and pull the ligaments running from them taut so that the leg was straight and rigid. It would probably still take his weight, but neither the knee nor the ankle would bend.

Just then he heard the main door of the building open and two sets of boots marching around the corner. Joseph grabbed the grill and pulled himself up so that he was standing on his injured leg, the right leg of his trousers hanging down empty. He manoeuvred himself into the shadows and raised up the TrueStep, holding it in his hands like a baseball bat.

The sounds of boots squelching in the mud stopped for a second, then quickened as the men saw the guard and ran towards his smoking body. Joseph watched through the grill as they both crouched next to the guard. As one checked for signs of life, the other sprang up, and Joseph pulled away from the door as he ran towards it. The man peered through one of the gaps into the darkness and then snatched a set of keys from his belt, unlocking the padlock outside.

The bandit set one mud-covered boot in the door and, just as he realised that Joseph was standing next to him, felt a blue aluminium foot slam into his throat. He fell noiselessly onto the stone floor, quietly choking and clasping his hands around his neck.

Hearing something, his companion left the guard and ran to the door, where Joseph was waiting. He looped his bound wrists around the bandit's neck and pressed against his windpipe, counting the ten seconds of struggle it took before he fell to the ground and didn't move again. His partner, still gasping on the floor, took another blue foot to the cranium before he too became still.

Joseph dragged the bodies of the men from the doorway, hopping backwards and piling them in the corner. He took one of their guns and slung it around his neck. Then he tore off the right leg of his trousers at the knee and stepped into his battered leg, feeling the seal instantly suck to his flesh. When it was comfortable, he limped outside into the rain and grabbed the blackened body of the guard. His burnt face looked up at him, permanently drawn into a startled frown from the moment he'd been catapulted up like an unwilling firework, and Joseph noticed the top of his cigarette pack still poking out of his shirt. It was a brand sporting an orange pack, now blackened with soot. When he had reunited the guard with his friends, he took out the hot cardboard box and flipped it open, glumly inspecting the seven charred and crumbling sticks inside it before tossing it onto the wet floor, cursing.

Next chance he had, he was definitely buying some cigarettes.

But first, he had to steal a truck.

BARBECUE ON A BOMB

Laos

ASHLEY AND Caterine sit on the bamboo floor and watch Sarat working silently in front of them. It is now evening, dark, and he has built a small fire in a deep metal trough made from the shell casing of a thirty-year-old bomb split in two. 'Barbecue-on-a-bomb' he had said, as he lugged the heavy cylinder in from outside. There were hundreds of them, he had told them, scattered all over the countryside surrounding them, remnants of the war. He had even pointed outside, beyond the ridge where the little girl had been singing, at a gun turret embedded in a ditch, unmoved since, three decades earlier, it flipped from its tank like the lid of a saucepan under the blast of a nearby shell.

The fire has dimmed to charcoal embers, but it is still warm and thin smoke drifts up into the air of the room as Sarat shifts them around. He has chopped up thin strips of red meat — neither Caterine nor Ashley have chosen to ask him which animal it came from — and spread them on the crude grill he has placed across the bomb casing, where they begin to sizzle and fry.

In a deep, battered aluminium frying pan, he throws in what looks like onions and a mixture of beans. On top of them he sprinkles green herbs and chillies he has chopped in a plate by his feet. Stirring them with his fingers, he places them on the side of the grill, where they immediately start to cook and mix their own fragrances with that of the cooking flesh. While this is happening, he checks the bamboo steamer in which he is cooking sticky rice over another small pan of boiling water.

Ashley tries to focus on Sarat as he springs around the fire, crouching on his ankles. He knows that if he looks into the embers he will sleep, so he watches Sarat working, his speed too quick to allow him to drift off. The smells that are filling the room have started to reach his nose and tickle his consciousness, helping to keep him awake.

They are quiet for a while; the rain has stopped and things have begun to chirp outside. Then Sarat speaks.

'Bad dreams.'

Ashley looks up.

'How did you know?' he says.

Sarat smiles as he turns the meat.

'Caterine? Did she tell you?'

Caterine raises her eyebrows, but doesn't look up from the glowing coals. Sarat shakes his head. Then he puts his hands to his mouth and lets out a quiet scream, his face twisted in mock fear. Caterine turns to look at Ashley.

'I didn't need to. You were screaming a lot when I brought you up to the village, not awake, but screaming your lungs out. The villagers were scared, but Sarat said we could stay in here tonight. It's his house; he's building it for him and his wife. They're staying with her mother till it's finished.'

'Thank you,' says Ashley, 'but I don't need to, I have a guest house in Vang Vien paid for. I think.'

Sarat shakes his head.

'Too much rain,' he says. 'Too muddy, I will take you back tomorrow. I have to take some people on the river, if the storm has left.'

Sarat checks the meat and sees that it is cooked. He lifts it from the grill and splits it evenly between three large, thick leaves. On top, he puts three spoonfuls of the onions and beans. Next to that, he places lumps of thick, steaming sticky rice. He passes a leaf each to Caterine and Ashley, taking the final one for himself and crouching back on his ankles to eat.

Ashley looks down at the food. It smells good, but he hasn't stomached anything properly for days and is afraid of covering Sarat's new floor with vomit. Caterine nudges him, chewing and nodding her head encouragingly. He inserts two tentative fingers into the leaf and lifts out a strip of meat, dripping with stock from the beans. He turns it in the light and watches the steam rise from it, before taking a small bite from the end. The moment it touches his tongue, an overpowering surge of flavour floods his mouth and his stomach heaves. But it is a dry heave and the feeling passes, so he starts to chew. The meat is tough, but tasty, like game, and the sauce is rich and warm. He takes another bite, bigger this time, and feels his stomach steadily take in the food.

'When we got you in here, you slept for a while longer,' says Caterine. 'It was fitful, but without any screams. I told Sarat about you, that you had been having nightmares, that you weren't sleeping. He took that very seriously, and told me he used to have nightmares, too.'

Sarat nods, frowning and chewing on a large mouthful of meat and rice. 'Bad dreams,' he says.

'Then I found out his name, and that he runs the canoe trekking company in town. I couldn't really believe it; he told me the story of the Sleeping Cave, pretty much word for word, just as my friend had done.'

Ashley finishes his mouthful and swallowes with pain.

'Well,' he says, 'like you say, you bump into people, don't you?'

Sarat puts down his leaf and wipes his mouth. He lookes at Ashley inquisitively.

'What you dream, Ashley?'

'Caterine didn't tell you?' says Ashley, managing to swallow another mouthful. Sarat shakes his head.

When Ashley has finished telling Sarat about his dreams, every last bit of them, he has finished his meal. He places the leaf in front of him and sits back with his hands wrapped around his knees, looking into the dying light of the coals in the barbecue bomb. He has been talking for only four or five minutes, but he feels drained and dizzy. The act of talking might not have been enough to cause this, but the subject matter certainly has. Talking about it has been no catharsis, and his fear was ever more present. His fever feels worse too, and he shivers and winces as he stares into the fire.

Sarat has not said anything yet.

Ashley looks up at him. He is still crouched back on his ankles, his knees level with his shoulders and his hands wrapped around them, staring into the embers.

'Well,' says Ashley. 'What do you think?'

Sarat raises his eyebrows.

'What *you* think?' he replies.

'I think…' says Ashley. He shakes his head once. 'I don't know what to think any more.'

Sarat nods grimly and picks some rice from his bowl.

Later, when it is dark and Sarat has cleared away the bomb and returned to his wife, Ashley lies on the bed, his blanket wrapped around him and Caterine sitting next to him.

'What are you thinking?' she says.

'I don't know what to think any more,' says Ashley. 'I'm sick of feeling like this. Sick of not wanting to go to sleep. I'm tired.'

'I know, you should get some sleep.'

She stands up from the bed and pauses.

'Do you…do you want me to stay with you?'

Ashley doesn't answer.

'Only there's a bed in the other room…makes no difference to me.'

Ashley is still silent.

'I'll go there, shall I…'

'I'd like you to stay,' says Ashley at last. Caterine nods and slowly returns to the bed. It squeaks as she lies down next to him.

'You know what you said when I met you in Chiang Mai?' says Ashley as he gives her some of the blanket.

'Which bit?'

'About the reason you were here.'

'Oh…'

'What is it? The reason I mean?'

'How about I tell you another time,' she says. 'It's a long story…Ash? Ashley? Are you asleep?'

ABSOLUTELY, WITHOUT QUESTION, THE FIRST TIME

Laos

THERE HAD only been twenty feet at most between the open door of Joseph's cell — now a temporary tomb for his three assailants, whose disappearances were sure to bring more of their colleagues outside soon — and the truck in which he'd been kidnapped. It took him five minutes to cover the distance.

It would have been an easy hobble, were it not for his prosthetic becoming submerged in mud halfway up its buckled shin with every step. It reminded him of those first agonising steps he had taken on his first false leg, that crude wooden stump cobbled together in a farmer's shed. It was a vulnerable journey, his disability making him feel more like a sitting duck than it had ever done before. If any of the half-wits inside had decided to take that opportunity to find out where their friends had disappeared to, they would have had time to stand and watch Joseph struggling for a bit, maybe smoke a cigarette, sigh, stroll back to get their rifle and then blow him clean out of the mud before he had had a chance to even show them the business end of his own stolen gun.

Nobody had come out, though, and he had, eventually, reached the door (which was open) behind which there was the ignition (keys still inserted), which would start the engine, which would drive the wheels that would get him the hell out of the jungle and, somehow, on the road to Luang Prabang.

But plans had changed.

Just as his hand had reached the handle, he had heard a noise. Three tiny, descending sobs. He froze momentarily, rain streaming down his face, imagining that it was just the mating call of some small exotic bird or gigantic, randy bug. They had killed her. He had heard them shoot the child.

But there was the noise again. *Sob-weeee…sob-waaaaa…sob-woooo.* It was definitely human — the girl was still alive.

A major part of Joseph's collective consciousness, the part that was relieved just to have made it across the mud; the part with bruises and broken bones; the part that pulled triggers and tightened ropes around jugulars; the part that he thought was all that had been left after he had watched his wife die in the burning wreck of his Mercedes…that part wanted out. It was prepared to cover its ears and shut its eyes and la-la-la-la-la, just get into the truck and fuck off.

But some trembling bud of emotion overruled it, and he unhinged his fingers from their grip on the door handle, turned and faced the direction of the noise. It was coming from behind the building. Joseph growled and lumbered back across the mud.

When he had passed the generator, he saw a thin ventilation gap in the wall just above his head. Joseph balanced his real leg on a rock and peered through it into an empty room, lit only by a dim bulb that crackled and glowed under the meagre current. The girl was huddled in the corner, hugging her shins and nestling her kneecaps in the sockets of her eyes.

'Hey,' he whispered.

The girl unplugged her knees and looked up. She was tired, confused and scared. She missed her father, missed her mother. She pulled back even further into the corner and made a wary noise.

'Shh,' said Joseph. 'It's all right, we're going to…'

There was the sound of coughing from the shack. Joseph froze and prepared himself, but there was nothing more.

'It's all right,' he repeated. 'We're going to leave now. Wait there.'

He looked around the room. The girl was in the corner

opposite the door, which must have led into the main room of the building, but there was also another door that led into the generator room.

'Shh,' he said again, and dropped from the rock.

The rain was lighter now, but the mud was still thick on the ground. It was full of litter, bags and empty beer bottles poking through the surface like disinterred bones. Joseph used the wall to steady himself as he moved back to the generator room. It was walled by wooden slats like a coal shed, and the gate to it was unlocked. He let himself inside.

The generator took up most of the room. It was an ancient petrol engine mounted on the ground, a shuddering pile of rusted metal, oil and duct tape threaded to the wall by dangerous-looking cables and wires. The fact that it worked at all was a wonder. On a rotten wooden shelf by the window sat an ashtray and a box of matches. Joseph lurched towards the ashtray. Empty. He tossed it back on the shelf in dismay and looked down at the ground. By his feet was a canister with a spout. He picked it up and sniffed it: petrol.

Suddenly there were noises outside and Joseph ducked down behind the engine, stuffing a fist in his mouth as the pressure on his damaged shin suddenly doubled. He watched through the slats as three of the men ambled across the mud from the front of the building to the trucks. Two of them got into the second vehicle, but the other made for the first. *No*, thought Joseph. He saw the man open the driver's door and step inside. His one chance of escape. In the time it had taken him to return across the mud to the girl, he could have been in that vehicle and away down the road. Now he would be trapped in a generator room, just waiting for the moment when one of the others noticed his room was full of corpses.

This was a fine time to grow a set of morals.

Joseph had never kidded himself about the fact that what he did for a living was anything less than morally corrupt. Likewise, he had never suppressed the knowledge that the reason he did it was because of a decision he had made on a snow-covered ledge twenty years ago. In the space of sixty seconds, one single conversation less than twenty words long had turned his world upside down. It had burst something deep within him, a reservoir of hope that just flooded away.

He had been driving, smiling, sucking in one last breath of courage before he told her, explained to her about what he did, what the Mafia had made him do and about how it was all going to change. They were going to start again, live somewhere else, perhaps in a different country where they could raise their child away from the danger he had brought close to their family. But Anita had got there first. Before he had a chance to begin, out of nowhere she had broken the silence and admitted her own guilty secret. Five deadly words.

'The child is not yours.'

She had bowed her head. Silence, just the whistle of the Mercedes' engine as the words settled in Joseph's mind. And then, a snowy mountain road covered with blue skies and fresh hope had suddenly become flooded with rage. Jealousy had poured from him in spiteful, pointed curses, his fists slamming the wheel as Anita bowed her head and cried. Then jealousy had met another car coming towards them around a steep, tight bend and everything was the sound of tyres and metal.

The two cars had swerved to avoid each other, their Mercedes veering first away from the cliff edge and then towards it, away from the ditch on their right. The car had spun, then hit something that tore through its side and smashed into Joseph's leg, sending him flying, broken through the freezing air.

Waking from momentary unconsciousness, Joseph had opened his eyes, clutched his mangled leg and looked down upon his burning car from the ledge onto which he had been thrown. The other car had sped off in panic, disappearing away down the mountain road, but he could see Annie inside the burning wreck, hammering the windows and clawing at the mangled door. His last memory of the event was an explosion, and as he slipped back into icy unconsciousness, he prayed for oblivion.

But his prayer was not answered. He had been found, taken in, nursed in a child's room. For days and weeks, he had woken to pain and fever. The two memories of his wife's admission and sudden death had orbited around each other as he lay nauseous in a strange bed. They had spun faster and faster, compressing into a single point of pain that he had carried with him ever since. Aside from his leg, he had recovered physically. But the pain had eaten him up, destroying his morals, one by one.

They weren't meant to grow back, his morals. He didn't want them to grow back — not just because they were now costing him his escape plan, but because if they came back, then they were sure to bring a whole lot else with them; memories that would not have aged well.

Joseph watched through the slats as the man in his truck rummaged around in the glove compartment for something. Then he closed his eyes with relief as the man left the cab and slammed the door with a wallet in his hand. He heard the other truck's passenger door open and shut, and the three men skidded off down the road.

That left six.

After he was certain nobody else was coming outside, Joseph stood up slowly and made his way round to the other door. It was solid wood, bolted and padlocked. He picked up a long metal pipe standing in the corner and inserted it into the lock's shackle, twisting it in an attempt to break it off. But the bar was too weak and it snapped in his hands, causing a clang, a rattle of the door and a whimper from within the room. Joseph cursed and shut his eyes tightly, trying to deaden the noise with his own blindness.

Then he picked up a screwdriver lying on the shelf and went to work on the door hinges, but they were rusted, stuck fast in the thick wood and couldn't be shifted. Seeing no other way of opening the door, Joseph stepped back and aimed his gun at the lock. The noise would alert the men, but if he was quick he could grab the girl and gun them down before they had a chance to fire. If he was quick.

He prepared to fire. It had to break on the first go, he couldn't afford for there to be any more than one bang before he was inside. He angled the barrel so that the ricochet would be away from him. He felt the trigger under his finger, but just as he was about to squeeze he noticed something hanging from the doorframe. A set of keys. He closed his eyes and swallowed, lowered his gun and gently lifted them down. The fifth one he tried opened the lock and he replaced them on their hook with one shaking hand.

Once inside, he shushed the trembling child and after several attempts managed to convince her to leave her corner and follow him. She took his hand again and let him lead her outside, where he whispered something to her. Not knowing what else to do, she stood quietly shivering in the rain and watched Joseph as he rummaged around in the mud and drew out an empty bottle. He filled this with petrol from the canister and stuffed a rag from his pocket down its neck.

Then he picked up the matchbox and carried it and the bottle very slowly around the side of the building, where he took out a match, lit the rag and threw the bottle through the window.

Driving from the exploding building was not easy, given the state of Joseph's remaining leg. Even when he was clear of the six screaming men — on fire and shooting their guns wildly at the truck as it swerved away — pressing the accelerator with his prosthetic foot while pumping the clutch with his left to negotiate the muddy road was agonising. The little girl looked up at him with alarm as he grimaced and yelled with every gear change.

When he was sure they were free, he slowed down to a more

comfortable speed. They were still within the jungle, on a narrow dirt track covered by trees. The rain collected and then poured from their canopies in concentrated bucket loads, causing warm, wet explosions in the mud and on the truck's roof and blowing refreshing spray through the open window and onto Joseph's face. They had been driving for about ten minutes and there had been no turn-offs or directional decisions to make, just the muddy road going steadily downhill. A heavy mist obscured his view through the foliage, over the ledge to his right — for all he knew, it could have been a sheer drop. He looked down at the girl, who was still glaring up at him doubtfully.

'It's OK now,' he said. 'Bad men gone. We're safe.'

The girl said something squeakily at him that sounded like distrust. She stuck out her bottom lip at him as if he had just denied her a puppy.

'What? What's wrong?' said Joseph, looking between her and the road. 'I mean apart from the obvious.'

She opened her mouth again and made another sound, kneeling up and hitting the dashboard with her palms. Then she sang some notes, or said something else; Joseph couldn't work out which.

'You must be thirsty,' he said. 'I know I am.'

He rummaged around in the driver's door pocket but found nothing. Then he looked on the floor by the girl's feet, where a half-drunk bottle of water lay in the dirt. He reached down across the girl, causing her to squeal and him to shush, and picked it up, taking a swig himself to check what it was before handing the open bottle to her. He swilled the liquid around in his mouth. It was warm and tasted of plastic, but just what his throat and tongue had been crying out for since the crash. He swallowed and watched the girl grip the bottle with both hands and gulp down great mouthfuls of it. When she was done, she made more sounds, less resentful ones this time, and shook the remaining water around so that it splashed from the top. Joseph snatched it from her and finished off the dregs, then shoved it back in her open hands before she could register it had gone.

With his thirst eased, Joseph wondered what else the truck could offer him. He looked down at the glove compartment, upon which the girl was beating the empty bottle.

'Excuse me,' he said, as he leaned over her and pulled the handle. She yelled and bashed the bottle on his arm instead while he felt around inside, glancing up occasionally at the track. He found a bar of something sticky and opened it, taking a bite, which he immediately spat through the open window. He handed it to the girl, who dropped the bottle and began sucking it, and then he pulled everything out of the compartment and onto the floor and the seat between them. There were maps, wrappers, empty drinks cans, a broken watch, three wires, washers and screws, a bent tin of oil, a book with the cover ripped off and various scraps of paper. There was also a box of matches, and everything was covered in tantalising specks of tobacco. But there were no cigarettes. Joseph growled.

Just as he was stretching his hand down desperately to feel for the possibility of a discarded packet beneath the seat, something on the seat caught his eye. It was a piece of paper with a black-and-white photograph poking out from underneath another. He pulled it out. The photograph was of himself, grainy but recognisable, walking from a building he couldn't place and wearing a suit he couldn't make out. His beard was short, which meant that the photograph was recent, taken in the last three months. Joseph stared at it. He was closing his jacket with one hand and looking across his shoulder to the left. The fact that he was level with the camera and the proximity of other people in the picture meant that whoever took it could only have been twenty yards from him at most. He cursed himself for missing it.

Suddenly the surroundings fell into place. He was leaving his bank at Marble Arch, and the briefcase in his other hand — he never usually carried one — told him it was when he had had that meeting about his mortgage. A complete waste of time, Joseph had decided upon a vat of Oxy-10 in which to drown the acne-faced trainee spod he had been allocated. It was less than seven weeks ago, four days after his clumsy job in Dollis Hill.

Underneath the picture there were some words scrawled in Lao, presumably about himself. It was no accident that he had been found by the bandits after the bus had crashed. Somebody knew he was going to Luang Prabang and wanted him to be captured. He folded the paper and stuffed it in his pocket.

They drove for another twenty minutes, during which time the girl fell asleep. The track gradually began to open out and become steeper, and Joseph realised that they were cutting naturally down into the valley to their right. Eventually they came to a T-junction with another road with a better surface, but still only single track. Looking at the sun, he quickly calculated that it ran north to south, so he turned left – north – in what he hoped was the direction to Luang Prabang. After a short while, Joseph spotted something ahead by the side of the road. It was a shack, with a sign up next to it unmistakably advertising coffee, food and — most importantly — cigarettes. They needed more water, some sustenance, and he wanted nicotine. Perhaps the owner could show him how to get to Luang Prabang.

Joseph prepared to pull over, but as he turned into the left of the road, he suddenly saw another truck approaching them from the other direction. He stared at it as it drew closer. It was army green and three familiar figures sat in its front seat — the other truck returning from whatever mid-afternoon errand bandits had to do in Laos. He looked to his left as he slowed at the shack. It sailed by almost in slow motion, and he saw with dismay that a man was leaning in its doorway, a cigarette tucked between his lips, smoke curling up from its tip like velvet. He nodded at Joseph and smiled. Then he looked out of the other window as they met the other truck coming towards them, also in slow motion, three startled faces clocking him as they passed.

Joseph slammed down his TrueStep on the accelerator and pulled out onto the road again. He looked in his rear-view mirror at the truck, which had screamed to a halt and stalled. It became smaller and smaller in the mirror, but before it disappeared he saw it turn, skid away from the shack and speed after them. The road was long, straight and flat, and Joseph pumped through the gears until they were at what had to be the truck's top speed. The engine roared and rain lashed in through the open window and streamed back across the windscreen like tears, impervious to the frantic wipers. He glanced down at the girl, still curled up asleep with her arms around the empty plastic bottle.

The other truck was gaining on him and there was no sign of any turn-off or main road approaching. The men had guns and so did he, but driving was difficult enough without firing as well. They, however, had two free sets of hands and soon they would be upon him. Joseph took one final look in the mirror and made a decision. He pulled on the handbrake and turned full lock right, spinning the truck around and stopping to face his pursuers.

At this stage, if he hadn't been so preoccupied, Joseph might have appreciated his surroundings. The air was full of warm, falling water, and everything around them, other than the muddy road, was vibrant green. About thirty metres down the slope to what was now their left, a wild river frothed and flowed and drank up the rain thirstily. Its colour was rich and deep, at the point where brown met red, as if some secret jungle chocolate factory had suddenly had to jettison its stock. The word 'lush' was invented exclusively for places like this. But Joseph was busy.

'Sorry,' he said to the little girl, and pushed her out of the door.

She squealed and looked up from where she had woken on the muddy roadside. The truck's wheels span noisily in the dirt and it hurtled back up the road they had just come.

Joseph faced down the approaching truck, staring straight ahead, watching three pairs of eyes widen as the two trucks approached each other. There was only one rule to the game of chicken: do not leave the road. Joseph did not break it. The other truck did, to its cost.

He stopped and reversed back to the tree. He was surprised they had given in so early, even more surprised that none of their bullets had hit him. In all honesty, he hadn't expected to come out of that as well as he had.

He got out of the truck and lumbered towards the other one, bent and steaming in the jungle. He opened the door and looked inside. Only two were left, the third having departed the truck through the windscreen and who now lay broken around a tree. One of the two who were still in the cab was dead, his gun having fired in the impact and put a bullet or two through his forehead. The other was semi-conscious, slumped and bloody against the broken steering wheel. Joseph pulled him back by his hair.

'Who do you work for?' he bellowed in the driver's ear, who half-opened his eyes and groaned.

'Tell me who paid you to find me!' said Joseph. He pulled the photograph from his pocket with his other hand and pushed it into the man's face.

'Who gave you this?' he shouted, shaking the man's head in his fist. 'Who the fuck gave you this?'

The man groaned again and closed his eyes. Joseph put back the photograph before it became too wet. He pulled up his gun and held it to the driver's temple.

'Tell me or I'll kill you. KILL YOU, UNDERSTAND?'

The man shook his head and gasped, mumbling something.

'WHAT? WHAT DID YOU SAY?' said Joseph furiously above the rain.

The driver mumbled something again. Then his eyes shot open and he croaked, his head relaxing in Joseph's grip, his hands falling down by his side.

Joseph muttered a curse and released his grip on the dead driver's hair. Just as he was about to slam the door on him, he spied a packet in his shirt pocket. He snatched it and opened it up. All fine and healthy cigarettes, a handy lighter nestled in there too. He shoved one hungrily between his lips and walked back to the truck, shielding it from the rain and flicking his thumb against the flint as he walked back to the truck. But just as the lighter threw up a tiny bulb of flame, he heard a noise.

Sob-weeeee….Sob-waaaa…Sob-wooooo.

He looked up and saw the girl. She was standing by the roadside, alone, tired and frightened, crying hopelessly in the rain. Her dress was drenched, water was pouring down her face and drowning her tears, and she was hugging the empty water bottle as if it were a teddy bear. Joseph, feeling an instinct he had never felt before, limped as quickly as he could across the road, fell to his good knee and put his arms around her. She gripped his T-shirt with her tiny hands. While she bawled into his shoulder, he shushed and stroked the back of her head and kissed her scalp as the cigarettes he had dropped behind him slowly disintegrated in the mud.

This was definitely, absolutely, without question, the first time Joseph had ever hugged a child.

REALITY FROM FANTASY

Laos

ASHLEY WAKES uncomfortably, but not to the sound of screams. The air in the room is sodden and hot, every part of him is wet with perspiration and he wonders how long he has been steaming. He opens his eyes and waits for the room to arrange itself sensibly. It is light, and the rain has stopped, but the air outside still seems tense and edgy, as if trembling on the brink of another storm. Caterine is standing by the window, her hair still ruffled by sleep. Her silhouette reminds Ashley of when he first saw her, weeks ago now, on the train.

'Good morning,' she says.

Ashley peels his tongue from the roof of his mouth and makes a noise.

'How are you feeling?'

'Shite,' says Ashley, shivering once. His fever is still high, his back aches and his eyes are stinging in the air, dry like pebbles. But he feels different, more rested, and his mind no longer feels like it's squashed in a vice. He can focus; he can remember things without feeling dizzy. He remembers what he dreamed last night.

'At least I slept,' he says, getting painfully up on one elbow.

'I didn't hear any screams,' says Caterine.

'Don't worry, there were plenty of dreams,' says Ashley, but his mouth suddenly flickers. 'Not just of her, though…'

Caterine opens her mouth, but at that moment Sarat hops in from the road, a bunch of squat bananas in his hand.

'Morning morning,' he says. His cheerful mood makes Ashley wince. 'Banana?' he says, offering one to Caterine, who takes it.

'Ashley, do you want a banana, my friend?' Sarat holds one out to him like a fat, yellow thumb. He watches Caterine peel hers slowly, some of the ripe pulp bursting through the skin. He shakes his head and sits up, holding onto the mattress with his hands and looking down at his knees.

'OK,' says Sarat, breaking one off for himself. 'The storm has gone. Probably. I think.' He gives the sky a token inspection through the window and bites into the banana.

'And the roads are dry, we can go back to town now.'

The road back to Vang Vien is not as dry as Sarat suggested. It's a dirt track, which has overnight been churned up into two feet of muddy trench, and his pick-up truck struggles and slides along it like a dog wiping its bottom on the carpet. Ashley and Caterine sit opposite each other on benches in the back, bracing themselves against anything with a grip as they're jostled around. Ashley tries to focus on the floor, breathing deeply to stave off the nausea brought on by the truck's movement. He is aware that Caterine is watching him attentively, and now and again he looks up at her and she smiles with one side of her mouth. On anyone else, it would be a smile of helpless sympathy, one that says 'I want to help you but I can't. How frustrating for us both'. But there is a fascination in her eyes, a kind of distracted, scientific curiosity mixed with something sexual that kills any pity in her face. It makes Ashley feel like he is being encouraged, dissected and molested all at once. Each time he wants to smile back, but only manages to blink his eyes. He hopes it doesn't make him seem dismissive.

A full night's sleep, although still laden with dreams, has lifted Ashley's fatigue to the point where it is no longer chronic. He can think, and his mind has already started to shuffle through facts as if they were the contents of an exploded filing cabinet.

He tries to do a simple sort, reality from fantasy. He knows he is ill, he feels like he has been ill, although he cannot pinpoint when it started. He scans back over his memories and tries to remember a time when he felt normal. The past few weeks are dead, and he can't remember a thing apart from buses, strange sounds and worried faces. Chiang Mai: there was nothing normal about that, although he doesn't remember having a fever either. The train to Bangkok: again, nothing normal there. He thinks back to Bangkok itself, and further back to the islands, but nothing makes sense from back then, memories are disjointed, chained together, the gaps between them filled in with suppositions and fictitious events. Even their subject matter, their main character, him, seems like a made-up entity. A snapshot, a frozen image like the birthday-card dreams from his childhood. A made-up memory: is this what he's taking back home?

Home. The thought suddenly fills him with a dreadful emptiness. To think back that far seems like recalling a time he never really lived in. Shoes he never walked in.

Ashley has left the building.

Sorting through fantasy and reality is not working. His nightmares seem more vivid, more tangible than the life through which he has walked. Witches, caves, curses and the lecherous demon spirit of a tortured girl-child: ridiculous, but the fear is more real than anything remembered from his waking life. He thinks about Sarat's story, and what he had told them about his own struggle with nightmares. After his sacrifice outside the cave, the dreams had faded, he had told them. Not at first, but after a few weeks they had given in and fallen away. Since then he had only taken his treks into the higher caverns of the Sleeping Cave, never down to the deeper caves. Ashley holds his head and shakes it, just as the truck pulls onto a smoother road.

'We're here,' says Caterine, as the truck's brakes squeal and the engine splutters out. Ashley looks up and recognises the main street of Vang Vien: quiet, the usual cluster of dreadlocked, baggy-trousered travellers mooching about like apes in a pit.

'Sarat has to take a kayaking party out, so he's going to brief them and give them their kit, then he's going to take us to a doctor. OK?'

Ashley nods and looks out of the canvas awning at the open-fronted shop outside which the truck has stopped. It is built around a large, covered area filled with tables and chairs, with a bar in the corner. Along one side are propped seven or eight single-seat fibreglass canoes, yellow and blue, and next to them their oars and life jackets. At the front, above the entrance, is a sign that says 'ST's Kayak School', and below it is a large board covered with pictures of Sarat with previous treks: happy, tanned, western faces giving thumbs up and smiles. Sarat appears at the back of the truck and opens the hatch.

'Stretch legs, I'll be twenty minutes, then we go to the doctor.'

He helps Caterine out and Ashley jumps after her, his knees buckling as he hits the ground. Sarat grabs his arm.

'Sarat,' says Ashley, 'are you going to the Sleeping Cave today?'

'Yes,' Sarat nods slowly, still gripping Ashley's arm.

'Then I want to come with you. I need to see it.'

'Don't be silly,' says Caterine.

Sarat's nod turns into a slow shake and he frowns.

'No Ashley, I don't think so, not today. I'll take you another time.'

'We'll see you in twenty minutes,' says Caterine. 'Come on, Ash, let's go and get some tea.'

Sarat turns to go, but Ashley grabs him by the shoulder.

'Sarat, I need to come with you.'

'Ashley, you cannot. I cannot. You are too ill; please, you must wait. When you are better, then I'll take you.'

Sarat smiles, looks at Caterine and walks into his shop and starts briefing the five kayak students who are waiting for him. Ashley watches him leave, feeling cold and worn. He feels Caterine's hand on his arm, but he pulls away and goes to look at the notice board. Next to the smiley pictures there is pinned an open brochure with a map of the route Sarat takes on his tour, the Sleeping Cave marked by a large black dot at the end of a yellow, broken line on the river.

When Sarat returns, his five students are kitting themselves out in jackets and practising their oar strokes. He opens the tailgate to the truck and lets Ashley and Caterine climb into the back, then drives them to the end of the strip and up a small track to where he says there is a doctor. They get out themselves and then he drives away, leaving them next to a small door in a white, two-storey building at the end of the track.

'Sarat said it was the third one down,' says Caterine, inspecting the set of buzzers. 'Ash? Where are you going?'

Ashley is halfway up the track, trudging back to the main street. Caterine darts after him.

'What are you doing?'

'I'm going to the cave,' says Ashley. 'You don't have to come with me.'

'You're not going to the cave, you're coming to the doctor.'

'I'm going to the cave.'

'Ash…'

Ashley stops and turns.

'Listen to me. You don't seem to understand. Every time I close my eyes, every time I sleep, a horrific, rope-lipped dog bitch terrorises me and tries to get me to fuck it, and I'm not sure how much longer I can resist. Did you hear me just say that? I heard me just say that, and I still don't believe it. If I'd heard myself say that a month ago, I would have punched myself, but then I can't remember what I was a month ago, I can't remember who I was. I've lost myself.'

Caterine shakes her head and closes her eyes.

'You're ill,' she says, 'you have a fever, your dreams are a product of that. Succubus is just a term for something that people didn't understand before now. Come to the doctor, maybe he'll have something you can take.'

'You don't understand. I wasn't ill when they started; I was fine when I met you on the train. Something has happened to me, and whatever it is it seems inextricably linked with a cave. I don't have anything else to believe in, don't you see? I have to go to that cave, I have to see what's in there, I have to see what I feel when I'm inside it. You can call it facing up to my fears if you like. I call it lunacy. But it's the only thing I can think of doing, and I don't think any pills are going to clear up what's in here.'

Ashley taps his temple.

'But you're sick, Ash.'

'I've felt worse, believe me, much worse, usually when I'm asleep.'

Ashley quickens his pace and turns the corner into the main street.

'Even if you wanted to,' says Caterine, 'Sarat won't let you have a kayak. He's probably gone by now anyway.'

'There are other ways of getting there,' says Ashley. 'You can stay here or come with me, it's up to you. Either way, I'm going.'

'This is ridiculous,' says Caterine as they reach the river. Ashley drops his tyre next to the water's edge.

'I told you, you don't have to come,' he says, kicking it in.

'How do you know where the cave is anyway?'

'I looked on the map, it's about two miles past the bathing area we're supposed to stop at. Probably at about the point when the storm started and you saved me. Thanks again, by the way.'

'But Sarat will catch up, he'll stop you, he won't let you go in there in your state.'

'No he won't, he starts about a mile upstream.'

'But he's in a kayak, we're in tyres.'

'Then we'd better be quick,' says Ashley, dropping back into the black ring with a splash and kicking off into the water.

'Ash!'

Caterine throws in her tyre and jumps in behind him, paddling out with her hands.

'You can't do this! You'll kill yourself!'

'I *am* doing it and I don't care.'

Ashley feels energy for the first time in a long time. It is a nervous energy, dirty and thin, but it feels like life coming back to him, raw and unfettered. He tries not to think about the fact that he's on an inner tube, heading downstream for a deep cave in which a demon — in which he doesn't fully believe — is waiting for him. Whatever he's doing, it feels right.

For a while they float peacefully, spinning gently in the current without a word. They pass the cliffs, and the point at which Ashley guesses he fell asleep the day before, but suddenly they hear a huge crack above them that echoes out across the valley. It creates a vacuum of sound, a long silence during which they freeze and stare at each other.

Then another sound, quieter, a rustling at first, then a hiss, and finally a roar, as ten million gallons of rainwater fall on top of them, drenching them and hammering into the river.

'Brilliant,' shouts Caterine through the rain. 'Now will you stop?'

Up ahead on his left, Ashley sees the bathing area, a small stretch of bank from which a crowd of young, half-dressed village women are clambering out of the water to rescue their discarded clothes from the rain. A small sign hangs from a post about three metres into the river — a black ring circling an arrow, dictating the point at which those bearing tyres should exit.

'Last chance to bail out,' says Ashley calmly.

Caterine shakes her head.

'Fucker,' she says, blowing water from the tip of her nose.

They pass the sign and continue down the river, the current immediately feeling stronger and their pace quickening. The even ripples on the surface soon turn into tight folds and eddies, short strips of fast water that drag in the tyres and spit them forwards like darts from a blowpipe. The rain is even stronger now, rattling on Ashley's already throbbing scalp and blinding his red eyes. Behind him, Caterine makes noises that oscillate between worry and anger, until she settles on a mid-pitched growl — aimed directly at the back of Ashley's head — that does the job of both.

Above the din of water, Caterine's agitation and the thudding of blood in his brain, Ashley tries to concentrate on the bank, cross-referencing its shape with that on the map at Sarat's shop. Having just passed the landmark of the bathing area, he guesses that the steep northward bend they are now on should soon fall down into a near vertical southward drop. This should then flatten out into a straight westerly for a mile or so, before curling northwards again. Then they should reach an opening to the Sleeping Cave. They reach the apex of the bend and, shivering, Ashley peers through the wall of water. A few hundred metres ahead, he spots the tip of the southward turn and nods to himself.

There is nothing left to do but float. Another round of thunder roars about them and echoes from the cliff faces towering to their right. Ashley instinctively looks up, shielding his eyes from the rain and taking in a short gasp of air as he sees the three shoulders of rock brooding above him. Although he remembers them from the previous day, they seem different. He tries to put his finger on the reasons why, but there is nothing there to touch. Even through the cloud falling around him, they seem more detailed, more intricate, more focused and he realises that each face is different from the next. The first is tall, grey slate, slippery and skewered with arrow-like trees; the second is a strip of rust, cratered with gigantic finger-shaped holes as if a rock-climbing giant had once scaled it; and the third is flat, diagonal and black, with a jagged brown triangle down its middle like wallpaper torn from a fire-scorched wall.

Ashley watches them with marvel as they scroll past him. He feels a dazed calm come over him and suddenly realises the reason why they look different: he is not in the picture. The difference between his image of the cliffs now and the recollection of them yesterday is that he, Ashley, is not physically there, bobbing around in a tyre in the corner as if his memory was a camera hovering constantly behind his right shoulder. He was exhausted yesterday, of course. Ashley winces. But all of his memories are like this, at least those which make any sense to him now. He remembers the train to Chiang Mai, meeting Mehdi, meeting Caterine, Bangkok, the islands, catching the plane from London, his leaving party, sitting at his desk at work, drinking in bars, moving house, studying, playing football, snowboarding, having sex. He is always there in the picture. Either his face or body in full frame, or the back of his head, the curve of his grin, his facial expressions in reaction to events, as opposed to the events themselves. It is a black spot, horrible and irritating, like a tall person sitting in front of you in the cinema. He wants to brush himself out of the way.

He tries some closer memories: waking up this morning, eating with Sarat and Caterine the night before, watching the little girl sing in the torrential rain. Not a trace. He has disappeared from view, and memory at once seems fuller and more alive as if he has swapped from fish-eye to wide angle. He looks back up at the mountains and smiles.

Suddenly, behind him, Caterine's noise becomes a series of yelps and sentences. He's sure one of the words is 'Sarat', two are definitely 'look', several are derived randomly from 'fuck', and many more are his name, followed closely by 'wanker'. He turns around. Behind Caterine's wet grimace he sees some small blue and yellow shapes on the water. It is Sarat's kayak party paddling down the river towards them at speed.

For a moment they lose sight of them and Ashley realises that he and Caterine have turned onto the long westward stretch of the river, but very soon Sarat reappears at the bend, closer, his five students behind him. Ashley tries to make them out. At the back are three girls close to each other, then another girl following behind a man who is directly behind Sarat. The three girls are falling behind, and Sarat doubles back swiftly, powering upstream until he is behind them, shouting words of encouragement at them and showing them his stroke in the air. The girls are laughing uncontrollably, but seem to be on that edge of hysteria that is about to produce tears. Two of them are trying to row towards the opposite bank. Sarat weaves around them, trying to herd them together like sheep, but panic is beginning to set in.

Ashley's tyre is beginning to lose control and whirl awkwardly in the mess of wild currents. Each time the kayak party spins into view, he turns his attention to the front two kayaks, which are almost upon them. There is something familiar about them, something uncomfortable. During one spin, the man in front looks up and spots Ashley. By the time he comes into view again, his face has developed a phosphorescent grin and his rowing has quickened. Thunder rumbles above and he shouts something. Ashley's eyes widen in disbelief. With every turn of his tyre, he locks his sight on the figure approaching him through the sheet of rain, flicking his head around with every rotation like a ballerina in mid pirouette. As the kayak draws up, Ashley gawps.

'Ashley!' says the grin. 'What the fuck, man! Get out of here, no way! Fuck! Dani, baby, look who it is! Fuck!'

Ashley manages to steady his spin, reeling back in his tyre with horror.

'Mehdi,' he stammers, 'what the hell are you…'

'What? I can't hear you, dude! This rain, huh! Fucking crazy!'

Mehdi lets out a long, piercing whoop and thrusts his paddles deep into the water. Daniella follows behind him, smirking, her long, tanned arms driving her past Ashley.

You just fucking bump into people.

Suddenly, there is a cry and a splash behind. One of the three girls has capsized and is being dragged across the river by a cross-current. Ashley watches Sarat paddle after her, but her empty kayak hurtles on towards Ashley and Caterine. Ashley looks quickly downstream, where Mehdi and Daniella are becoming smaller and smaller, then back at the stray canoe as it finds its way towards him. Just then, Caterine lets out a yell of her own as she hits a strong current that whisks her past Ashley and pushes her into an uncontrollable spin. Sarat is way upstream now, trying to drag the girl from the water, and Ashley seizes his chance. He raises himself up in his tyre and pounces on the kayak as it passes, landing with a crack on his ribcage and almost capsizing it again. He cries out in pain, but manages to lift one wet leg into the fuselage and then drags himself inside, grabbing the oar — attached to the boat by a string — from the water.

Ashley looks ahead, trying to find Caterine. He scans the frothy water from bank to bank, rainwater dripping from his eyelids and dribbling over his lips. He spits it away and spots a tyre, empty, being tossed around by the river, just as he hears two screams simultaneously from behind and ahead. Looking back, he sees another of the girls in the water, her kayak having abandoned her and taking its chances alone like Ashley's. He looks ahead again and sees the source of the other scream: Caterine, bobbing up and down in the brown water, her arms waving desperately above her head. Ashley grips his oar and begins to paddle.

For a few minutes Caterine is tossed randomly between the river's banks. Ashley comes close to reaching her several times, but just as he is about to reach her she disappears below the water and resurfaces seconds later in a different, unexpected place. Ashley pushes himself faster, realising that he is racing the will of a strong undercurrent that could drag Caterine down to her death.

At last he pulls up close to her and plunges in his hand before she goes under, grabbing her wrist and hauling her over the bow. She gasps for air and splutters and he pulls her aboard, trying to steady the overburdened boat as she struggles to get her limbs aboard. For a few moments Ashley lets the river decide their direction as they both catch their breath. Then, at the bank in front of them, he sees the second canoe. It is caught, stranded with its nose wedged between the branches of a tree. The current on this side of the river is still strong, but not as ferocious as its opposite bank, and Ashley dips in his oar to turn them towards the tree, Caterine still slumped face down over the front breathing heavily. The tip of the canoe bangs into its sister with a hollow thud, and Ashley grabs hold of a branch to steady them. He touches Caterine's shoulder.

'Can you get in?' he says. 'Caterine? The kayak will capsize with both of us in it.'

Caterine makes a noise and struggles over the yellow fibreglass. Ashley helps her and rolls her into the neighbouring craft's seat, where she lies back, gasping.

'Stay here,' he says, making sure the canoe is still lodged firmly in the tree, and pushing his own away from the bank and back into the river. He looks quickly behind, where he sees the dim figure of Sarat successfully landing all three girls onto the bank. Then he looks ahead to where the bank gives way to a sheer rock, into which Mehdi and Daniella are disappearing. Ashley grits his teeth and paddles.

The entrance to the cave is low and tight, and an inexperienced paddler might damage his kayak on its walls if it wasn't for the strong stream of water flowing directly between them. As it is, Ashley is picked up effortlessly by the current and sucked straight out of the stream. Immediately he is in darkness, and the sudden loss of vision combined with the enclosed space makes the roar of the rain and the river even louder. His kayak shoots forward under the new concentrated current, white noise rushing in his ears and blackness all around him. Ashley tries dipping in his oar one paddle at a time, but the speed of the water only causes him to turn violently left and right, throwing him off balance and almost overboard. He decides to let the water take him, and tries to catch his breath.

The current tugs him roughly around bends like a carriage on a ghost train. He can hear voices echoing quickly between the walls: Mehdi and Daniella. He hopes their presence means there is nothing unexpected coming, like a waterfall, although a small part of him hopes to hear a grunting yelp and a splash.

Slowly, Ashley's eyes begin to adjust to the light. He's in a narrow tunnel, but it's gradually opening out and the ceiling and walls are moving further apart. All around him is dim, yellow rock and at some parts of the walls the water meets a flat bank on which Ashley considers trying to steer towards so he can moor his kayak. But he hears the voices up ahead, laughter, and he allows himself to float on.

The sound of the rain outside has started to fade as Ashley moves further into the cave. Now all that is left is the reverberation of a million ripples and plops of water all around him.

Behind him, above the wet, chaotic noise, Ashley suddenly hears a rhythmic splashing. It gets closer and is soon joined by a voice.

'Ashley! Ashley, what you doing?'

Ashley turns and sees a light bouncing around in the dark as Sarat approaches him. Soon he has caught up.

'What are you doing here?' pants Sarat. 'You should be at the doctor! No good! No good! Silly! There's a storm!' Sarat shakes his head and the light strobes around the walls. 'I should not come out today.'

'Sorry,' says Ashley. 'But I told you I had to come.'

'No going back now,' says Sarat. 'No paddling up that current. We have to go through the cave, come out on mountainside. Have you seen others?'

Ashley nods ahead, allowing Sarat to overtake him, the small light strapped to his forehead illuminating the cave further.

'Follow me,' says Sarat.

'OK.'

Before he entered the cave, Ashley didn't know what to expect. Part of him thought that some dread would grip him, thought it might be like entering one of his dreams again where he would have to confront something terrible in the dark. The other part, the part that doesn't believe in anything, was unconvinced, and now the first part is beginning to agree. It is just a cave.

'Yes?' says Ashley.

'What?' says Sarat.

'What do you want?' says Ashley.

'What do *you* want?' says Sarat.

'Nothing, you started it.'

'What you say?'

'You said my name.'

'No, I didn't.'

'Oh, what did you say then?'

'Nothing.'

'Hmm.'

They continue downstream, the current still strong and the tunnel widening. Sarat has begun to paddle, and Ashley does the same to keep up.

'What?' says Ashley.

'Huh?' says Sarat.

'Come on, I definitely heard you that time, you said my name. 'Ash' you said.'

'Ashley, my friend, I said nothing. Now keep up.'

'I definitely, definitely heard…there. Didn't you hear that? It was loud…and again. Stop fucking with me, Sarat.'

'I no fuck with you Ashley, I only fuck with my wife. It's probably the echoes, your name sounds like water. Why are you whispering anyway?'

'LIE WITH ME.'

Ashley's heart drops.

'Are you telling me you didn't hear that?' he whimpers. 'That didn't sound like water, Sarat, that sounded like…'

'Shhh,' says Sarat, sticking his oar against a rock and grabbing Ashley's boat. 'I think I heard something.'

'Thank fuck for that,' says Ashley.

'Laughter, coming from down there.' Sarat points to a tunnel leading off left from the one they're in. 'The other two must be down there. That's the wrong way; that goes deeper, not out! We'll have to get out before the waterfall and walk up through the rock. Stupid, why you all so stupid?'

'So you didn't hear…'

'What?'

Sarat lets go of Ashley's boat and pushes it angrily across the stream towards the second tunnel.

'Never mind,' says Ashley.

He hears it again.

'ASHLEY. LIE WITH ME.'

He gulps and curses, but shakes his head of it and carries on. It is getting louder; he can hear it next to his ears as if something is in his boat. Sarat holds up his hand and stops again. For a while they both pause, their oars jammed into the rock before Sarat speaks.

'No…no good at all! Very bad indeed!'

'What?' says Ashley.

'Wrong tunnel, they've taken the wrong tunnel! Very bad tunnel!' Sarat jabs his finger in the direction of yet another side tunnel to their right. Ashley hears voices coming from its mouth.

'What's wrong with it?' says Ashley.

'Very bad tunnel! Waterfall! Very high!' Sarat pushes himself off again, throwing his kayak into a sharp ninety-degree turn into the third tunnel.

'Shit,' says Ashley, and follows.

In a few seconds, Ashley hears the sound of water rushing ahead once more. It's a loud, constant, long roar, the sound of lots of water falling a great distance. Soon, he can make out figures ahead lit up in Sarat's light, the bright blue and yellow of a kayak and Daniella's white vest top. He hears a shout of alarm ahead, then a crash, then a scream, then a muddle of voices in panic. As they get nearer, Ashley can see Daniella with her hands over her face, still screaming and heading towards the waterfall. Sarat ducks his head and drives towards her, crashing into the right of her boat and pushing her across to the bank of rock on the right. They struggle for a while, Sarat pushing back against the current, trying to steady them both and ground the boats.

In front of them, Ashley sees Mehdi's boat, horizontally lodged between the rocks on either side of the waterfall. He is tipping slowly over to his right, staring straight down into the abyss below. He is not making any kind of grunting sound, just a whimpering repetition of the first letter in 'help'.

Ashley paddles as fast as he can towards the precipice, peering at Mehdi in Sarat's flickering light. He reaches him quicker than he expected, almost crashing into the kayak and sending Mehdi tumbling, but he drives in his oar vertically to the bed of the stream, turning so that the nose of his own boat is lodged against the left-hand rock.

'Give me your hand!' says Ashley, stretching out his oar.

Mehdi whimpers, looking at Ashley in terror.

'Very slowly, grab the oar,' he repeats.

Mehdi blinks and gradually reaches out his left hand. His fingers almost touch Ashley's paddle when suddenly his boat shifts and scrapes against the rock. He yelps and recoils, creasing up his face and sobbing.

Ashley leans forwards, but he is too far away to stretch out the oar again. Very carefully, he begins to climb out of his canoe and along its bow.

'Mehdi, look at me,' he says. 'It's all right, relax, I'm coming to get you.'

He shifts his weight onto his front, wincing as he feels his damaged ribcage bend. He grabs the rock in front of him.

'OK, now grab the oar.'

Mehdi keeps whimpering, stationary, his eyes closed.

'Mehdi! Grab the oar! Now, for fuck's sake!'

Mehdi's eyes open and he lets out a squeak before lunging forwards with his hand again. This time he reaches the oar and for a moment the two balance motionless and speechless, neither pulling. Then, without warning, Mehdi tugs desperately at the oar, Ashley counteracting by pulling back, lifting Mehdi out of the boat and into the water, where he clings to the rock and watches Ashley — who has been pulled forwards — lose grip and fly across the noses of the two kayaks and down, face first over the waterfall.

~1978~

THE DIARY OF CLAUDETTE FERRIÈRE

19 MARS 1978

We tried to help Joe walk again today. He got as far as getting his stump in and standing like yesterday, but Doctor Moreau didn't even get a chance to tighten the straps before he fell out of it. Papa caught him this time, and I saw specks of blood on the bandage around his stump.

Afterwards, I wanted to read to him about the *Atacama Desert*, where it never rains but people still live, but he said that he didn't want me to today, so I read to Madame Beaufort instead.

20 mars 1978

Joe couldn't even get his stump in the leg today. He fell over before Doctor Moreau even had a chance to stand the leg up.

21 mars 1978

Papa has finished the sledge and he showed it to us all in the engine shed. It is just like new. He has fixed it with fresh pieces of timber and the runners aren't rusty any more but are shiny and clean. We were all impressed, apart from Joe, of course, who couldn't leave the house. I don't think he would have been happy to see it even if he could have. Papa said that as soon as the snow stopped coming down as heavily, they would take him down to the village.

After I told him, he said that he wanted to try walking again. This time he managed to stand in the leg without crutches and Doctor Moreau managed to tie the straps onto his waist. He wasn't shaking as much this time, and his face didn't look like he was in pain, he just seemed to be concentrating really hard on balancing. It worked, and he stood there for ages just staring down at his feet. Then he took his weight off his real leg for a second, which made him flinch so he set it down again. After a few seconds he tried again, only this time he put his leg forward to take a step. But it was too much for him and he fell forwards howling, knocking the vase of ferns from the mantelpiece and all the ornaments behind it.

We all picked him up and made 'well done' noises, but I could tell he was angry at himself. What must it be like not being able to walk?

22 mars 1978

Two steps today! He almost made three, but before he could, the new leg buckled under his weight. Doctor Moreau put his hands to his head and said 'I knew those springs should have been tighter, Victor!' and took it away to fix. Joe was almost smiling when we took him back to the old family room, because it wasn't his fault he fell over this time.

23 mars 1978

Three steps today before the leg buckled. Doctor Moreau thinks the springs aren't strong enough, so he and Papa went to the engine shed. When they came back there were two new black springs on it Papa found from bits of an old, broken-down tractor he still kept. Now he says the leg would hold a horse without buckling.

24 mars 1978

Joe walked the entire length of the sitting room today! Madame Beaufort and Doctor Moreau held his hands while

Papa stood at the end and watched with our arms crossed. It was strange to stand there next to Papa looking at three strangers in our house walking slowly up our sitting room. I am getting tired of people I don't know living with us. Even so, I don't want Joe to go, which he will when the snow has stopped, and I know that Madame Beaufort will be here for longer after he has gone.

As for Doctor Moreau, I am sure there are sick people in the village that need his help more than we do.

25 mars 1978

Finally! The snow has stopped!

The moment Papa saw the blue skies this morning, he went to work at clearing all the drifts away from the door to the yard, and by lunch time we could open the door and climb up the long slope again and stand on top of the surface. It felt so good to feel sunshine and smell the fresh air again and it felt like the snow had gone for good. Everywhere down to the valley was thick with bright white icing like a giant cake, and Papa said that he could see a route down already, and he showed me where the roads in the village had been cleared, which meant that the snowploughs were out and that they could take Joe to Grenoble.

I was happy and sad, because I know Joe has to go, even though I don't want him to and I know he doesn't want to either. I think he is scared of something that he shouldn't be scared of, and that once he is better in Grenoble he won't want to be on his own any more and he'll want to go back home. Papa said they would leave tomorrow.

After feeding the beasts and digging some more of the drifts and eating lunch, we all went for a walk around the farm on the fresh snow. Joe had been practising walking inside, which he can do now without any help, and he said he wanted to try outside as well. It took him a while to get up the slope, but he managed it without too much help, and Papa said it was the tread on the tyre he had stuck to the foot that had helped. When he was up, he looked happy to be outside, and I realised that he hadn't left the house for almost seven weeks. In the bright light, his skin looked so pale you could almost see through it and onto the bone, but even after just a few minutes in fresh air his face caught some colour and his cheeks went red.

As we were standing there, Zeet suddenly came out of nowhere, running up the bank by the cattle shed and worrying our legs. Then he saw Joe and stopped dead. He didn't know what to make of his leg, and he did a few dances in the snow and flattened himself on his belly before letting out his loudest bark. He wouldn't stop; he just stood right in front of him and barked as if he didn't know what to do.

'Maybe he wants me to throw it for him,' said Joe.

'Shut up, Zeet! Be quiet! Leave him alone! Bad dog!' I shouted, but he didn't listen.

'ARRÊT!' said Papa, and this did the trick as it always does.

We walked around for a bit. Joe said that he was finding it easier to walk, although the springs were so tight now that every time he took a step it made a clanging sound. I told him he sounded like the metal man on *The Wizard of Oz.*

'The one without a heart?' he said, and I nodded.

'I'd rather be the lion, I think.'

'But the lion was a coward, silly,' I said.

'Yes, that's right, I'd forgotten,' he said, and then he asked me which I would rather have – courage or heart. I told him I didn't know and it was a difficult question, but that I would think about it.

This evening, we all sat around by the fire and didn't say a lot. Papa packed bags for Joe, Doctor Moreau and himself and said that they were to be up early to make a good start down to the village. Then we had some cocoa and went to bed.

Since then I've been looking out of the window at the stars, which I haven't seen since the snow started, and thinking about Joe's question and whether or not it is really a proper question at all. The moon is bright and is lighting up the whole valley and its blanket of snow. You can't see anything but white, so if you didn't know what was there then you might think it was as big as an ocean or as small as a garden. The sledge is outside, ready for them to take Joe down to the village. I wonder if I'll see him again.

~2003~

BIG SPIDER

Laos

IT TURNED dark very quickly in the jungle roads south of Luang Prabang. One hour after Joseph had won his chicken match with the last of the bandits, he found himself on a narrower road again, driving under a heavy canopy of trees and black sky. He had not turned off the road, but was beginning to think he should have done. It had twisted slowly west, and the only part of it he could see was the dim arc of rushing dirt illuminated by his weak headlights. He held out no hope of spotting any side roads.

The girl next to him was asleep, fitful and shivering beneath the least bloody jacket he had stolen from the men in the truck. He had tried to dry her as best he could, unsure of what was the most effective and least inappropriate method of drying somebody else's child in the middle of the jungle, but the absence of a towel or a blanket meant that she was still damp.

Joseph pulled to a stop and turned off the ignition. The truck's protective bubble of sound and light quickly became engulfed by the dark chattering of the jungle. A thick blanket untouched by light. Sounds of things too close.

Joseph stared at nothing and thought. Somebody wanted him captured. Who? Ideas rolled over slowly in his head like clothes soaking in a washing machine, each time coming to rest at the same conclusion. It could only be Byron. He was the one who had sent him on this job; he was the only one who knew he was here. He was the only man who could have had the motive. It was the Dollis Hill fiasco. This was his idea of some clever payback: send him out to some shadowy corner of the world and into the clutches of a gang of bandits he had tipped off. He should have known he wouldn't have been so forgiving, should have known that only Byron could come up with such clumsy wrath. Maybe he had paid them extra to keep him alive and incarcerated for a while before they killed him. They must have been waiting for him at the airport, wondering how they were going to stop him from getting on the plane. Turned out they didn't need to bother. With first the plane strike and then the bus crash preventing the need for any hold-up, all they had to do was collect.

He snorted quietly to himself as he realised what he had just been thinking: that Byron was the only man with a motive. Joseph had potentially hundreds of enemies lurking in his past from the people he had killed, people who might have taken the deaths of their husbands, sons and lovers personally if they could only find out who had caused them.

But there was no question of it, the trap had to have been set by Byron. He should have sensed it when he told him about the job. Byron had never sent him anywhere further than Frankfurt for a job, least of all to collect some shady diamonds from an unknown corpse.

The thought of the corpse sent that wayward, distant memory creeping slowly up his back again. He shrugged it off. *That* would have been impossible.

Joseph gathered up the temporal bearings that had been spilled by the last twenty-four hours and found that they placed him on the evening before the day the corpse was due to arrive in Luang Prabang hospital. If indeed there was a corpse, of course — maybe that had been part of the joke. He had no choice but to find out. If there wasn't, then it proved Byron had been up to no good. He still had to find his way to Luang Prabang.

But he was in the middle of a jungle with no idea how to get to there. He had almost a full tank of petrol, having syphoned some off from the crashed truck, but very little idea what to do with it. It was dark. The rain had stopped, but it was still wet outside. He had an orphan in his care, who was badly in need of some dry clothes and food. He was injured, and — he was irritated to discover — tired. Above all, he was screaming for a cigarette.

He thought back to the little shack he had passed as he encountered the other bandits. It was dark, but it couldn't be that late yet. Maybe it would still be open; they would have cigarettes, food and water, and directions to Luang Prabang. He started the ignition and turned the truck around, driving back in the opposite direction.

He drove for another hour, desperately searching for a pinprick of light in the distance that heralded the little shack's oasis of nicotine and sustenance. There was nothing but black road, but all of a sudden something rushed by on the right that wasn't a tree. Joseph braked and reversed, and the shack came into view, dark and deserted.

'Shit,' he said to himself in the dark.

He parked the truck in front of the shack, angling it so that the headlights lit up the ground around it. It was small and wooden, with a corrugated tin roof and a padlocked door that Joseph easily broke down. Inside was darker than out, the truck's meagre light not wide enough to spill that far inside the doorway. He tried to make out shapes, walls, tables or cupboards, but there was nothing to illuminate them. He held out his arms and walked slowly forwards, shuffling and scraping a few steps before his right hand touched something by his hip. He stopped and stroked it. It was a wooden surface, like a tabletop, and he turned so that both his hands were upon it. He then used it to guide himself sideways along it, patting his hands around for any objects that might be resting there. He felt a pen and some paper, a cardboard box containing things that felt like chocolate bars (of which he took a handful and shoved in his pocket), a plastic bottle, which he shook and then hurled to the floor irritably when he found it empty, and something that might have been a tape measure. When he came to the corner, he guided himself round so that he was on the other side of what he guessed passed as the shack's counter. Instinctively, he threw out a hand behind him, expecting it to land triumphantly on a full rack of cigarettes, tobacco and cigars like you might find in a petrol station or newsagent. But it was just wooden wall. He replaced his hand on the table and began to traverse back along its surface.

As he did, his foot kicked something metal, which made a dull, wobbling clang as if liquid were inside it. Steadily, he crouched down and knelt on his left knee with his prosthetic stretched out to the right, gripping the object with both hands and feeling rust crumbling from it in his fingers. It was a tin bucket, and he lowered his head over it like a drunk with a toilet bowl and took a sniff. Joseph was half expecting petrol or paraffin fumes or worse, but there was nothing strong or unusual about the smell. He inserted a hand, hitting liquid about two-thirds of the way down and dabbling a finger around in it. He was so thirsty, his mouth and throat still as dry as dust, and it felt cool and watery. Very cautiously, he took a handful and held it to his face, sniffing it again and hesitating before slurping it up with his lips.

It tasted metallic, but was refreshing enough, although there were bits in it, which suggested it wasn't clean. Perhaps it had been collected from the nearby river. Joseph took another handful and wiped his mouth. As he stood up, his hand brushed something else next to the bucket that felt plastic. He clutched at it and felt the unmistakable shape of wrapped, plastic bottles crammed together in a multi-pack and bound with cellophane. He tore one of them frantically away and stood up, landing it on the table in front of him and feeling for its cap, which he twisted off. Pausing and remembering the foul sweetness of his last pre-packed Laos drink at the airport, Joseph held the bottle to his nose and sniffed for the presence of anything floral. Nothing appeared and he took a small sip, feeling a bulb of tasteless, lukewarm fluid hit his tongue. He blew a whistle of relief and knocked back the bottle, gulping it down until half of the water inside was gone. Then he replaced the bottle on the table and caught his breath, before reaching down and lifting up the rest of the pack.

Seeing as his feet had been the most productive in his exploration of the shack, he kicked his left one about some more next to where the water had been and it soon hit some other packaging. He found some other wrapped goods and took a handful of them as well. There were some other boxes, but none was the long, rectangular, hard-packed carton he was searching for. Where did this bastard keep his fags?

Joseph searched the rest of the room, blind as before, but found nothing apart from a few more buckets, some puddles, more stone wall and an empty cardboard box. He disturbed a rat at one point, which squeaked and scampered across his TrueStep and away from the light seeping through the doorway. Various other movements and scuttlings were enough to make him give up his quest for nicotine, and he grabbed the water and fled to the truck.

Once inside, he carefully placed the water on the floor by the sleeping girl and turned on the cab's internal light. When he looked down he saw a gigantic tarantula gripping onto his T-shirt, staring up at him with eight black eyes.

Joseph yelped and sprang out of the cab, landing heavily on his buckled TrueStep and almost falling, but steadying himself with his left foot and brushing madly at his chest. He felt the spider fall onto his thigh and screamed again, shaking his leg and throwing wild punches at it until finally it fell to the ground and trundled away in the dust. He then did a small dance, patting himself all over his torso, back and shoulders and shivering before he calmed down and stood motionless, crooked, panting in the dark.

After a minute, he shuddered again and returned gingerly to the cab. The girl was awake and sitting up, looking at him questioningly through sleepy, half-closed eyelids. He closed the door quietly.

'Big spider,' he whispered.

Her body wobbled and she fell forwards onto his lap. Joseph recoiled slightly, raising up his hands as if she were another tarantula. Then he gradually lowered them, pulling the jacket around her shoulders and cradling her with his left arm. He looked down on her for a while, wondering at the simple spectacle of a child asleep in his arms. *This should have been twenty years ago*, he thought.

The crash reared up suddenly in some corner of his memory, more vividly than it had done for a long time. He felt the violence, the heat from the flames, the sickening pain in his leg, the dizziness around his head as the car exploded and he fell unconscious, the cold air, cool snowflakes landing on his face like baby spiders, the feeling of a big hand on his shoulder and two big arms hauling him off the ground. His heart lurched and the memory faded.

He ran a single finger softly through the girl's black and matted hair, then turned off the light and rested his head against the truck window.

Joseph woke, as he always did, to the sound of tyres and metal. Then, a fingernail tapping impatiently upon glass.

He was sat up rigid in his seat, panting and sweating and clutching his chest. He turned towards the window and saw the stern face of a little old man looking up at him, the hand that wasn't tapping behind his back. Joseph rolled his eyeballs two degrees and saw the door to the shack hanging off its hinges. Then he rolled them back at the man, who squawked something angrily up at him.

Joseph relaxed his tensed body and stretched out his arms. His ribs smarted from being kicked, and his leg was still sore, but what was most uncomfortable was his throat, still coarse with thirst. He reached forwards and picked up the half-bottle of water from the truck floor, which he drank while watching the old man still tapping on the pane. The girl snuffled and shifted on his lap and looked up at him, so he offered her the bottle and she drank some too. Then she sat up fully, looking out at the dawn light and quietly shivering.

'Good morning,' said Joseph. He touched her forehead and felt it burn beneath his fingers. Then he stroked back the hair that was stuck to her face.

The old man made another squawking sound and Joseph threw him an irritable look, swinging the door open violently and making him stagger back in the dirt. He got out and faced the man, who pointed back at his shack and said something calmly.

'I'm sorry about your door,' said Joseph, reaching down into the second secret compartment of his twisted prosthetic leg and pulling out a slim wallet.

'English?' said the man.

'Yes, I speak it,' replied Joseph.

'Why you break my door?' croaked the old man, putting his hands on his hips. 'My door. Why you break it?'

'I'm sorry. You weren't here and we were thirsty.' Joseph glanced over his shoulder at the truck as he opened his wallet, and the old man followed his eyes back to the girl, who was looking through the window at them both, her hands against the windowpane. His face lit up.

'Aaaaah!' he said, grinning and waving. 'Sabaidee!'

The little girl ducked down from the window, out of sight. Joseph handed a stack of notes to the old man.

'For the door and the water. And the chocolate,' he said.

'Chocolate?'

'Whatever it is.'

'Aha,' said the old man, folding up the notes and quickly putting them in his shirt pocket. 'Kop Jai. Thank you.'

They stood before each other for a while, the old man with his hands behind his back, eyeing Joseph up and down with a strange mix of suspicion, fear and amusement. It was very early in the morning, still and quiet apart from a few chirps and wing flaps from the jungle. The sun was up, but barely making it through the heavy, wet mist that hung around everything. Everything that could be seen within the dome of visibility it offered was either grey or green, apart from the old man's shirt, which was a vibrant, nauseous red.

He bobbed on his feet a couple of times, taking in the bent, blue metal of Joseph's leg, his torn and bloody clothing, his bruises and wayward, grey beard. Sensing that he wasn't coming across particularly well, Joseph instinctively flattened down his hair and cleared his throat.

'The girl…,' he said, '…she needs a hospital. I think she has a fever.'

'Aaaah,' whispered the man. 'Fever? Oooooh.' He frowned solemnly.

'Yes. I need to get to Luang Prabang. Can you tell me how?'

'Luang Prabang?' repeated the old man slowly.

'Yes…'

'Noooo problem,' he said laughing, raising a finger in the air and immediately returning it behind his back. He bobbed again.

'OK….' said Joseph. 'Could you show me? Perhaps you have a map?'

'Map, yes,' said the old man, and stayed where he was, smiling and bobbing. Joseph looked at the shack expectantly.

'Could we…' started Joseph. The old man frowned, then smiled.

'Cigarette?' he said.

It was too early in the morning for Joseph's heart to slump. But it did. He shook his head.

'I don't have any,' he said.

'I do,' said the old man. 'Come inside.'

There was a fanfare in Joseph's lungs.

Inside the shack, Joseph inhaled deeply on a cigarette brand he had never heard of from a pack that the old man retrieved on a stepladder from a shelf high above the counter. As the smoke streamed down his trachea, he felt every vessel in his body bristle and his spine shiver as it was drenched in the colossal tide of nicotine. He exhaled and closed his eyes. It tasted foul, but it was the best cigarette he had ever had. The old man lit one for himself.

'First one morning,' he said. 'Always best.'

Joseph nodded, examining the smouldering tip with genuine affection.

'Luang Prabang, huh?' said the old man, and gobbed noisily in the pail by his feet. He pulled out a map from another shelf and stretched it on the table, sniffing.

Joseph froze and stared in horror down at the tin bucket.

'About fifty mile…south…'

'That bucket,' said Joseph, who was still looking at it.

'Hmm?' said the old man, leaning over the map and scanning it with his eyes.

'Do you always…'

The old man suddenly snorted up another huge round of phlegm and fired it down into the grimy liquid, which sploshed around the sides of the bucket under the impact.

'What you say?' said the old man, smacking his lips and looking up from the map at Joseph, transfixed by the rippling, filthy water. His lip trembled.

'…nothing,' he said.

The old man waved them off, smiling, and Joseph pulled away quickly into the growing light of morning with the map resting on his lap. He waved a hand briefly in the mirror.

'What?' he said to the girl. She was looking up at his grim face, head cocked.

WHAT IT WAS NOT

THE YOUNG man's eyes opened to a silent, black world. Pure, unbroken darkness swamped the air, obliterating all shape and shadow. He blinked once. His breaths were slow and shallow. There was no feeling, no thought, no memory. Just the empty, numbing darkness all around him, protecting him like an unborn child.

The sound of flowing water seeped into Ashley's consciousness. Ripples moved softly from left to right beneath his feet. Slow and steady drips sounded in his right ear, then echoed somewhere to his left. Beyond, the soft roar of a river, safe and distant.

The feeling was…

The feeling was…

It was not what it was, but what it was not.

It was not life. It was not London. It was not the hot rage of a street. It was not work. It was not ambition. It was not money. It was not shares. It was not cars. It was not neglected friendships. It was not lust. It was not excess. It was not greed. It was not pride. It was not vanity. It was not a drunken blowjob in a sixty-pound taxi. It was not snorting cocaine from the clammy leg of a netball captain from Sussex. It was not wasted time. It was not the pretence of youth. It was not the embellishment of every single moment of his life. It was not the deep yearning for something, anything, anywhere but where he was. It was not the feeling of always wanting more. It was not the feeling of sickness in his own skin. It was not the feeling of hunger growing with every mouthful. It was not the face of his mother. It was not the smell on his father's coat. It was not boxes or watches or crystal glasses or half-empty bottles of champagne falling down a kitchen sink or leather jackets or torn expensive T-shirts or unread books or unheard CDs or Bang & Olufsen or Harpers or Queen or Gucci or Armani or Porsche or Ferrari or Krug or objects or things, things, things and more things. It was not shame. It was not pain. It was not weakness. It was not fear. It was not Buddha. It was not Allah. It was not God.

It was not.

It.

Was.

Not.

Ashley lay in watery silence, the dull pain in his right arm the only thing telling him he was still alive. Although he had fallen into deep darkness and deep quiet, he felt as though he had suddenly emerged from an ocean into a colourless and empty sky. It was a place without noise, without thought, without feeling. A place without time, without consequence. There he let himself float in a pure and infinite sea that rolled gently around him, out towards a nameless horizon. All of his time — all of time — was deep below. Centuries of thought and distraction swam beneath the surface like shoals of tormented fish.

He lay on cold stone, floating in this passive sea. Not listening, but allowing sound to enter his ears. Not seeing, but allowing the darkness to flow across his eyes. Not feeling, but allowing the pain in his arm and chill from the rock to run slowly through his nerves. Not thinking, but allowing the twenty-five-year dust cloud of thought that had raged inside his head to freeze, fall and settle like snow. As it did, one thought remained, simple and bright and hovering before him like a young star: he would never go back beneath the surface.

Do not go back.

Do not return.

Voices. Shouts in the distance. His name called in panic.

Then further into the darkness. And sleep.

YOU AND YOUR LEG

THEY ARRIVED in Luang Prabang by mid-morning. The bandits' hideout had been further away from the crash site than he had calculated, actually north of the town and some fifty miles into the jungle. It had taken him five hours to follow the old man's directions on his gob-splattered map, by which time the sun had burnt away all trace of moisture in the air and left it dry and baking. Despite the stratospheric temperature, the girl still lay curled up in the jacket, shaking with fever. They had finished almost all of the water from the shack, and Joseph had polished off the entire pack of cigarettes.

The country had changed so much in the miles they had driven and, as they drove, Joseph witnessed the jungle visibly relinquish its wild hold over the land to the softer rule of field, stone and water. He had expected to find Luang Prabang dull and basic, a shanty village of sticks and mud, but instead he drove into a peaceful, rolling town full of gardens and wide, colonial streets lined with whitewashed villas. In the centre was a small hill teeming with manicured plants and trees — a reminder of jungle tamed. A stone staircase wound its way up to the top, where a small temple looked upwards and around to the surrounding country, basking in the sunlight and the daily prayers it channelled from within.

The riverfront was washed with the same calm, full of quiet fishermen on one side and open-fronted, mosaic-tiled bars on the other. It was long and paved, curling around the glittering water like the serene smile of a Buddha. At one end of it lived the hospital, a flat building set back from the road and surrounded by gates and a garden. Joseph pulled up and stopped the truck.

He carried the child through the front doors and walked up to the reception. His mud and sticks expectations had placed his idea of the town's hospital somewhere back in the eighteenth century, but he was surprised to feel the bliss of air-conditioning wash across his body and shoulders and the smell of modern medicine greet his nose as the doors closed behind him. It was not a grand place, but it felt clean and peaceful, a place where you might just get better. The floor was shiny and a wide window at the back of the reception filled the room with light. There were a couple of wooden seats and a dog-eared sofa in the corner on which was sat a plump young woman with a bandage round her foot. She was too engrossed in a magazine to notice the arrival of anyone else, least of all a one-legged foreigner carrying a sick child. Corridors to the left and right of the reception promised wards and treatment rooms. There were even staff. Doctors, nurses…

'What is happening here?'

A short man with a shock of jet-black hair appeared before Joseph. His white coat was starched and gleaming.

'Doctor…' said Joseph.

The doctor reached out and took the child from Joseph's arms. His face was calm and expressionless, but he eyed Joseph warily up and down — first at his leg and then at his sweat-stained, dirty face. He turned and set the child down on the reception desk. She was quiet and still shivering with her hands crossed in her lap. The doctor bent over her, making soft sounds and gently feeling her brow.

'What happened?' he said with his back still to Joseph.

'There was a crash,' said Joseph. 'A bus crash on the road from Vientiane, two days ago. We were the only survivors.'

The doctor looked round briefly and gave Joseph's leg and face another going over.

'How do you know?' said the doctor, examining the girl's eyes.

Joseph paused.

'I was there, the bus span off a mountain and blew up.'

'How do you know there were no survivors?' he said, checking the girl's ears.

'There were bodies scattered all over the ground.'

'Did you check them all?' He took a stethoscope out of his pocket and placed it on the girl's chest, smiling at her. 'Did you make sure they were all dead?'

'What?' said Joseph. 'Look, we crashed and I found her crawling around the wreckage. There was no rescue party so I took her and found my way here.'

'In two days? It was only three miles.'

'I got lo…how do you know it was three miles?'

'The crash was just outside Luang Prabang, and there *was* a rescue party. Five survivors. Strange that they didn't find you.' He eyed Joseph suspiciously.

'As I said, we got lost. What are you accusing me of exactly?'

The doctor took off his stethoscope and replaced it in his pocket, stroking the girl's forehead. He turned back to Joseph.

'I'm going to take a proper look at her,' he said, picking up the girl. 'I'll send someone back to check on you and your leg.'

Joseph watched as the doctor made off down the corridor, the girl looking blankly back at him as they disappeared.

'You have a prosthetics expert?' he called out.

'Not that one, the other one,' shouted the doctor. 'It's bleeding very badly.'

MY FIRST ONE WAS WOOD

THE WARD in which Joseph lay was small, with eight old beds around its walls, steel-framed and topped with saggy mattresses and bright, stiff sheets. Each bed had a plastic fan attached to the wall above it, the germ-carrying air conditioning banned from anywhere but the reception. They were each on full power, whirring quietly like distant lawnmowers, rotating between left and right so that they swept brief gusts of warm air from the open windows around the faces beneath them.

His torn and useless clothes (apart from his boots) had been disposed of at his request, and his TrueStep had been taken away by the nurse, despite his protestations. It didn't even carry his weight properly any more, and he could feel the metal weakening whenever he put weight on it. He had been allowed to have a shower in an adjoining room and now lay wearing nothing but a white T-shirt and some linen trousers that had been on the pillow when he came back. The trousers' legs were rolled up so that both legs were exposed — one a stump, the other now sporting a dressing where the bullet had grazed his shin. There were also plasters and bandages on various other parts of his body, including his head and areas where he didn't remember having been injured.

In the seven other beds lay six Lao men sleeping and, next to him, one young and tired-looking western man reading a book. Outside, he could hear light traffic, the occasional two-stroke engine spluttered past.

He finished the rest of the noodles and vegetables he had been given and put the bowl on the bedside table. He rubbed his brow. He felt anxious. It felt good to be clean and dry, but it was already noon and he didn't want to be in the hospital any longer than necessary. He needed to find the morgue and determine whether it really was planning on playing host to a dead body full of diamonds today, and if so who exactly was coming to collect them. He also faced the threat of another ambush. If Byron had set him up with the bandits, he was sure to have found out that he had failed soon enough. Lying up in hospital without a leg was not where he wanted to be waiting for whatever backup plan the little prick had lined up.

It all seemed so unlikely, that Byron had gone to the lengths he had in order to have his wrath satisfied. It was strange and elaborate, not the work of a man who had once driven a blunt letter-opener up an employee's nose for killing the wrong person.

The doctor who had met Joseph at the hospital entrance came into the ward and walked towards his bed, carrying a bag. He drew the tatty private curtain around, pulled up a seat next to him and sat down.

'How is she?' asked Joseph.

The doctor smiled thinly.

'I am sorry,' he said at last.

Joseph looked surprised.

'I did not mean to accuse you of anything,' the doctor went on.

Joseph slowly shifted himself up in his bed.

'Well, you didn't,' he said. 'Not exactly. Although I've never been welcomed into hospital like that before.'

The doctor nodded.

'It is not the first time I have seen a white man and a local child around here.'

'Oh,' said Joseph, frowning and adjusting his pillow. 'That's what you meant when you said you were going to take a *proper* look at her.'

The doctor nodded again.

'My name is Doctor Mookjai,' he said.

'Joseph.'

'Sommai.' The doctor's eyes fell on Joseph's stump.

'Your prosthetic is very badly damaged,' he said.

'Not for the first time,' said Joseph. 'It's stood up to quite a lot in its time. Table legs, a few falls…'

'Bullets?' said the doctor.

Joseph said nothing.

'It took a hard blow from something,' the doctor continued. 'It is a shame for such a nice leg. The XC1 is a remarkable model. What happened?'

Joseph answered him with a blank stare, resisting the temptation to fold his arms and betray his defensiveness. Instead he diverted him with a new question.

'How do you know so much about prosthetics?'

'One of my areas,' answered the doctor, his eyes still fixed on Joseph. Both said nothing. A man groaned a few beds up from Joseph.

'So,' the doctor went on. 'I examined the girl.'

Joseph shifted in his bed.

'She's fine,' said the doctor, answering the change in his expression. 'She has a high fever and she was very dehydrated but we have her on a drip for now. One of the other survivors recognised her from the bus and said both her parents were on board as well. They will be in our morgue now, I expect.'

'What will happen to her?' said Joseph.

'We will look after her, try and get in touch with her relatives in the villages between here and Vientiane.'

'If she has any.'

'If she does I will find them,' said the doctor. 'My family are from near there. Now, how are you?'

'Fine,' Joseph shrugged. 'As you can see, I've had worse injuries to worry about in my time.' He rubbed his right stump.

'How did it happen?' said the doctor, leaning over to inspect it.

'Car crash,' said Joseph flatly. The doctor smiled.

'Hmm,' said the doctor, smiling. 'That is a novelty.'

He peered intently around what was left of Joseph's leg as if he were inspecting the engine of a new car.

'All of the ones I have dealt with are from bombs,' he said.

'Landmines?'

'Yes, landmines and bombs.'

'I thought that was mainly in Cambodia?'

The doctor sat back in his chair.

'Two million tonnes of explosives were dropped on this country during nine years of the Indo-China war,' he said — not for the first time in his life, thought Joseph.

'That is one plane load every eight minutes, like a decade's worth of Blitzkreig. Some just hit the ground without a sound. Thirty years later, a child comes along and…'

The doctor shrugged and swept back a strand of black hair from his brow.

'Someone gets their legs blown off every two days here. Half of them are children.'

'And they all get prosthetics? That must be expensive.'

'It would be if they all got legs like yours, but they don't. The legs we give them are very basic; single joints, plastic bodies. Still,' he shrugged, 'it's better than it was — children used to have to make their own out of bamboo before we set up.'

'My first one was wood,' said Joseph.

'Hmm,' the doctor nodded, looking suspiciously back at Joseph. 'Not any more though. As I say, a remarkable model. At least it was. Now, not so good.'

'I guessed as much. Don't suppose there's any hope of fixing it?'

The doctor shook his head.

'I do not know much about computers, but the AI chips are burnt and the titanium rods have lost all their strength. I am surprised you made it. Something must have hit you quite hard.'

His gaze held Joseph firm.

'But,' he said, finally. 'It is none of my business. Here.'

He reached down into the bag and pulled out a clumsy-looking, angular, white plastic limb.

'It's the biggest one I could find,' he said, smiling and offering it to Joseph. 'Nothing fancy.'

Joseph took the leg and examined it. It was no better than his first one and the knee joints were a bit loose, but it looked like it would get him around. He thanked him, fitting the straps of the leg to his stump.

'What are you doing?' said Sommai.

'I'm putting on my leg,' said Joseph, wriggling his stump into the worn seal of the leg. 'I'm leaving now.'

Sommai reached down and snatched back the leg, standing back from the bed.

'Give that back, please,' said Joseph. He leaned on his stump and reached up at the leg. 'It's very important that I leave right now.'

Sommai held the leg out of reach.

'No,' he said. 'No…not until you tell me who you are and what you are doing here.'

He looked back through the curtain, then back at Joseph.

'*I know you were shot*,' he hissed.

Joseph sat back and fumed.

'Like you said,' he said at last. 'It's none of your business. What do you care anyway?'

'I care,' said Sommai, shaking the leg at him, 'because the only people with guns around here are bandits, thieves and murders, and for all I know you could be involved with them.'

He yanked the curtain shut again.

'People like that don't usually come to our hospital, they have their own ways of looking after themselves and I am glad of that. I do not want people like that…people like you…in my hospital.'

He glared at Joseph and pointed the leg at him.

'I do not want trouble on my ward.'

'Then give me the leg and let me leave,' said Joseph, holding out his hand.

'Not as simple as that,' he said, raising his voice. 'Just because you leave does not mean you will leave without a trace. Who is after you?'

He looked back over his shoulder again.

'How did you get shot?' he whispered.

Joseph lowered his palm and tightened his lips.

'Sit down,' he said.

Sommai sat down and blinked. Joseph lent forward and lowered his voice.

'Listen to me,' he went on. 'I'm not going to tell you a thing about myself. Not about where I come from, what I do, why I'm here or how I got shot. All I can tell you is that I pose no threat to you or the hospital.'

Sommai went to stand up, but Joseph continued. 'But I have reason to believe there is somebody in or near this hospital who poses a threat to me, and wants to find me.'

'In that case, I am calling the police.' The doctor tried to stand, but Joseph grabbed his coat by the sleeve.

'No,' said Joseph. 'You can't. Please understand me, somebody has set me up, and for all I know they could well be involved with the local police anyway. Where's the morgue in this hospital?'

Sommai faltered.

'Why do you need to know that?'

'Because I think whoever is involved is going there today. From what I know, which isn't much, it is a young woman. They will probably be here to witness an autopsy, but that's not the real reason they're here.'

The doctor was silent. He sat down slowly.

'What did you say?' he said.

'And if they aren't involved,' said Joseph, 'then they might be in danger too. You have to let me leave.'

Sommai said nothing, just stared at Joseph, weighing up what he had just been told.

Eventually he blinked.

'You will stay here, Mr Joseph,' he said. 'I do not want you moving from this ward.'

With that, the doctor stood up and opened the curtain, walking quietly from the room with the leg tucked firmly beneath his arm.

'Shit,' said Joseph. Then, 'What do you want?' at the young and tired-looking man beside him, who had put down his book and was looking at him very seriously indeed.

BLACK SHADOW

MYLO SLID stealthily along the wall behind Luang Prabang hospital. He was a tall man, but quiet and nimble. Stealth was what he did: he lived and breathed it.

He looked at his watch. It was just past one in the morning, yet shafts of white, sterile light from the three windows above him cut through the dark, hot air of the night. The source of the light was the hospital morgue, and it would normally have been closed at this time: a cold, temporary tomb, a physical purgatory for the bodies that filled the cells in its walls. But this evening, as Mylo knew and expected, there was life inside.

Bulbous moths and insects clattered hopefully around the high sills of the windows. A small, pale lizard appeared as if by teleportation, four inches from where it had previously been camouflaged. It paused, a fly as big as its head now broken between its flat jaws, then swallowed its prey in three rapid spasms of chews and gulps. A web vibrated in the corner of one window as a beetle flew head first into its sticky core. A fat, black shadow pounced upon it, cradling it in its front legs and setting to work on the creature's terrible cocoon. All around, jaws clicked and snapped as little hunters baited and harvested the abundant night air. Mylo watched the silent microcosm above him; tiny lives nourished and extinguished in moments, quiet, unscreaming, yielding, vivid and beautiful. It calmed him, even though his blood was already cool and impassive, his breathing perfectly controlled.

A sudden shadow flitted across each of the three shafts of light, first one way, then back. Movement. Mylo blinked away from the brief distraction and turned his attention to the door further down the wall. According to the map he had memorised, it would open into a storage area housing waste awaiting collection from the morgue. Another door lead from this into the morgue itself.

Slowly he drew a silencer from the breast pocket of his jacket. He edged beneath the windows and towards the door, screwing the black, metal cylinder onto the barrel of his gun.

Progress down the corridor from Ward G to the morgue was slow. There were three reasons for this: first, it was late, and the Luang Prabang hospital budget did not extend to lighting up empty corridors after dark. Second, Joseph did not have any prosthetic or crutch to hand, and so he was walking on just his injured left leg. Third, the person helping him was Ashley Gritten, and Ashley Gritten had a broken arm. Caterine and the rescue party had found him two days previously, unconscious at the bottom of the cave. Although his nightmares had stopped, he was still unable to sleep for any period of time and had managed just three hours since arriving at the hospital. He was visibly and audibly exhausted, and his voice was barely a whisper.

'I still don't understand why you want to go to the morgue,' said Ashley. 'It's already too late for visitors…what do you expect to find in there?'

Joseph gave him a disdainful, sidelong glance, a look that was wasted owing to the lack of light and the fact that Ashley's eyes were almost entirely shut anyway. The young man lumbered along, supporting the right side of Joseph's body with his good shoulder, but at first glance it would have been difficult to tell who was helping who.

Their conversation in the ward had been brief. Ashley, who had overheard Joseph and the doctor, had initiated it by asking what sort of trouble a young woman who might possibly be visiting the morgue could be in. Joseph's reflex demand to know what business it was of his had clammed up Ashley, which made Joseph angry, since it was his one and only lead on the whole situation. His lack of a leg, however, and therefore any agility, meant that he had been unable to assert any physical pressure on the young man. Instead, he had threatened to garrotte him in his sleep if he didn't tell him all he knew. Ashley was afraid not for himself, but for Caterine. In some vague hope that he might determine what was going on, he had fed Joseph some information: that the girl was coming to the hospital to see her father, and then to see him.

He had refused to give him Caterine's description, however. Even her name would have singled her out as being western. It had been decided that this information would be traded only for Ashley's inclusion in whatever plan Joseph may have formed to find out further details. A further selling point of this condition had been that Joseph, again, had only one leg.

Joseph had tried further threats, but they seemed to be wasted on the kid. He didn't seem to be…altogether there. In the end, he had reluctantly agreed that Ashley help him to the morgue later that night to investigate. He had then tried to sleep, but found himself jumping out of unconsciousness the moment he entered it, like a toe from a cold bath. He had noticed that Ashley, too, was experiencing a similar torment. Eventually he had shaken him awake and they had both quietly left the ward.

'I expect we'll find dead bodies,' muttered Joseph between hops. 'One in particular,' he added. 'The one she's here to visit.'

'Her father? You think…Ca…her father's…dead?' said Ashley.

'That remains to be seen.'

'You think she's…here to…pick up her f-father?' said Ashley like a drugged sloth.

'Not her father. Just what's inside him.'

'What? But…she's…what's inside of him? What do you mean? Why would she…why here in Laos?'

'Why not here in Laos?' said Joseph. 'Are you saying she's

not from Laos?'

'…I didn't say that.'

'Hmph. Yes you did, although I'm pretty sure I knew that anyway…Christ, will you be careful?'

'Sorry.'

'I don't know if I'll find anything in there of any interest. Hopefully nothing. Let's just say I have a bad feeling, something I've had right from the start and that I want to lay to rest.'

'What kind of bad feeling? What sort of trouble is she in?'

'Shh…quiet.'

The pair froze next to a discarded bed as footsteps approached the corridor crossing theirs fifty feet ahead. Joseph pulled them into the deep alcove of a doorway and made Ashley stand flat against the frame.

'Be very still,' he said, clutching Ashley's trembling arm. 'Try not to breathe if you can help it.'

The footsteps grew louder and stopped with a squeak and a shuffle as a security guard came into view at the junction. He took one look down the corridor and flashed his torch along its walls. There was a pause; Joseph and Ashley held still, and then the guard continued on his route.

'OK,' said Joseph, 'I think we're OK.'

They continued up the corridor for several more hops before Joseph signalled for Ashley to stop. They were outside a door.

'This is it,' said Joseph.

WHERE ARE THE DIAMONDS?

SOMMAI PULLED the sheet up so that it covered the face of the body on dissecting table. He sighed and stretched as he moved across to the steel bench beneath the windows of the morgue and set about cleaning his blades and needles. He was glad to have finished. It wasn't the late hour that bothered him, nor the fact that he was alone. Despite the disturbing nature of his conversation earlier with the patient in Ward G, Joseph, he had still chosen to work late. He preferred it. It reminded him of his days as a medical student. He liked the quiet, the stillness, the absence of life and movement. When the white noise of the day subsided, it left hours of unruffled peace; time for him to concentrate and focus on the job in hand.

It was not the time of day, his solitude or the nature of his work. It was the fact that he had never before had to work with the body of someone he had known, a friend.

He understood why Elmo had asked him. They had been friends for a long time after all, almost from the day that Elmo had arrived, lost and haunted, in Luang Prabang those twenty years ago. Sommai had just started at the hospital, glad to have found work close to home. The north wing of the building was being renovated, and Elmo was one of the labourers on the site. Sommai saw him every day, working silently beneath the sweltering sun. He was fairly difficult to miss, being the only western face in the dusty rabble of builders. He was quiet, kept himself to himself. He did not have the wiry, coarse bodies of the other labourers. They poked fun at him, laughing at him, and he laughed back though he never got the joke. One day, Sommai joined Elmo as he sat on a wall eating his lunch by himself. He asked in English for a light, Elmo obliged, and they began to talk. Neither spoke much in the way of a common tongue, English at first, then more Lao as Elmo learned from his co-workers, but he had instantly been an easy man to like, whatever the language.

They became friends, and when Elmo began talking of staying longer in Laos, perhaps of hanging up his boots and settling, Sommai was the first to encourage him. He helped him with documents, pulled some strings in passport offices, found him work, introduced him to friends, women. Elmo was grateful. He trusted Sommai, and some years later as they sat one summer drinking cold beers on the riverbank, he told him about the secret inside his gut, his 'little cargo' as he called it. Sommai had not taken it seriously at first, laughing off his friend's insistence as a drunken joke, but Elmo had persisted until Sommai, as much to quieten him as anything, performed an examination himself. Sure enough, there were what looked like five uncut diamonds lodged deep in his abdomen. Sommai was stunned, incredulous, and Elmo made him swear to keep secrecy, which of course he did.

Sommai was devastated when Elmo became ill, but he shed no tears. Instead, he offered counsel and help as a doctor and friend, talking him without sentiment through scenarios and options, weeping quietly for his friend only occasionally, and only when he was alone. He was not surprised when Elmo elected to leave Laos to be with his family back in Italy, but neither was he surprised when he asked for his body to be buried in Laos. He knew how much he had grown to love the country, and how many friends, like Sommai, would miss him when he went.

The extraction of the diamonds had been Elmo's idea. It would be a simple procedure on a dead body, a five-minute job that Sommai could easily arrange and perform himself without anyone needing to know. When Elmo's body arrived back in Laos, the body would need to be stored in the hospital anyway, and, as a senior resident, Sommai could take care of things discreetly. He could do it without leaving so much as a stitch.

It made sense, since he was the only one who knew about the diamonds and Elmo's paranoia had prevented him from wanting anyone else to know but a trusted friend. But it troubled him to be asked. Despite his years as a surgeon, debasing the lifeless body of a friend was not easy.

Still, it was done now. Elmo's last wish of his friend had been carried out and the 'little cargo' had been collected by the girl just moments before. She was prettier than she looked in the photo given to him by Elmo; a sad expression, bewildered. Sommai did not blame her.

He still did not quite know what to make of his conversation with Joseph. It had worried him, of course, put him on his guard, but the hospital was well secured and the job had been done. Still, he resolved to check on the strange patient before he left for the night.

He stretched his shoulders again and wiped off his scalpel, replacing it in the leather case laid out in front of him. This he folded carefully and placed inside the top pocket of his coat. Then he reached forwards to turn off the lights. One by one, the three fluorescent tubes were extinguished, leaving the room bathed only in stark moonlight. Sommai turned to leave.

A cold barrel of steel pushed into the back of his neck, followed by the knuckle crack of a pistol's hammer cocking. He froze.

'Don't move, please,' came a voice behind him. 'I'll take that, thank you.'

A brown leather-gloved hand reached around Sommai's front and plucked the leather case from his pocket.

'The most important thing now is for you to stay calm,' said Mylo, applying more pressure to the surgeon's neck. He spoke clearly and precisely in a firm, friendly voice. 'This gun is very powerful and its bullets are much faster than you…*I* am much faster than you. Your brain is on overdrive. Your heart is pump,

pump, pumping adrenaline. You don't know what to do. You feel there is something you *should* do. Please listen to me when I tell you that there is not. Tell your brain to relax, your heart to slow down and close your eyes.'

Sommai was shaking, his breathing nervous and tight. Mylo took some pressure off the gun and placed his other hand on Sommai's shoulder.

'Relax now,' he said. 'Deep breaths, come on, breathe with me…in…'

He took a loud, long drag of air. Sommai did not respond.

'IN….' said Mylo, inhaling again and pushing the gun harder into Sommai's neck. This time Sommai responded, with a weak gasp of air.

'…and out…' Mylo exhaled, yoga-like, as Sommai released his own quivering breath in tandem.

'Good, now again…in…'

They repeated, twice; Mylo's breaths deep and powerful, Sommai's nothing more than a nervous tremble.

'Good. Better?' he said. Sommai nodded.

'Good, good, now put your hands face up on the bench in front of you where I can see them. Now, please.'

Sommai placed his hands on the cold steel, and looked down at his own shaking palms.

'Thank you, you're doing very well, a little further forward please…excellent, thank you.'

Sommai felt the metal leave his neck, and heard a rustle behind him.

'Now, the diamonds. Where are they?' said Mylo, replacing the gun to Sommai's head.

'I…' stammered Sommai, 'I don't know what you're…'

Before he could finish, he felt a sharp nick in his right forefinger as Mylo darted forwards and drew one of his own scalpels along its length. Sommai gasped and looked down in horror. For a moment, there was nothing but a pale line in the skin, then a sickening gush of dark blood seeped out and spread out from the open wound like an oil slick.

Sommai screamed in pain and drew back, clutching his hand, but Mylo slammed him back against the bench. From somewhere he had torn a strip of thick gaffer tape, which he wrapped tightly around the bleeding finger as Sommai struggled in his grip.

'Again, hands on the bench, face up,' said Mylo, stepping back and replacing his gun into Sommai's neck. Sommai's knees had buckled, and he stood barely upright, struggling for air and hunched over the bench, still holding his hand to his chest.

'On the bench, please,' repeated Mylo, jabbing the gun against the base of Sommai's skull. The terrified surgeon yelped and obliged, flipping his hands over into the place they had already been.

'Now,' said Mylo calmly, 'once again, where are the diamonds?'

Sommai, out of sheer fear and confusion, began shaking his head.

'Please,' he said, 'I…'

Mylo sprang forward again and drew the knife expertly through the skin between Sommai's left thumb and forefinger, pulling his captive forward and slapping another strip of heavy tape over the wound. Before Sommai could even draw breath for another scream, Mylo had dropped down and inserted the scalpel through the back of the left knee of Sommai's trousers, and into the soft flesh beneath. He twisted it ninety degrees, then yanked it sharply to the right.

Sommai felt something twang in his leg and shrieked in pain as it gave way. Mylo caught him and lifted him upwards, holding him there while he wound two, three circles of tape tightly around his bleeding knee. Then he pushed his entire weight against Sommai, trapping him against the desk and slamming a hand across his face, silencing his screams. Spittle few through Mylo's fingers as Sommai drew fast, spluttering breaths. He pushed the gun hard against his temple, and Sommai squeezed his eyes shut.

'Now,' said Mylo. 'This time think. Any word that is not a location, any movement that is not a nod or gesture in the right direction, will result in me using this blade to find parts of your body that cause you so much pain you will wonder why you were born. So tell me, take your time, no rush, where are the diamonds?'

Sommai opened his eyes and rolled them about desperately, trying to see the man whose face was next to his, or the gun that was jammed against his head.

'Mmmph…' he said.

Mylo slowly retracted his hand from Sommai's mouth.

'Yes?' he said.

'You're….you're too late,' said Sommai, catching his breath. He felt a movement.

'No!' he shouted, 'I mean it, they're not here.'

His face crumpled and tears of pain and despair began filling his eyes. His chest twitched and shuddered as violent heartfuls of blood pumped again and again through his body. He felt the three raw, constricted wounds spike with pain, one after the other, with each surge.

'They're not here,' he repeated, squirming, 'please…please don't hurt me again…please.'

Mylo pulled back and released Sommai, who fell forward, weeping against the bench. Over his shoulder, Sommai saw his tormentor tap the tip of the silencer twice against his front teeth, his other hand holding the scalpel loosely upwards, the way a painter holds a brush.

'Not here?' he said. 'Really…'

Mylo eyed the covered corpse on the table beside him and the steel blade in his hand, fresh dark pools of blood puddling on its edge. He put away his gun and pushed the point of the blade against the side of Sommai's neck.

'So where are they?'

'Gone,' gasped Sommai. 'They're gone, I swear.'

'Yes, WHERE?' said Mylo as he dug the scalpel into the surgeon's flesh.

Sommai swallowed, feeling sharp, wet heat on his neck. He tried to steady his lungs.

'Who are you?' he breathed.

'WHERE.' Mylo shouted, pulling the knife down sharply and opening the wound.

Sommai squeezed his eyes shut and gripped the sides of the bench, bracing himself. Then he relaxed as he resigned himself to the only course of action he could take.

'I don't know,' he sighed.

For a second, Mylo remained still. Then he grunted, a row of white teeth widening in the dark.

'Ha!' he said.

He adjusted himself, standing back and pushing hard against the back of Sommai's skull so that his neck was exposed and taut. He placed the blade expertly into the hollow at the top of the spine but just as he was about to cut, he heard something. Voices and footsteps outside the door. He retracted the scalpel.

'One word, one noise,' whispered Mylo in Sommai's ear. 'You die.'

Keeping the blade against Sommai's throat, he pulled him back into the shadows towards the door.

Ashley looked at the squiggles on the door's white sign.

'How do you know this is the morgue? Do you speak Laos?'

'No, I memorised the hospital floor plan.'

'…h-handy,' said Ashley. 'Right…' he continued, trembling, drawing on some dribble of energy deep within. 'I've…helped you, now tell me what's going on. What are we expecting to find in here? Why is Ca…the girl…in trouble? What do you think she's done?'

'I don't think she's done anything, it's what might get done to her I'm worried about,' said Joseph, pushing the door open. It was dark inside, but there was light enough to see the table in the opposite corner, and the unmistakable shape of a sheet-covered corpse on top of it.

'What?' whispered Ashley. 'What are you talking about? What's going to get done to her?'

'I told you, I don't know for sure. Anyway, why are you so worried about her? Are you and her…?'

'No,' snorted Ashley.

'Just good friends, eh?' Joseph released a dark chuckle. 'Don't kid yourself, just good friends don't come with breasts. Certainly none of the ones I've had.'

'She saved my life,' said Ashley.

'Oh,' said Joseph. 'And I expect you feel some duty to try to do the same for her?'

'Kind of. If she's in any trouble, I want to at least let her know.'

Joseph managed to get Ashley walking again, slowly towards the corpse.

'Well, that's not the worst basis for a relationship, I suppose, but I'm afraid I can't promise you anything. At best, this is all a waste of time. At worst, you'll be in as much danger as her.'

'What do you mean? How do you know all this, and how do you know Caterine?'

'Caterine?' said Joseph. 'Is that her name?'

'…f-fuck.'

Joseph gripped the hem of the sheet in his hand.

'…w-what's your relationship with her…?' said Ashley, resigned to his slip-up.

'None,' said Joseph. 'It's him I have a relationship with.'

He whipped back the sheet and revealed the hollow face beneath it. Ashley made a noise. It took Joseph a couple of seconds to strip back the years that had aged it since he had last saw it, not to mention the pallid, soulless expression of death that now met him. But it was him. It always had to have been him.

'*Had* a relationship,' breathed Joseph.

'Who?'

'Elmo, Elmo Ollandi.'

'Who's he?'

Joseph studied the shadows, the deep recesses of his eyes, the pale skin and the thousand blemishes and craters that littered it. The last time he had seen it had been at *Amico's*, the day before Elmo left. Three months before his holiday with Anita. Three months before the crash.

'A very old, very dead friend.'

'Oh…I'm sorry,' said Ashley.

'I said *old* friend,' said Joseph. 'He's not any more. Hasn't been for a long, long time.'

'Fall out, d-did you?'

'No. We never got the chance.'

Joseph stared at the face, flitting through memories he hadn't flitted through for years. The restaurant, Elmo, the piano, Anita, the diamonds. He was never sure whether he had ever truly forgiven — or believed — Elmo when the diamonds had failed to reappear. To have such wealth sitting useless in your best friend's gut was too much for him to bear. After all the risk and worry they had endured, something had to be blamed, and why not him, the one who had panicked and swallowed them in the first place?

Still, it was only money — their friendship might have at least endured that. Maybe one day they could have even laughed about it. But it wasn't the diamonds; they didn't matter.

'The child is not yours.'

Those were what mattered, those five little words going seventy miles an hour on an alpine pass. She didn't have to say anything else; he knew it was Elmo.

On the evening that Elmo had swallowed the diamonds, Joseph, then Fidelio, had been sitting in the corner with Pepe. That's why he had swallowed them in the first place, the idiot, he'd thought they were in trouble, thought they'd been found out. But they hadn't, everything was going well, just as it had been. In fact it was better. Pepe had offered him an opportunity, some work. Just him; low risk, high pay. He had accepted it, done it and taken home the money to Anita like a proud hunter.

There had been more opportunities, more jobs. He had found, to his surprise, that the work excited him. But it had also taken him away for longer and longer, away from Venice, away from Anita, away from Amico's. She had questioned him, but he never answered. He was making money, so why should it bother her now?

And the longer he had spent away from her, the more time she had spent with Elmo, the friend who played piano and picked up his ex-girlfriends like half-drunk glasses of wine. Now he had picked up his wife.

'The child is not yours.'

He didn't have to ask whose it was. He *knew*.

But Anita had died in the crash, taking her betrayal and Elmo's child with her. Since that moment, Fidelio had become Joseph, a different person. He had never seen Elmo again.

Now it seemed that Elmo had moved on, too. This girl, at the very least she was someone to whom Elmo had entrusted his strange legacy. Perhaps it was her inheritance; perhaps she was Elmo's daughter. It seemed to make sense.

Joseph swept back the sheet to Elmo's waist. He was surprised to find a minuscule cut near the base of his abdomen, freshly stitched together.

'He's been opened,' said Joseph. 'They must have already extracted them.'

'What?' said Ashley. 'Extracted what?'

'Listen,' sighed Joseph, turning to Ashley's tired and confused face. 'The girl, it's not important what her name is, but we have to find her now. I believe she has something that somebody else wants. I don't know who that somebody else is, but I'm almost certain they ambushed me and tried to kill me, and I was on my way to collect what she has. Please, do you know where she is?'

Ashley churned the odd collection of half-facts in his mind like thick glue in a broken bowl. He tried to examine each one, but they were sticky and untenable. Eventually he resigned himself to the only two things he knew. For whatever reason, Caterine was in danger, and he had to help her. The man next to him, although it was still uncertain whether or not he could be trusted, seemed to have her best interests at heart. He also knew more about the situation than Ashley. He sighed.

'She's staying at the Riverfront Guesthouse,' he said at last. 'By the harbour.'

'OK,' said Joseph, nodding. 'OK, we need…'

Before he could finish, the door by the bench burst open. Joseph and Ashley swung round as Mylo appeared, holding Sommai out in front of him and a gun to his head.

'Riverfront Guesthouse,' said Mylo, apparently to Sommai. 'By the harbour…now we all know.'

Joseph eyed Mylo in the shadows, trying to make out his face.

'Who are you?' he said.

Mylo squinted back at Joseph's gaunt face. Another grin stretched across his face.

'Hello, Joseph,' he said. 'I apologise for underestimating you. I honestly did not think you would make it here. So much for the local workforce, eh?'

Sommai stood unsteadily in front of Mylo, breathing short, sharp breaths. His eyes darted between Joseph and Ashley.

'You…' he said. 'What is happening? 'Who are you all?'

Mylo, as if he had forgotten his captive, turned and pushed him forwards.

'I am sorry,' he said. 'You may go now.'

Mylo stood back, his gun still pressed firmly against Sommai's temple, but before he could squeeze the trigger, Joseph threw himself forwards, hopping once and springing into the shadows where Mylo stood, pushing Sommai clear of Mylo's aim and back towards the door. Mylo caught Joseph in mid flight, sweeping the butt of his gun against his head. In the confusion, Sommai scrambled to his feet and made for the door. Two muffled shots echoed against the steel bench as Mylo fired two bullets after him, but they drove harmlessly into the door frame. He spat a curse after the terrified doctor as he escaped, hobbling down the corridor from the morgue.

Ashley, suddenly wide awake, gripped the table behind him, unable to speak. Joseph lay before him, unconscious on the floor. The door Sommai had disappeared through swung back and clicked into its frame. He watched in horror as Mylo turned slowly to face him and walked forwards, stopping in a shaft of moonlight and allowing the cold, cruel features of his face to be illuminated in the white, smoke-filled air. Gently, Mylo pulled a few strands of black hair from his forehead and fixed his eyes on Ashley's exhausted, horrified face. There were shouts in the distance: Sommai alerting the security guards.

'Time to go,' said Mylo. He cocked his head and frowned, as if concerned.

'You look tired,' he said, raising the gun above his head. 'You should sleep.'

FIVE TINY PEBBLES

CATERINE PULLED the straps of her backpack tight and scanned the dark room for any belongings she may have left. She had arrived in Luang Prabang two days ago, delivered Ashley safely to the hospital and then killed time until she was due to meet the man who had called her after Elmo's death: his friend, the surgeon Sommai. She had planned to stay in the town longer, at least for a few days while Ashley recovered. But now she had collected her dubious inheritance, and things had changed.

Sommai had insisted on her meeting him at night, entering the morgue through the door around the back of the hospital. They did not say much to each other, pleasantries, some shared nervous humour about the strangeness of it all, sadness at Elmo's death, wishes of good luck. The whole thing had taken less than five minutes and, before she knew it, she was back outside, stealing through dark, empty streets with a small bag of diamonds that had been inside her father for a quarter of a century. They made her feel criminal, weighing down the lining of her pocket, tugging at her attention and making her check her every movement and quieten her footsteps. They made her want to disappear into the shadows. This must have been how Elmo felt, she thought.

They sat innocently on the small dressing table. Five tiny pebbles, and yet they loomed over Caterine like monoliths.

Now she had to decide how she was going to carry them back home. Neither Elmo nor Sommai had thought to give her advice on that. She thought briefly about ditching them. It would have been easy enough, but then what would have been the point in coming all this way? There must be some way of getting them home. They were small, sure enough…

Noises began seeping through the thin, wooden walls from the room next door: the whimpers and grunts of a couple in copulation.

Caterine opened the side pocket of her pack and fished around in the debris of used underwear, socks, tickets and pens. Eventually she pulled out a square packet, which she tore and opened. She took out a round, greasy rubber disc and unrolled it into its natural tubular shape, letting it hang in front of her as she contemplated the prospect of spending the next forty-eight hours with a condom, tied up and heavy of stones, worming through her intestine. She grimaced.

Then, out of the corner of her eye, she spotted something. Tucked into the edge of the mirror on the dressing table was a torn slip of paper with a name and a telephone number scribbled across it: the surgeon's contact details. Caterine lowered the limp condom and tossed it at the metal bin beneath the table, where it stuck against the inside like spaghetti. Then she pocketed the piece of paper and the stones, lifted her rucksack and left the room.

Down the unlit, bamboo corridor she walked, past the next room where the sounds of copulation crescendoed and quietened to coos and strokes and giggles, past two more rooms, a cracked sink with a rusty mirror smeared with shaving foam, a dusty, plastic plant, an ancient framed poster of a Thai movie and down the rickety stairs. At the bottom she reached the reception area. There was no light on, just cool, white moonlight bathing the piles of old books, cushions, glasses, ornaments and badly assembled chairs and tables. On one cushion was a middle-aged man, the owner. He lay snoring with his legs spread, his arms folded and a dry flannel covering his eyes. Caterine paused, placed money for the two nights she had stayed on the counter and tiptoed past the man.

From a nearby shelf, a mangy cat suddenly darted in front of her. Caterine stifled a gasp as it clattered underneath a table on the tail of a gecko. She froze as the man stirred and grunted, then returned to his sleep. Caterine walked quickly to the open door and out into the night.

It must have been 2am and the only sounds on the early streets were the whips, cracks and buzz saws from insects in the trees that lined them. She turned left down the short lane towards the river, where she hoped to catch some late taxi boat north up the river. She would call Ashley somehow and apologise for not sticking around, but right now she had to keep moving until she felt safe. Keep moving, just like her father.

She stopped dead. Had there been a rustle? She held her breath and listened, hearing only her own blood in her ears, waiting for some rat to scuttle out across the lane. There was nothing. She walked on. Then, again, some movement in the shadows, footsteps, something large, *she saw it.* She stepped two paces back, and the object followed. Caterine swung round to sprint back the way she came, but before she had taken a step, a strong arm had engulfed her, yanking her back. She screamed, but was stifled by another large hand holding a cloth across her face.

'Shh,' said a voice. Acrid fumes, dizziness, then darkness.

A BULLET TO THE HEART

JOSEPH WOKE, as he had not done for two decades, to absolute peace and quiet. He kept his eyes closed and allowed his brain to feel around for any scattered memories of its recent past. Then he lifted his chin from his chest, wincing immediately from the pain in his neck and the back of his head. He tried to put a hand to it, but found them both tied behind the chair on which he was sitting. He straightened up, slowly, and opened his eyes.

A long, narrow face looked up at him, filling his vision. It was blue in the low light, and its prominent nose drew a hooked shadow across one smooth cheek. The eyes were dark, apart from two white glints of light, and a thin grin of bright teeth drew out from the mouth as Joseph squinted in surprise.

Mylo puffed two satisfied bursts of air through his nostrils and stood up from where he was crouching. Joseph watched him walk away and lean over a large bag, from which he began to pull objects and toss them on a long bench that ran the length of the room. It was not a small room, perhaps fifty feet long and half as wide. What light there was seeped in through high windows that ran around three of the walls. The floor was stone, the walls patched together with wood and corrugated metal, apart from the fourth, which was a large garage-like sliding door. There was another small door in the opposite wall. From the ropes, hooks, poles and engine parts that hung on the walls and lay around the ground, he was in some kind of boathouse. Outside, below the hum of insects, Joseph could hear gentle ripples of water lapping against the riverbank.

'Wh-what's going on?' said a shaky, female voice behind

Joseph. He turned suddenly, revisiting the pain in his neck, and realised that there were two seats behind his. All three made a triangle facing out from the centre of the room. Ashley was to his left, asleep or unconscious, and to his right was the owner of the voice — a young woman.

'It's OK,' he said instinctively.

'Who are you?' it trembled. 'W-Why am I here? Why are my hands tied?'

Mylo stopped and turned to look over his shoulder for a moment. Hearing nothing more, he returned to his search.

'Somebody…somebody tell me what's going on,' said the girl.

There was a snort from Ashley's seat as he woke and lifted his head. He sniffed a few times and cleared his throat.

'Ashley?' whispered the girl desperately. 'Ashley, is that you?'

'Yes,' he croaked. 'Caterine?'

'Ashley, what's happening? Why am I tied up? What are you doing here? Who's talking?'

Ashley began to speak, but Joseph broke in.

'Keep quiet,' he whispered. 'Both of you. Don't say anything.'

The girl sobbed a few times into her chest.

'Ha!' cried Mylo, standing up with something small in his hand, a bag. He held it up to the light, then emptied it into his palm. After fingering through its contents, he returned them and placed the bag on the bench. Then he turned to look at the three captives, his hands on his hips as if pondering what to do next. Eventually he strode over to the chairs, past Joseph, to Caterine. She trembled as Mylo gently lifted her chin, examined her face, then let it drop. He moved to Ashley, who was still groggy from unconsciousness. Mylo looked pitifully at the young man, shook his head and sighed. He gave his face a hard, glum slap, and walked back round in front of Joseph, where he stood silently, his arms crossed.

'Byron, am I right?' croaked Joseph.

The wide, white grin reappeared.

'In a manner of speaking,' said Mylo.

Joseph nodded.

'How much did he pay you?' he said, some part of his brain registering that his kidnapper's accent was Italian.

'Hmm,' said Mylo, wagging a finger as if he was playing a riddle. 'Not quite. Try again.'

Joseph frowned. The obvious answer to all of this was that Byron had paid one of his peers to dispose of him, abroad being a safer location to do so than in his own back yard. Nobody else knew he had gone to Laos. Unless…

'You paid *him*?' said Joseph.

Mylo smiled and snorted again, returning to the bench and picking up the bag.

'You know,' he said, his voice rattling off the metal walls. 'Life can always, and will always… run. Faster. Than. You.'

Each word matched one of the four steps Mylo made back to Joseph. He held out a hand in front of his face and, slowly, he opened it. Joseph looked down at the five sizeable diamonds in his palm, then flicked his eyes up to Mylo, who snapped his hand shut and pulled the diamonds to his chest like a child with sweets.

'Always,' repeated Mylo, grinning.

Joseph's eyes flickered. His body was tense with nervous energy and he felt the rope dig into his wrists. He tried to relax and sort through the questions in his mind.

'What do you want with me?' he breathed, trying to keep calm. 'What do you want with them? Who are you?'

Mylo tucked his hands behind his back and leaned forward slightly.

'People don't just disappear…Fidelio,' he said. 'Their hunters just stop hunting.'

He fixed Joseph's eyes, watching as he absorbed what had just been said. Eventually he stood to his full height, sighed and began strolling slowly back and forward in front of his captives.

'You know,' he said, 'You could have just walked away. You

didn't have to run.'

'What?' said Joseph. His pulse had picked up when he heard his old name. It had been twenty-five years since he had heard it last. Whoever this was, he was Italian and he knew about his old life. That could mean only one thing.

'All you had to do was ask,' Mylo continued, still strolling and gesticulating, 'just say that you didn't want to work for us any more. What did you think we would do? Kill you? Blackmail you?' He stopped suddenly and turned to Joseph.

'Kill your wife?'

Joseph flinched and turned his face away, every nerve ending in his body straining to struggle out of its constraints. The mention of his wife was like a sharp jab to his stomach, so long ago had he or anyone ever talked of her. He felt violated; this stranger from Italy talking about his old existence, his old love, of what had been torn away, of what had been amputated from his life…

But he resisted, he could show no signs of struggle or discomfort, not this early in the game.

Mylo smiled and continued walking up and down the room. He tossed and caught the bag occasionally, as if it were a dog's ball and he were strolling in the park.

'Too many films, Fidelio, too many films. We aren't how you imagine us. My people would have let you walk; they may have even given you a goodbye party. After all, you weren't that important, you weren't…family.'

Mylo glanced momentarily behind Joseph.

'How do you know me?' said Joseph. 'I don't remember you.'

'The problem is, you did run,' Mylo said, ignoring Joseph and sucking a jet of air sharply through his thin lips. 'And that's not so good. That showed you didn't trust us, and if you didn't trust us, how could we trust you? We went looking for you. Not me, of course, you were before my time. A man called Pepe, I think it was.'

Mylo distracted himself by playing with the bag. He seemed

bored by the conversation.

'Anyway,' he continued, 'when your wife returned to Venice, we questioned her.'

Joseph's ears pricked, his blood surged with a belch of sickly adrenaline as if he had fallen a hundred feet on a rubber wire… *when your wife returned to Venice…*

'She was in bad shape, but alive,' said Mylo. 'Very upset, apparently; very scared, poor woman. She told us of the crash, of being rescued and waking up in a village thinking she had died, of spending weeks in Grenoble hospital while a fierce blizzard raged up in the mountains…all very dramatic…'

Mylo smiled down at Joseph, plucking the top of the bag.

'But she knew nothing of you. You had gone, disappeared, *poof…*' Mylo flashed his fingers. 'Into the storm, as it were.'

He smiled and tipped his head towards Joseph in mock respect.

'We had no reason not to believe her. She was a broken woman. The only thing that kept her going, she said, was that she had not lost her child.'

Joseph's blood surged again. His eyes bulged as the words delivered another slug to his gut. She had survived…they had both survived. He squirmed in his seat, dizzy; hot nausea rising in his belly.

'No,' he said through his teeth, shaking now, 'no.'

Mylo's face gave a brief twitch of confusion as he saw Joseph's reaction. He frowned, then a morbid grin crept across his face.

'You did know…didn't you?' He darted across to Joseph and leaned down, horrified and fascinated, like a child watching a dying slug. 'You did know that she kept the baby, you…'

Mylo straightened up and gasped, his hand to his forehead, still grinning.

'Oh my, Fidelio…' he whispered, '…you didn't even know that *she* survived, did you?'

Joseph stopped struggling and let himself slump forwards.

He looked down at Mylo's feet, stunned, sick, and for a few seconds there was silence. Mylo eventually broke it, by spinning on his feet and letting out a great, theatrical cry. He returned to pacing, faster this time.

'All this time!' he said. 'You didn't even know! You didn't even check to see if she was alive!' He slapped his palm to his forehead again in disbelief and stopped at Joseph's feet, where he crouched down once more, shaking his head and looking up at him.

'You must have really, really wanted to disappear, my friend,' he said, stifling a small laugh.

Joseph kept his gaze fixed upon the ground. He was numb again; empty. He allowed himself to think back to the crash. He had seen the explosion, hadn't he? He had seen her die, hadn't he? There was no way she could have escaped…was there? He shook his head free of the memories. He had dreamed them so many times since that they made no sense: they were intangible and unreliable, useless. They didn't matter any more.

'Why now?' he said quietly. 'What do you want with me now?'

Mylo puffed through his nose and stood up again.

'Good question,' he said. 'About fifteen years after your disappearing act…Don Antonelli…your boss, remember? He was killed. He was my sister's father-in-law and I had been working for him for five years, which is why you don't know me, Fidelio. Anyway, his successor took over. He wanted to run things a little differently, said that the business had too many loose ends, you know, grudges not satisfied, assets misplaced, debts unpaid…' he swung a hand at Joseph. 'People unaccounted for. He said it made us look unprofessional, and that we needed to send a message to our competitors. Every book was reopened, reinvestigated. I got you.'

Mylo stopped pacing and leaned back against the bench. He was no longer excited. His breathing was slow and calm and he fixed Joseph with a cool stare as he talked.

'I started in the Alps, in the place where you crashed. I pretended to be a journalist writing a story. They were very helpful, the people there, nice people. I liked them. They told me of the storm that blocked the valley around the time of your accident. A few said they had heard of someone being taken in on a hillside farm, someone with a serious injury.'

Mylo glanced down at Joseph's stump.

'A winter storm, a stranger on a farm, an amputation…all very visceral, very poetic, don't you think?'

Joseph looked up wearily at the dark figure in front of him. Mylo had placed the small bag down on the bench and had picked up something else, a canister. Something sloshed about in it as he held it innocently down in front of him and continued to talk.

'I went to the farm. The young woman who lived there was…not so helpful. She knew you, she knew you were alive; I could feel it. But she didn't trust me. I tried to be more… persuasive, if you like, but she gave me nothing.'

Joseph felt another twang of fear and frustration from his insides. Claudette, the young girl who had looked after him…

'What did you do to her?' growled Joseph.

Mylo ignored him and began playing with the top of the canister, screwing it and unscrewing it absent-mindedly in his fingers.

'The only thing her resistance told me was that you were alive, somewhere. After that, I just had to search, and you weren't that hard to find. Made quite a name for yourself, didn't you, *Joe*? Quite a natural, by all accounts. Odd that you would end up moving in similar circles to the one you had run from. Then again, maybe you wanted to be caught.'

'What did Byron have to do with this?' said Joseph, seething for countless reasons, for Anita, for Elmo, for their child, for Claudette, for this stranger in front of him, for Byron, for his own incompetency in falling into this trap.

'I watched you work for a while, traced you to Byron, talked to him. He wasn't so keen to give you up; seems you were valuable to him.'

Mylo reached back with one hand and picked up the bag of diamonds, shaking them like a little bell.

'But then,' he said, 'everyone has a price, no?'

Mylo grinned again and swung away from the bench, holding the canister behind his back. Its contents glooped around inside as he walked back towards Joseph, excited again.

'A colleague of mine, he was given another loose end to tie up: some diamonds missing from a pickup,' Mylo said, nodding back to the bench.

'He got a tip-off on a body here in Laos. He thought he was a smuggler, you know, a swallower? Pretty common in this part of the world, although mostly with drugs, not diamonds. Anyway, it turns out he was wrong. His name cross-referenced against yours: Elmo Ollandi, your old friend from Amico's.'

Mylo smiled again as he watched Joseph's reaction to yet another reminder of his past.

'Don't be surprised, my friend, I know more about you than you think,' said Mylo. He straightened up again and resumed pacing.

'So, we offered the diamonds to Byron in exchange for you, and he accepted.'

'The bus crash, the kidnap,' said Joseph. 'That was you, too?'

'Of course,' said Mylo. 'The plan was to keep you out of the way while I collected the stones, so I hired some local muscle. My mistake, really; I underestimated you. It was a good thing Byron told you where I would be, so to speak.'

He grinned his grin and returned to the bench.

'Why would you choose me over the diamonds?' said Joseph. 'It's been over twenty years, they're far more valuable than an old cripple like me.'

'Such modesty,' tutted Mylo. 'And anyway, Byron won't be receiving his payment. Why would we give him anything for something that is rightly ours? Now we have you and the diamonds, two for the price of one.'

He frowned suddenly and put the canister down by his feet.

'Of course,' he said, pulling something from his shirt pocket, 'there are always complications.'

He opened what looked like a passport and ambled back across to the three chairs. He walked past Joseph and stood in front of Caterine.

'Caterine Genovese,' he said, reading aloud. Caterine kept still and silent, the revelations of what she had just heard still ringing in her ears.

'That's *your* second name, isn't it, Fidelio? Nice that your wife kept it, even after you were gone.'

Mylo turned the passport in his hand and looked at the photograph.

'The image of your mother,' he said. 'The image of your wife, Joseph.'

Sickness and disbelief coursed through Joseph. He slumped forwards, trying to take it in.

The child is not yours.

This was the child, the one who would have been his, the product of the betrayal that had cut his life in two. He felt the warmth behind him, the trembling fear as she sat like him, prone and tied to the chair.

'As for you,' said Mylo, turning to Ashley. 'I wonder who you are…?'

He examined his face with concern for a few moments, then ruffled his hair and stood up.

'Right,' he said, clapping his hands and striding back to the bench. 'To business.'

He picked up the canister and began unscrewing its cap. There was a sudden friction in the air as Mylo stopped talking. Joseph felt Ashley's feet shuffle uncomfortably and heard a whimper from Caterine. Dawn was near, and shafts of low sunlight were finding their way inside the boathouse.

'Let these two go,' said Joseph. 'You have me, you don't need them.'

'Sorry,' said Mylo. He pulled the cap from the canister and began pouring the contents around the floor in front of him, across the bench and up around the chairs. Joseph winced as the smell of petrol fumes reached his nose, and Caterine and Ashley began yelling and struggling as it reached theirs, too.

'They're only kids,' said Joseph, louder now. 'Let them go, you already have what you want, they're useless.'

Mylo continued to distribute the petrol quietly around the chairs, gradually closing in on them and splashing it liberally over their legs and torsos.

'No!' screamed Caterine as she felt it drench her flesh, but Ashley was quiet, the only signs of his discomfort being the continual rattles and bangs as he struggled in his chair.

'No loose ends, no witnesses, no more unaccountable assets,' said Mylo, avoiding eye contact with them. 'New rules,' he finished, and tossed the empty canister to one side.

Joseph began struggling now, gritting his teeth and glaring up at Mylo.

'Fanculo!' he said, 'Let them go!'

But Mylo frowned and began patting his shirt and trouser pockets, ignoring Joseph's shouts, Caterine's terrified howls and the desperate banging of Ashley's chair. At last, he clipped his fingers in frustration.

'One moment, please,' he said, and strode across the room and out of the far door.

After a minute, Caterine's wailing had quietened to frightened sobs, though Ashley continued to struggle violently, but without sound, in his chair. Joseph heard a car door opening and shutting outside, then some whispered curses from Mylo and another door opening. He guessed they had another minute or two at most before he returned with a flame. There was only one thing left to do.

'Your mother,' he said quietly. 'How is she?'

Caterine's sobbing became short, trembling breaths.

'Dead,' she said finally. 'She's dead.'

Joseph hung his head again.

'Why didn't you come back?' said Caterine. Her voice was calm, but full of fear and ice. 'I lived my life thinking you were dead.'

'I…' stammered Joseph, 'I thought the same about you, and your mother. I thought you had both died…but Caterine,' he said, nervous at the name he had only heard for the first time a moment before, 'I am not your father.'

'I know,' said Caterine. 'But you could have been.'

Joseph nodded sadly.

'In truth,' he said, 'I always knew…even before we left I always knew.'

He turned his neck to look across his shoulder.

'That it was Elmo, that Elmo was your father.'

Caterine began to cry again.

'I don't want to die,' she sobbed.

'They were so much more…' Joseph began, but was interrupted by a sudden cry from Ashley and a bang from his chair. He and Caterine swung their heads round towards the noise and saw Ashley, trembling in the chair, with his hands out in front of him.

'You're free,' said Joseph.

'How…?' said Caterine.

'I…I don't know,' said Ashley as he struggled for breath, 'but I think having a broken arm and an enormous amount of morphine helped.'

He held up his right arm, half of which had bent almost at right angles to the rest of it. His struggling had re-broken it, allowing him to slip out of the bindings. His face went pale.

'Oh my God,' he said, 'I can't believe I…'

'Never mind that,' said Joseph. 'You're free, get up and grab me that hook on the bench.' Daylight was starting to fill the room properly now, outlines of shadows becoming proper shapes. Joseph nodded towards a rusted, sharp end of a boat hook that was lying on the bench in front of him, and Ashley stood up and staggered dizzily across to it, holding his twisted arm to his chest. He picked up the hook and took it to Joseph.

'Cut through our ropes,' said Joseph. 'Quick, we don't have much time.'

Ashley bent down, almost fainting when he saw his own splintered arm again, and went to work weakly on Caterine's rope. He dropped the hook twice in the pools of petrol, each time making a loud clang and a splash.

'Quickly!' said Joseph.

Eventually, the rope came free and he started on Joseph's, but suddenly there was the sound of a car door slamming from outside and footsteps approaching.

'There's no time!' said Joseph. 'Give me the hook and sit back down, both of you pretend to be tied.'

Ashley put the hook obediently in Joseph's hand and staggered back to the chair, just as Mylo reappeared at the door and paused. He looked at them for a moment and Joseph adjusted the hook in his hand, glaring back.

'Matches,' said Mylo simply, holding up a small cardboard packet. 'I forgot matches.'

Mylo strode back across to them and plucked one from the box. He held its tip to the rough strip and smacked his lips impatiently.

'Last words, I suppose?' he sighed. 'Fidelio?'

But Joseph was elsewhere, faraway, looking somewhere into the middle distance. His expression was blank, and his thoughts were not of last words, but of three dimensions, of the space around his body, of contortion…

'No?' said Mylo. 'Suit y…'

With a thundering growl, Joseph suddenly tore his hands underneath him. He felt tendons snap and twang in his good leg as he pulled it across the chair and down onto the floor. Now he was standing, roaring on one leg, his hands still tied to the chair above him. Mylo looked back in horror. He struck the match, but it broke and fell to the ground. He began fumbling in the box for another, but before he could find one, Joseph had smashed down the wooden chair on top of his head, splintering it and freeing himself from the bindings.

Mylo fell onto the petrol-soaked ground and his gun slipped from his belt. Joseph dived upon him and sunk the rusty hook into the flesh of his thigh. Mylo squealed in agony and struggled against Joseph, who silenced him with an elbow to the face. Mylo, stunned, struggled silently on the floor with the two pains in his nose and leg. In this vacuum, Joseph turned and saw Ashley lift Caterine from her seat.

The sight of her face hit him like a bullet to the heart. Her mouth, her eyes, her form: all her mother's. It felt like a long-healed wound had been torn apart, and Joseph reeled as a thousand sweet and bitter memories bled through it; a dizzying, raw torrent of hatred, joy, jealousy and love.

'Go!' shouted Joseph, 'Go now!'

They looked down at him, sprawled on the stone ground, his stump swinging wildly as he gained purchase with his other leg and tried to claw himself upright. But Mylo had come to and was crawling for his gun, which had spun away across the floor. On the ground behind him were the diamonds and the matches. Joseph picked up both, tossing the stones to Caterine, who caught them.

Joseph took a match carefully from the box and watched as Mylo stretched for his gun. He placed one against the sandpaper and fixed Caterine with a steady eye.

'Go,' he repeated. 'Go, now. Please, Caterine.'

For a second the three were locked in the moment, each unable to move from it, until the sound of Mylo's pained grunts became a roar as his right hand met with the metal of the gun.

'GO!' growled Joseph, striking the match. The sulphur flared, white and orange, a gasp of flame settling at the tip of the tiny stick. Ashley tugged at Caterine and they span on their heels, sprinting towards the door. As they reached it, Caterine, still running, turned to look across her shoulder. Joseph was hunched in the growing light of the dawn, his face lit by the weak glow of the single match in his hand. He was balanced on his knee and bending like a priest, mid blessing, above Mylo, who was reeling back, bleeding, struggling to load his gun and kicking his feet silently against what was to come.

They were twenty metres clear of the door when they tripped and fell face first into the dirt bush that separated them from the water's edge. Ashley pulled Caterine over and held on to her as they both looked back in horror at the small, silent building. For a moment there was nothing, just dawn light and quiet broken only by the ripple of waves from the river and the snore of insects in the jungle. For a moment, they thought that it was over, that some struggle had ensued, that no bullet or flame would be required.

But then what was dark became fire and light. What was quiet became two loud shots ringing out across the riverside. They shielded their faces as the shack and the morning exploded around them.

~1978~

THE DIARY OF CLAUDETTE FERRIÈRE

26 MARS 1978, 3:36 in the morning

I haven't slept since I went to bed. Slowly the whole house has filled with snores. Madame Beaufort doesn't seem to mind Papa's noises, because she makes even louder ones herself, and all I can hear from downstairs is Doctor Moreau whining in his sleep like a puppy. I was about to get up and read, but just as I pulled back the covers, I heard the handle to the front door open and I pulled them back and ducked under the bedcovers. I was frightened; I thought a madman was trying to break in and kill us, but then I heard the door close again and some footsteps outside, which meant somebody was going out, not coming in. They were slow footsteps, and in between each there was a clang and a squeak like an old mattress.

I jumped out of bed. What was Joe doing outside?

I stood at the window and watched him hobbling up the slope, wearing a big coat and carrying a bag on his shoulders. He got to the top quite quickly, but then he slipped and struggled and his bag fell down to the door and he had to go and get it. When he reached the sledge he stopped and put the bag on the back of it. I opened my window and he turned round, almost falling over.

'Joe!' I whispered, but it was a loud whisper that echoed around the yard. He stared at me for a while, and I could see his breath billowing in the cold air.

'Go back to bed, Claudette,' he said.

'What are you doing?'

'Go back to bed,' he said again, and then tied the bag tightly to the back of the sled. The snoring next door had stopped suddenly, and I thought that maybe Papa was awake and was getting his clothes on to go and get Joe back inside, but then I heard two splutters and it started again, even louder than before.

'Papa will be angry,' I hissed.

'Tell him I'm sorry,' he said, as he walked round to the front of the sledge and started pulling it forwards.

'You can't make it on your own. Please don't go, you might die!' I said as he walked slowly away, clanging and squeaking.

'I have to try, Claudette. Now go to bed.'

I watched him for a bit, wondering what to do or say, and he had just about reached the end of the yard when I called out to him as quietly as I could.

'I've been thinking.'

'I said go to bed.'

'About your question.' He stopped and turned around and looked at me across the yard.

'About whether it's better to have courage or heart.'

'What do you think, then?'

'Well…I don't think you can have one without the other. It takes courage to love, and love makes you brave.'

He didn't say anything, just stood where he was, wonky like an old scarecrow. Then he nodded and waved at me once, and pulled the sledge away.

But just as he did, Zeet came out from nowhere and scampered up the side of the slope. He saw Joe and started barking again, a loud bark that would wake anyone in the middle of the night. Joe panicked and stepped backwards, almost falling down the slope as Zeet began snapping at his leg and snarling. Papa might wake at any second.

'Stop it, Zeet! Shut up!' Joe kept saying, but every time he did Zeet's bark just got louder and angrier.

I had a thought.

'Zeet,' I whispered, as loud as I could without shouting. 'ARRÊT!'

I heard my whisper echo around the yard, and Zeet stopped and sat down quietly, licking his chops and looking up at my window. Then the house, which had become quiet, filled with snores once more. 'Arrêt,' I said to Zeet again.

Joe picked up the rope on the front of the sledge and looked at me. I looked back at him and that was how we were for a bit. I wonder if I will see you again, I thought.

'I wonder if I will see you again?' I said, out loud.

He stopped what he was doing and turned around and smiled at me. My heart felt funny, Mama, and he winked at me, then turned away and limped behind the engine shed. I saw him push off with his hands and the sledge carried him very slowly over the snow-covered paddock. I felt like reaching out towards him and shouting or running after him and telling him to stay. But I could not move. By the time he reached the snow-covered fence, he was flying north towards the forest at the end of the valley, and I watched him until he became too small to see by the light of the stars and the bright blue moon, and then the darkness swallowed him up whole.

~2058~

ONE HAND RAISED IN A WAVE

The French Alps

I LET the diary rest on my lap and readjusted my eyes. It was past dawn, and strong sunlight was streaming into the old woman's — Claudette's — study. I jumped up from the chair and looked out of the window, causing the dog to jerk awake and release a loud bark to show he was concentrating. Outside, the snow had stopped: where there had been cloud, there was now bright blue sky; where there had been blizzard, there was now still, crisp air. I could see far down the mountainside to the villages, towns and lakes in the valley below. The snow was still high and drifting, but there was nothing to trap me any more: I was saved.

I sat down and ruffled the head of the dog, wondering what I should do first. Then I looked back at the diary. I flicked through the pages from the last entry I had read. After Joe had left, the entries seemed to be spaced out more. After a while, they dwindled and eventually gave way to empty pages. I let the blank sheets shuffle past until I reached the back cover and was about to put the book down when I noticed a brief flash of writing on the last page. I turned back and found one last entry. It was written in spindly, adult handwriting and was dated three days before…

I don't know who he is or where he has come from, but he is staying in MY room.

That is the second time I have written that sentence in my life, and I sincerely hope it will be the last. It is the strangest thing — yet again, another lost young soul needing shelter from the storm. So many memories, my love, so many memories.

He is ill, but getting better, I think. He has no injuries, at least not like yours, and he seems strong. We shall have to see how long this storm lasts.

I was worried when I found him. The blizzard made me think of you, and of the visitor who came calling all those years ago, asking about you. He was an unkind man, cruel, and he tried to hurt me when I refused to talk about you. I never told you how much.

But he was stupid as well. He didn't know that Papa would be back early from the village, didn't know he would be carrying a gun. I laugh now when I think of him running from the farm, tumbling and tripping down the hill, Zeet at his heels. He never came back.

But you did, didn't you, my love? So long after you left, you came back to me. You were so worried about me, the little girl you left behind. Bruised, wounded and weary you arrived, in from the storm.

I am not far from you now, I think. It is cold, and I am old now.

I closed the book and put it down. The dog was up and wagging his tail, blinking in a shaft of warm sunlight. I could see all around the study, now that it was light. I saw pictures I had not seen before, framed photographs of a young woman, of Claudette. One was of her crouched low to a muddy track in khaki shorts and weathered boots. She must have been in her thirties, her blonde hair was swept back and tied sharply in a ponytail, and she was leaning forward, focusing a large camera lens on something in the distance. Another was of her beaming in a crowd of laughing children, all looking up and reaching out to the camera. In the background were blue skies, trees and the huts of a tribal village. The same camera was slung around her neck.

Another picture was framed in yellow trim. It was a close-up of Claudette, older now with lines around her eyes and mouth, but most of her face masked by a camera, which she was pointing directly out of the picture. In the lens of the camera was a bright reflection of Earth in space, and beneath it was written '*Claudette Ferrière, Photographer of the year, 2012.* Above, in white letters, *National Geographic.*

I picked up another picture that was on one of the

bookshelves. It was only small, and set in an old wooden frame. It was of the farmhouse, I guessed, but in warmer weather. There was no snow; only lush grass, blue skies and green peaks of mountains spreading out to the horizon. In the foreground, almost upon the camera was the side of Claudette's grinning face and her outstretched hand holding the camera that was taking the shot. Next to her, peering up into the frame, were the eyes of a young girl. They were creased up with pleasure as she clung to her mother and reached out to the lens.

In the background, barely visible at first, there was a figure standing on the porch to the house. It was a man wearing shorts, a shirt and a wide-brimmed hat. He leant against the doorpost, smiling, one hand raised in a wave, his right leg — a prosthetic — crossed across his left.

I stared at the photograph for a while, absorbing the happiness. Outside I heard voices, and the sound of engines powering against the snow.

Ash Trés says: how are you?

Damien says: shit.

Ash Trés says: what's up?

Damien says: i lost the fucking henley acct

Ash Trés says: sorry to hear that mate

Damien says: ur sorry? i bought a fucking house last week now what am i going to do?

Ash Trés says: sure you'll work something out, you always land on your feet

Damien says: yeh right so what u up to dikhed?

Ash Trés says: im feeling better, had a rare strain of dengue fever apparently

Damien says: dung fever?

Ash Trés says: you heard. doc says it reached my brain, if i hadn't gone to him i might be dead. broke my arm too.

Damien says: :-0

Ash Trés says: that's what i said

Damien says: where r u?

Ash Trés says: still in laos, we're going south

Damien says: we?

Ash Trés says: just a friend

Damien says: cock sucker, what u take me for?

Ash Trés says: gotta go, we're catching a bus in ten minutes

Damien says: whats she like?

Ash Trés says: speak to you some time soon, good luck with the house

Damien says: big tits?

Ash Trés says: bye

Damien says: please tell me you fuckd her you dik

Damien says: ash? u there?

Ash Trés is offline and may not respond.

EPILOGUE

Laos, 2003

SOMMAI STEPPED out onto the hospital porch and sat down on the step. He shuffled along so that he was away from the light and the orb of bugs that buzzed and snapped beneath it. Then he set down his crutch and lit a cigarette, sucking the warm mixture of smoke and morning air deep inside of him. It was still dark, but it would not be for long.

The police had been as good as useless, and he had not expected anything else. Their questions about the attack in the morgue had been lazy and routine. He could not give them a full description of his assailant, nor of the young patient who had gone missing. It was only Joseph whom he could describe with any accuracy. As he did so, he watched the young officer write just three words on his pad: *western, one leg.*

He had told them nothing of Elmo or the diamonds.

There had been a fire later that morning in a nearby boathouse on the river. A body had been found, too badly burned to be identified. All in all, Sommai guessed it was too much to investigate for too little reward.

He did not know what had happened to the young woman. He had talked to the Riverfront Guesthouse and the owner had told him that she had left before dawn, a pile of notes left on the reception counter. There had been no trace of her since. He hoped beyond hope that she had made it away in time.

His injuries were only minor, aside from his leg, which had required a small operation. He had refused the offer of extended leave to recover. He always felt better about things when he was working.

Sunlight began to spread across the hospital gardens and Sommai already felt the wet heat of the day on his hands and face. He took a last drag from his cigarette and squashed it against the concrete step. As he got to his feet, he saw something on the step beside him that he had not noticed in the dark: a small brown package taped tightly shut at both ends. He picked it up. It was light. There were no stamps on it and a single word for an address: *Sommai.*

Sommai looked around. There was nobody there. Nobody in the gardens and nobody in the street outside. He opened the package and shook out its contents into his palm.

In an instant he had made a tight fist of his hand and clasped it to his chest. He glanced around again, frantically looking for a sign of anyone watching. Seeing nobody, he opened his hand again. It held five large diamonds. They were instantly familiar; he had held them in his hand just three days before.

Sommai sat on the step and gawped at the glittering stones that were cradled in his hand, his mind swimming with questions and possibilities. The sun slowly climbed, and by the time he had shaken himself from his trance, the garden had filled with golden light and the long shadows of trees. Carefully, he replaced the diamonds in their package. As he did so, he saw a note. It was handwritten on a scrap of paper.

From Elmo
Buy legs

THE END

FROM THE AUTHOR

Thanks for reading *From the Storm,* I really hope you enjoyed it. If you could spare the time, I'd be very grateful if you could post a review on Amazon or Goodreads. And feel free to let me know what you think in person by dropping me an email at adrian@adrianjwalker.com - I'd be happy to hear from you.

You can also sign up for my newsletter here:

http://www.adrianjwalker.com/storm

I'll send you exclusive short stories, some of which feature characters from this book. You'll also find out the *second* a new book is published.

Thanks again for reading.

Adrian

THE END OF THE WORLD RUNNING CLUB

THE ULTIMATE RACE AGAINST TIME THRILLER

When the world ends and you find yourself stranded on the wrong side of the country, every second counts.

No one knows this more than Edgar Hill. 550 miles away from his family, he must push himself to the very limit to get back to them, or risk losing them forever...

His best option is to run.

But what if your best isn't good enough?

"Ridiculously gripping straight from the start." (Jenny Colgan)

"A page-turning thriller with a pace as relentless as the characters' feet hitting the pavement. A deft look into the mind of a man who needs the near-destruction of the world to show him what truly matters." (Laura Lam, *author of False Hearts*)

"A really fun, engaging, exciting, and compassionate take on a familiar scenario: the apocalypse. Highly recommended." (David Owen *Carnegie longlisted author of Panther*)

Out now on Del Rey.

ACKNOWLEDGEMENTS

All characters appearing in this work are fictitious. Any resemblance to real persons, living or dead, is purely coincidental.

The story of the *Sleeping Cave* is based upon one I was told by a tour guide in the amazing country of Laos. It has been embellished for the purposes of this book and as far as I know there is nothing bad lurking in the caves of Vientiane other than their recent history.

I would like to thank my father, Norrie, sister, Rachel, father-in-law, Bob, and friend Fraser for their help and encouragement. I owe special thanks to my wife, Debbie, for pushing me to complete this book.

Printed in Great Britain
by Amazon